HIDDEN IN PARIS

CORINE GANTZ

BLOODHOUND
— BOOKS —

www.bloodhoundbooks.com

Print ISBN: 978-1-5040-8550-2

To my three men.

PROLOGUE

PARIS, TWO YEARS BEFORE

*J*ohnny dressed like a Frenchman these days, Annie noticed. The cut of his sport coat was flashier than anything he would have worn in the States. As usual, Annie's curves, the good ones and the not-so-good ones, overflowed from her burgundy Chantal Thomass dress in a very un-French manner.

They kissed their boys goodnight, and asked the sitter to put them to bed before ten. Then Johnny pushed open the massive front door of their Parisian Hôtel Particulier, and from this simple push, his stiffness, Annie knew Johnny was mad. At what, or whom, she did not know. She just hoped it wasn't at her.

The night air, humid and warm, caressed her skin as they walked in silence on rue Nicolo under the old-fashioned street lamps. She put her hand in Johnny's but he let go of it after only a minute. "You drive," he said, stopping in front of her minivan. "You hold your liquor better than I do."

Annie drove. He sat in the passenger seat. She rolled her window all the way down, dangling her bare arm, and caressed the air as she drove down rue de Passy towards Trocadéro. This was June 21st, the summer solstice and night of the Fête de la Musique. This was a night for dancing in the streets, a night of ivresse and amour, and Annie's great hope for the night was to get a little bit of both.

In the passenger seat, Johnny sat and cringed at the usual mess of candy wrappers and kids' broken toys.

"You all right?" she asked tentatively. Johnny only shrugged.

Rue de Boulainvilliers and Avenue Mozart bustled with people on foot. In the streets, the collective mood was electric. A woman moved her hips to the rhythm of a bongo, while the drummer's blond dreadlocks swayed against his back as he played.

"Let's go dancing after dinner," she said. "We have to go dancing on a night like this."

Johnny didn't respond.

From Place Rodin, notes of jazz floated in the air. At Place Costa Rica, that odd man with the rickety tuxedo, the one she had seen whistling opera at métro Ranelagh, bellowed "Nessun Dorma" as he stood in the middle of the sidewalk.

"You don't seem all right," she said again.

"Annie. We need to talk."

When they were done talking, her whole body was trembling. Johnny was quiet, his hands resting on his lap, his chin down like a falsely repentant child. She could not make it to the Champs-Élysées. She parked the minivan as best she could on Avenue Victor Hugo and rested her elbows and her forehead on the wheel, her heart pounding. It was a struggle to think straight, to breathe right. An instant later, rage overtook her. She felt herself grabbing junk —toys, her cell phone, an old map, anything she could get her hands on—and launching them at Johnny. He had his arms up, a three-hundred-pound gorilla victim of domestic violence.

"Annie..."

"Get. Out!" She screamed.

"Listen..."

"Get out of my car!"

"Annie, you better calm down," he said in his warm reasonable voice, a voice like expensive red wine. But his hand was already on the door.

She launched out of her seat, threw herself at him, pummeled his shoulder. "Get out!"

Johnny got out of the car, shut the door and she watched his silhouette disappear into the night.

She drove aimlessly. Her senses had abandoned her. She drove, not seeing the streets, not hearing the music. She drove for an hour or more and wept like a child.

For an eternity, she circled the block around her house, unable to find a parking space through her tears. Home. She needed to be home. She removed the five-inch Manolo Blahniks she had purchased just for this night, and walked barefoot toward the house, thankful for the cool asphalt under her bare feet. Then she sat at the bottom of the stone steps, cried some more, dried her eyes, and walked up the stairs.

On the other side of Paris, Johnny and his brother Steve were leaving the bar rue des Pyrénées. They were laughing. Steve could barely walk. Johnny took the wheel of Steve's Jaguar and veered left towards the Périphérique, all tires screeching.

By the time Annie entered her house, Johnny and Steve were already dead.

CHAPTER 1

JANVIER

 en years ago, back in the land of cheeseburgers and donuts, Annie didn't give a thought to what she ingested. These days, Food with a capital letter; thinking about it, talking about it, preparing it and ultimately gaining an unacceptable number of kilos on it—at least unacceptable by Parisian standards—was pretty much the obsession. In fact, the day before she must have hit some kind of gustatory bottom when she bought the Bible du Beurre on an empty stomach. This was a cookbook solely devoted to butter, a bible to its ode no less. Last night, after putting the boys to bed, she had mustered the nerve to peer at the croissant recipe. Had she cringed when she discovered that those innocent-looking pastries she had wolfed down without the slightest suspicion over the last ten years were essentially composed of 99% butter? Absolutely. Had this stopped her from jumping straight into the preparation of her own croissant? Apparently not.

So maybe this was her therapy. Butter. She needed the butter, she reasoned, and wads of it. She needed the butter because she was grieving.

That is, of course, if what she felt was indeed grief, and not rage. She preferred that it was grief and not rage that had made her gain thirty pounds and growing since the night of the accident. She preferred that it was grief and not rage that had kept her from remembering to put on lipstick or going to a hair salon in years. No matter how anxiously she stared out her window, Paris stubbornly refused to wake up. It was six in the morning and there was no sign that daylight would ever break. Today, again, she'd awakened at four, feeling restless and lonely. Lonely enough to seriously contemplate creeping up three sets of stairs and shaking the kids awake for an early breakfast at the crack of dawn.

She was still in her bathrobe, uncombed, unwashed but the shower would have to wait. The water pipes tended to scream like a cat in heat at the slightest provocation and the kids needed their sleep. So she searched the walls and high ceilings of her kitchen for a task, preferably a brutal one, to occupy her for an hour. But the ancient tile floor was already immaculate. Her collection of colorful flea market finds well organized on the open shelves. On another shelf, nuts, grains and legumes arranged by color in glass jars did not need another rearranging. Chicken soup already simmered on the antique stove, and on the Carrera marble countertop were the twelve adorable miniature croissants prepared last night, all virginal and doughy, ready to pop into the oven, and her mouth.

With the gentle bubbling of the soup as soundtrack to her morning, and the smell of yeast, cooked vegetables and fresh brewed coffee wafting through the kitchen she grabbed a cookbook and her well-used French-to-English dictionary from a shelf, sat at the massive farm table in the center of the room, and flipped through the cookbook's pages impatiently. Finally a photograph of a fish encapsulated in something white caught her interest. Bar de mer dans sa croûte de sel was the name of the recipe. Just to make sure, her fingers hunted the pages for the word croûte in the dictionary.

Crust! Salt Encrusted Sea Bass. The recipe called for one kilo of coarse sea salt from the Guérande region –– the use of lowly table salt apparently a punishable offense in French cookbooks. The recipe looked impossibly difficult to prepare or shop for. Perfect. She grabbed the Pokémon calculator and punched in numbers. Ten years after moving to France, she still converted recipes from French to English, grammes to ounces, and centilitres to cups.

It's not that she could not learn, it's that she had her own insubordinate way of doing things. Food residues on the calculator cracked and popped, and she took satisfaction in the revelation that her calculator too was en croûte.

The prospect of the recipe made her feel better suddenly. Perhaps she would end up spending the day planning, shopping, and preparing a baked sea bass that no one would eat, but at least she would be busy enough for her mind to shut up. Especially she would not think about money, or the absence of it, for a little while. And maybe it would muffle the perpetual match of ping-pong playing in her head where the ball never stopped and no points could be scored. Because now that Johnny was dead, it would forever be his responsibility, her responsibility, his fault, her fault, his betrayal, her betrayal, back and forth for all eternity.

The accident had, in a way, been the result of a simple mathematical equation: Alcohol + Speed = Death, and no one in his right mind would say that luck had anything to do with it. But all the irreversible things that were said that night... now that was the unlucky part. Knowing, and pretending not to know, was what gnawed at her heart, rotted her spirit and haunted her nights.

❧

A distant tap came from the front door. Lucas! In the same instant, she remembered she had not locked the front door the night before — again. Oh mon Dieu, and Lucas was going to let himself in and sulk over the contentious topic of her négligence alarmante. Of course he could have simply entered through the back door and into the kitchen like everybody else, but no, he had to check the front door to make a point. Whoever gave him that mission was anyone's guess. Besides, this was the sixteenth arrondissement of Paris, and a private street mind you.

She heard Lucas struggle with the front door, wiggling the doorknob just so, then the pushing of the warped door with all his weight, which was how most things worked, or failed to work, in her house. How he liked to point out how run down the house was! Which she took as a criticism of how she ran her life in general.

Annie straightened the powder pink, heart-infested terry bathrobe the boys had given her for Mother's Day. The robe was a disgrace in every way and made her look like a tub, but what's a mother to do? They'd pooled their allowances to buy it. She quickly flattened her hair with her hand before Lucas could glimpse what her boys dubbed the "momhawk" and braced herself for her French friend's righteous indignation, and for the inevitability that he would be wearing cashmere, be clean-shaven, and smell deliciously of Habit Rouge by Guerlain, while she reeked of soup and looked like one of those vagrants who wander the streets of Paris talking to themselves and wearing pink bathrobes with hearts on them.

A gust of January wind entered with Lucas and he wrestled with the door to close it. He blew on his fingers, tucked his hands in the pockets of his black coat, and shuffled toward the stove like a penguin in a very affected show of self-pity.

"Oh give me a break!" Annie said.

Lucas approached the stove, sniffed the boiling soup with suspicion, put his hands over the heat of the pot for a few seconds before removing his coat and folding his lanky body onto a kitchen chair. "Do you have any of that very bad American coffee?" he finally asked. Lucas's English was good but his accent was thick enough to trip on. Annie rose from her chair and turned her back to him mostly so that he wouldn't see her smile —she was after all, officially mad at him, and he at her. She grabbed a Mickey Mouse mug from the cabinet, and moved the coffeepot from the countertop to the table, all the while worrying about the size of her ass in that bathrobe. She did not exactly slam the mug on the table, but she wasn't gentle either, as she poured the coffee for him.

Lucas, she needed to remind herself, had her best interests at heart. He was here because he knew of her insomnia, and of everything else. Almost everything else. He was here to have a cup of coffee before work, and, she suspected, to check on her and make sure she was going to get dressed that day, and maybe comb her hair all the way through. And his plan usually worked: nothing like a terminally elegant French man's eyebrow raised in disapproval to whip you into shape and send you to the shower.

She often wondered why Lucas still bothered with her, and just as often, and especially today, why she bothered with him. Since Johnny's death, she had kicked plenty of well-intentioned people out of her life. Better alone than in bad company she told her boys. And yes, it did occur to her that she might be the bad company.

Lucas inspected his cup for food-borne bacteria, or perhaps for the words to his next sentence. "You're firing the messenger," he said.

"Killing! We say killing." Here they were again. She felt anger rise in her like the steam of an old-fashioned engine. Lucas was truly gifted at pissing her off. It was not some old anger, oh no. It was fresh and new every time. And no—she was sure of that—it had nothing to do with Lucas escaping the accident when Johnny had not.

Johnny had tried to talk Lucas into going out that night but Lucas had wanted to stay home and watch the Fête de la Musique safely on television. The best way to resist Johnny was to play dead, so Lucas had not picked up the phone. "Steve and I are coming to get you," Johnny's recorded message said. "You can't experience life on the TV, you inbred prick."

Surely there would have been no accident had they not gone to pick him up, but Lucas could never be blamed for this. The papers had called the ten-car pile-up a blood bath. Too much alcohol in the system had perhaps delayed Johnny's reflexes. Alcohol, or being preoccupied with the fight he'd just had with her. No, she did not hold Lucas responsible; it would have been misplaced. She only wished she could apply the same logic to her own sense of self-blame.

The reasons she was angry with Lucas —furious in fact— had nothing to do with the accident and was absolutely, one hundred percent Lucas's fault for minding what was unequivocally her business and for trying to control her life.

Lucas dropped a sugar cube into his coffee, stirred, brought the cup to his mouth, and looked around as if dismayed at having landed in Annie's kitchen again. "Ideally, you would put the house on the market in February," he said, not looking up.

Annie felt that prickly sensation she got in her nose before she cried. She pointed in the direction of the trays on the counter, three neat little rows of two-inch pots under the bio lights. "My tomato seedlings?" she said, not meaning to raise her voice, but there it was: the screech. "What about them? Do the seedlings mean anything to you?"

"There is..." Lucas said before pausing, "no miraculous way to come up with the money it takes to raise three children in a trendy Parisian neighborhood."

"I'll get a job," she said coldly.

Lucas looked at his well-groomed nails. "You may lack marketable skills."

"Skills, skills," she mimicked, in her best rendition of Peter Seller's French accent. "I'm the mother of three boys under nine. I have skills coming out the Ying Yang. And I was the valedictorian at my school! Does that tell you anything?"

"No," he said with sincerity.

Of course, it didn't, she realized all too well. It meant nothing in France, and ten years after the fact and with no work experience, it didn't mean much in the States either.

"The house is all we have left since the tragedy."

"The tragedy's three years old, Annie."

Everything that was wrong with Lucas appeared to her, like a newly produced Technicolor, 3-D version of the same old film, starting with his aristocratic posture, his grave face, the hands he waved as he spoke. So annoyingly, snootily, abjectly French! Her eyes lingered on his jugular area. "Two and a half years! The kids are nearly as raw and fragile today as they were when Johnny died."

Lucas looked at her. "You are. You are, maybe. The boys are doing fine."

"No one is fine! We are scarred! We are scarred for life!" Her voice broke and before she could do a thing to stop it, she was hunched over the table, crying softly. Lucas unfolded from his chair, fetched a tissue, and handed it to her. She ignored the tissue; instead, she grabbed a dubiously clean sheet of paper towel from the table and blew her nose with it. He stood next to her and tapped her back awkwardly. Her tears did not deter him for long, already he was putting his hand on her arm and saying, "Annie, you must sell or the house will be taken away from you and you'll get nothing. You can't pay the mortgage. I am sorry, but financially, you don't have a choice."

Annie dabbed her eyes with the paper towel and sprung to her feet. "The hell I don't!" she said. Relieved to see the tears had stopped, Lucas sat back in his chair and watched her as she proceeded to hurry around the kitchen, opening and slamming cabinet doors, gathering flour, butter, and eggs before whacking the ingredients onto the kitchen table one at a time.

Lucas raised an eyebrow. "What are you doing now? You are making what? You are making a cake?"

Her teeth clenching hard enough to break a molar, she measured three cups full of flour and threw them in a heap onto the table, glad to see a small cloud of flour invade Lucas's space. He waved the cloud away as she dug a hole in the center of her preparation and chucked spoonsful of soft butter onto the mixture.

"C'est beaucoup de beurre, non?" Lucas offered.

"I have tons of choices, myriads of choices in fact," she said as she cracked egg after egg and dropped them into the mixture from high up, plop, plop, making a mess with determination.

"Please sit down for a minute. Stop with those eggs," he pleaded.

"It's the eggs or your skull, Lucas. And taxes are due! And electricity!" She practically yelled. "And I am keeping the fucking house!"

"Your monthly grocery expenditure alone," Lucas began, "Which, by the way, is quite extravagant."

Was Lucas still talking? It came to her like a vision, right there, at six thirty in the morning. All of it came together: the perfect little crescents of dough on the countertop, Lucas in his designer suit, moving his mouth, the children still asleep upstairs, the Mickey Mouse mug, the open cookbook, the gooey mess on the wooden table. She raised her dough-coated hands and held them in mid air. She had flour in her hair, a wayward expression on her face.

Lucas looked at her. "What?"

"I'm having an idea, that's what." Annie said, wide eyed, and at the same time white as a sheet and looking ill.

Her mind was made up that same instant.

CHAPTER 2

*S*omewhere up rue de Cambronne, a truck blocked both lanes. Deliverymen unloaded boxes methodically, indifferent to the honking and the wrath of drivers. Jared watched from the window of his apartment, his forehead glued to the cold window as he tried to wake up and piece together the source of his headache and hangover. He was pretty sure he had not spent the night alone but there was no sign of a woman anywhere. This would make things difficult if and when he saw her again. Merde, he thought.

He peeled little bits of red oil paint off his forearm. Obviously he had painted last night. It was two in the afternoon, and he doubted he'd get any hot water whatsoever, only the lukewarm trickle that would leave him with a sense of being punished for the previous night's excesses. He remembered that his last razor blade had died on him in mid shave and that he was out of cigarettes. The shower and the shave would have to wait. The red paint was sprinkled all over his hair, face, and even his chest like he had been playing paintball in the nude. He tried to scrub it off but the water was too cold. He found last night's clothes scattered around the bedroom, which confirmed that there had been a woman, ran wet fingers through his hair, and walked out of his apartment.

The building manager, in her robe and slippers, was already onto him, her diminutive body creating a barrier in front of the elevator. "Bonjour Madame Dumont!" he called out merrily as he made a rapid 180-degree turn towards the stairs. The furious steps of the old lady's slippers on the wood floor pursued him. "Mais c'est l'aprés-midi! You think it's morning? Well it isn't. And you think it's still December maybe, but this is January and the owner wants her January rent."

"Not the morning? I thought, since you're wearing slippers?" he added with a flirtatious smile. "I like this color on you, by the way."

The building manager almost blushed, giggled, and then came back to her senses. "The rent! La propriétaire wants her rent!"

"Bien sûr, Madame Dumont. Demain," he said as he zoomed down three sets of stairs.

Jared slowed down the instant he came out on the street. He stepped into the corner Café Des Artistes where he stood at the zinc counter, foraging his pockets for money.

"Salut, Jared," Maurice grunted. He noticed the red paint on Jared's face. "Did you slit someone's throat this morning?"

"Salut, Maurice. The usual." Jared counted his money. "Hold the croissant," he said. "Oh, and one pack of Gitanes."

"Pas de croissant?"

"Not hungry," he lied.

Maurice would have had a dignified look to him if it weren't for old acne scars on his cheeks. Unhurried, he wiped the liquor bottles and replaced them on the shelves behind him one by one: Alcohol de Framboise, Grand Marnier, Courvoisier. There was nobility to the repetition of this task and Maurice was in no rush to serve Jared, or anyone. He finally pushed a pack of Gitanes in front of him like a reward for good behavior. Jared opened his first pack of the day, put a cigarette to his mouth, and clicked open his Zippo lighter that smelled of airplane fuel. Maurice placed a café au lait and three paper-wrapped sugar cubes in front of him. The cigarette smoke slowly made its way above his fingers as he sipped coffee amidst the sounds of the coffeemaker, orange juicer, and furious honking outside. He jumped when he realized Maurice had been talking to him.

"The job interview!" Maurice said with unexplained animosity. "How did that work out?"

"Didn't go."

"You didn't go? It was almost a sure thing!"

"I'm not desperate enough to serve appetizers in a tux at one in the afternoon," he said, then noticed Maurice's fitted white shirt and bow tie.

Maurice murdered him with one look. "Maybe you should have kept that rich girlfriend, the one that bought all kinds of stuff."

"She wasn't rich, just well dressed."

"If she was still your girlfriend you'd be ordering a croissant right now," Maurice shrugged. "Imbeciles in tuxedos have a sense about those things."

Jared tossed crumpled euros on the counter, took a last draw of his cigarette, dropped it to the floor, and crushed it with his foot before walking out.

Maurice stepped from behind the counter with a broom and began sweeping the dozen or so cigarette butts that littered the café's tiled floor. "Connard!" he whistled between his teeth.

"Crétin!" Jared mumbled as he walked towards the métro station.

On the street, old people's eyes widened at the sight of the scarlet paint on Jared's hands, hair, and unshaven jaws. Schoolgirls giggled, and women steadied their gazes. Jared walked for a long time. He left the smell of spices and exhaust pipes of his neighborhood, and walked down boulevards and avenues. A half hour later, he was moving through the pristine streets and imposing architecture of the seventeenth arrondissement and came to a halt on rue Montsouri in front of a stately three-story building. He rang one of the three buttons of the intercom. Lucas D'Arbanville. He pushed the button over and over until he heard Lucas's cry over the intercom.

"Who in the world is making this awful racket?"

"It's me."

"Will you please remove your finger from the bell? I'll let you in!"

Lucas opened his apartment door wearing pressed jeans and a Lacoste shirt in a rare shade of mango. Lucas who was in his mid-forties and compared to him looked the picture of health and self-grooming, took one look at him and burst into laughter. "You look absolutely revolting! And what is that smell?"

Jared turned back and started down the stairs.

"Please come on in, Jared, I was just being humorous."

"I'm not in the mood."

"Oh and does it show!" Lucas said, still laughing. Jared turned to leave again.

"No, no, come on, my boy." Lucas grabbed Jared's arm and pulled him inside his apartment. They kissed each other on both cheeks. "I'll make us some coffee."

Jared took in the apartment. Lucas collected Empire furniture, a style that fitted him. He had inherited most of the pieces, but those he had purchased were just as exquisite. There was a watercolor by Henry Miller on the wall opposite his couch, a wild choice for Lucas, maybe an indication that Annie was having a positive impact on him. On the other walls, some very old school paintings, and then, of course, the three large canvases Lucas had bought from him, from the time Jared's oil abstract paintings sold before they dried. On the mahogany desk laced with delicate gold incrustations, an open laptop, a few sheets of fine stationery, and an uncapped Mont Blanc pen were the only signs of human activity. Jared went to sit in the kitchen out of respect for Lucas's prized furniture. He put his hand to his pocket to retrieve his Gitanes but changed his mind.

"I need a cigarette," he said as he dropped into a chair.

Lucas followed him into the kitchen. "I'm working on quitting. I don't have any."

Jared gave him a desperate look.

"All right then, I do have a few packs strictly for emergency," Lucas sighed. "This is an emergency, right?"

"Merde, it is."

Lucas turned on the espresso machine and foraged in a kitchen drawer. He retrieved a brand new pack of cigarettes, and handed it to Jared.

"Marlboro? Light? You're buying the American dream and its bullshit in one fell swoop. She's got you brainwashed."

Lucas ignored the comment. He labored over the complicated machine and then retrieved a wooden box filled with delicate espresso samplers that looked like designer chocolates. "Blow the smoke away from me," Lucas said. "If Annie smells cigarettes on me, she'll never believe I am really quitting."

They sat facing each other at the kitchen table, sipping espresso out of tiny coffee cups without a word. Jared pretended not to notice that Lucas was smiling fondly at him, as Lucas always did when Jared was working his hardest at being a jerk. For a moment, there was only the sound of spoons stirring coffee. Then Jared tried to make amends.

"So how's your love life going? Gotten into Annie's pants yet?"

"Jared, I love you, but you are getting on my nerves. You barge in here rudely, smelling terrible, you demolish my doorbell, steal my last pack of cigarettes, then you insult Annie, and you insult me."

"I'm having a bad day," Jared shrugged.

"So it seems."

"I'm hungry. I need money. I need an exhibition. I need a place to stay. I need a shower that works. I need a girl."

"As a thirty-year-old heartthrob, that last item shouldn't pose too much trouble."

"I mean I want a real girl. Someone who matters." Jared had to confront Lucas's blatant amusement. "I know, I know. That's a first," he said before Lucas could.

Lucas got up, took butter, strawberry compote, and organic orange juice out of the refrigerator, and brought all this plus half a baguette and a serrated knife to the kitchen table.

"Am I really hearing my godson beg me for advice on matters of the heart?"

"Oh please."

"May I at least, feed you breakfast then?"

Jared accepted, wondering again why Lucas, a man so unlike him, so unlike anyone in his life, still persisted in not giving up on him.

Annie sat at the ten-foot-long table in the center of her Parisian kitchen feeling sick to her stomach at the thought of what she was about to do. She had been sitting like this the entire morning while the kids were in school, and now it was time to pick them up for lunch, only she had not prepared lunch. The cold soup on the stove had undoubtedly become a giant Petri dish by now and the baked sea bass was no more than a faint idea from a distant past. The decision was made and that was that. She felt the nausea of someone about to plunge into the void.

She got up and turned on the heat under the soup pot. She'd boil it; hopefully bacteria would get the message. She desperately needed to ingest something liquid, thick, warm and salty like amniotic fluid before she could give birth to her action. Her subconscious must have known she should prepare chicken soup for her future nauseated self.

She loved her kitchen most. It was built some two hundred

years ago, when aristocrats seldom ventured into the servants' quarters. For this reason, it didn't have the formality of the rest of the house. A glass door opened to a small garden with a beautiful stone fountain in the center, and remained open all through spring and summer, making the garden a natural extension of the kitchen. In the warm season, Annie grew every type of herb and the best tomatoes this side of the Seine River. Raspberries climbed wildly along the south-facing wall and an ancient apple tree trained as an espalier produced the sweetest apples of a variety not found in markets. She needed only to step outside her kitchen to help herself. Her own private Garden of Eden. Even now in January, when the plants were dormant and the door to the garden was closed, light flooded in through the glass panes making the kitchen the brightest and most inviting room in the house.

This decision was so unlike her. Or was it? The thing was, there was a before and there was an after to who she was, and she did not know in which category to fit this decision. The person she had been before Johnny's death might have been capable of handling such a decision, but what about the new self, the one that had settled in lately, the one she did not like very much? What was the new self capable of? But really, wasn't the new self, the darker, angrier, more mistrusting self more real, more true to who or what she really was?

She had made terrifying decisions before. The last twelve years of her life, for example, had been the consequence of a single word uttered at the end of a single meal. She had been twenty-three then, and Johnny twenty-eight. He was about to finish grad school and she had three years to go. They were having dinner in a rather seedy Italian restaurant near the campus. Her foot gently rubbed his crotch under the red-and-white-checkered plastic tablecloth. He looked more than ever like Redford in Butch Cassidy and the Sundance Kid. Gorgeous and mischievous. Impossible and irresistible. Outside, the Indian

19

summer was ablaze. They had met at a party. She had made him laugh. Her old self had been silly and free. There had been several months of wild lovemaking and very little studying. They were as physically compatible as two people could be. Two days into what was not yet a relationship, she had known that she was helplessly in love with Johnny, but boy had she worked valiantly not to show it. She was no nitwit; Johnny was an academic star, captain of the Lacrosse team, and voted most likely to weaken ladies' knees. She was wise enough to know he was only hers temporarily. They had been dating for six months, and they never talked about the future. She had never broached the subject of the future, never planned one.

The evening her life changed forever they were, in fact, having what she believed to be their last week together. Johnny was moving to France to become a partner in his older brother's import firm in Paris. Sitting across from him over gooey eggplant parmigiana, Annie was as heartbroken as she appeared nonchalant.

Johnny poured wine into her glass and handed it to her, waited for her to take a sip. "So?" he said, a half smile on his lips. "You want to get married?" She swallowed the wine and coughed, "Do you mean in general? I guess one day, with the right man, at the right time."

"No, not in general. I mean the two of us. This week."

Yes, her stomach dropped indeed. Sank down to her ankles, as a matter of fact. She felt her cheeks burn crimson, as sweat sprang from every pore of her skin. Her shaken response came from the heart. "Me?"

Johnny laughed at that one.

In the Italian restaurant, life moved at a different speed now. Johnny took her hand, placed something in it, and closed her fingers over it. What did she hope to find when she opened her hand?

"Is this some kind of sick joke?" she said, trying to contain the head-to-toe trembling.

She opened her hand. In her palm was a thin gold band.

Across from the table that was now the center of the universe, Johnny looked at her, a bemused expression on his face. "So, what's it gonna be?" he said, tilting his head like a cocker spaniel. "Wanna get hitched and move to Paris with me?"

"I... I will have to get back to you on that," Annie answered, her throat already constricted.

"All right, go ahead," he said. And a second later, "so?"

She laughed, and the same time tried very hard not to cry. If this was a practical joke, she was a dead woman on campus. But she could not hold the tears. "You're not serious."

He had taken her hand, and slowly, incredibly, placed the ring on her finger. "Very serious. Come on, just say yes, don't leave me hanging like this."

And then came the single word that changed her entire life.

"Yes," she sobbed.

They were married a week later so that they could move to France as Mr. and Mrs. Roland. No big wedding, and she couldn't have cared less. The opportunity to work with his brother as soon as he graduated had to be grabbed. Johnny had learned French for years in preparation but Annie knew not a word of French except for bonbon and voulayvouparlay. Her parents disliked the France idea just as much as the Johnny idea. Her mom, especially, was frantic.

"You hardly know him!"

"Well, does one say no to winning the lottery?"

"You did not think this through. You're willingly putting your hand down the meat grinder, that's what you're doing!"

"Oh come on mom, the French can't be that bad."

"I'm not talking about the French, dammit! This... adventurer... your education!"

This was the first time she had ever heard her mother curse.

It turned out that her mom and dad, who got most of their exercise from arguing about virtually everything, united beautifully in disliking Johnny. They insisted Johnny was self-involved, unreliable, and immature. Annie wondered if it had anything to do with the fact that Johnny was too handsome, and that a man who surpasses his wife in beauty has to be immediately suspicious. She wondered if she did not think that herself.

It was a whirlwind time of which she had little recollection. A promising (and expensive) education ended abruptly. She met Johnny's parents for the first time the day of the civil wedding. Tearful goodbyes followed at the airport.

And overnight, or almost, she was a married woman living in Paris. Her sheltered and, up until now, mostly academic life transformed immediately into chaos, confusion, and very hard work. She had to learn an entirely alien language in a particularly alien culture. She had to figure it all out on her own, learn her baguette from her ficelle, her Roquefort from her Reblochon. She had to learn to live without her family. How she missed her family. Without friends. How she missed her friends. And how hard it was to make new ones when you suddenly found your ability to communicate reduced to that of a trained chimpanzee. She had to learn to take care of a husband who worked all the time. Then, so fast, she had to figure out how to raise one, two, and then three children. Heck, she had to learn to take care of herself. She had to learn to make beds, wash laundry, shop, cook, take sick babies to the doctor, and drive through Paris with a stick shift, the whole thing en français!

Her parents had been wrong. Everyone had been. Their ten-year marriage proved it. Yes, Johnny had been immature, independent, but in a way that made every day an adventure. And he wasn't unreliable at all. She trusted him.

It had taken her ten years to feel halfway settled in her new life. And then Johnny died. His death was terribly sudden.

Gruesome. Shocking to all. None of it felt real or possible. Her pain had been abject, the despair of the children intolerable, but also—and this within days of his sudden disappearance from her life—it became clear that she'd never had a normal maturation from young woman to adult. Since arriving in France, she had relied almost entirely on Johnny for everything that took place outside the house. It was in Johnny's nature to take charge, and she had found it easier to let him. She had let him sweep her off her feet, transplant her to Paris, keep her barefoot and pregnant. She was good at being a mother, possibly a mother to the exclusion of everything else. Johnny did the rest. He and his brother Steve had thrown themselves into their business and worked relentlessly at growing it. He traveled a lot in and outside France and handled every aspect of their personal finances—something she would come to bitterly regret after his death. He bought and drove fast cars, dressed more French than the French, became an expert in wine, and because he needed to entertain large groups of people for business, he spent entire evenings in the best restaurants around Paris.

She never much liked the concept of entertaining to improve business, but one day she got the idea that she should entertain those people at home. At least by inviting people over, she and the children got to see Johnny. Via forced practice and also because she found it fun, she soon became an accomplished cook.

By the time Johnny died she had done little in France besides making babies, nursing, pushing strollers, and cooking. When he suddenly disappeared, she was lost again. Once again she had to figure out everything else. Some things never got figured out. The question of how to keep the business going, for example, never got solved. The business was shut down and with it all hope for an income. Another aspect of her life she had not been able to figure out yet was how to recover from more subtle losses: her carefree nature, innocence, playfulness, and the luxury of trust.

She was tough now, tough as in strong, and tough as in hard. She was a tough-as-nails mother, and tough-as-nails femme au foyer, or what Americans call a homemaker. She couldn't argue the making part. She was making that home all right, if it killed her. Two and a half years later she was no longer the soft mother, the round-hipped and milky-breasted creature protected and taken care of by a man. She had become a she-bull that everyone (beside her children—hopefully not her children—and the indefatigable Lucas) feared and avoided. She had become the Sarah Connor of remodeling projects, as rough as the skin on her hands, as heavy as the bags of plaster she hauled up the stairs, and as hard as the planks she fed into the circular saw. She was busy building herself and the children a house out of something stronger than brick; something strong enough to never again let pain in. That home—that house—was her Great Wall of China, her Maginot line. It was her refuge and her jailor, her passion and her foe, her salvation and her demise.

She rubbed cream on her hands where the skin was the worst. She did everything herself in the house. No job too small, or too big. The very table she sat at was an example. She had painted it a warm tone of red, painstakingly varnished it, and had nearly passed out from the fumes. The stairwell was another example of her work, reconstructed plank by plank, so were every chair, couch and sofa in the house: scavenged, reupholstered and the woodwork refinished by yours truly.

The soft January light flattered and caressed every surface of the beloved kitchen. The carrera marble countertop, she kept in perfect shape. The ancient tile floor, she had regrouted herself with a hundred-year-old recipe that mixed sand, glue, and pigment. The glorious three-oven eight-burner AGA range, she had recomposed piece by piece.

The light and the silence of mid-morning gave the kitchen the wistful feeling of an old painting. Those were lonely hours before the boys came back from school. Maxence was nine now,

Laurent seven, and Paul five. They walked to school at the Lycée International, a few blocks away from the house. Thanks to the French education system, they came home for lunch daily so that she could do what she did best—feed them and smother them to death. In exchange, the boys gave her life meaning and purpose.

The enemy was Thinking. No, the enemy was Time, or having too much of it when the kids were at school, especially now that Paul was in kindergarten. Too much time bred too much thinking and that she could not have. Her next therapy, she had already decided, would have the combined benefits of being cheap and brutal. She wanted to refinish the maple wood floor in the entryway, a task that included, but was not limited to, sanding, gluing, restoring, tinting, varnishing, coughing, and crying. But projects didn't solve everything; as her arms and fingers moved, so did her mind, and in pretty tight circles, too. And projects ended. Once the floor was refinished, then what? And now that she was utterly and desperately penniless, now really what?

Money had come to them via Johnny's side of the family, in the form of a substantial inheritance at a time when the dollar was worth a whole lot more. She and Johnny had visited dozens of places, penthouses with pools, and apartments with views of the Trocadéro or the Eiffel Tower. The real estate woman wore skin-tight suits and stiletto heels and walked with each foot precisely in front of the other, as though there were cliffs on either side of her. Annie became excellent at imitating her behind her back to make Johnny laugh.

They saw the house on a spring day. The stiletto woman had shown it to them as an afterthought. "It came on the market this morning. I haven't seen it, but look at the listing, an eight-bedroom townhouse with a private garden in the heart of the sixteenth arrondissement? There is work, it says. But the street alone is a gem," she had assured them with a whisper that indicated that awe and respect were de rigueur. "It isn't authorized to through traffic. There is a gate to the street."

"A Parisian's take on the gated community," Johnny pointed out.

"I'm against it on principle," Annie said.

But as soon as the three entered the street, bird songs and the smell of jasmine replaced the noise and smell of traffic. The street was lined with centuries-old gnarled sycamores, and the trees' tender spring leaves filtered light like in a meadow. The real estate woman's ankles bent in frightening angles on the cobblestone pavement, and Annie admired one more time the way French women surrendered to the enslavement of elegance.

The houses on the private alley were all hôtel particuliers, town houses, which really looked like miniature castles to her eyes, with their beautiful facades and moldings, handsome roofs and tall windows framed by well-kept wooden shutters symmetrically placed on either side of impressive front doors. One hôtel particulier was lovelier than the next. They had been built in the Haussman era and been kept up with respect to the protected historic monuments they were.

All except for the house in front of which the real estate woman was standing. She pointed an accusatory finger towards it. "What a pity. Quelle honte, non?" she said and turned toward them. Johnny made a sour face and looked at Annie.

Annie paid no attention. She was in the process of falling in love. Her face showed it before she knew it herself. This hôtel particulier was the very definition of ramshackle. Windows were broken, shutters missing, and the roof seemed to have collapsed in places, but Boston ivy and wisteria laced the stone walls and added softness to the architecture, giving the house a wildly romantic air. The owner, "Une folle avec ses chats" as defined by the real estate woman, had lacked funds but steadfastly refused to move. She had recently died inside the house and had been discovered there, dead among her cats a few days after the fact.

The gruesomeness of the visual and the condition of the house made it borderline unsellable.

"We'll take it," Annie had said.

Johnny had looked at her with amusement. "Do we know that there is an actual inside to this place?"

The stiletto woman, seeing Annie's face, started to work on Johnny. With time and money, she insisted, it could become the quintessence of class and luxury in terms of Parisian living. The woman and Johnny spent an inauspicious amount of time trying to open the door, but when they did, Annie thought she had entered Ali Baba's cavern.

The house had soaring ceilings, original crown moldings, and crumbling chandeliers that had seldom been violated by a dust broom. Years of wallpaper layers fell in patches, and the smell of cat urine grabbed the throat like a claw. There were only two bathrooms, both with impractical claw-foot tubs, broken bidets, cracked faucets, and exquisite mosaic tile Annie knew instantly she would never tear down.

The house was purchased. "With time and money" became the motto. With time and money, the fissured stucco could be restored. With time and money, the wood floors could be brought back to their original luster. With time and money, the stories could be connected with proper working stairs. There had been no plan for time or money to run short.

She now saw things as they were: Johnny had been the world to her, and now the house and her boys were her entire universe. Within the confines of the house, no matter how limiting or punishing it might be, she felt safe. Only in her house did she see herself as master of her life. At home cooking, building, scraping and sanding, she felt capable and purposeful. Focusing on what was still a constant—the house and the boys—she did not need to let questions in, questions about Johnny, questions about what would have come of her had Johnny not died, questions also, about her own worth, the risks involved in loving and trusting someone, the validity of a life devoid of trust or love. Since that night two and a half years ago, she had become like someone with a fear of heights condemned to live on a rooftop.

Her decision, for someone who had so carefully avoided the exterior world, might seem out of character, but in fact it allowed her, with what she considered to be a modest adjustment, to keep the status quo. She would get to stay home. All she really wanted was to stay home like the old woman who had died amongst her cats.

CHAPTER 3

*L*ola opened her window wide to improve the master bedroom's Feng Shui, but then she remembered that article in the yoga journal on Southern California's air being the worst in the nation, so she closed it. Surely it couldn't be true about Bel Air, with all those trees? They must be talking about the Port area, or the San Fernando Valley. She unrolled her mat and sat on it for a few minutes of meditation. She bit her lower lip, felt it still hard and sore two days after the injection. Coming from the kitchen downstairs were the sounds of a coffee grinder and pans being moved around. Serena, the maid, was preparing breakfast. Lola straightened her spine and closed her eyes. I'm breathing in. I'm breathing out.

The way Mark moved inside the walk-in closet, Lola knew he was getting himself worked up. "Why can't I find a goddamn thing in this house?" he said.

She relaxed her arms and laid her hands, palms up, on her knees. I'm breathing in. I'm breathing out. Whatever was needed was always elsewhere, far away and rarely in the expected place because the nanny and the maid were always in competition when it came to running the house, organizing closets and cabinets according to their conflicting senses of logic. Lola didn't have what it took to demand that things be put in any specific place or done any specific way. Instead, she forever adapted, forever navigated her "staff." She wasn't a very good hostess, or housewife, or "CEO of the household," or even "wife on duty," titles Mark called her for fun.

"Lola!" Mark called. She got up and escaped to her bathroom. In front of the mirror, she tapped her lips with the tip of a finger. They felt like wood. Did she look better or ridiculous? On the walls, her face graced the covers of Cosmopolitan, Elle, and Marie Claire. Twenty years of her life relegated to the walls of her bathroom.

This last year, all the headaches with Simon had probably cost her triple in the looks department, but she was lucky to have good bone structure. Her ink-black hair was cut short in a trendy style. She was tall and thin with imposing boobs—paid cash, as Mark liked to say. She was almost forty and still turned heads.

Leaving Mark to his struggle, she tiptoed out of her bathroom and descended the stairs dressed for yoga. The sound of pans in the kitchen resonated inside the stairwell. Maybe it was the height of the ceiling, but no amount of rugs could muffle the odd echoes. Mark liked the mansion pristine, all 7,640 square feet of it. He had said she'd never lack anything. He was speaking of material things, of course.

In the kitchen, Tamara, the twenty-five-year-old nanny from South Africa, was feeding Simon in his high chair. Lia was only half dressed for school, and her hair wasn't combed. Lola had helped her nine-year-old select two outfits for the day, to circumvent early morning meltdown, but Lia was wearing yet another combination, and now was stabbing her spoon into her cereal bowl and not making eye contact. Is anger genetic or learned? Lola kissed Simon, took a mini lick of a speck of pudding on his cheek. "You taste delicious today," she said.

"Mom, that's disgusting," Lia said.

Lola kissed the top of her daughter's head. Mark's call came from upstairs and tore through the silence of the house like skid marks on white linoleum floor. "Where is my fucking Donna Karan shirt?" Everyone in the kitchen—Lola, the kids, Serena, and Tamara—froze for a heartbeat.

"It's right in the closet," Lola called out.

"Not that one, dammit! The white one! Where the hell is it?" Mark yelled from the stairwell. She smiled at Serena, who could barely look at her. Simon flailed his arm at his mother. "Up me."

"I'm not carrying you, love. You need to finish breakfast."

In an instant, Simon had wriggled his way out of the chair, threatening to make it topple over. "Up me! Up me!" Tamara picked him out of his chair and set him down.

The pediatrician didn't know if what Simon suffered from were nightmares or night terrors. What difference did it make? Last time Lola had taken Simon to the doctor, not knowing where to start with the list of things that worried her about him, she had felt like a complete idiot. The doctor had looked at her intently and prescribed a lot of love and a very soothing environment. It made Lola feel as though she was an abusive mother and he knew it. She had done what was prescribed and kept Simon in the house with the nanny most of the day. She limited their outings to visits to the nearby park and had stopped mommy and me classes. Obviously, preschool was out of the question.

Simon's hands were covered in chocolate pudding and she lifted him in mid-run before he hit the white upholstering of the kitchen chairs. She didn't need a fight between Serena and Tamara over who would be responsible for cleaning that stain. Simon's furious little body jerked as Lola held him under her arms and carried him towards the kitchen sink. Mark's voice thundered from the upstairs bedroom. Lola sat Simon up on her knee by the sink. As she was running warm water over Simon's hand, it suddenly dawned on her that the shirt Mark wanted was still at the cleaners. She felt dread, wiped Simon's hands with the cloth Tamara handed to her, thinking rapidly.

"What about the Armani shirt, honey?" she called out with the hint of a shrill in her voice. "Or what about that other one that you wear all the time? They're clean, pressed, and ready to go."

She heard Mark running heavily down the stairs. He appeared in the kitchen, his face red and half a dozen white shirts on hangers in his hands. Tamara and Serena stepped out of his way. He came to an abrupt stop on the other side of the kitchen island to face Lola. "Are you saying my white shirt hasn't been cleaned?"

Lola put Simon down and gave him a gentle push, which resulted in Simon wrapping himself around her leg. "What about the two brand new ones, you know, the..."

"I'm about to have an extremely important meeting," Mark, roared. "The one thing I ask is to have the proper clothes available!"

Lola looked at Tamara in a plea for her to take Simon out of the room. Tamara, on instinct, was already motioning for Simon to come, but Simon tightened his grip on Lola's leg. Tamara tried to pry him off with no success as Mark stepped toward Lola and inched close enough that she could smell his toothpaste breath and see the pores on his face. His handsome, freshly shaven face, tanned skin, bleached teeth, the face of a winner. "Are you incapacitated in some way I should know about?" he sneered.

Lola glanced at the clock, at Simon wailing in Tamara's arms, then at Lia who was entering the room timidly to get her shoes tied, and then back at the clock. Mark looked at Lia. "And what do you want?" Lia looked down at her dangling shoelaces. "Nine years old and you can't tie your own shoes? Is this whole family handicapped, or what?" Lia bent down and tied her shoes. "I need that shirt!" he screamed. "Get me that shirt!"

"It's at the cleaners," Lola said. "I'll be back in no time at all. I won't even make you late."

Lola could see Mark's rage feeding on itself. "You've already made me late! I get no support in this house. I carry your ineptitude on my shoulders!"

Had he been physically abusive, maybe things would be clearer. The way it went, it was all so confusing. Later today, they might call what just happened "blowing a fuse." They might even laugh at it. She would laugh at it. But for the moment, she was scared, but of what? Perhaps of what Simon and Lia were hearing, of what Mark might do or say? Scared, perhaps that he might be right about her.

Her silence had a way of making him even more furious, but she didn't know what to say, especially with the children in the room. The angrier he got, the more she became paralyzed.

"Please calm down," she pleaded finally.

"Why should I?" he screamed.

She searched for words, a reason to give him. "Because I...I can't handle it?" she finally said. Yes, it was formulated as a question, and in that question, she got her answer.

"What is it you can't handle? Is it your basic role as my wife?" He lowered his voice and talked in her ear between clenched teeth, showing that he was enough in control of himself to spare the children. "If you can't handle it, get yourself a fucking divorce. That's what all your girlfriends are doing, sucking their husbands dry, those gold diggers. I don't even know what you're fucking waiting for."

Divorce, that word. Here it was again, used in vain. It occurred to her finally that Mark was no longer talking about shirts, but about her turning him down for sex again earlier that morning. Her basic role as a wife.

Lia was standing near the front door, suddenly ready for school. A miracle. She had managed to comb her hair in front although the back of her head was still a tangled mess. She had found her backpack, her jacket even, and had put them on. Her little face was pale and tight. Simon's wails were like a siren in the background. He was still fighting his way out of Tamara's arms. Serena was wiping the granite kitchen counter with ardor.

"I'm getting the shirt," Lola said, and a moment later, she and Lia darted toward the front door. Simon managed to break free and grab Lola's leg again, so she picked him up, held him tight, and snatched her purse. The three of them sprinted toward her car while, still in the kitchen, Mark was thrashing shirts and hangers around the room.

Once in the car with the doors shut, an overwhelming sense of relief enveloped Lola. All she needed to do was get the shirt, drop it off at home, and then drive to school. It wouldn't take more than ten minutes. Lia would get a tardy at school, but so be it.

She drove slowly along the driveway. I'm breathing in. I'm breathing out. Cleansing breath. Yoga breath. The worst part of the morning had passed. Tonight, Mark would probably act as though nothing had happened, or else he'd make a joke about it. The frustration over Lola avoiding sex would probably never be discussed. Mark would calmly explain what he was really angry about. He would give her the list of the ways in which she was failing him, and she would believe him. I'm breathing in. I'm breathing out. That night, they would have sex.

She swallowed the urge to cry. Serenity. She said the word silently. I have a choice about how I feel. I have a choice about my words, and I have a choice about my thoughts. She glanced back to look at the children in the rearview mirror. Lia was sitting tensely upright, her face pale, and her mouth tight. Simon was chewing on the sleeve of his sweatshirt and it was soaked. She turned onto Sunset Boulevard, accompanied by the creeping feeling that was with her everywhere lately and that she wasn't able to name.

Althea allowed herself the apple that had been the ever-present center of her thoughts all morning long. She went to the bare kitchen where she had never prepared a thing but tea, and opened the refrigerator. Lemons, apples, baking soda. She took the apple to the coffee table, the only table in her apartment, and placed the apple on a large plate. She turned on the TV and, as she watched, cut the apple into quarters, then quarters of quarters with long, dexterous fingers that felt foreign to her. Over the next half hour, she chewed the apple slowly, making herself aware of the minutest sensation.

Later, on the way to her parents, she didn't pass another soul. Half of Ohio had been battered by an ice storm, and the wind was merciless. She walked close to buildings for shelter as her long red hair battered her face like a whip. She was light enough to be carried away by the wind. Light and small, but never light enough or small enough. She would soon be twenty-five but exhaustion and anxiety made every step feel as though she was closer to eighty.

She stood in front of the door for a few seconds, and finally let herself in. Her dad's glasses sat crooked on his face as he slept in front of the blaring TV. Althea wondered when her dad had started taking naps before lunch. Sounds were coming from the kitchen. Her mother, Pamela, was cooking. Althea gathered her strength and put her hands on the doorknob. In the kitchen, her mother's body had the familiar stiffness as she moved around with heavy steps in a state of contained exasperation. Althea tried to not look at her thighs or her prominent stomach. The kiss she deposited on her mother's cheek wasn't acknowledged.

"What took you so damn long? Now we won't be able to eat until one o'clock! Now the entire day will be off. We won't be hungry at dinnertime!"

Conscious of the fact that she had deliberately arrived late, Althea didn't ask why any of this mattered, since nothing would happen between lunch and dinner. Those were criminal thoughts, unacceptable thoughts. "I'm not that hungry at all. Maybe a small salad and we could eat right away?" she blabbered. "I'm making Duck à la orange! It's French. There is a sweet orange gravy, and I'm making a noodle pudding to go with it." She gave her daughter a piercing look, her face like a permanent warning. "Your favorite."

By coming over only once a week, Althea deprived her mother of her only joy, which was to feed her. "Thanks, Mom." she said, and wondered how she would swallow that thing.

"Peel these oranges, will you."

Althea curled up on a kitchen chair, took the sharp knife her mother handed her, and began cutting a shallow groove in the peel around each orange. She detached each peel with her thumb and laid it on the table, one orange peel spiral after another, and racked her brain for something interesting to say. "Sandra told me she overheard I wouldn't receive a bonus this year. Anything she can say to upset me."

"Sandra? Is that the girl with the gorgeous skin?" her mom asked.

"That's the girl who's jealous of me, you know, because of her obesity."

Pamela grabbed the orange peels from the table and dumped them into the trash can. Althea's mind raced, madly searching for what in that story had displeased her mother. She handed Pamela the last peeled orange and laid both hands flat on the kitchen table, the knife set vertically between her hands. There had been no such exchange with Sandra; in fact, she had never spoken to her in five years at the company. Sandra was just a person in a cubicle. Althea was here to give her mother a reason for living by swallowing her food and bringing her the exterior world. But she felt so disconnected from the exterior world herself that she had to make things up as she went or there would truly be no point in her coming here week after week. "Sandra has no self-control with food. It's tragic!" she said.

"But she has such a lovely face!" Her mom always sided against her, defending perfect strangers.

"She's a backstabber," Althea protested weakly.

"Everyone is a backstabber to you."

Pamela dipped the raw duck into a casserole where margarine and oil had begun to bubble up and turn brown. Grease particles exploded around the stove. Althea recoiled in her chair.

"How's that ex of yours behaving these days?" Pamela said. "He could be spreading nasty rumors about you."

"Tom was a loser. You were so right about him."

"I told you it wouldn't last," her mom said, delighted.

It was true that pretend-Tom had to be dumped. It was getting too pretend-serious, and Althea was running out of plot for that character. The break up gave her an excuse to skip a few visits to her parents while she grieved the imaginary relationship. Those few weeks without the dread of the parental visit had been a relief. She had felt lighter at first, but then heavier than ever when she realized her parents did not feel the urge to call or visit her. Were they too depressed, too deadened or too selfish to bother themselves with her wellbeing? For as long as she could remember, it had been her job to worry about theirs.

At lunch, Althea devoured everything and flooded her mom with the required compliments about her cooking. Twice during lunch, Althea excused herself and went to the bathroom to vomit. When she got back to the table, flushed, neither parents lifted their gazes from the TV set.

CHAPTER 4

*I*f Annie rented out three rooms, she'd make enough to cover all her expenses. Renting out the fourth room would be gravy. It solved so many problems, it was a thing of beauty. No need to sell the house, no need to move, no need to work, no need to go back to school. And like Lucas would probably say—and she could hear him from here—no need to go out of the house ever again. Her plan would keep her financially afloat, and terrifyingly busy, which was the name of the game. As a bonus, the plan would freak Lucas out. A thing of beauty indeed. The plan wasn't without a glitch. She would be forced to deal with actual people. Actual people invading her space. That nagging thought kept buzzing about her head but she waved it away angrily like she would a mosquito.

In the kitchen, she adjusted the angles of the grow lights over the seedlings. Her chest fluttered with anxiety, her brain on overdrive. Could this be done? It had to be done. Had to. In her head, she rehearsed what she would tell Lucas. Trying to virtually convince him helped her convince herself. The fact that he would be against it fueled her determination. There would be people, yes, people. Strangers, in her home. Didn't she used to be gregarious? What had changed? Was this the new her? The permanent her? Strangers would be fine. Just fine.

The first miniature tomato leaves were unfolding already. She had grown vegetables even when Johnny was alive. She liked to get her hands in the dirt, a primeval compulsion of hers she had not discovered until adulthood. Johnny had loved to poke fun at her ordering of rare seeds in the dead of winter, at her schlepping of store-bought soil and organic fertilizer. Later, in the summer, he'd say, "Could you pass the fifty-euro tomato slices please."

Growing the seedlings was her way of fighting winter blues. Tomatoes, especially, gave her a sense of hope. Tomatoes meant summer, sunlight, heat, the children home from school for nearly three months. She clipped a few leaves with her nails. The scent of tomato leaves suddenly threw her back to a few summers ago, her on her knees picking tomatoes in the garden. She was tired, hot, and dirty from the gardening but loving it, loving being eight months pregnant, with two little kids running around, loving living in France in her beautiful house, but furious at Johnny for being gone all the time, for not helping more. Johnny had been nearly impossible to fight with. He was the kind of man who could charm you out of wanting to kill him. But that day, she had had it. He was gone on a seminar for the weekend, again. This combined with all the evenings when he didn't come back from work until late in the night. She was tired of being a single mom and tired of his excuses. Yet she remembered her anger at him transforming to joy when he surprised her by arriving in the garden dressed in a white cotton shirt and cream linen pants.

"I remember you," she had said. "You're my husband, the one supposed to be at a seminar all weekend."

"I'm blowing it off."

"You are?"

"I felt like being with you."

Oh, those sweet words. But not this time. No, this time she

was mad. "How come you're dressed so fancy? You look suspiciously gorgeous."

Johnny had lifted her, taken her in his arms, tipped her backwards and planted a kiss on her lips. "You're the gorgeous one."

She had tilted her neck back to be kissed there and whined. "I'm fat."

Johnny whispered in her neck. "You're pregnant. What? Didn't anyone tell you?"

"Pregnant? I thought it was the damned French food," she had moaned. "I hate the French."

He puts his hands all over her. "I like to have yummy things to hold on to."

In the light of her bio bulbs, Annie shivered. She cleaned up the dirt around the pots, added the emulsion of fish and kelp and wiped her hands on her jeans. Her fat jeans, without the excuse of being pregnant. She wasn't exactly morbidly obese; maybe thirty pounds over her ideal weight, but even her ideal weight was unacceptably plump by Parisian standard. The chance of her finding someone, a man, so to speak, who'd be into her the way she looked, was, unlike her, pretty slim. Not that she was looking. Besides, this was Paris. Every woman out here was more put-together, more flirtatious, and more self-confident than she was.

She contemplated the neat little rows of seedlings. At least something in this kitchen was growing in height rather than width. These days, she felt a different kind of kinship with her house: she identified with it. Like her house, she badly needed some T.L.C. Like her house, it required just the right kind of person to see the beauty within. Like her house, she appeared to stand strong, but cracks were appearing everywhere. Like her house, it felt that just below the surface, everything could erupt or unravel without notice.

Ten years into the remodel, the house was greatly improved, livable, full of charm, but still falling apart at the seams in too many places. Even the plumbing was antique, though not in the noble sense of the word. But Annie didn't mind the imperfections. Her house was like a demanding child, and she was going to love that child, take care of that child and above all else, accept it just the way it was, leaky plumbing and all.

The question was: would her tenants share her taste for charm and whimsy over modern comfort? Her decision to not rent rooms to French people had been immediate. She'd had enough of their cigarettes, and their complaints. Complaining in France, as she had discovered over the years, had nothing to do with negativity. Au contraire, it was the sign of a discriminating mind. Complaining was an art form here. Her house was her turf, and she intended to remain the complainer En Chef. Not only that, but a French or even a European tenant would have all those annoying rights, whereas she would have no problem kicking out a fellow American if things didn't work out. And because of the language, renting out rooms to Americans was the logical thing to do.

She had feverishly typed numbers on her calculator all morning. She needed three tenants to make the money work. She had four rooms she could rent out, but could do with three tenants. She was also sure of one other thing. They had to be women. She wasn't sure she liked women strangers so much better than men strangers, but women felt safer as far as having them under her roof and in contact with her boys. She had boasted to Johnny once, "I can beat the shit out of any woman, if need be."

"Or given the opportunity," he had suggested.

So maybe she had been antisocial even before Johnny was gone? Had she been less angry then? Her mind was teeming with images of perfect tenants. Why did they all look like herself, plump, in their late thirties, dowdily dressed, hair troll-like? The ideal woman would be single, of course. Not an adventurer. Maybe she had a child. The thought of additional children in her home reassured her. Kids running around, that was the salt of the earth. In her head, she was composing an ad, the kind of ad that would appeal to just the right person. A woman in need was something she could wrap her mind around. Not someone too needy, but someone vulnerable. Someone gentle. There had to be women out there looking for a chance to start fresh, and not everyone was the fighter that she was.

She would open her home, help them out. It would keep her busy, and if it all worked out, this spring, her tomato seedlings would find their home in the backyard again. But first, she had to face Lucas.

"Well, of course this is indeed the worst idea I have ever heard," Lucas said. "Une très mauvaise idée." He coughed, took out a handkerchief and dabbed his eyes. A real-life handkerchief, Annie wondered in amazement. Lucas recouped, put on his reading glasses and ceremonially opened his menu. "I'm told the braised foie gras is divine," he said.

They were sitting at one of the most sought-after tables at Gourmet des Ternes, a restaurant as expensive as it was exclusive, and one of the perks of having Lucas as a friend. At the next table, quintessentially chic Parisian women chatted as they ate. Annie stared down at her white blouse for stains and realized the last wash had shrunken it a bit and her boobs were threatening to burst out. They very well might before the end of the meal. The waiter took their order with the manner of a funeral director. Lucas matched his tone, prompting Annie to stuff her mouth with too much bread. When the waiter left, she spoke with her mouth full. "For months now, you've been telling me I need to do something about my financial situation, and now that I do, you're pissed."

Lucas stooped as though he carried France's national debt on his shoulders. "I said do something. Not do anything. Strangers are going to invade our—your life, and once they're here, living here, you won't have any way to get rid of them."

Annie swallowed her bread and held her chin high. "I'll select them very carefully."

"On the phone? Carefully on the phone?"

"I can tell a lot about people on the phone. I'm pretty perceptive."

Lucas shrugged for the tenth time in the conversation; a very French expression of disapproval combined with exasperation, adding to that shrug a grunt and an eye roll for added weight.

"I am. Don't patronize me."

"C'est une très mauvaise idée," Lucas said, almost desperately.

The appetizers arrived, crudités for him, and for her, foie gras and another half a pound on each thigh. She watched Lucas eat and had to hide a smile. Lucas was slightly inbred, but in a good way. He wasn't bad looking at all. He had style, definitely. He was tall, lanky, and awfully proper. On paper, he was a catch, but he gave out that subtle vibe, an interesting mix of womanizer and gay-in-the-closet, a type found a lot in Paris.

Lucas had been Johnny's good friend, and she had known Lucas for twelve years now. But it was only since Johnny's death that Lucas had become a friend to her. When he was Johnny's friend, she had mistrusted him. Too well dressed, too blue blooded, a playboy who had never married and wasn't committed to anyone in particular. And then there was the politeness, the careful diction, the insistence on kissing her hand like she was the frigging queen of England, and all those big words, which she now realized were not an affectation. Was it his fault he'd had a semi-aristocratic upbringing? But now that they were friends, the other side of Lucas had revealed itself: the humor, the hilarious naiveté, the patience, the unwavering dependability, and what she valued most, the blunt honesty.

Lucas lived alone in an atrociously expensive apartment in the seventeenth arrondissement. Old Madame Dubois cooked his meals and pressed his laundry, as she had done for the last twenty years. Lucas had love interests, but too many of them. His excuse was that he was forever searching, relentlessly hunting the perfect woman. The relationships lasted long enough for him to regale Annie with stories that involved mystical themes such as his sex drive and the size of his penis—large, allegedly.

"And how are you planning on finding lodgers?"

"I ran the ad in Chicago, L.A., and Cincinnati papers."

"Americans!" he moaned, "Pourquoi?"

"Chicago because of the Bulls, Los Angeles because of the Lakers, and Cincinnati because of the Reds. I had to start somewhere."

"This is doomed. Doomed."

Reminding herself that this was actually a fight, Annie took the high road for once. They were, after all, in an exclusive restaurant. She made her voice calm but firm.

"You've always been very supportive. I need you to help me make this work. I've made up my mind."

Lucas's pale blue eyes were sad for a moment. He brought the fork to his mouth, chewed slowly, and said, "You and the boys could come and live with me. You could rent out the house until it sells."

Calm but firm, she thought, then she yelped, "Three active boys and me, your sloppiest friend, living on top of each other in your annex of the Louvre?" To demonstrate her sloppiness, Annie made a big gesture that tipped her precious glass of Château Margaux. The red wine had barely hit the white table cloth when three waiters materialized, one to fill her glass, one to place a napkin over the injured tablecloth, and the third possibly to serve as a kind of visual shield. An instant later, they had disappeared.

For a moment, Lucas seemed to consider the image of Annie and her boys ransacking his apartment. "If your house sells as well as it should, you could rent a two-bedroom outside Paris and live reasonably well on a small income."

"Outside Paris! La banlieue?"

"My dear, have you become one of us Parisian snobs?" Lucas expertly weaved crudités onto his silver fork and added, "That of course takes into consideration reimbursing all your credit cards and the backlog of electricity and telephone. I was thinking, perhaps a translating job, something that would allow for a flexible schedule."

"Translating? In the suburbs?" She had spoken too loudly. The women at the next table looked at her ever so slightly, then looked away.

"A snob indeed." Lucas said.

Annie felt her eyes moisten. She hated that about herself. She got so frigging teary. "My house is my life and you know that."

"I know, I know," Lucas said softly. "But look at you. You could extend yourself outside the house, have a real life. You are still young. And pretty." Annie shrugged off the notion, but Lucas insisted. "Yes, yes, you are. You could make a nice life for yourself. Find companionship perhaps?"

Annie rose one eyebrow. "Companionship?"

"At the very least you must consider the silver lining of your financial crisis. This might force you to drive again, to take classes, maybe travel."

"What possesses you to think I want those things? I'm perfectly content with staying home."

"Content perhaps. But happy? Are you happy?"

"What's happy anyway? My house and my kids around me are all that I need."

"What about companionship?"

She shook her head. "What the hell, Lucas? Companionship? You want me to get a dog?"

Lucas hesitated, as though the word cost him to pronounce; "Un homme?"

"It's a myth perpetuated by men that a woman cannot be whole without a man. I don't need a man. I have a man." She caught herself. "I had a man. I don't believe the perfect man will come knocking at my door twice. That's another myth. And besides," she said grabbing Lucas's hand, "I have you. Why would I need a man?"

"Yes, you have me," Lucas answered, looking away.

"This is a good idea and you know it," Annie said.

"Don't do it."

Annie finished her glass. "I'm doing it."

She left the lunch not having convinced Lucas, but suddenly resolute. Of course, she would not do anything without talking to the boys first, particularly Maxence. No, she did not need his authorization. But the truth about their financial problems was going to come out sooner or later, and this was the alternative solution to moving. They'd understand that. Maxence would say "double you tee eff." WTF was his new thing. Where had he learned that? Irritating because he had found a loophole around swearing. She could not justify forbidding him from pronouncing letters, and now all three kids were saying WTF about everything.

At pick-up time, she waited for them on the other side of the street facing the school to avoid the mob of moms and conversations. She waited and watched the pretty French mothers, always in pairs or small groups, rapidly talking or laughing, always stylish and lovely. She watched them from the other side of the street for a long time wondering what they could be talking about. What could be so enthralling? They were taking their children to the park probably, or to each other's houses. Her own friends were all in the U.S. and she sometimes communicated with them, but not often. Since she arrived in France, she had not felt the need for women friends. Johnny had been all she needed, and she had been too busy having babies to notice the empty space. Now she noticed it but it was too late.

She had forgotten how to make friends, found it terrifying, in fact. And French women were still a mystery to her; their way of relating so different from what she knew. But it was not only because they were French. Annie found that she mistrusted women, the cattiness, and the competition, a leftover from having to keep women off Johnny.

There was the sound of a school bell and almost simultaneously the large wooden door opened and children poured out of the building. Colorful coats, hats, backpacks, boots, strollers, and umbrellas mixed in with the sounds of voices. She saw her boys finally and her heart leaped. They had found each other as they always did before getting into the street. She waved for them to stay put and crossed the street. Maxence, her eldest, her nine-year-old little man, so young but so frighteningly mature was holding each of his brothers by the hand.

They walked back home and she listened to their day and let them talk her into a stop at the pâtisserie. The strawberry tartelettes, were ridiculously expensive with strawberries being so entirely out of season, but she said yes.

"You said it was too expensive yesterday," Maxence pointed out.

"It's cheaper today."

"It's the same price. Look: 2.5 euros each."

Annie sighed. "I'll have one too after all," she told the boulangère.

Once at home, she set the tartelettes in front of each boy, cleared her throat and told them about her plan. Paul and Laurent seemed uninterested at best and more into counting the remaining strawberries on each other's tart. She asked, "What do you think? Do you have questions about this?" Paul and Laurent looked at Maxence for clues.

Maxence made a gagging face like he had swallowed something horribly bitter. "For how long?"

"We don't know, baby. They pay month-to-month. I'm hoping they'll stay six months, maybe more."

"Six months!" he wailed. His brothers chewed in silence, watching Maxence. Maxence was the one she had to convince. He was the alpha dog of the pack.

"We're not doing it because it's fun," she said.

"It's not going to be fun at all," Maxence announced. The way he said it, he actually looked like Lucas. She wondered if the two had been speaking.

"Okay. We're doing it because we don't have a choice, then."

"I thought you told me we always have a choice."

She sighed. Semantics and her eldest! Her changing moods and frazzled actions drove him mad. Maxence was too pragmatic, too mature. Maybe that's why she tried hard not to talk to him like the adult he pretended to be. She called him "baby" more so than the younger two. She gathered her strength for one of those courteous, reasonable, very grown-up arguments that always left her exhausted. "The choice," she said, "was to sell the house or have tenants. We chose to have tenants."

"Who's we?"

"We, well, of course, I...Lucas and I decided..."

Maxence rocked from side to side on his chair, hands in his pockets, the tartelette still sitting in front of him untouched. Annie adored his unruly hair, his freckles, his stubbornness.

"One, Lucas is against it," Maxence said from a corner of his mouth.

"How do you know that?" she cried out.

"It was me," Paul said triumphantly. "I heard it! I told them!"

"You knew? You knew I was planning this and told me nothing?"

"Two," Maxence continued, "Lucas doesn't make the decisions. You do."

Touché. She took a deep breath, "Then I guess this was a unilateral, unanimous decision between me, myself, and I."

Maxence calmly bit into the pastry. "And what if your unanimous decision is ruining your kids' lives?"

"Guys, I'll make it up to you," she whined. "Somehow, I swear I'll make it up to you."

"Can we get the Internet?" Laurent asked.

She looked at her boys. Was it a furtive sign of complicity she was reading in their way of avoiding looking at each other? "What's going on around here?"

"And we really want to get cable, Mom," Laurent said. "We really, really, really need it."

CHAPTER 5

*A*t the bank, she signed her name, Althea Hoyt. The Bank of America teller handed her the handwritten piece of paper. There was the number: exactly $50,000 in her savings. She had just withdrawn the $351.23 to make that number cleaner. Althea was drawn to evenness, and she was going to spend $351.23 on something for herself. She put the bills and coins in her wallet and said thank you to the teller, aware of his stare.

Saving all this money had been challenging. She was single but had quite a few expenses: the rent for the apartment, apples, tea, cable, and telephone. She was low maintenance, always had been. She had sold her car and put the cash, insurance, and gas savings for the month into the savings account. Now she walked everywhere, saving money and, especially now that it was winter, burning calories with every step. Althea was not saving for any reason in particular. Saving was the goal, and now she had met that goal. Her savings were not affecting anybody else. She was alone and was leaner that way. Unattached. Detached. Light. Invisible. She wasn't hurting anyone, bothering anyone.

Outside the bank, the frigid wind dragged trash and muddy leaves in circles on the pavement. She sat on a bench, took off her leather gloves slowly, and observed her long white fingers for a moment. The usually busy downtown was empty. Passersby walking against the wind and wrapping themselves in their winter coats came and disappeared. She rubbed her face with her icy hands trying to feel something.

She had reached her goal. She had fifty thousand dollars in the bank and just over three hundred fifty dollars to spend on herself. She didn't know what to do next. What did people do with fifty thousand dollars or three hundred and fifty? She needed nothing, and desired not a material thing.

She lifted her emaciated body off the bench and began walking against the wind. Why walk? To go where? The problem was that at this point, she didn't want immaterial things either. Not love, or happiness, or a family. All she wanted was to be thin and that cost nothing. She had no want for anything money could buy or for anything money couldn't buy. She didn't exactly want to die. She already felt dead.

Before Mark came back from work, and while Simon and Lia were watching cartoons — Goodness gracious how many cartoons were those children watching? Hours each day? — Lola called their friend Lou Driver, who happened to be their attorney. Lou was one of the best, most ruthless lawyers in L.A. Lou, as Mark said, was the best. She tried to control the shiver in her voice when his secretary interrupted a meeting to let her speak to him.

"I'm so sorry to interrupt you Lou, it's just that I don't know what to do anymore. Mark mentioned divorce this morning again. I'm wondering, I mean, what are my rights?"

Lou laughed reassuringly. "Your rights? Oh Lola, honey, there is absolutely no need to be so dramatic."

"But I—"

"Take a breath sweetie. Mark is a reactive kind of guy, that's all. He's brilliant otherwise. Brilliant. And I know for a fact that he needs you far more than he shows. I've known him for twenty years. He is crazy about you."

She hesitated. How much could she reveal without betraying Mark? "He has these ups and downs," she tried to say.

Lou interrupted. "Every couple has ups and downs. You're the only woman for him and you know this."

"But he gets so angry, and for no good reason sometimes. And every time he tells me that if I'm not happy, I should divorce him."

"He's under a lot of pressure, that's all. I've known that bull-headed husband of yours long enough to assure you that he doesn't mean a word of it. And I personally won't pay any attention to this divorce scenario until Mark himself calls me."

When Lola hung up the phone, it was clear in her mind whose side Lou would be on in case of a divorce. And Lou was "the best."

Dread almost brought her to her knees. She stood at the kitchen counter, feeling numb, numbing herself for Mark's return. She turned the pages of the Los Angeles Times. The travel section. Maybe that's what they needed: a beautiful vacation! Maybe they could bring the nanny. Hawaii, Tahiti, Paris... Three small lines of text lost in an ocean of cruises and Club Med photographs caught her eye.

Start over in Paris! Lovely rooms in a beautiful private home. Nurturing environment. Children welcome. Affordable. Meals included. Best area of Paris. English spoken. Call ****

She heard Mark's Hummer coming up the driveway. She threw the newspaper in the recycling bin and rushed to the window to watch Mark come out of the garage. Her heart went wild in her chest when she saw the bouquet. She was forgiven!

But by the time he had turned the doorknob, barely a minute later, her mouth was dry and her head pounding.

Mark walked in the front door, dumped his jacket and briefcase into Serena's hands, and handed Lola the bouquet. He was handsome and tall even compared to Lola, who was five-eleven. He gave her his most dazzling smile and asked, "So, did you finally get a grip on your responsibilities?" He was being humorous. Lola stared at him. Her body stiffened further as Mark hugged her and grabbed her butt amorously. "Oh, you can't still be mad about this morning?" He said.

"Is the, the, the...divorce cancelled?" she stuttered.

"Baby, what divorce? I'm the one who overreacts around here, remember? Such a silly girl!" He gave her a gentle tap on the forehead. "You know I'd be a condemned man without you. I'm under a lot of pressure," he said, and he walked away calling, "Could a hardworking man get something to eat?"

A lot of pressure. Lou's exact words. Were the flowers Lou's idea? In the kitchen, she opened the refrigerator. Her breath was shallow. She pulled a plastic container out of the fridge, placed it on the counter. For a long moment, she stared at the lid in her hand. She finally set it down, walked towards the recycling bin, took the travel section out, folded it, and hid it in one of the kitchen drawers. By the time dinner was made, she was essentially gone. Thousands of miles away.

From the sofa, Jared scanned the room for a discreet way out through the wall of bodies undulating to the music. Beautiful Parisian men and women were crammed around tiny tables or lounging as if swallowed by the red velvet sofas that looked like gigantic mouths.

He had come here with the intention of persuading a girl to come home and have sex with him, but it was taking too long.

The girls wanted to stay until closing, be flirted with, have a couple lines of coke but he had run out of momentum. At this point, he wanted to get the hell out, immediately and alone. He extricated himself from the red sofa and two girls plunged in the warm spot where his body had been. The sofa-mouth became a knot of bare arms, sexy legs, drunken giggles, and hands that hung on to him and tried, like a playful octopus, to draw him back in.

He labored his way through the crowd. The weather report had mentioned snow. When he finally reached the front glass door of the wine bar, he rubbed a finger on the condensation and peeked into the street through the small clearing he had created. No snow. He found his coat beneath three others on a hook near the door and put it on. He searched his pocket unsuccessfully for his scarf. Had the scarf been lost, he would no longer be accountable for it. But the raggedy orange scarf made by his mother when he was twelve was not the kind of object he could deliberately leave behind. He searched the floor, the hangers, and in the process found his hat. No snow and, now, no scarf. At the other end of the wine bar, he spotted the scarf around the neck of a girl whose name he had forgotten. He had felt shackled to her for part of the evening, but then she had moved on to someone more responsive.

Seething and bundled up like an astronaut, Jared made his way towards her. "Au revoir, beauté," he said as he slowly unraveled the scarf from her neck and gave her a soft kiss on the neck. She arched her back like a panther, turned, and clutched his arm. "Jared, où vas tu?"

Jared took her in his arms so she'd let go, and she went soft. "I'll be back," he lied.

"I'll wait right here," she breathed.

At last, Jared opened the glass door and the frigid air rescued him. He screwed his hat on and walked away in long strides, drinking up the icy night air. The street was lively at this late hour, still early by Parisian standards. The smell of the restaurants he passed reminded him he was starving. Greek, Vietnamese, Italian, he didn't need to look up to know their ethnicity. He stopped at a Greek hole-in-the-wall and ordered a lamb sandwich. The man cut slivers of meat from a hanging roast of lamb and let them fall onto the baguette. He paid and ate the steaming sandwich as he walked briskly. He walked for half an hour until he reached rue de Cambronne, deserted from traffic and free of store lights at this time of night. He noticed the pounding of his own heart, watched the little clouds coming out of his mouth with every breath. He stopped in front of the building where he lived; its eighteenth-century Parisian architecture, both classic and ornate. Jared inserted the old-fashioned key in the keyhole and pushed open the wide wooden door. The familiar scent of the building's staircase, hundreds of years of wax and patina combined with soup, home-cooked meals, the scent of centuries, welcomed him. Five flights of stairs, and he was home.

He let himself into his apartment and turned on the light of a bare light bulb. As he walked into the room, he stripped off most of his clothes—his coat, his hat, his scarf, followed by his sweater and T-shirt—and let them drop to the floor. Jared ignored the scarce furniture and the books, boxes, and trash scattered around the room. He took off socks and shoes and threw them wherever they would land.

He stood in front of a table thick with grunge, food residue, and paint stains, and stared at the tubes of paint on the table. After a while, he opened a few, dropped dollops of oil paint into a plastic plate, and blinked at the canvas, the largest he could afford, one meter by one and a half meters, but still, it was too small. He opened the turpentine bottle and rummaged through a shoebox for a decent brush. There must have been well over fifty unusable brushes in the box. All coated with dried paint. Ruined. Jared painted until five in the morning. When he could hardly stand, he cleaned off his hands with turpentine and a dirty cloth. He then searched the floor for his coat, wrapped it around his body, and let himself fall on the couch. He sat and stared at his work until it became blurry, and then he fell asleep sitting up. The brushes sat in paint in the plastic plate.

❧

The room smelled of detergent and vomit from last night's misery. Althea was cold to her core despite the sweaters and blankets. She was stiff on her bed, reading the same words over and over. She licked her chapped lips for the fiftieth time. Her lips were getting worse, but she had stopped using lip balm because of its fat content. She had been so bad last night.

She read the small ad again, six little black lines of text, and shook her head to chase it away. She'd read that ad a dozen times already, trying to dismiss it, yet her gaze kept drifting back to it, until she was forced to stop long enough to feel "it." The silly words in that small ad were like a promise of something. Reading the paper became increasingly difficult. Any reading required racking effort, but this morning, she was cold, and there was a picture of a lagoon somewhere in the Pacific Ocean on the first page of the travel section. The title of the article, "Alone in the Sun. Go and Discover Your Inner Fish," floated in lagoon waters. In the heart of a seemingly endless winter, photographs of the heavenly island seemed nonsensical. Warmth and beauty and a shallow translucent sea accessible to no one. For Althea, realizing that going there would have been anybody's dream was a blow, because she was incapable of such a dream. The picture had no impact on her, the words had no meaning. Go? She had no strength. Discover? She had no curiosity. Alone? She cared for no one. In the sun? She had no interest whatsoever. Tropical Paradise held no promise of well-being to her.

But again, her weary eyes drifted away from the lagoon pictures and towards the small print ad buried amongst many.

Start over in Paris! Lovely rooms in a beautiful private home. Nurturing environment. Children welcome. Affordable. Meals included. Best area of Paris. English spoken. Call *****

Althea couldn't peel her eyes from the bold letters. "Start over in Paris." What did it mean? Whatever it meant, it spoke to a desire she didn't know she had, and lately, the faintest desire was like an oasis. Every word in that ad was a little caress that stirred up an incomprehensible longing.

She had studied French for many years. Also Spanish, German, Latin, and Italian. Althea had a peculiar gift for languages. That and drawing, her two useless talents. She'd had some indistinct plans of going to France, years ago, but as usual, more realistic and sensible plans had been carried through. Althea wasn't going anywhere. Her mom needed her. As far back as Althea could remember, her mom had repeated, "Had it not been for Althea, I would have killed myself long ago." Althea tossed the newspaper into the trash. But now something was happening, in spite of herself. Something extraordinary. The small, soft wing of a desire fluttered in her heart.

She authorized herself breakfast. Two liters of very black tea, unsweetened. Two apples cut in quarters. She would eat, slowly, methodically, over an hour while watching the Food Channel. She'd go back to the trash long after breakfast and forage for the cores and eat them, and this would leave her overwhelmed with shame and panic. But when the cooking show ended, instead of cleaning up after breakfast, she observed her fingers dial for the operator to find out what time it was in Paris. She went to the trash can, and instead of the apple core, she retrieved the travel section of the paper. She dialed the number and sat on the corner of her table, with the receiver nudged between her ear and her shoulder while her arms were crossed over her chest in an attempt to protect herself from unknown enemies. There were a dozen rings, and the space between the rings became eternities. Althea was going to hang up and suddenly a woman's voice, so close.

"Allo?"

"Hello? Do...do you speak...English?" Althea asked.

"I sure do. Don't mind the heavy breathing. I was all the way upstairs and had to run down to get the phone. Tripped over the damn rug! Who's this?"

"I'm sorry you had to run...fall," Althea stammered.

"Nah, I like to live dangerously. What's your name?"

"Althea Hoyt." Althea waited for a second. "I'm sorry."

"Are you kidding? Anything to bail out of my kids' homework! What do you want to know, Althea?"

Althea. That was her name. Why did it sound different in this woman's mouth?

"Well," Althea asked, improvising. "Is this a bed-and-breakfast? How much do you charge? Do you still have a room? Is month-to-month okay? Is it furnished? I am...I'm thinking of taking a...sort of...sabbatical."

CHAPTER 6

*W*rapped in her red poncho and sitting on the cold grass of the soccer field, Annie watched her boys and Lucas run with the ball. She was gathering pebbles in her hands. Amazing the quantities of stones that were heart-shaped when you started looking. Maxence was getting stronger she noticed. He could keep up with Lucas's pace. The four of them playing soccer in the park was a bittersweet sight. Johnny had been too busy to do these kinds of things with the boys. He had meant to, but later. Everything was always for later. Johnny was a big talker, a man of promises, often broken ones. But the promises he made were made with gusto; with such details and enthusiasm that you could almost trick yourself into thinking they might actually come true. Future adventure-filled voyages in mysterious locations, future gourmet picnics by the moonlight, or future epic soccer games. She should have forced him to not miss out on the kids. But who was she to talk; she who at the moment sat on the ground collecting pebbles, lost in the past, entirely incapable of getting up and playing with her children?

Lucas, in his Adidas shorts and knee-high socks, his skinny legs surprisingly hairy, was cleverly mastering the triple task of convincing each kid that they were beating him. Lucas threw his hands up in surrender. "I need a break. Jouez sans moi," he said, and he jogged towards her and sat down, his breathing no heavier than after a stroll. The kids ran towards them, high socks and knees covered in mud, breathing like freight trains.

"You're just afraid we'll beat the crap out of you!" Maxence said.

"The poop out of you," Annie suggested.

"Let me catch my breath. Je suis crevé," Lucas said. Maxence turned around, kicked the ball hard and ran. Paul and Laurent sprinted after him.

"Her name is Lola and she lives in Bel Air!" Annie said.

"Qu'est-ce que c'est?"

"Hello? Fresh Prince of Bel-Air?"

Lucas shook his head. "A prince?"

"Will Smith? Men in Black?" Lucas's expression was genuinely clueless so she gave up. "It's in or near Beverly Hills."

Lucas made a sound of recognition. "Ahh!"

"She sounds so nice. Very normal. Just a mom with children, you know, like me. I kind of fell in love with the idea of that, you know, a lost mom with a daughter and a toddler boy, and me helping her out."

"And the father?"

Annie considered the pebbles in her hands and had a vision of herself chucking them at Lucas. "Out of the picture. An abusive monster. Horrible."

"Did you fall in love with that, too?"

"That what?"

"The notion of an abusive husband?"

Now her eyes were resting on much larger stones. "What is that supposed to mean? Of course not! I gave her some advice."

"Such as?"

"I told her she needed to follow her instinct and put some mileage between them."

"Is all this her instinct, or yours?"

Annie sprang to her feet like a jack-in-the-box. "I don't like where this conversation is going, so I'm ending it. I'll be at home." Annie walked away fuming, her poncho bouncing with each step. She left the field and didn't turn around. What a French asshole! She trotted towards the house, crossed boulevard Suchet and made the turn after Musée Marmottan, and grumbled all the way to La Muette. They'd be better off on the soccer field without her anyway

The reality was that the other calls she had received for her ad were no good. And she did not receive that many responses at all. There had been the retired couple from San Francisco who wanted to stay for a year because they had read A Year in Provence, and it had messed with their heads. Rental agencies had called who wanted her money, and she had dismissed the lone men sent to work in France for a few months. There had also been a wealthy couple looking for a true French experience that included fax, cable, high speed internet, and a TV in the room. They'd asked if there was a hot tub. She had snapped that this was Paris, France, not Paris, Vegas. But really, she was horrified at the thought of people coming in and complaining about her place. Her house was low tech, and she wanted it to stay that way. A computer would be nice one day, maybe. The teachers sure were putting pressure on her, not to mention the boys' obsession with it. But she certainly refused to get cable. TV was bad enough as it was; who needed more of it?

So, when Lola finally called and did not ask her about complicated things such as DSL, HBO, DVD, and VCR, Annie had to have her. "I'm not sure what I'm looking for," Lola had said. She was blowing her nose occasionally and Annie did not know if she was crying or had a cold. "I'm not even sure I should come to France. It would be for a short time, very temporary." But in the next sentence, Lola said, "I might need a school for my daughter. Are there international schools nearby?" Lola said she loved France but did not really speak the language, calling her French an embarrassment.

"Well, in that case, don't even try your French here. You'll get lynched!" Annie said. When Lola gave a throaty laugh, something genuine and childish, it reassured Annie immensely.

Lola had also sounded confused and undecided, so when the issue of the bathroom was raised, way too soon in the conversation, Annie was sure it would be a deal breaker. "Do the rooms have their own bathrooms?"

"Well, it's not exactly like that. This is an old house. It kind of lacks... amenities." Annie had braced herself. "There are eight bedrooms, but only two bathrooms. As a matter of fact, you might have to share a bathroom with other tenants."

"Share?"

"Well, take turns, of course. Anyway, don't you think hygiene is way overrated in the U.S.?" she had joked.

"Well, that's true," Lola had responded, like this made perfect sense.

Annie was on a roll with lame-ass jokes "Worse comes to worst, the kitchen sink is huge."

Lola had laughed again. "Bathing is in the kitchen? Oh, I feel better now!"

Only this was not entirely a joke. During the summer months, the boys used the kitchen sink as a pool of sorts. They climbed in and out, into the garden, back to the kitchen, leaving puddles of water and mud everywhere. The same tub was at times the place for earth experiments. Once, she found a tadpole in it. No need to get into that.

"It is a crazy thing," Lola said. "You wrote 'start over,' and I couldn't get the ad out of my mind. This is totally intuitive. I'm mostly, like, an intuitive person."

Oh great, she thought. A new agey L.A. wackjob. She breathed in, and then spewed out her response: "Don't over think it, dear. Grab your kids and pack your bags. Don't take too much. Your clothes will seem irrelevant the instant you see what people wear here. I've got toys, towels, métro tickets, and I'm a mean cook. The best bathroom has a wonderfully large tub, and I am the proud owner of a bubble bath collection." She had said that fast and in a high-pitched tone, like a damn insurance salesman. She cringed and waited. Lola gave a big sigh. "This sounds so, like, nurturing. And Paris is so beautiful in the winter." Annie did not think Paris was so damn beautiful in the winter. "Oh, like, totally," she said.

"I can't get any sort of fresh start in L.A. My husband would talk me out of it," Lola said, blowing her nose again. This time, Annie was sure she was crying. "He can be very persuasive. I can't say no to him."

Annie had to ask. "How does he feel about your separation?"

"Well," Lola seemed to consider how to respond, "it's really been years in the making. Mark has resigned himself to the idea. I'm sure."

"And he's fine with you going to another country?"

"Well, this would be temporary, of course."

"Of course," Annie said. "When a woman decides to leave, it is always the right thing to do," she said, forgetting that she knew nothing on the subject. She decided to appeal to Lola's intuitive side. "We have instinct, and something tells me you've been fighting yours for a while." And by then, she had managed to convince herself that what she was truly being helpful.

§~

"I'm making roast beef for lunch. It was on sale so I said, 'Why not!'" Pamela chirped.

Althea contemplated the idea. Red meat. Meat on sale. Rotting meat. "Great!" she said flatly as she took off her coat. On the counter, the meat was thawing. She wondered how long it had been sitting there. Many times, as a girl she had sat for what seemed to be hours in front of her cold plate unable to lift the fork to her mouth, until her mom, in furious exasperation, slapped her across the face and sent her to finish her meal in the bathroom. It was the ultimate punishment as well as the only way out for everyone. There, Althea would cry in despair and relief and tip the plate of food down the toilet after staying in the bathroom for a respectable amount of time to avoid suspicion. Then she would wait there in dry sobs until Pamela came to free her and give her the profuse love that always came after the storm. In the end, her mother had the last word since Althea had apparently eaten all her food. The last word, but not the victory.

During lunch, sometime between the roast beef, the rice pudding, and Althea going to the bathroom to vomit, Pamela revealed to her husband the barely formulated concept that Althea had immediately regretted sharing.

"She should take a cruise instead. At least she won't get any of those diseases they have overseas."

"Cruises are for old farts like us," tried her dad.

Pamela rolled her eyes to the ceiling. "Your father has no idea what I'm talking about. You spend two or three days in one city, say, Vienna and..."

"Vienna's not in France; it's in Germany," Henry said.

"Anyway, Germany might be better. Cleaner. The French think they're better than us, after everything we've done for them."

"Dad," Althea asked, "isn't Vienna in Austria?"

Her father looked up from his plate. "What, sweetheart?"

"Vienna's in Austria."

"Forget Vienna, Althea," her mom cut in angrily. "Your dad has no idea about geography and never has."

The day dragged on painfully. Her dad went for a nap and she accompanied her mom on a walk, their weekly walk in a park deserted by humans and pigeons alike. France was not brought up again. Later, when she was alone in the kitchen folding her laundry on the counter and smelling each item before folding, Althea was surprised to see her dad come in.

"Your mother is talking to the TV—the TV, for Pete's sake!" Standing next to her, her father looked frail. These days, his hands always seemed to shake ever so slightly. He was holding a neatly folded piece of paper between his fingers. Watching him, she felt suddenly drained.

"This idea of going to Paris, I think it's a good one," Henry said abruptly. "You need a little fun, a little adventure, you know."

"I'm probably not..."

"You were the best in your French class at school I reckon. That's a talent, languages."

"It's just a silly idea," she said, powerless.

Her father waved his hands impatiently, the piece of paper still between his fingers. "You can't keep coming here week after week to watch us watch TV. You've got to stop spending your weekends walking your mom around town, sweetheart. Our life is what it is," he chuckled unhappily. "We sure messed that up real good. But yours...."

"Oh, Dad, don't."

He gave her a stern look and handed her the piece of paper. Althea unfolded it with great difficulty, which had nothing to do with her hands or her brain function and everything to do with the chance she might suddenly become unable to hide her despair. It was a check for one hundred and fifty dollars.

"That should cover the airplane, no?" he asked anxiously.

She couldn't look at him. When she finally did, she saw his eyes were as wet as hers. She gave him a hug and only said, "Thanks, Dad, I think I'll do that."

"Now, go pack. Don't look back, she might catch you!" Henry added with a nervous laugh.

Althea put the check into her wallet, arranged her clean and folded clothes into her bag, and said goodbye. She walked home for an hour in the frigid night, but she did not feel the cold this time as thoughts of Paris buzzed through her mind.

❧

Lola's heart was pounding. She locked her bedroom door even though Mark would be in Atlanta for several more days. She dug deep into the drawer, tossing lingerie to the side and removed a large brown envelope. She sat on her bed trying to calm the shaking of her hands; breathing in, and spread out the contents on the white silk comforter. The sound of her heartbeat seemed to resonate against the cathedral ceiling of the all-white bedroom. She inspected the contents of the envelope for a long time, trying to absorb its meaning, incredulous for having gone this far. Had she tried to stand, her knees wouldn't have supported her. Three tickets. Three passports.

She had given the nanny and the housekeeper the day off so she could pack. Tomorrow, the taxi would be here to pick them up at 6:00 AM. In the cab, she'd tell Simon and Lia that they were going on a surprise vacation. On a school day? She had to lie to Lia. She couldn't take a chance. She was being duplicitous, lying to her own daughter, stealing her. But is taking what is yours stealing?

Three weeks ago, Lola didn't question her life, like the worm not questioning being stuck at the end of a fishing hook. Nor did she really question the validity of Mark's criticism of everything she did. Three weeks ago, she had only ached to become who Mark needed her to be. And then, almost overnight, she stopped being able to tolerate any of it.

She had to keep her momentum because she had a tendency to forgive, to see the good side of people over the bad. For the last few days, every bit of Lola's energy had been spent pretending everything was as usual and planning the trip. The stars were aligning nicely. The end of January was the time for traveling abroad. Her astrologer assured her that she would not get such a perfect planet alignment again until 2022. Things were all pointing in the same direction. It didn't even feel like she was making decisions. But all the while it didn't seem quite real either. She was going through the motions, accomplishing a little more towards her unfathomable goal every day.

The passports were still good since their trip to Mexico. Mexico. That was in August, five months ago. She and the children had been so sick amidst the coconut trees and the warm ocean breeze. They'd suffered from terrible stomach problems, except for Mark, who was never sick and who'd had a wonderful time going deep sea fishing every day. She took care of the kids while her own sickness had sent her to the bathroom every hour for days. She'd lost weight to the point of being emaciated. Mark came back with a glorious tan.

Going to France couldn't possibly be any more difficult. In fact, without Mark sending everyone into a panic in preparation for the trip, it all seemed to go remarkably smoothly. The pull that small ad in the paper had had on her was confounding. Whenever her resolve weakened, she'd merely go back to the envelope, retrieve the cut-up page of the Los Angeles Times, and read the ad again. Each time, she'd feel joyous like a small child. She always loved surprises, and secrets! She knew none of this was properly examined, was not without consequences, and was wrong in a way. But she was doing it.

Lola folded the page of the paper and placed the stack of euros, the three passports, and the three airplane tickets back into the manila envelope. In her modeling days, Paris had always been her favorite city. To Mark, the world outside of the U.S. was narrowed down to Mexico and the Bahamas. He would never find her there.

CHAPTER 7

FÉVRIER

*A*nnie's stomach cramps had not eased since the night before. Going three miles per hour on the périférique while Lucas moaned about the wheels of her minivan, made her feel even more sick to her stomach. She did not want to talk and was thankful for Lucas's silence. Through the rain on the van's window, she was suddenly taking a sobering look at France through what she figured to be a Bel Air resident's eyes. Gone were the charming cafés, the flower shops, the statues, the parks, the architecture. All she noticed now was the dismal weather, the pollution, and the endless string of rotted cars filled with people with rotted teeth. Paris was nothing but a dump and soon it would be all in the open.

What struck her was how little movement there had been in her life in the last two years, how very still things had been. For one, since Johnny died she had stopped driving. It had not been a conscious decision, but a profound, inexplicable aversion. This was the first time the van was out of the garage since. She reasoned that she had been traumatized by his car crash. It was only natural. But then why did she not even want to see the van. If she needed something from the garage she'd send Maxence or Lucas to fetch it. Lucas periodically insisted she needed to work on the issue, but she dismissed it. In the rare instances when she needed to get out of her neighborhood, she simply took buses. The day before, she had surprised herself by insisting that Lucas pick up Lola at the airport using the van. Lucas had raised an eyebrow.

"Why?"

"I can't very well ask her to take a cab, can I?"

"I don't see why not."

"I want things to go smoothly. I want them to feel welcome and at ease."

"What about me being at ease?"

She pushed Lucas with both hands toward the garage and she let him lift the metal curtain. "Let's air out the monster, see if it can still roar." Lucas turned toward her looking offended. "I hope you are not referring to my private anatomy."

In a few minutes, they would be at the international gate where Annie had come off the plane as a newlywed. Had she really once been the kind of person who flew over oceans, drove in unknown cities, moved to new countries?

"I am missing work for this?" Lucas said. "I just don't see why you could not drive on your own."

"I don't feel capable of driving, I told you a million times that I'm not ready."

"You are capable," he said. "And you're ready."

"When I'm ready to drive, you'll be the first one informed."

Later, as she stood in the dense crowd that faced the international gate at Charles De Gaulle Airport where Lola and her children should have appeared a long time ago, she was back to feeling more anticipation than fear. There were people everywhere, people doing things, going places and she was right in the thick of the action. She was waiting for an unknown woman to become part of her life. She could not help but feel proud of herself for breaking that spell with the van, and for making this tremendous plunge towards the unknown. But an hour after the airplane was shown to have landed, there was still no sign of Lola. The colorful pageant of people and families from every country, race, nationality and social stratum had stopped being interesting a long time ago and she was back to being tormented by stomach upset and cold sweats. She scrutinized the crowd till her eyes hurt. What did they look like? Could she possibly have missed them? There must have been dozens of mothers traveling with children. Had she not seen her sign? Annie no longer had the gumption to hold up the cute little homemade sign she had coerced Paul and Laurent into constructing. Children's letters and coloring. Cute as a button. The idea behind the sign was to give a warmer, more friendly reception than the one she felt capable of voicing.

She turned to Lucas. "Could they have missed their connection?" Lucas, still busy feeling sorry for himself, only shrugged. "Shit, this is not normal. Maybe this is the wrong airport! Lucas, please, make sure we're in the right place. This could be a disaster. And I'm begging you to stop giving me the cold shoulder! This is stressful enough." Dragging his feet, Lucas went to ask. She wanted to wring his neck.

She now had to push and shove to remain in the front row because the crowd had grown for the arrival of international travelers who were making their way slowly up the ramp. She was beginning to feel claustrophobic in the stench of sweat, perfume, and cigarette smoke that engulfed them all.

Faces—hundreds of faces, strange faces—lit up when they recognized someone familiar. Saris, suits, turbans, shorts, and flip-flops. People pushing carts covered in mountains of mismatched parcels and luggage. Everyone looked so strange. One woman caught Annie's attention. She was quite an incongruity, a stunning woman with high cheekbones, a pale face and dark glasses. She could have been six feet tall or appeared to be amid this rather low-rising crowd of French, Asian, and Arabic men and women. She wore her black hair closely cropped, her face was chiseled, her lips very full, and her skin like porcelain seemed to glow from the inside. Annie wasn't the only one to gawk. The oversized sunglasses and the floor-length, mocha-colored cashmere coat, mocha cashmere turtleneck, and mocha cashmere boots made her look like she might have been a model in the midst of a photo shoot. Annie racked her brain for a clue and forgot all about what she was here for. Surely this was someone famous, maybe a French *actrice*. Not Chiara Mastroianni, not Carla Bruni...the woman continued walking up the ramp and pushing a cart piled high with Vuitton bags.

It was only when she passed right by that Annie noticed that a toddler and a girl of about nine were at her side, both children beautiful and as blond as the woman was dark-haired. And suddenly it hit her. Lola? The shock of this realization hit her at the same instant as the enormity of the disaster struck her. Quick! Toss the sign into the crowd! Sprint out of the airport, and run, run, across fields and across towns all the way home? There was still time. "Down to earth" she had told Lucas to describe Lola. Not from this earth was more like it. But Lola had sounded so normal over the phone.

She looked anything but normal. It was as if Wonder Woman had landed in the airport with her skin-tight American flag outfit and her golden lasso. This was impossible. Impossible! This woman, this creature would find a hotel, she'd find another home, she'd find another place in which to start over or whatever hellish reason she was here for. She needed to turn around and go right back into the pages of Vogue from which she came. She'd be absolutely fine. She'd be better off, in fact. This woman did not belong in her world, in her life and she sure as hell didn't belong in her house.

But instead, Annie found herself elbowing, pushing, and shoving to make her way toward Lola, and lifting her homemade rickety little sign high, wriggling it pathetically and wailing "excuse me, excuse me." Terrible humiliation ensued. Lola kept staring right above the sign. There she was, plump and barely over five-feet tall on her tiptoes right next to a goddess who could not see her! Finally, Annie practically shoved the sign in the woman's face, cleared her throat. Her voice came out, high on helium, "Lola?"

Lola looked down, the African gazelle to the aardvark, recognized her name on the sign. She looked at her through her impenetrable sunglasses. "Annie?" The crowd moved in slow motion. "Welcome to France!" Annie said in one hysterical breath, and the world resumed normal speed. "I was worried sick about you. What happened?"

Lola took off her glasses. She had beautiful pale green eyes and looked like she had been crying. She bent down slightly to speak closer to Annie's ear. "They held us up at immigration," she whispered. "We looked suspect to them, I guess, a single mom with two kids. They were rude and..."

Her little boy wailed "Mom, up me, up me!" He was pulling on her arm. She looked at Annie and her eyes filled with tears. "For a moment there, I thought they wanted to send us back. Then, suddenly, for no reason, they let us go. I don't get it."

Annie was entirely confused by Lola's vulnerability. "There is nothing to get, honey," she said, patting Lola on the sleeve of her soft coat. "Welcome to the best France has to offer, starting with abuse of power and arbitrary decisions. You're going to love it!"

"Right now, all I am is terrified," Lola whispered even lower. "I'm so thankful to see a friendly face."

"Me?" Annie said.

Six feet tall women in cashmere have nothing to fear, she thought. But Lola did look terrified. "Your worries are over now," Annie said, believing herself. "I'm going to take care of you and your adorable children." She turned to Lola's children and gave them a wide smile destined to convey warmth and motherly self-confidence. The girl's face was scrunched up and closed and she did not make eye contact. The boy was hanging on to his mother's coat with both hands now and looked like he was going to climb up the coat like a monkey. Lola lifted him into her arms and the boy buried his face in her neck. "I bet you can't wait to get to your new home!" Annie said with all the jolliness she could muster.

"Our vacation home," Lola whispered and looked at Annie worriedly.

"Your nice vacation home, of course," Annie said. "Do you know I have a boy your age? I have three boys in fact."

"I hate boys," Lia shrugged, "They're stupid."

"Not mine. They're grade-A boys, I promise you that." Annie took mental note to brief the boys about potential fires of hell if they acted out.

Like the sighting of a buoy in the middle of a rough sea, Annie spotted Lucas cutting through the crowd and advancing toward them. When he saw Lola, Lucas opened his eyes wide and, for Annie's benefit, simulated what seemed to be a miniature heart attack by covering his chest with both hands in a very French gesture signifying that he was love struck. He shook Lola's hand, introduced himself and began to speak to her and the children in English without the slightest hesitation or intimidation, and Annie breathed an immense sigh of relief. Lucas was going to save her ass and make this whole thing possible.

In the car, Annie decided she was going to pretend that she was fine. She wasn't going to show anything to anyone, not even to Lucas. But she suspected Lucas knew all too well what was going through her brain, that old rascal. For one, she could not come up with anything clever to say and the van had fallen into an uncomfortable silence where all Annie could hear was the sound of her thoughts furiously galloping through her head. The van was beat up. A disgrace. There were crumbs and toys. Why had she not noticed before? Why didn't she listen to Lucas and let them take a damned cab? That way, the first thing Lola would have seen of her life was the house. She had never felt more intimidated. Then the van was caught in a bad traffic jam and they were hopelessly stuck past a run-down industrial suburb. Lia and Simon fell asleep in the back seat. Lola was still wearing her sunglasses and she stared in silence at the suburb, which had never looked more sinister. In the cars surrounding them, lower human life forms chain-smoked and honked their horns. Annie suddenly hated Parisians and all things French. The rain, as on cue began to fall hard. Lucas turned on the windshield wipers, which stuttered and creaked and began to go up and down, trailing with them a puzzling black substance.

"How interesting," Lucas said dispassionately. "The rubber of the blades appears to be crumbling."

"Of course not."

"The windshield wipers have lost their elasticity, I believe."

Sure enough, the wiper blades were rapidly disintegrating into tar-looking residue that mixed with the rain on the windshield into nauseating muddy streaks. Lucas scooted down to see the road in the lower ten inches of windshield where the wipers halfway worked and began driving in that position. Did he have to do that?

She picked at her nails, removed dried dough, and rummaged her brain unsuccessfully for something to say, careful to avoid Lucas's side glances. Oh, she knew precisely what he was thinking. Lola had to be the most beautiful woman either of them had ever seen outside television. And Lola would never, ever, fit in her house.

Lucas scooted back up finally and looked at Lola in the rear-view mirror. His voice breaking the silence like a giant fart. "Is this your first time in France?" he asked. Shut up, Annie thought. Shut up!

Lola tuned her face away from the window. "I've come here for work, but never more than a couple days at a time."

"What kind of work?" Annie asked, bravely turning around and looking at Lola.

"Modeling," she said. Annie's spirit dropped down to her ankles. Of course, modeling! "I was much younger," Lola added. "I love Paris," she said, and removed the sunglasses she had put back on. Her eyes were red and swollen. "Sorry about the glasses," Lola said. "I didn't want the kids to see me all emotional. I was fine in the airplane, but now, after the immigration and everything…"

Annie had never considered whether her children should or shouldn't see her emotional. Heck, if they saw her only when she wasn't emotional, they'd hardly get to see her at all. She thought of something to say. "Please don't look around; it's the Périphérique, on the other side of this freeway is la banlieue; the Paris suburb! That will depress you even more. Wait till we get to my house. Everybody loves my house!"

"I'll do a scenic detour," Lucas declared.

"Lucas, they're exhausted," Annie protested weakly.

By the time Lola's daughter woke up, Lucas was driving past Place de la Concorde, rue de Rivoli, Jardin du Luxembourg, and the Louvre, and Annie didn't try to stop him. Lola said "Oh, Lia, look at the beautiful old buildings. The Eiffel Tower. This is it, Lia! We are in Paris!" Lia looked unimpressed, but on Lola's face was a touching expression of hopefulness and vulnerability. Whatever kind of woman Lola might be, Annie understood that she was before everything a mother. And in that single way, she and Lola were the same.

§

Lola felt drained of all strength. What had she done? But she needed to be strong as Annie introduced her boys who uncrossed their arms to shake her hand gravely. Simon showed no sign of waking up, so Lola carried him over her shoulder fast asleep from room to room, conscious of the three pairs of eyes that followed her every gesture and, of course, of Lia's anger at her. The way Annie's boys bombarded her with questions inquisition style and argued with each other confused her. Was she making a good impression on them? "Your baby, there," Laurent told her. "He's drooling all over your shoulder."

"So, Einstein," Maxence answered. "That's why he's a baby. Duh!"

"How tall are you?" Paul, the five-year-old, asked.

"That's rude to ask." Maxence said.

"You're rude," Paul responded.

"Put a lid on it, all of you," Annie said, and, to Lola's surprise, the three boys did.

Annie took Lola and Lia up the creaking stairs and made a dramatic pause, her hand on the knob of a room. "Lola. I'm giving you the pink room, but I must warn you, it's not for the faint of heart." They entered a large room basking with warm light. Lola felt a bit of a shock at the sight of the almost entirely pink room. In the center was a smallish canopy bed with a powder pink gauze curtain. The window that opened to charming rooftops was draped with sumptuous candy-color striped silk. The only furniture was a miniature desk painted glossy red, an antique armoire lacquered in black, and an armchair covered with raspberry velvet. "I reupholstered it," Annie said, like an apology. "With vintage fabric. It's a bit like stepping inside a box of valentine chocolate, this room, no? But I had fun. It's my girly-girl room."

"I love it," Lola exclaimed, meaning it.

"The walls were a piece of work. Took me forever to mix the plaster evenly and get just the right shade."

"Did you make that?" Lia asked, pointing to slightly darker polka dots painted haphazardly on the walls.

"Not finished yet."

"And that?" Lia showed the gauze veil on the canopy, which was covered with miniature silk daisies. "I used hot glue, stupidly, and the glue kept on melting the gauze. A real drag. In typical fashion, instead of stopping and getting the right glue, I continued. When I start being creative, I'm possessed."

"It's pretty," Lia said.

Lola took notice of this rare show of endorsement. "This is charming and lovely," she insisted.

"Well, it's...me," Annie responded. "I bet you guys are accustomed to the best."

The children's room did not get the same response. The room was barely large enough for the two children's beds and the large trunk between them. The smallness of the room and the low, slanted ceiling gave it a tree house feel. The wallpaper added to the effect with a mossy shade of green adorned with rather gory hunting scenes, dead ducks, guns and scattered feathers.

"I'm not sleeping here," Lia exclaimed.

As on cue, Simon started whimpering.

"The room's plenty ugly, I must admit," Annie said matter-of-factly. "It's got the previous owner's touch, and I never got around to decorating it."

Lola tried to put Simon down, but he climbed up her body like a small marsupial and reassumed his position. "Oh, it will be just fine," she said.

"I hate this place. I'm still not sleeping here," Lia said.

"They're starting to feel the jet lag," Lola apologized.

Annie looked at Lia. "Think of it as a blank canvas. We can make this room anything we want it to be. Sky's the limit."

Lia considered this. "Pink like the other one?"

"If you can convince my boys. They hate pink. I personally think it's the new black."

"I like purple, too."

"Only if you help me. I can't do it by myself," Annie responded.

Lola watched the exchange between her daughter and this perfect stranger with incomprehension and a maybe a tinge of jealousy.

"How did this materialize?" Lucas cried out in delight an hour later when Annie placed a steaming dish of chicken lasagna and a large Salade Niçoise in the center of the dining room table. "The way to a man's heart is through his stomach," Annie said for Lola's benefit. She did feel a touch of pride at her planning skills. She had prepared the lasagna and washed the ingredients of the salad the day before, then warmed up one dish and tossed the other with homemade vinaigrette, and a meal was ready to eat within a half hour of arriving from the airport.

It did not get easier to find things to say during dinner. But thank heavens for Lucas who spoke at length about various American presidents, foreign policies, current art exhibitions in Paris that she had to not miss, the weather, and whatnot. Lola responded the best she could, eating with one hand, an impressive balancing act since Simon was back to sleep over her shoulder, but she spoke charmingly, making every effort to seem approachable and tried, unsuccessfully, to include her daughter in the conversation. Meanwhile, Paul and Laurent goofed off throughout dinner and Maxence wasn't making eye contact or speaking. But since Annie was herself having trouble making eye contact, could she blame him? Maxence was staring, and that was rude, but then again, what was she doing? She did not so much look at Lola as detail her inch by inch, goggling at her, counting the pores on the skin of her nose. She found no flaw, though she wondered about that mouth. Where did she get that mouth? Was it from an Angelina Jolie body part catalogue? Whoever had mouths like this? And her breasts were huge. Huge!

After dinner, Lola took Lia and Simon to bed and Annie walked Lucas to the door. "Your job here is done," she whispered to him. "Very well done. Please be back tomorrow at 6:00 AM sharp for further assignments."

"Would 4:00 AM be too soon?" he whispered back. "As a matter of fact, I never want to leave this house again."

"Oh, she's that hot, huh?"

"There's something too perfect about her makeup, though," he said, whispering lower. "And her nails are strange."

"How strange?"

"They seem fake."

She laughed, "They are fake."

Lucas opened his eyes wide, "How can one fake nails?"

"Never mind. It's an American thing."

"Her lips," he said wistfully "are... pornographic. And those breasts..."

"Always the poet," Annie laughed as she pushed him out of the house. She rounded up the boys and together they tiptoed upstairs, whispering and giggling, unclear as to how to navigate a house that already smelled and sounded different. In bed, peeking from under his blanket, Maxence said, "Aren't they weird? I think they're really weird." She straightened the cover and moved the hair away from her nine-year-old's eyes. "What's so weird about them?"

"How do I know?" Maxence shrugged.

"How tall are they?" Paul wondered, his eyes closing already.

"It's time for bed," she said. She went from Maxence, to Laurent, and then to Paul for kisses and hugs.

"I love you a gazillion," Paul said in her neck.

"I love you a googolplex," Annie whispered back.

Annie went back downstairs to clean the dishes, relieved to be finally alone with her thoughts. She filled one of her Japanese cast iron teapots with water. Each time Johnny had come back from Japan, it was with a teapot, each one a small piece of art. "For your collection," he would say.

"Why do you call it my collection? It's your collection," she remembered saying.

"It's my collection for you."

"I think I should come along the next time you go to Japan. Choose a collection for myself."

"Next time? What's the big hurry?"

She put the teapot on the stove and began cleaning the dishes. Of course, she never ended up going to Japan, but that's hardly what bothered her. What bothered her is that she no longer had any desire to. Here she was, encouraging strangers to start over, but the fact of the matter was, she was stuck in her solitude, her circular thoughts that revolved around a single day less than three years ago. She rinsed a pan and moved it to the drying rack to the right of the sink.

"Your water is boiling," said Lola's voice.

Annie jumped. "Oh goodness, I didn't hear it. I didn't hear you come in."

Lola was wearing jeans and had taken off her makeup. Her face looked a bit strained from lack of sleep, but beautiful. "Didn't mean to make you jump," she said as she took the pan from the drying rack and began to wipe it dry. Annie cringed in horror. Now, during her teatime? Her solitude, invaded? "You don't have to do that!" she said rather bossily. "You must be exhausted. Go to bed!"

Lola seemed nonplussed by her tone. "I want to," she said nonchalantly. "I could use a cup of herbal tea too." She took a wet plate from Annie's clenched fingers and began drying it. "I guess I'm the one who gets to sleep in the duck room tonight. Lia and Simon are sound asleep in my pink bed. So," she added, "Lucas doesn't live here, then?" Annie was appalled. Did she want to make conversation now? "Heck no!" She said.

"Have you ever been married?" Lola asked.

"Once," was Annie curt response.

"You're divorced?"

Annie's answer came out sounding rehearsed. "My husband, the love of my life, was killed in a car accident two and a half years ago. D.O.A." Lola looked at her and stopped wiping. "I'm so, so sorry," she said. "So am I, believe me," Annie said, removing her plastic gloves. She resigned to the fact that her solitude was ruined for now. Would any place in the house be safe from now on? She offered Lola a cup of tea, and the two of them stood at the sink. Annie did not invite Lola to sit down in the hope to hurry things up. Maybe she should have. Lola was tall enough to make her—along with the entire kitchen—seem smaller. And shouldn't she have looked worn out from all those hours of traveling? Instead, in her jeans and white shirt, she had a calm, groomed air about her, a quiet loveliness and effortlessness that was mesmerizing. Annie's inadequacy flared up in a big way. Lola pulled up a chair and sat at the kitchen table without being invited to. Of course. This was her house now. Annie sat down too, feeling defeated. "If you want to call your husband, or ex, or someone this is the perfect time," she told Lola. "It will be morning for him."

Lola took a sip of her tea. "Truthfully, I'd like to postpone that a while."

Annie had a vague premonition. "What do you mean by a while?"

Lola seemed to be stalling. "What do you mean?"

Annie looked at her significantly.

"Mark should be coming back home from Atlanta in two days," Lola finally said. "I wrote a postcard and mailed it to him from New York where we changed planes on our way here. So…"

"So?"

"So, with a little luck, he'll be fooled for a while."

"You. Did. What?" Annie gasped.

"I sent a postcard from—"

"You did not take your children and fly to another country without his okay, did you?"

Lola stared at her cup. "Well, it's very complex," she said with a bit of a rattle in her voice.

Annie's heart began pounding. Was she harboring fugitives? "You're not doing anything illegal, are you?" She had sounded terribly accusatory and belligerent and regretted her forcefulness immediately. Lola opened her mouth to answer but Annie spoke instead, trying to soften her stance. "You did say on the phone that he was abusive."

"It's a question I keep asking myself," Lola said. "What's the definition of abusive?"

"Is he physically violent?" Annie asked. At that point, she needed Lola to say yes.

Lola hesitated, looked away. "He, yes, he is violent... Can be quite violent, yes," she said. "But he is very remorseful each time. That's the thing about him, he always comes back and apologizes. I have to give him that. But then, he does it again. The situation at home was getting unbearable. He is so unpredictable. And it's gotten so much worse with the stress of having children." She lifted her face. "You know what I mean. Men get so jealous of the attention."

"I know precisely what you mean," Annie lied. The boys had been nothing but a strong, wonderful bond between her and Johnny. "You poor thing, and the children! How bad is the hitting, I mean, is it hospital-bad?"

Lola's eyes filled with tears and she looked away. Annie had clearly been tactless, grilling her about something very painful like this must have felt like the Inquisition. "Frankly, I'm here to try and not think about Mark for a while, get a fresh start and..."

Annie had to ask. She had no choice. "Just promise me you're not doing anything illegal coming here."

Lola thought for a long moment. "I…I told him I was moving to New York. I'm not doing anything wrong by moving to France instead."

"Was there ever a restraining order against him?"

Lola looked at Annie. "Oh, definitely. I can do anything I need to protect the kids. I'm allowed."

They sat in silence. Annie felt the weight come off. There was a restraining order. The husband was a bad guy. This was not illegal. She was doing a wonderful deed, helping a woman start over.

"I love him, you know," Lola said.

Annie knew exactly what Lola meant; she knew the ache. She could feel it in her throat, so she made a joke out of it. "I don't mean to be rude, but what part of him is so lovable?"

"Well, he's gorgeous, mainly!" Lola said, and she had such a contagious laugh that Annie had to laugh too. It was in that instant of silliness that an imaginary veil lifted and Annie's preconceived ideas about Lola were thrown out the window.

That night, Annie lay in bed not sleeping, but not exactly anxious either. Maybe this could work. Maybe this would work.

CHAPTER 8

*W*arm water was slowly filling the bathtub. Naked in front of the mirror, Althea watched her emaciated shoulders, her hollow stomach, her hipbones, her legs like tortuous sticks, her knees like giant knuckles. What had happened to her? She had only wanted to be thin. Her mother had told her again, as she was saying goodbye, that she looked like a concentration camp victim. But if she did look so terrible and sick, then why would her mother do nothing about it but insult her? Of course, it would not be fair to blame her mother for what she was about to do.

Her dad had given her that check to go to France and this was as close to communication as they were going to get. He was encouraging her to go away, but did he not mean it figuratively as well? Did he possibly want her to run for his own sake rather than hers? Her parents were not equipped to save someone like her from herself.

She looked at her studio apartment through the open door of the bathroom where she stood; the curtains, the refrigerator, the mirror, the computer, the neat stacks of files and papers, the bowl full of apples that said, "Eat me, eat me," but never, ever, fed her. She felt no physical pain besides hunger.

It would be like going to sleep. There would be no real pain there either. In fact, all she could imagine was relief. She would slowly become weaker, and then fall asleep. The tub was nearly full. In a few minutes, life would sweetly drain out of her. On the side of the tub was the sharp knife she used to peel apples, the knife sharp enough to make this effortless. She considered the knife for a minute, touched the blade gently and felt its power. She turned off the faucet, the bath now full, and stepped in the warm water. She lay in the water and looked at her wrists. If only there was someone she could ask one last question. If only there was someone, somewhere who would be able to tell her how to get out of this skin. Someone who could tell her that things could be different.

She let go of the knife, jumped out of the water, wrapped herself in a towel and got out of the bathroom. Her whole body shivered now with cold and fear. She turned the pages of the paper, searching for the ad. She finally found it, her fingers shaking out of control, and dialed the number of that woman in France.

Annie felt herself pulled out of the womb of slumber with forceps. For an insomniac such as herself, being woken up in the middle of a deep sleep was unwelcome to say the least. In the dark, she felt clumsily for the ringing telephone on her bedside table.

On the line, the voice was barely a whisper. "It's Althea," it said. Althea? The young woman from Cincinnati who had asked many questions about the ad three days ago? Annie let her head sink in the pillow, her hand softened its grip on the receiver and she nearly let sleep engulf her. "It's the middle of the bloody night here, darling."

"I don't feel...good. At all." The voice was plaintive, like a small child sick in the middle of the night.

What was that, transatlantic night therapy? Annie mumbled, "Honey, what's wrong?"

"I think I want to die," said the murmur.

An icy tingling traveled Annie's spine and she sat up in a jump. "Non, non, non, non, non," she said in French. "Nobody's dying!" Why call her for God's sake? "Where are you right now?"

"Home."

What was that supposed to mean? Not to contradict someone suicidal. Could she call 911 from France? Of course, she couldn't call 911 from France. "Are you okay right now?" Annie asked, speaking fast. "Right this minute, are you bleeding anyplace? Did you swallow anything? Is someone with you?" Sweet Jesus, why call her?

"I can't live like this. I really can't." Althea said blankly.

"Not on my watch! None of that," Annie's neurons fired and bubbled, connecting thoughts, searching for the right things to say. "Are you coming to France, honey?"

"I... don't think so."

"Oh, yes you are! Listen to me, why don't you just pack your things, go to the airport, and stay there until a seat is available. You have a passport? Right? Okay?"

"I do... but I don't..."

"Oh, come on, give it a chance. You just call a travel agency and... forget it, my bad. Bad idea. No, just go to the airport and stay there until a flight becomes available. This time of year, you'll have no problem getting a flight. Take a direct flight, you hear me? To Charles de Gaulle Airport. It's spelled C.H...."

"I know how it's spelled."

"And call me, anytime, collect, it doesn't matter, and tell me when you'll arrive. I'll be at the airport to pick you up."

"I'll try."

Annie shrieked. "I'm counting on you, Althea! Don't let me down, sister."

There was a long silence on the line, then Althea's voice, flat. "Okay."

"Good, very good, now give me your address and number." But before she could finish her sentence, Althea had hung up.

Annie stared through her dark bedroom. WTF! WTF! She put her head in her hands. For all she knew, that woman was carrying a deadly virus. Or, more likely, she was dangerously unstable. Oh, this was bad. Very bad. She'd never hear the end of it with Lucas. She looked at the clock. 4:00 AM. Couldn't the inconsiderate have attempted suicide at a more convenient time? She got out of bed, wrapped her robe around her, turned on the light in her room and went to her linen closet to find sheets for Althea's bed. She would give her the orange room. To cheer her up.

One day, Lucas thought, he would tell Annie that contrary to what he had told her, he was not an early riser. Every morning he fought the blaring alarm, confronted Paris's pitch-black glacial streets and drove in a semi-comatose state, all this to spend what amounted to perhaps thirty minutes of alone time with her. But these were not minutes he ever wanted to miss.

"You will not believe this." Annie told him the instant he entered. Lucas removed his coat, folded it over a chair and sat at the kitchen table. The mug was already there. Coffee, in a mug. Only in America, he thought, not for the first time. Stoical, he began sipping the terribly acid brew, taking pleasure in watching Annie move in the kitchen. Today she wore those jeans he liked on her. She had such a lovely, feminine figure, not like those brittle Parisiennes that were his usual lot.

The hour before the boys woke up was their special time

together. Now of course Annie had no idea just how special, and for this Lucas had no one to blame but himself.

This morning, Annie was in a good mood he could tell. "Lola left the U.S. in a hurry and is hiding from her husband!" she said excitedly. "He's a monster! Years of a violent marriage. Lola is a mess. She's a complete mess." Annie did not seem the least bit upset about this, he noticed. In fact, she seemed more than in a good mood. She was upbeat.

"What are you making?" he asked.

"Brioche."

"Ahh! Brioche," he said. He got up, discreetly emptied the contents of the mug into the sink, and came close to her. He looked over her shoulder as she stretched the smooth golden dough and folded it over itself with complete economy of movement. Her hair was in her eyes as always, and Lucas thought of tucking it behind her ear for her. He could feel the heat from her body and the smell of yeast. Both had the tendency of working on him like an aphrodisiac, the yeast and her scent, always the same soap scent that smelled to him better than any perfume and he began to feel his erection. He folded his hand over his crotch and continued watching her hands as she worked the dough.

"Lola says she still loves him. What a crock of shit!" Annie's eyes twinkled. "A mess, I'm telling ya!"

Lucas took a slight step back. "Why do I get the premonition of an impending circus?"

She gave him a dirty look. "What?"

"There will be Lola's drama, and then your drama about Lola's drama."

Annie shrugged this off. "How old do you think she is?" she asked, her hands vigorously working the dough back and forth in a cadence of pushing and flapping. Flour was all over the floor, even in her hair. Above her lip was a little bit of sweat. Lucas sat down. "So?" she insisted. "Take a guess! How old do you think she is?"

"Well, hmm. Maybe twenty-five? Or thirty?"

"You know what?" Annie said, placing the dough in a brioche mold and covering it with a cloth, "I have extra dough, I can make cinnamon buns."

"Cinnamon buns," he repeated.

"It might sound harsh, but I have trouble respecting someone who's been such a pushover for so long. On the other hand, leaving everything behind was maybe very courageous of her."

"You, harsh? No," Lucas said with what he meant to be pointed sarcasm. "What is that American expression? You don't have a harsh bone in your mind."

"You mean, in my body." She took it literally and seemed pleased. "Well, I haven't gotten the precise information out of her, but I bet she is older than she looks. She told me about her life, and I was adding in my head. She's definitely older than I am." Annie turned off the coffee maker with flour-covered hands, poured coffee into a small cup, placed it in front of Lucas and pivoted back to her baking.

From his chair, Lucas watched Annie's profile concentrated on the effort of rolling raisins and cinnamon into the dough. He did not pay attention to much of what she was saying as she went on about Lola and her husband. His gaze followed her, and his mind wandered. Annie looked particularly sexy today. He would lift her hair and kiss her neck, and then he'd caress her buttocks lightly, then more insistently. She would start moaning...

"Couldn't he?" Annie said.

He jumped. "Couldn't he what?"

"Couldn't her husband find out where Lola went by asking the airline?"

This Lola conversation was getting tedious. Lucas drifted back into his reverie. "Possibly."

"So, the Althea woman, you know, the suicidal one, called me finally and she will be landing at eight AM, which means I'll really need your driving expertise tomorrow morning again, by the way. I'm giving her the orange room in the attic. It's cheerful. I'd better get going on the cleaning."

"I'm not going to the airport again." He remembered the attic room. He would carry Annie up to the room and unbutton her jeans...

"I won't be able to walk for a week," he heard Annie say and he nearly fell off his chair. "I beg your pardon?"

Annie stepped toward him, holding her sticky hands up like a surgeon after scrubbing.

"Hellooo? Earth to Lucas? I'm saying could you please bring the vacuum cleaner upstairs. It kills my back every time."

Lucas got up and walked to the closet where the vacuum cleaner was stored. "I was wondering," he said. "You said you wanted four tenants?"

"Three now that Lola is renting two rooms. Why? Do you have someone in mind?"

Why did Lucas have to make things so difficult? Annie was thinking the next morning as she scanned the airport crowd for her new tenant. They both knew he was going to help her out, so why the charade? Her thoughts were interrupted and she instantly knew that the young woman coming up the walkway was Althea. Red Hair, she had said, and boy did this fit the definition. But the strangeness of her appearance? Annie had expected someone who looked depressed. What do people look like when they are depressed? They'd look like Annie did: normal. They wouldn't look like this. This was something else. Something she clearly had no name for.

In the airport, people stared, as French people do, at the red-haired young woman who was advancing toward them. When

she had first come to France, the stares had made Annie feel
furious, violated. The staring included gazes that swept from feet
to face and back down, taking in every detail, whispered
comments, little face and hand movements. Men looked at
women in sexual ways, and women looked at other women in
critical ways. It was the way it was and had always been. It was all
done in a very conspicuous way. A rude way, possibly? Annie
didn't know any better anymore; it had taken her a while to get
used to it, but not long to emulate.

"Look at that specimen," Lucas said with impeccable timing.

"Oh, shut up."

"What?"

"That's her, that's what."

"Carefully selected, over the phone, specimen!" Lucas said
smugly and she did not have the energy to kick him in the shin.

Her hair was the first thing Annie noticed, and how she
recognized her. "I have a lot of long red hair," Althea had said.
Hair was hardly the fitting word. This was a mane, alive, profuse,
lush, that came half way down her back and moved as one curly,
bright red mass. But that hair of hers was all that seemed alive. As
she walked up the ramp in her black sweater and black jeans, the
young woman appeared breakable, lost in her clothes and in the
world. She walked slowly, hesitantly as though she might retreat
and run away any moment. There was something of a pre-
Raphaelite painting about her. Not a healthy pre-Raphaelite. She
wore no makeup and her high cheekbones accentuated the
triangular shape of her face. There were dark circles around her
gray eyes, and her mouth was pale enough to blend with her skin.
But even with serious mascara, lipstick, and some color, she
wouldn't have looked right. At the end of Althea's long emaciated
hand and collection of thin bones under translucent skin was a
single suitcase. It was the hand that alarmed Annie the most. The
hand was not right either. It alarmed her in ways she couldn't
have put into words.

Annie should have waved, called her attention, but she found herself needing time to adapt and gather herself. She crossed her fingers like a schoolgirl as she walked towards Althea, hoping it wasn't her, knowing it was her. "Althea?" she called.

"Annie?" Althea smiled. She had the mouth movement down, but her eyes were not smiling.

Nervousness kicked in. Annie cringed at her own glibness, which had a life of its own. "Welcome to France!" she clamored. "We are so glad to see you. Did you have a nice trip? Here is Lucas. He's got a horrendous French accent. He sounds like Peter Sellers in the Pink Panther," she added with a big fake laugh. "His English is actually pretty decent, but you'd never know 'cause you can't understand a word he says."

Althea shook hands with Lucas and blushed intensely. Annie had never seen someone turn so red, so fast. That made her want to get rid of Lucas at once, but then she'd be stuck without a driver. Althea crouched in the middle of the airport and opened her suitcase, foraging for something. Annie whispered to Lucas "Elle est très timide. She's very shy." Lucas groaned and rolled his eyes.

"La panthère rose, hmm?"

Althea retrieved a small package, closed her suitcase, got up, and handed it to Annie.

"This is for you," she said.

"Oh, dear, you didn't want to...need to, have to I mean," Annie said as she fumbled with the wrapping. Did that woman have parents, a family who would take her back? The package contained a bottle of expensive perfume, Nina Ricci's L'Air Du Temps.

"Oh, honey," Annie exclaimed. "Are you crazy? I mean... insane? Sick. Hum, huh...this wasn't necessary!"

"I wanted to," Althea answered with an enthusiasm that felt forced. "This is so nice to come to the airport and pick me up so early in the morning, especially with the traffic. I'm sure I really should have taken a cab. This is so inconvenient."

Annie and Lucas waited for Althea in front of the restroom, and it occurred to Annie that they could escape and Althea would never find them. She didn't even have the address. Lucas's look of contrition encouraged Annie to convey her anguish. "She's skin and bones," she said.

"You're speaking to her as though she is a child. A retarded child," Lucas said.

"I'm certainly not," Annie snapped.

"My dear, this, honey, that."

"That's how American women talk to each other. You're just not used to it, that's all."

"Well, I would stop," he said.

They walked out of the airport and towards the garage. Annie was ruminating over Lucas's comment. What a jerk. She decided to aggravate Lucas by sitting in the backseat with Althea and shouting the address: "Onze rue Nicolo, dans le seizième, s'il vous plaît, driver." Lucas stuck his tongue out at Annie in the rear-view mirror.

"Quel gamin!" Annie giggled.

"Tous les hommes sont des enfants," said Althea.

Annie wailed, "Haaaa, she speaks French! Lucas, we're so busted! Have we said anything totally embarrassing so far?"

"Non, rien Madame," she answered like a good child. "So, this is Paris!" she said, looking at the inside of the airport garage with apparent ecstasy.

Remembering her experience with Lola, Annie believed a disclaimer was in order. "First we'll go through the suburb. The good stuff is coming up. If you're not too tired, we'll take the scenic route, won't we, chauffeur?"

"Your husband took time off work to pick me up. That is so nice."

"That's not my husband, Heavens forbid! My husband passed away several years ago. A tragic accident. I haven't driven since. Lucas is a doll to give us his time, nonetheless."

"I... Apologize. Thanks. Sorry," said Althea, who continued to blush unexpectedly at Lucas.

The entire way back, for a whole forty-five minutes, Althea spoke, seemingly without breathing, about her sudden decision to visit France, taking a sabbatical from her exciting career, saying goodbye to loved ones. She spoke in a rapid, excited, enthusiastic tone. Annie noted that Althea was saying all the right things, as if she really wanted to be liked, or blow smoke on the real issues that made her come here. Had she forgotten their middle-of-the-night conversation? Less than thirty-six hours ago, her life didn't seem so rosy. Maybe she would get real once Lucas was gone.

They left the suburb and Lucas made the same detour through Paris he had for Lola. But unlike Lola, Althea hardly looked out the window and said not a word about the city. More bothersome, she hardly looked at Annie. Instead, she stared straight ahead as she spoke, lost in her words as though she was reciting a lesson.

§.

After showing Althea the house and then her room, Annie ran back down to the kitchen to make lunch. The boys had walked back from school by themselves for the first time. Already, Annie could see the massive changes to their routines, and how it would affect them. Of course, Maxence was old enough to bring his brothers the few blocks from school to the house. But to walk back alone only to find their house invaded by Lola and her children? She shuddered. No, this was better than moving to the suburbs, better than switching schools and her having to work a regular job. The boys would have ended up walking themselves to school then too. Life was hard. To expect it to be easy was to set everyone up for disappointment. It was a fine thing to empower Maxence. So why then did it feel like such an irreparable loss, a moment with her children lost forever, never to be recovered?

Lucas appeared in the kitchen. He clearly was expecting to stay for lunch. "This suicidal friend of yours seems to be in a jolly mood," he said smugly, "and she's quite the fascinating talker." Annie took a deep breath, opened the refrigerator door and stared at its contents without understanding. "She's weird."

"Possibly you had meant to say that she would drive all of us to suicide?"

"I'm a little down right now and could do without the sarcasm."

"Oh yes, honey, my dear!" he responded.

She turned to him, slammed the refrigerator door. "Lucas, why are you continuously trying to push my buttons?"

"Well, next time you need me, don't hesitate to push my button. The word 'chauffeur' is written on it!"

Paul entered the kitchen, came to his mother, hugged her tight around her waist, and then just as abruptly left the kitchen singing, "First-comes-love-then-comes-marriage-then-comes-baby-in-the baby-carriage."

Althea stood in the center of the tiny bedroom. The white ceiling slanted toward a small window from which she could see only the top of brick chimneys and the bare branches of a tree where a dozen sparrows were making a racket. The walls of the room were a golden yellow, the bedspread a vivid orange and crowded with pillows covered in brilliant fabric. On the bedside table was a bouquet of silk gerbera daisies.

She stayed petrified for a few minutes, and then stepped toward the desk under the window. One by one, she lifted the scented candles and smelled them. On a hook behind the door was a fluffy white terry cloth robe. She put the candle down and took the terry robe in her arms and held it close to her like a teddy bear. She sat on the bed. The bed was soft. Her fingers brushed against the bedspread. She needed to remove her coat. She needed to unpack her suitcase. A spiral of panicked thoughts started emerging, and she braced herself. But there were loud footsteps coming from the stairs, screams and laughs and a huge knock at her door. Before Althea could react, there were five children inside her room taking over the space. Two younger boys sat on her bed. A young girl with a frown held the hand of a toddler. The oldest boy looked at Althea suspiciously. "Are you a vegetarian?"

"Are you a Republican?" another boy asked.

"Mom hates vegetarians," the older boy continued.

"We're supposed to tell you that dinner is ready," the girl said.

"How long are you staying here?" Althea heard, but before she got a chance to answer, the children were galloping down the stairs, leaving behind two plastic swords, a wet but empty water pistol, and a crying toddler. Althea took off her coat, gathered the toys, took the toddler's hand, plastered on a happy mask, and walked downstairs with him.

Mark was about to demolish the plane's phone. "What do you mean they haven't been home?"

"No, Mister Mark. Miss Lola and the children are not home."

Mark gave a small nod to the businessman next to him, who, like Mark, sat in first class, sipped champagne and toyed with a top-of-the-line laptop. Mark lowered his voice. "When were they home? I've been calling for twenty-four hours!"

"I don't know, Mister Mark. They were not home yesterday either. Miss Tamara and I were here all day yesterday. I cleaned. Miss Tamara waited all day. Oh, and, hum... Mister Mark, Miss Lola's car is still here. And there is a... letter."

"What letter?"

"You want me to open the envelope, Mr. Mark?"

Mark growled inaudibly. "No, don't touch that envelope. Pass me Tamara." He thought for a moment. Tamara gossiped with all the other nannies in town. He was about to land and would be home within a couple of hours. "On second thoughts, tell Tamara to go home. Lola must have forgotten to tell you she was flying with the kids to...Vegas for a few days."

"On a school day?"

Why the fuck not on a school day? "We'll call you. Don't worry; I'll cover your pay. Oh, and make me dinner. I'll be at the house in two hours." Mark hung up the phone and saw that his hands were shaking.

CHAPTER 9

*I*t was always fascinating to watch her children from the particular angle of being a fly on the wall. The key was to not interfere, to play deaf and dumb. Annie continued waxing the wood of the staircase banister, a silent task that allowed her to snoop on what was going down. She observed Lia through the bars of the banister. Notwithstanding the angelic face and long golden hair of a maiden, Lia was mighty. Her eyes shone with fury as she stood in the living room, standing as tall as she could make herself, arms crossed, chin high. "My dad is very rich," she was saying. "We have a really big house, much bigger than yours. And we know tons of famous people."

"Like who?" Maxence said.

"Like Rosie O'Donnell. Her kids are in my school."

Maxence, who was only a month older than Lia, stood a full head taller than her and used it to his advantage. He looked down. "Rozy what?" he said, detaching each syllable. "Never heard of your Rosy-O-Josy." Lia opened her mouth to respond, but Laurent cut her off and trumpeted, "Rozy-O-Jozy…Rozy-O-Jozy…" Paul echoed his brother, "Rozy-Oooo-Jozy!"

"Well, you couldn't have heard about her, could you?" Lia cried out victoriously. "You don't even have a TV!"

Maxence, Laurent and Paul seemed stunned by the blow. They turned their head toward the small cabinet where the house's diminutive TV was under key.

"We do too have a TV!" Paul blurted out. "Liar!"

Laurent sang, "Liar, liar, your ass is on fire."

Lia twisted her mouth for an instant. "I have four TVs, all plasma. We even have one in the kitchen, just for the maid. And we have, like, five thousand channels. You guys are poor."

The word stung Annie. Her boys had no concept of being poor. They were not poor. The little bitch had no right to make them feel inferior. This was only a financial crisis. Johnny had been a good provider. It was her fault. She should not have been obsessed with keeping this damn house. She was a horrible mother.

Laurent screamed, "You're lying!"

Maxence, meanwhile, appeared perfectly composed. "Even if we had three billion channels, we wouldn't watch them," he said. "We're not zombies like you Americans."

Lia's face and fists tightened and she was evidently close to tears. "When my dad comes, he'll slap you around until your teeth fall out. You little Frenchie Fries will go wee wee wee in your pants and stuff your mouths with rotten frogs."

Maxence raised an eyebrow as a response, but Laurent could not rise above the infamy. His brother and personal hero was taking a verbal beating, and by a girl! "Shut up!" he screamed at the top of his lungs.

Should she intervene? Her own blood was boiling. Too poor? She'd show her.

Maxence only shrugged. Did he look like Lucas doing this, or was it her imagination? "It looks to me like you're stuck here for a while without your rich Daddy this and Daddy that. And tonight..." Maxence made a dramatic pause and gave his brothers a meaningful look. "Tonight, we'll see who is peeing in their pants, right, guys?" Laurent, Paul, and adding insult to injury, little Simon, who had been witnessing the exchange in silence, nodded their heads in hopeful unison. "In the meantime, live in fear," Maxence added. And he simply walked away with Laurent, Paul, and Simon in his footsteps.

Annie crawled up the stairs hoping she had not been seen. A moment later, Lia was coming up the stairs, dragging Simon, whom she had reclaimed, by the arm. She stormed past Annie, barged into her mom's bedroom and slammed the door.

❦

Lola had been hunched over the miniature desk for over an hour, staring at a sheet of paper half covered with crossed-out sentences, her attempt to write the letter to Mark that stubbornly refused to be born. This was the letter where she would set the record straight and tell him everything she had been too paralyzed to say. She had left him and taken the children. She was doing something both morally wrong and likely punishable by law, but still easier than writing him this letter. The letter would open a dam. Things would be said that might destroy him. For example, what if he found out that she had been faking orgasms? What if he found out that his anger — or was it her anger? — made his touch unbearable? What if he found out that the way he treated her and the world in general made her want to puke? Wasn't disappearing less horrible than the truth? There was a balance in their marriage but it had been a balance based on lies. The truth, if it came out now, would reveal that she had been a complete fraud. Also, once the dam was open, then she might discover Mark's truths about her, those things he could tell her that she may never recover from. He might tell her that she was looking old. That he didn't desire her. That she was dumb. That she was good at nothing. That she had no talent, no value, no worth. That she did not challenge him, and that was why he treated her the way he did.

The moment she put the pen to paper, those anxious thoughts screamed like Furies. She ached to drop the pen and deal with the situation the only way she knew: by pushing it away from her thoughts. She put the pen down. What she should do now is go through the house and hopefully find Annie busy with some chore, and maybe help her, chat with her about everything and anything. Maybe she would be able to tell Annie about all this one day, but not just yet.

The door to her bedroom opened suddenly and Lia barged in, holding Simon by the hand. Lola gathered her papers quickly out of sight. Lia was crying, and so was Simon. Lia let go of her brother. "What's up sweetie pie?" she asked Lia.

"I want to go home! Right! Now!" her daughter screamed. Lola reached one arm out towards Lia who jerked back. "I hate it here. I want to go home!"

"Angel, we've barely been here half a day! We have yet to get out of the house and be tourists, which I was just about to—"

"I hate you!" Lia hollered, and she pushed Lola's shoulder, hard. Lia's rage was uncontainable. She looked precisely like Mark when she was furious. The same redness in the face, the same tightened fists. Lola made a movement to dodge the push, but not really. "I don't want to go anywhere. I want to go to the airport, right now!"

"That's somewhere! There is hope," Lola teased with a smile.

"You shut up!"

Lola recoiled, looked at her daughter's face in horror. Her heart sank so deep she thought she might burst into tears. Lia looked at her, almost as horrified as she was, and then she was the one who burst into tears.

"I want Dad right now!" she said, her voice drowning in tears.

Lola held back a gesture to wipe Lia's tears off her cheek. What if Lia pushed her again? Then where to go from there? "We are not going to see Daddy...for a little while, love," she said. Lia continued crying but didn't ask any questions. Was it possible she knew? Was it possible she didn't want to hear her mother's reasons? "I just want to talk to him!" she cried. "It's night over there. He's probably sleeping. We'll call soon." Lia threw herself at her, or was it into her arms. The only difference was that after she had thrown herself at her with all her might, Lola opened her arms and held Lia against her. Lia was shaking and crying uncontrollably. On the rug, on the wood floor beside the bed, Simon was rolling back and forth gently bumping his head on the baseboard and humming to himself.

"We're all tired right now. It's the jet lag. Things are going to be all right," Lola said. Still holding Lia tight, she opened a free arm to Simon, hoisted him onto her lap and kissed him again and again on top of his head. Maybe Lia wanted to be calmed down by her, and maybe everything would be okay.

"I hate you!" Lia said in a small voice. But she let her mom take her in her arms and rock her for a long time while she wept.

Hunched over her cutting board, Annie chopped parsley and juiced lemon for the salmon stuffing as she rehearsed imaginary conversations with Lola and Althea. What was she going to talk about with these women, day after day, week after week? The weather, check. Children and school, check. Parisian idiosyncrasies, check. She felt the stress in her shoulders, in her jaws, even in the way she murdered her herbs on the chopping block. If she didn't slow down, she was going to cut herself. Finger-stuffed salmon, check.

Maxence walked into the kitchen and stood next to her, stiff and serious. Precisely the way a nine-year-old shouldn't be. "Those people are all creeps," he announced without preamble. It had been three hours since the kids had their fight. This was very much like Maxence to mull things over like this. Not like Lia who obviously had ratted on him right away. She washed her hands, sat on a chair and pulled Maxence towards her. He stayed there but this was no embrace. "Can't you try to make it work for your poor old mommy?" she asked, knowing it reeked of manipulation. Maxence raised an eyebrow, waiting for the rest of her bullshit with an air of bafflement on his face. He reminded Annie so much of his father that she wanted to cover him with kisses, although she didn't have such fond memories of her arguments with Johnny.

"You want me to put up with this mean girl and that screaming baby for six months? And now some woman gets my room in the attic? You promised!"

"What promise? I said I would think about moving you to the attic."

"Plus, we have to see their stupid faces at breakfast, lunch, and dinner. As if we don't see enough strangers with Lucas coming over all the time."

Right, right, right, and right again, she thought. "Wrong, Maxence, this is wrong. You like Lucas, you said he was fun!" she exclaimed, all too happy to divert the issue to Lucas.

"When I was young, yes. Now he gives me the creeps big time, sniffing around you and all that."

"Lucas is not sniffing a thing," Annie said, with all the indignation she could summon. "And I've known him since before your birth, so he is certainly no stranger."

"And the woman who got my room. She gives me the creeps."

She thought of Althea's gaunt face, her black clothes, her silence alternating with bursts of verbal diarrhea. "Name one thing that doesn't give you the creeps, Maxence."

"Well, the four of us being home by ourselves, for one," he said, lowering his eyes and turning his face away slightly.

That her pre-teen would favor being home with his brothers and little old her brought tears to her eyes. "Maxence, we're in this together, you hear me? We need money and this was the only short-term solution that made sense. I'm thinking of going back to school, maybe pass the bar exam here."

Saying those words, she thought of the Dr. Seuss rhyme: I said, and said, and said those words. I said them. But I lied them. "Renting out rooms will buy us time, that's all. Hopefully, in the meantime, you'll start getting along with Lia. She is without a dad, and you know better than anyone what that feels like."

"Yeah, I guess so," Maxence said. He was rapidly breaking down in the face of his mother's unbending logic, her irrefutable arguments.

"One thing, though," he added.

"Yes, sweetie pie."

"Could we at least get a real TV?"

"A TV?" she repeated. "We're low tech. We're very low tech," she added, suddenly unconvinced. She thought of Lia's words. You're too poor.

"A really big screen TV, Mom? Pleaaase, Mom?"

"But where would we put it?"

"And cable."

"What would you need cable for?"

Maxence shrugged this off. "Without cable, there is no point."

If she got the kids a television, she would be getting off easy. True, she would be manipulating her own flesh and blood. "Okay," she said.

Maxence jumped up and down and into her arms. "You're the best mom ever," he said. She tried to keep him in her arms a little longer, but already he was out of her room calling for his brothers. "Guys, guys, we're getting cable!"

It was only later, several hours later, that the thought occurred to her that she might have been had.

CHAPTER 10

A week later, reality had sunk in and Annie was ready to move out to the suburbs if that's what it took to get away from the nightmare of having renters.

The weather hadn't helped; glacial rains alternating with sleet and the occasional hail had kept them cooped up in terrible ways. Battles were being fought on all fronts. She was at war with the housework, a fight she was rapidly losing. Oh, there was cleaning, so much more cleaning, and cooking, so much more cooking. This combined with nights spent dwelling on cold feet and self-doubt. Exhaustion showed on her face. Also, she was angry, and that was showing on her face as well. Sure, her finances had perked up nicely. Sure, she was making money to cook and clean, things she had previously done for free. But now she felt like an employee in her own house and therefore resented what she had previously done happily. She was also at war with her boys, who, sensing her weakness, worked her to get maximum benefit out of the situation. The boys were acting out, mirroring Lia's obnoxious behavior and tone. They were fighting with each other, and together against Lia who in turn provoked them and her mother every way she could. There was yelling, physical fights, and plenty of self-righteous tears.

Althea was all right in the end. Yes, Althea was good. In her absent way, she was nearly the perfect tenant. Not a sound came out of her room, no music, no shuffling of chairs. So silent, in fact, that there had been times when Annie wondered if she should make sure Althea wasn't dangling from a rafter. But at dinnertime, Althea appeared normal, if not hyper. She dutifully came down to the dining room, sat in the spot she had chosen for herself at the end of the table, and alternated moments of stunned speechlessness with bursts of animated yapping. Althea could talk a lot, but not, per se, converse. She answered questions tartly and never asked questions or showed interest in the people around her. Her way of being at dinner was to monologue while playing with the food on her plate. From the cost of airline travel, to the weather, to the toll of high heels on the back, no mundane subject was left untouched. What Althea didn't do, apparently, was get personal. Was she suicidal? No, Annie didn't think so. What did suicidal look like anyway? Wasn't everyone suicidal to some extent?

But if Althea left her alone by hardly leaving her room during the day, Lola, alas, seldom remained in hers. If she had pictured tenants paying rent and occasionally passing her in the staircase and saying a cheerful, helloooo, she had been naive. It wasn't like that at all. Lola, her children, their scents, their things, their needs, and their presence was everywhere. It was an invasion in the most obvious and pernicious way. Not an inch of the house was off limits except for Annie's bedroom, which she now kept locked and where she ran to for refuge to pull her hair out in peace several times a day. Annie could not take a step in the house without coming face to face with the six feet tall übermodel. Even the kitchen was no longer safe, with Lola insisting on helping her despite her two left hands, and her annoying insistence on making conversation. Lola, contrary to

Althea, made every effort to get personal and did not seem to read Annie's clues that she wanted to be left alone.

The pièce de résistance in this dismal week had been Simon's night screams that woke up the entire household. By now, everyone in the house was ready to bite someone's head off, except, of course, Lola, who appeared to have the most infuriatingly sunny disposition. At first, she had wondered how long Lola would sustain that behavior of unending sweetness before the varnish cracked. But the varnish was not cracking. Could it be that this was no varnish? Who was Lola? She was not the prima donna Annie had imagined when she first laid eyes on her at the airport. Neither was she a brat, not in the least. She did not seem to want to be the center of attention. She was not a rich bitch. A week into putting up with Annie's cold shoulder, everyone's angry moods and all kinds of abusive behavior from her children, Annie decided Lola had to be some sort of saint. A saint who, for incomprehensible reasons, seemed to want to become her friend.

Just as Annie was arriving at the conclusion of sainthood, something happened that forced her to reassess. It took place on the first day of clear sky in weeks. Lola had suggested they all go for a walk. A good idea; the kids were going berserk. Everyone was. Before she could stop her, Lola was running up the stairs to tap at Althea's door and invite her to join them.

They walked down the stone steps, all eight of them, she and her three boys, Lola, Lia, Simon, and Althea. The weather was crisp and cold. The neighborhood's mostly 1850s and later Haussmann style façades shone, as though brand new. Annie took a breath. Only a step away from the house and already she felt lighter. She and Lola carried the stroller down, careful not to slip on the icy steps. Althea didn't budge to help with the stroller, just like she didn't budge with the cooking and hardly budged with the cleaning, though she kept her room meticulously clean and the bathroom was always cleaner after she had been in it than before.

"We haven't seen Lucas," Lola said, pushing the stroller.

"He is skiing in Courchevel."

"So, he lives his own life?" Lola asked.

Annie thought it was a strange question. "I know, the nerve of him."

"It's the French way," Lola quipped. "I'm sure it's healthier."

Healthier than what? Annie wondered. "Let's go to Parc du Ranelagh. It's very close."

They walked on the crowded sidewalk of rue de Passy. Well-dressed mothers held the hands of their children bundled up in elaborate tiny coats, scarves, and hats. Annie had never managed that, well-dressed children. Or a well-dressed self. Johnny had picked up that Parisian flair like he'd been born to it. His wardrobe was meant to dazzle. Italian suits, tailor-made shirts, thousand dollar shoes. He had walked proudly in this neighborhood where bejeweled old ladies walked their prized dogs and where perfumed men in trench coats walked quickly, looking straight out of Vogue Homme.

"How do the French learn to be elegant?" Lola asked, maybe reading her thoughts.

"It's that stuff they put in red wine."

"Even the French dogs are more elegant than American dogs, no?" Lola mused.

"There's even a je ne sais quoi to the way they sniff each other's butt."

They walked on Chaussée de la Muette and soon entered the Jardins du Ranelagh. The three of them must have been an odd sight, each one an extreme of the female body spectrum—Lola the Amazon, Althea the waif, and she, feeling as tall as she was wide in her unflattering but oh-so-comfy red poncho, trotting between them like a miniature pony. She found herself in control of the stroller and it felt good, even with someone else's child in it. The wheels made a comforting swish sound against the wet sand of the path. She had carried three babies inside her, then in carriers. She had pushed their strollers, always carrying, holding, pulling, lifting, pushing, and now she missed the constant physical contact she had taken for granted. She used to be a physical kind of girl. These days, she had to respect the boys' desire and need for more separateness, but the result was that she didn't get to touch or be touched too often. She felt increasingly physically separated from other humans, and emotional separation did not feel so far behind.

The giant beech and ash trees were bare and majestic, the air crisp and clean. Street noises became muffled and then disappeared. She felt the tension in her jaw ease as they walked and the children ran ahead. They passed neat rows of boxwood and life-size antique sculptures of goddesses, and through the bare branches of the trees, she admired the ornate details of the neighborhood's architecture. With the cars out of sight, they could well have stepped back in time a hundred years. Annie pointed to the Musée Marmottan, the impressionist museum and vast collection of Monet's work, and the green wooden barrack where the traditional puppet Guignol had been an attraction for generations of Parisian children. She felt strangely proud. This was her city.

Could it be that Althea was paying no attention to her city? Her park? Althea was walking with her head down, looking at nothing but her own feet and keeping her hands close to her chin to hold the collar of her flimsy coat. Meanwhile, she spoke in poor Lola's ear, explaining that she used to bite her nails but had read it is bad for the enamel of her teeth. What? Annie wanted to say "you're in Pa-ris! Forget your frigging enamel for a minute." How could Lola bear this? In the last few days, Annie had attempted to exchange meaningful looks with Lola every time Althea went into one of her soliloquies. She did so in obvious ways by rolling her eyes and tilting her head back in expressions of utter boredom. To all of this, Lola appeared entirely impervious. She showed no sign of annoyance, and nodded in concentration at Althea as she walked. Lola looked so rested, so much more serene and relaxed than she had a week ago. It was interesting how, in the space of a week, Lola had stopped wearing makeup and had taken to moving about the house in leggings and socks. Now she wore jeans and a down jacket that had belonged to Johnny. A wool hat was screwed on her short hair and she walked like a boy, hands in her pockets, looking up and around and smiling to no one in particular. The absence of a husband was doing her good. Annie wished she could be so lucky.

They arrived at the playground, which was filled with children, mothers, nannies, and French conversations, and then walked around to a quieter area with an empty stone bench facing the winter sun. On the bench next to theirs sat a carefully made up elderly woman. Her hands were covered with large rings and twenty or so pigeons surrounded her as she fed them remnants of a pastry. The kids ran to the jungle gym and Simon watched the pigeons, mesmerized. He seemed to put a great deal of thought into it, then toddled towards the birds and faked a small kick in their direction. The pigeons flew away noisily, then landed a few yards away and walked right back to be fed.

"Méchant garçon!" the old woman barked at Simon. Simon's face turned pale. He pivoted on his feet and threw himself into Lola's arms.

"La ferme, vieille peau!" Annie yelled at the woman. She was telling her to shut up and calling her an "old skin," a sure bet of an insult to French women of any age. The old woman showed a fist in their direction, got up, and hurried away screaming. "Retournez dans votre pays!"

Go back to their country? Annie was disgusted. It was one thing to be mean to defenseless children, but open xenophobia? "Tes pigeons ont chié sur ta tête!" she screamed back. She then turned to Lola and Althea and explained, "I just told her that her pigeons crapped on her head!" She burst out laughing and was genuinely surprised when the two didn't laugh. In fact, all she read on Lola and Althea's faces was shamed bewilderment. "What?" she asked. The two only looked at their shoes. "Oh, I know just what you're thinking. I used to feel the same way. Why such gratuitous antagonism, heh? It's just France, that's all. The French are all about opinions and arguments. In fact, it's better to have a hideous opinion than no opinion at all." Because at least that's interesting! Annie thought, unlike Althea's dissertation on teeth and enamel.

Simon began to play sweetly in the sand while Lia, Maxence, Paul, and Laurent dangled from the jungle gym like a family of monkeys. Lola looked perfectly at peace with the moment, despite Althea's talking her head off. Annie observed how fine Lola's skin was even in full daylight and without makeup. She decided to interrupt Althea's rambling.

"I'm considering renting one last room to someone. It's an artist actually, a relative of Lucas who's going through a financial and artistic crisis." She paused. "But I'm kind of hesitating."

"About what?" Lola asked.

"Well, it's a man."

"Is that a problem? Not enough bathrooms?"

"I've known Jared for years. You'd want him in your bathroom. That's the problem," she said. "He's gorgeous, thirty years old, as French as they get, and did I mention gorgeous? He's broken many hearts, I'm sure. Do we need this?"

"My heart's long been broken. I'm safe," Lola laughed.

Annie looked at Althea who sat stiffly on the bench. "What about you Althea? Whadayathink?"

"Well, I... don't..." Althea seemed to choke on her words and she blushed. "I mean I don't feel... anything."

Annie braced herself for another one of Althea's stories. But instead, Althea's shoulders began shaking and her face went from beet-red to turnip-white. Her expression was one of terror. She looked up at them, and then said, out of nowhere. "I'm…sick…I need help." She then gasped, bent forward and buried her face in her hands. Huge sobs came like a wave from deep inside her.

Annie looked at Lola for help, only to find her reaction even stranger. Lola was stiff as a statue, and then she began to recoil and slide on the bench away from Althea. Althea's cries became louder, and to Annie's amazement, Lola walked away from the bench and went to play with Simon in the sand box. Lola had ditched her! Some Saint she was! What to do? What was this? Annie scooted close to Althea and did the only thing she could think of, which was to wrap one arm around Althea's frail shoulders, noticing just how frail the girl really was, hardly thicker than a twelve-year-old, and rub her back as she whispered, "You're okay, you're okay."

"I'm not okay," Althea murmured.

"That's exactly why you're here," Annie said softly. "That's why we're all here. That's why you came all this way to Paris, to get better!"

"I can't get better," Althea said, weeping.

"Are you, like…really sick? What is the problem?" Annie said, still holding her tight with one arm and waving impatiently for Lola to come closer. Lola approached the bench with great reluctance.

Althea lifted her face toward them. "Can't you see me? Just look at me! I am the problem!" she bellowed.

It seemed as though everyone, Lola, the children on the playground, passersby and their dogs, even the pigeons had turned to statues, all eyes and ears in their direction.

"At last!" Annie said.

"I don't see a problem," Lola said hastily.

"I'm without…hope," Althea sobbed.

"Well, you're in Paris now. A new life. A new you!" Annie suggested.

"I don't… think so."

"Bah, you're depressed, that's all." Annie suggested. "What about Prozac? Xanax? It doesn't make a dent for me, I'd be more of a horse tranquilizer type of girl, but you could try it."

"I have no desire to live," Althea said flatly.

Yikes. No desire to live? What did that mean? "It will probably pass," she said for lack of a better idea. "I've buried a husband, and look at me, I'm totally fine now." She looked up at Lola and gave her a look that said, "Say something!" But Lola had buried her nose in her turtleneck and was looking away.

Althea lifted her head. "I'm not going to be fine," she said with such absence of passion that Annie's arms covered with goosebumps.

On the way back home, Simon refused to climb in his stroller and instead took hold of Annie's hand. She liked the small warm hand in hers, needed it, as Althea spoke about things Simon was luckily too young to understand. There were no more talks about teeth, only about depression and hopelessness. Maybe this was better. At least it felt real. And Althea was no longer talking to Lola. She was talking to her. Lola, she guessed was the perfect person to go to when you wanted to say nothing at all. Oh, she would not have minded being off the hook. She dug furiously in her brain for comforting notions to offer Althea, who countered each and every one. Words were futile in the face of Althea's nihilism.

Far behind them in the street, having let the kids go ahead of her, Lola pushed the empty stroller, not even pretending to want to help. Annie could have maimed her. At last her house was in sight, her beautiful home. The carved stones, the massive front door, and the sculpted silhouettes of sycamores fed her strength and she started breathing again. Could it be that the beauty of the house, the street, of Paris was lost on Althea? How mistaken she had been. Paris was no bloody cure for anything, and she herself was the living proof of it.

The children climbed up the stone stairs excitedly. It was as though while all this was happening, the children had had a watershed moment and were now playing together. What had she missed? Simon looked happiest, still hanging on to her hand and taking large steps up the stairs. Inside the house, coats, gloves, and scarves were removed and the children ran upstairs to the bedrooms. That is when Lola finally turned to Althea and said brightly, "I know exactly what you need."

"Do you now?" Annie said, as sarcastically as she could.

Lola chirped, "A makeover!"

Annie closed her eyes in disbelief and ran up the stairs to take refuge in her bedroom.

Annie had learned at the school of insomnia that the later she stayed up, the less hours of loneliness she would endure in the wee hours of the morning. It was past midnight. She was physically drained but her brain had never been more alert. There was no peace in sight. She was running on panic mode. In her pajamas and bathrobe, she sat at the kitchen table with only the light of a small table lamp over her and a pile of cookbooks at her side as she took notes for the next day, ingredients, quantities, recipes, nonsense. Planning a meal was how she muscled through the crisis of self-doubt, how she mapped out her day, her year, the rest of her life.

She had to send these people back. She had to send them all back from where they came. Perfect Lola back to perfect Lola land, doing cheerleading or whatever it was she did there, and Althea back to her cave. They would leave and take with them their children, their death wish, their messy lives, and their huggable toddlers. Maybe she'd go back home to the States too, sell the house, give up on Paris, renounce huile de truffe and paté de lapin. She could resume the life she had interrupted ten years ago. She'd live at her parents' house, work at Starbucks, and go back to law school. Pass the bar exam. She wasn't too old to crawl back into the womb.

She came to the conclusion that if there was to be any sleep at all, she would have to get a glass of something first. She closed her book, turned off the light, and left the kitchen in the direction of the living room and the liquor cabinet. How pathetic she was to resort to drinking alone in the middle of the night. The house felt so symbiotic that even in pitch black, she could easily move about it without bumping into things. Maybe it was the house that was the womb? She advanced in the dark, hearing only the shuffle of her socks on the wood floor. She was surprised to find the door to the living room open because she remembered clearly closing that very door an hour before. She stood, on hold. Something was not right. She heard the wood floor creak somewhere in the room. Someone was in there. Her heart thumping, she felt for the heavy vase on the table and waited on alert, prepared to take hold of the vase and crack it on someone's skull. But then came the distinct sound of a bottle being uncapped. She moved her shaking hand to the light switch, adrenalin pumping, and turned on the light.

It was Lola in the act of nursing a bottle of rum. Lola's eyes widened in shock when she saw her, but she continued taking a long swig from the bottle, like a child determined to stuff as much candy into his mouth before his mother takes it away. Annie put her hands over her pounding heart. "You scared the living crap out of me!"

Lola moved the bottle away from her lips and began laughing, laughing and coughing so hard that tears sprang from her eyes. "I'm not an alcoholic, I swear!" she said between snorts of laughter. Annie gravely reached for the bottle and took it authoritatively out of Lola's hand, which made Lola laugh ever harder. "I must look sooo guilty," she wept.

Annie looked at her in silence, frowning, as Lola doubled over with laughter. She pointed to the bottle in Annie's hand. "I wasn't quite finished getting plastered," she said. Annie contemplated the bottle in her hand, wiped the top with her pajama sleeve, took a long swig, and coughed before handing the bottle back to Lola.

"Let's do this properly, shall we."

Annie turned to the fireplace and placed a fresh log in it. She went to the kitchen and came back with a plate which held small French cookies, ladyfingers and langues de chat, and then sank to the couch. Lola curled on pillows at the coffee table and poured rum in small glasses. They dipped cookies in rum, letting the alcohol and the fire transform the room around them. The walls, the framed art, the photographs of the children, and the antique furniture took on an orange glow.

"When's Lucas coming back?" Lola asked.

Annie shrugged. "I don't know."

"See, that's so French, so modern. I love it," She said, looking impressed.

Annie raised an eyebrow. "What is French?"

"You know, it's totally not codependent. You don't own each other." She gave Annie a playful look. "Is it true that French men are better lovers?"

"Johnny was American."

Lola looked dismayed. "Lucas? Isn't he your boyfriend?"

"Of course not!"

"But he came to the airport."

Annie laughed despite herself. "The airport, yes, that would be a telltale sign."

"I figured…"

"Am I supposed to deny in advance everything people might imagine?" She realized she had no reason to be defensive and softened her tone. "He's just a great friend of the family. There is nothing between us, of course."

"I could have sworn."

"Look, Lucas is a womanizer, and me, I'm one man's woman." She marked a pause, "One dead man's woman. Besides, Lucas is

rather out of my league, wouldn't you say?" Lola seemed to
consider that for a moment and didn't contradict her. That alone
pissed Annie off. You can never let your guard down around
popular girls. Popular girls get that way by being cutthroat and
eliminating the competition. And what better way to eliminate
the competition than to make them feel two inches tall. "Lola,"
she said, "I've been meaning to ask you a personal question. How
can you be so cold and collected in the middle of this marriage
crisis of yours?" Cold and collected. She was mostly referring to
Lola's behavior at the park. If Lola noticed her choice of words,
she did not let on.

"I don't feel calm or collected. I'm neither of those things," she
responded, her voice trailing a bit, the valley accent suddenly
apparent. Annie didn't know if it was due to sadness, or due to
the rum.

"This morning with Althea, you seemed very... composed,"
Annie said, tight-lipped.

"No way. I was totally, like, freaking out! I'm, like, the least
qualified to help anyone. I can barely help myself," she said, her
valley girl accent taking over. "I have no control over my life, no
control over anything, really. I'm put together and all but it's all
totally fake. Lying is, like...totally my life!" she added, biting her
lip like she might cry. Annie tried to read Lola's face.

"How much booze did you have?"

Lola widened her arms "A lot!" She continued in earnest.
"Guess what?" she laid her upper body flat on the coffee table
with complete abandon and whispered, "I'm not even a real
brunette!" Come to think of it, Lola's coal-black hair was
surprisingly dark for her complexion.

"That's your big lie? I'm pretty confident you won't burn in
hell for that one."

"No, no, you don't understand," Lola squealed. "I'm a tow
head. I'm a real dumb blonde! Look at my roots!" She leaned over
the table again and parted her short hair to reveal the odd sight of

a pink scalp and very blonde roots. "It was dyed black for a photo shoot ten years ago, when I modeled, before I met Mark. It gave me instant character." She snapped her fingers. "Poof, just like that! It's been my hair color ever since."

That would explain the green eyes, the pale skin, and the blonde children. "I'll bet you look stunning regardless of your hair color," Annie said, feeling magnanimous.

"Stunning, yeah, whatever good it does me. I'm thinking of letting it grow out. I really, really, really want to start over, you know. I want a new life. Completely brand spanking new. I don't want to be Mark's thing anymore. I don't even want to be his type." She sat straight, suddenly very serious, and whispered intently, "Some of the damage is irreparable, though."

"Like?"

"Like this," she said, jubilant. She unbuttoned her pajama top, flashed Annie her bare breasts, a pretty humongous set of fake breasts, closed her pajamas, and laughed like a hyena. Annie was speechless. "Not too organic, huh? Can you picture these enormities in Down Dog? They almost rub against my cheeks!"

"Doggy style?" Annie wondered.

Lola hollered with laughter. "Not doggy style!" She rushed to the floor, put hands and feet flat on the ground, her back and legs straight, butt elevated. "Down Dog! You know, in yoga?"

This was so interesting. Lola had fake breasts! Wait till she told Lucas. "I know why they invented yoga," Annie declared. "It's a hypocrite's excuse to go into obscene positions with impunity." And Lola's breasts did get in the way, but she kept that to herself. "I've done yoga," she continued. "It's boring, and in my case, embarrassing."

"Boring? Yoga?" Lola yelped. "Yoga is my life. You've got to do yoga." Then she looked about to cry again. "I hate these fake boobs. I hate them," she said, her voice trailing pathetically. "And what for? I mean sex has become so, like, bla bla bla all the time. What's the word?"

"Perfunctory?"

"The boobs were all his idea. He used to pay some attention to my... hmmm..."

"Vagina?"

"But now... it's like it never existed. He's too into the boobs. But really, the boobs, they're not me at all. Mark's into the one part of me that has nothing to do with me. These days our sex is so perfunctory, you know, that I'd rather not have it at all."

These days? The words did not sink in immediately, the alcohol having blurred the edges of her reasoning. Weren't Lola and Mark separated? She thought of pointing it out but instead said. "Maybe you should have let him know."

"Let him know what? That he's a lousy lay?"

"You could have taught him what you like."

"It's not like that... it wasn't like that I mean. I think it's more that all that good testosterone is used up with some twenty-five-year-old in his office."

"You've caught him cheating?" she asked.

"Do I need to catch him in the act to know what he's up to? He's got looks, power, and money. Of course, he cheats on me." Lola didn't seem angry or resentful. Was she past those feelings or incapable of them?

"My husband had looks, power, and money too," Annie said.

"They think with their dicks, it's scientifically proven."

Annie shook her head. "Oh no, not Johnny." She felt worn out by the alcohol and the late hour. She could have easily curled into a ball on the couch and fallen asleep right there.

"I hear adultery is de rigueur in France," Lola said.

"Johnny was American."

"Famous last words," Lola giggled.

This jolted Annie like a slap in the face and suddenly she was wide awake. How insensitive. Johnny was dead, killed for heaven's sake. She needed to shut the bitch up. "So, tell me Lola, what else about you is fake?"

"My name." Lola looked at her with naked vulnerability, her eyes almost imploring acceptance. "My real name is Laura. But there already was a Laura at the modeling agency that was booking me. I was only sixteen when I started modeling full time. I didn't even object to being given whatever name. I lost my name and my education. The money was too good to pass up. I didn't finish high school." Now Annie felt like a schmuck. Hopefully Lola didn't notice she had intended to hurt her.

"So, you've been Lola for…"

"I'm going to be forty."

"You don't even look thirty!" Annie exclaimed.

Lola pointed to her face. "Here and here, collagen. Here, here, and here, Botox. It wears off, you know." She had a small laugh. "If I don't keep it up, you'll see me age ten years over the next six months!"

"No shit!"

"Well, I hope not, but I'm pretty scared."

Annie, for the first time, saw Lola not for who she appeared to be, but for the person Lola must feel she was. Deep inside, the glamorous Beverly Hills model was still flat-chested Laura, the domestically abused mother of two screwed-up kids. Lola was a woman in transition, a woman who had too often bet on the wrong horse, a woman ambivalent about growing older. A woman not unlike herself.

The next day, Annie was hurrying through the downpour and entering the overheated sixteenth arrondissement bistro where Lucas ate lunch almost every day. She spotted Lucas at a table near the window and made her way between tables. She dropped onto the bistro chair and wrestled with her coat. "What's the Plat du jour?"

"Confit de Canard and scalloped potatoes." I took the liberty of ordering for you.

Annie took note of Lucas's ski tan. "How was Courchevel?"

"Une bouteille de Perrier," Lucas asked the approaching waiter. He folded his menu neatly. "Courchevel was superb. The powder was divine. What did I miss?"

"Everything!" Annie proceeded to describe the week, wondering all the way, but never asking, with whom Lucas had traveled. "My heart goes out to Lola," she said finally. "She really is a nice person, and genuine, no matter what she says about lying being second nature to her. And," she added smugly. "She looks great for being almost forty."

The plates arrived, steaming. Lucas put his napkin on his lap. "Sounds like you like her better."

"She's not such a bad girl."

"Blonde or not, breasts or not, she'll have no problem finding a man to worship her."

"Did I tell you she's almost forty?"

"You made that abundantly clear."

"That's because society doesn't give women a chance. For us, thirty-five is the beginning of the end."

"Her end has not come yet."

"Hmm," Annie said, looking at him quizzically. "Would I be wrong to assume that you wouldn't mind paying homage to her plastic bosom?"

"Only as a public service, to help her regain much needed self-confidence."

Annie shook her napkin angrily and put it on her lap. "Suit yourself."

"Are you angry with me?"

"Why would I be angry? I just think the last thing Lola needs is to be treated like a sex object, particularly by a French macho man who can't hold onto a woman for more than a week. "

Lucas put a hand over his heart. "I pledge to make it last more than a week!"

"You've got some nerve! What makes you think she'd want you?"

Lucas tried to appear humble as he said, "My reputation, as you know, precedes me."

Annie studied his face. Was he joking? The thought of pouring her water glass down his pants occurred to her, but she was thirsty so she brought the glass to her mouth. "Oooh I see, we must be talking about Monsieur Le Penis. I'll break the news to you, since you've been caught in a time warp. Size is nothing to women! Besides, I'm pretty sure you are not her type."

"I'm ze French man. We have an international reputation."

"Ze French male ego is at work, I see."

"Ze ego and Ze penis are always at work."

Annie smiled despite herself. "So? Who was there?" she asked.

"Who was where?"

"In bloody Courchevel, where else?"

"No one of importance," Lucas answered. Annie chewed and looked at Lucas intently, but Lucas only stared back.

CHAPTER 11

$\mathcal{T}$he cab stopped in front of Annie's house. At the moment, all Jared could feel was resentment. But when he lifted his eyes toward the house and took a breath, it was a breath of relief. There was something about this place, the maze of rooms, the toys everywhere, the loud kids, and that rare garden in the middle of the city that Jared had always loved. This was the house, the family he would have wanted to grow up with instead of the poverty and grief he had been dealt.

On warm summer nights, when Johnny was still alive, they had gathered there, he and many others to eat Annie's food, to drink large quantities of Bordeaux, to talk about politics, and to laugh. All of it ended, of course, after Johnny's accident. Annie was in shock and wanted to be left alone. Jared stopped visiting, and he hadn't been the only one. At a loss as to what the appropriate behavior should be, he had chosen to be a coward rather than a fake. Somehow, he got news through Lucas, and since he was kept informed, it had given Jared the mistaken impression that he had kept in touch. It was only as he handed cash to the cab driver that the reality of his desertion dawned on him.

Now, after three years of this, Annie was saving his ass. He carefully pushed away a confused mix of guilt and irritation. Being able to live here for very little money was a huge break. A gay couple from Italy was subleasing his apartment for a nice amount of cash until June. That money would keep him going for a while afterward.

In the street, the driver helped him pull his suitcases out of the cab, and Jared braced himself for Annie. But there she was at the front steps, waving at him. Jared hoped there'd be no sign of despair over Johnny's death, that it would be all clean and digested. Lucas had told him she had changed, that she was going through a difficult phase. Jared had trouble picturing her as anything other than the gregarious, witty and fun loving woman of three years ago. But he had changed too. What he was like three years ago had nothing to do with who he was now.

Annie threw herself into his arms to hug him, an American habit she had never quite replaced with the more French kiss on the cheek greeting. The American hug, too close for comfort made him feel self-conscious and he kicked himself for arriving empty-handed. Annie, hands on her hips and head cocked to the side, examined him from head to toe. She punched him playfully on the shoulder. "Still as good looking as ever! Hey, when was the last time you got a haircut? Lucas is right, you look a mess!"

Jared didn't know how to respond to what weren't questions. Yes, she was different. Entirely different, but how, he had not yet taken it in. Her face looked strained, her body, forgotten. She was wearing stained painter's overalls and her hair was held together in a haphazard ponytail. She was not wearing make-up but, just as Lucas had told him, she was still wearing her wedding ring. Lucas said she was not accepting Johnny's death. It looked to him like a part of her might have died along with him. He fumbled with words and vague attempts at pleasantness until Maxence, Paul, and Laurent stormed out of the house to greet him.

"The Man!" Maxence said as a form of greeting, and Jared felt his body soften. The boys were barely recognizable after two years, especially Paul, who was a toddler last time he saw him.

"There's a new secret handshake and a new password," Laurent said. They threw Jared a Nerf ball and pushed and shoved him into the house. Maxence whispered in his ear, warning him about the new people living here. All weirdos.

Inside the house, there were no obvious signs of sorrow. The entrance's wall, bright yellow stenciled with large orange suns, was basking in the light that came through the open door. Facing the front door was the dark stairway, and to the left, the living room with the fireplace where year after year he had lingered with Lucas and their then respective girlfriends. They had listened to Johnny's record collection and had drunk Tequila until no one could stand.

Annie waved the children instructions. "Help Jared with his stuff."

Gesturing for Jared to follow, Maxence and Laurent dragged the suitcases up the stairs.

"Can I go on your back?" Paul said.

"You remember that?" Jared hoisted Paul to his shoulders.

"I have a little surprise for you, for later," Annie sang as he started up the stairs. "That's all I'll say for now."

"Are we glad you're here!" Maxence said in French. He jerked the suitcase up from step to step using brute force. "Way too many girls here. It's becoming unlivable!"

"And they're stupid too," Paul added with passion as he strangled Jared with his legs.

"Shhh!" Maxence interrupted.

A silhouette was slowly descending the dark stairs, hesitant. Struggling to breathe and trying to take Paul's hands off his Adam's apple, Jared looked up right as her hair came to mask her face. Eye contact. Gray eyes he noticed, and then the shadow of her body coming down the stairwell. Jared's heart made a leap in his chest.

ॐ

Jared found himself in a small bedroom under the roof with the low-slanted ceiling. The walls, the bed spread, the furniture, the painted floor, everything a harmony of whites and creams, all conspiring to remind him of the very thing he was trying to forget: white canvases. A moment later, Annie entered his room without an invitation. He'd have to lock it from the inside from now on. "Are you ready for your surprise?" she asked as she surveyed the room where the contents of Jared's suitcase, mostly black clothes, were already scattered everywhere like shadows. "There are two other rooms on this floor beside this one. One's not usable; it's never been remodeled and it's full of junk. So, I was wondering if you'd make a deal with me."

Jared peered at her. "Depends."

"You get rid of the junk for me, clean the room, plaster it, dry wall it, whatever it, and in exchange for that, I'll let you use it free of charge and make it your atelier."

Jared looked out the window. The woman he had seen in the stairwell shared the floor with him. "I'm all right," he said. "Thanks anyway."

"What good is it to have an in-house artist if he doesn't have space to paint?"

"You've been talking to Lucas?"

"So, what if your work isn't selling? Neither did Van Gogh's."

"Old Vincent stuck with it and it eventually paid off." Jared brought a cigarette to his mouth and a finger to his temple like a gun.

"Please, don't smoke in the house," she said. Jared put down his lighter but kept the cigarette in his mouth. Annie had her hand on the doorknob. "I'm surrounding myself with people who have youth, beauty, intelligence, and talent but are too busy feeling sorry for themselves. Look at me—thirty-five, fast approaching forty, a dead husband, three kids, no marketable skills, and a house that's on the verge of sending me into bankruptcy but do you hear me complain?" She shut the door rather angrily and he heard her grumbling her way down the stairs. He lay on the bed and lit his cigarette.

❧

There were giggles and whispers in the dark staircase as Jared came downstairs for dinner later, but those stopped the instant the children saw him. The boys were sitting on the steps with a little girl and a toddler. They all looked at him in silence, moving to the side as he made his way between them.

"Bonsoir," he said.

"Bonsoir," Maxence said. The other children stayed silent and he felt strangely excluded. As he stepped into the dark hallway and away from the stairs, the children's whispers and giggles returned.

Jared walked toward the kitchen and opened the door to bright lights, loud conversations, humid heat, and the rising smell of Coq au Vin. Standing at the stove, all six stove burners going at once, Annie was like a percussionist, noisily opening and closing lids, stirring, adding ingredients, cranking up or reducing temperatures under bubbling pans of various sizes and shapes. Close to her, Lucas stood in her way, and she bumped into him every time she needed to get to the cutting board. The woman Jared had seen in the stairway was peeling vegetables and glanced briefly at him before disappearing in her task. Next to her was a beautiful woman with closely cropped black hair who flashed him a sexy smile.

"Jared! At last, honoring us with his presence," Annie exclaimed. "Lola, Althea, here is Jared, Don Juan extraordinaire and famous painter on a ridiculous sabbatical."

Unable to gather who was who, Jared gave a small "salut" in the direction of the women. Lucas poured a glass of wine and offered it to him. Jared went to sit at the table. The red-haired woman turned her face away and suddenly all he could see was her hair.

Lucas peeked over Annie's shoulder into a pot. "You left the rooster's bones in?" he pointed out.

"It's chicken," Annie said, chopping parsley at high speed.

"Coq au vin sans coq?" Rooster cooked in wine without a rooster. Lucas seemed to put a great deal of thought into his reasoning. "But then," he said "Don't you have to work around the bones as you eat. Wouldn't it be better to use a boneless rooster?"

"The bones give the dish its flavor. God forbid you'd have to put in the effort and work around the bones!" Annie turned to the dark-haired woman. "Lucas was born with a silver spoon, filled with boneless rooster, in his mouth."

"What do you mean?" Lucas asked.

"An American expression. Hey, why don't you tell Althea and Lola your theory on wrinkles, you know that bit about rich wrinkles and poor wrinkles."

Lucas turned towards the dark-haired woman. "This is not my theory. It's a known fact."

"Tell them," Annie insisted.

"Rich people's wrinkles are horizontal from time spent smiling in the sun, on a boat, or on a golf course," Lucas explained. "Poor people's wrinkles are vertical. Furrows between the eyes, creases around the lips, lines on the cheeks, lines obtained from a life of worries over financial woes."

"Interesting you'd say this in front of a widow on the brink of bankruptcy," Annie spoke to the women as witnesses. "Isn't this elitist, and revoltingly macho?"

"Elitist perhaps, but why is it macho?" Lucas asked.

"Because I'm approaching middle age, or will be in the next ten years." Annie looked at the beautiful dark-haired woman, who was laughing. "I guess this must be why women find him charming." Annie grabbed a large knife from behind Lucas. "I'm immune though. Lucas, please sit down, you'll get wounded standing there."

The beautiful woman extended a graceful hand towards Jared, which he shook. "Welcome, we're glad to have you," she said languidly. She was flirting with him, that much he recognized.

"Sorry. I don't speak English very well," he said, looking at the red-haired woman.

"I'll have to hurry and learn French then," she smiled. Lucas came close to her and whispered in her ear and the woman giggled. Lucas at his best. His approach seemed self-defeating if Lucas's goal was to seduce Annie. Annie, using a butcher's knife as long as her forearm was chopping mushrooms at great speed, ignoring them. The red-haired woman stood up and brought the peeled vegetables to Annie. She put the peels in the trash and left the kitchen without a word. Jared got up to leave the kitchen as well but Annie interrupted his motion by grabbing his arm.

"You better not have become a vegetarian or something," she said. "There is an endive and beet salad, and for dessert, a mousse au chocolat." She added, speaking to no one in particular, "Jared, he is too independent to be having dinner with us every night, but tonight, he is bestowing on us the honor of his company." Lucas was giving the shorthaired woman a wine tasting lesson, twirling her glass by putting his hand over hers; neither of them paid attention to Annie.

"What did you say her name was?" Jared asked Annie in a low voice so that the other two wouldn't hear.

"Oh, yeah, Casanova is waking up? Lola is married with children and Lucas has obviously claimed her for himself from the moment she landed here." She stepped toward the refrigerator angrily.

Of course, he wasn't asking about that woman. "Stop calling me Casanova and Don Juan. D'accord?" he said.

"Whatever you say, Romeo!"

❧

Johnny loved dinner parties and she had cooked for as many as twenty-five people almost every weekend. She had felt more comfortable in the kitchen while witty conversations in French darted around the dining room table. As intimidating went, Paris's advertising world was right up there with the Third Reich. Elitist, power hungry, and ruthless. She was left in the dust, among the internal political attacks and the sous-entendus.

But dinner that night, the largest dinner party she had hosted and cooked for since Johnny's death, was different. She was not retreating to the kitchen. The kids monkeyed around at the grown up table instead of being fed first and then sent to their bedroom. They drank several bottles from Lucas's family cellar, a wine collection that rested mostly undisturbed in the family's manor cave in Normandy, and the wine lifted spirits the way only fantastic Bourgogne could. The conversation, a blend of French and English had turned to everyone criticizing the United States, and Annie had taken on the role of its staunchest supporter. She who had been so critical of it while she lived there. Lola fell into easy laughs at everything anyone said. Johnny's dinner parties had always been filled with beautiful women as dependent on men's attention as if it were air or water. Annie had hated them, so why then could she not manage to hate Lola? Was it because Johnny wasn't there? Or was it that Lola listened to Annie intently and guffawed at her jokes?

Althea was the only one not speaking. She had stopped all manic talk since that day at the park. It was as though she allowed herself silence at last. She did not take part in discussions and did not seem very interested in what was said, but she did hide in her room as much. She hid in quietness and this suited Annie just fine. Now that Althea didn't try so hard, her face had relaxed and showed more vulnerability than tension. There was to Althea's face a romantic beauty, a charm that had not been apparent before. Charm was something so hard to put your finger on. You could be gorgeous and have no charm. You could be ugly and have charm. Everyone in this room had charm. Jared, of course, had a brooding charm. Even Lucas, that old rascal, was full of French upper-crust charm. Everyone was so darn charming, except, alas for herself.

After dessert, the children left the table to watch the brand-new television delivered and installed that morning. Once they had left, Lucas, who was always mindful of the children's ears, began regaling the adults with a renewed repertoire of salacious jokes and juicy bits about past hunts and fishing trips with ridiculously inbred relatives, all the while extolling the virtues of France. The thin line between patriotism and bigotry so often crossed in her own country was not something Annie suffered gladly. "The golden age of France died with your glamorous ancestors," she reminded him, just to see where it would lead them. "France is finished. Now all it's known for the world over is negativism and snobbism."

Lucas raised his gaze from his glass. "Annie," he said, "you are the Queen of understatement and verbal restraint." Annie smiled. Bourgogne helping, she had a glimpse of him from Lola's standpoint, or from any woman's standpoint, really. Lucas looked pretty good in his black slacks and grey polo shirt. His face was handsome, his smile charming as heck.

"Look," she said, "I love my French children and I like my French cheese on my French baguette, but collectively, the French are inbred and the society has been stagnating for eons."

Lola giggled into her Bourgogne. "From my perspective, the French are as attractive, as charming, as poetic as their reputation." She smiled at Lucas. "Besides, they value the enjoyment of life. That's a form of intelligence Americans don't have. We go so fast. We accumulate, spend, consume. We have abundance and wealth. Yet our lives miss the richness of being able to appreciate the moment."

Lola's platitude gave Annie satisfaction. "It's not because the French take their joie de vivre seriously that it makes them decent people. Actually, doesn't that make them pretty selfish?"

Jared played with his knife and the breadcrumbs on the white tablecloth. "Are you sure you don't want to pack your bags and return to that great country of yours? Or maybe they won't take you back. You are so French now, so nihilist," he said.

"That's why I blend in so beautifully in France. Being in a good mood is considered socially unacceptable here. Be optimistic and people look at you like you're a simpleton."

"That doesn't sound too good," Lola said with a pout.

"Neither is it even remotely true," Lucas answered, unruffled.

But she had hit a raw nerve in Jared. "How can you be so misinformed?" Jared said. "Please remind me, you received your education where? Ah, yes, in America!"

"Education, of course. That wild card! You French are such intellectual snobs!"

Lola raised her glass. "I, for one, intend to learn as much from the French as possible."

Jared took a cigarette and offered his open pack around the table. "So, you haven't answered my question, Annie."

"Please smoke outside. I'm enjoying my life in Paris on the sidelines of all this, as a voyeur, and I'm witnessing the unraveling of the French."

Jared folded his napkin, placed it on the table and walked out of the dining room without a word. Lola and Lucas whispered to each other and Althea went nose-diving into her plate. Annie wondered if she had gone too far. Through the window, she saw Jared on the front steps of the house, his wide shoulders silhouetted, then his profile as he lit his cigarette. He took a long drag and tilted his head toward the dark sky. When Annie looked up, she saw that Althea was watching Jared too.

§&.

After dinner, Annie held onto Lucas's arm as she accompanied him toward the door in a way that only she could see as sisterly. When Annie drank, she became a tad seductive, Lucas had noticed. But he knew better. She leaned against the front door, in the semidarkness, her hand on the doorknob.

"So, that was a nice evening, huh?" she said and she nudged him with her shoulder and stayed there. "It's nice to see you being the life of the party. Something tells me that you're not impervious to Lola's charm."

Annie was so short that when they stood next to each other like this, she had to lift her chin up to look at him. He had the urge to lift her up toward him. "A lovely dinner," he responded. "But I'm only coming to see you, as you know."

"Oh, come on. It's blatant that you're smitten." She looked at Lucas expectantly, her neck stretched up to read his expression. "Come on," she cajoled, "admit it."

Lucas stiffened, wondering for the hundredth time why women were in general so easy to get into bed, and why he became so thoroughly inept when it came to Annie. "I'm just being friendly," he said.

"You don't have to apologize for flirting with her. She's having a grand time," Annie mused, stepping even closer to him, close enough for him to smell her perfume—a cheap perfume she bought in grandes surfaces, something musky and wonderful, something full of promises. "If I were her, I'd have surrendered to your charm right then and there," she added. In the dark of the hallway, with the lamppost shining through the window as sole lighting, things seemed possible for an instant. "Alas," she said, stepping away from him suddenly and opening the front door. "You're going to have to try a little harder. Lola's convinced that she loves her moronic husband. She is so wrapped up in her lousy marriage that she wouldn't be able to spot a decent man if he came crashing down on her head."

Not unlike yourself, Lucas wanted to say. "Perhaps you spend too much energy thinking about your renters," he said instead. She looked vexed. "I'm concerned, that's all," she announced. "I'm concerned for Lola, and I'm concerned for Althea, as a matter of fact. It's what we call compassion."

The thought occurred to him to ask her to be concerned about herself, to be concerned about him, but there was no good place for this to go.

"Maxence has renamed Althea 'Madame de Gloom,'" Annie continued sweetly. "Did you notice she's got a strange way of eating?"

"No."

"Sometimes she eats and eats. Other times she doesn't even come down for dinner. She says she is not used to French food, it doesn't agree with her. But to eat nothing at all? Don't you think she's skeletal as it is?"

Lucas stepped outside. "Let me know if you need help with Madame de Gloom and Madame..." He looked for a word, "Bimbo."

"You're being unfair," she said, visibly pleased. "Lola's down-to-earth, not the snob you'd expect to find in someone so..." She paused, looking entirely disingenuous, "Perfect."

The conversation was back on them, always other people. He wanted Annie close to him again flirting with him, or did he imagine this? "She is gorgeous, and quite relaxed," he agreed.

Annie nodded gravely, but Lucas could tell she was fuming. "A little too relaxed. You know what she's been doing with her ex? I know there's a restraining order and all that, but she's been sending him postcards, through a friend of hers who lives in New York so he won't know she's in France. I think the later he finds out, the more chances Lola might have a wounded rhinoceros to deal with. I know that's how I'd react."

"Still," Lucas said, "does he deserve to be cut off from his children? Am I the only one who wonders about that?"

"Every time I bring it up to Lola—which, believe me, I do—she says she's going to write to him and spill the beans."

"Spill the beans?"

"Spit it out."

"Spit, ah yes," he said, having no idea what she was talking about. It was late now. The alcohol was wearing off; the window of opportunity was missed, if there had ever been one. "If I were you," he said, "I would look into Lola's story. Beans and all."

"My business is to bite my tongue, which does not come naturally to me."

"Those are your words, not mine."

Annie came close again, nudged him, and whispered against his neck. "Honey, I can keep quiet when I need to. I have my little secrets, you know. Don't think you have me all figured out quite yet."

Flustered, he changed the subject. "I ... hum ... I hope bringing Jared here was a good idea."

"Are you worried Jared will seduce Lola before you do?"

He had an epiphany. "Are you upset about the attention she is getting?"

"No. But I notice a lot of animosity coming my way."

"Animosity? Me?"

"Yes. I'm making a living. I didn't sell the house. You were wrong, and it pisses the hell out of you. How do you like them apples?"

"What are you talking about? What apples?" he said, baffled. And Annie pushed him out of the house and closed the door.

After dinner, Althea removed her clothes and folded them into the small cabinet. Everything fit exactly. She wrapped herself in the terry cloth robe and lay on her bed, waiting for the house to become silent so she could have the bathroom to herself. Tonight again, she waited until it was too late to call her mother. If her mom was angry with her or sad that she was in Paris, she did not say, but the phone calls to her mother filled her with dread.

From her bed, Althea stared out the window at the night. During the day, she stayed in the house, in her bedroom, coming down to the kitchen only to make tea. She did not want to see Paris. Not yet. What if it disappointed her? How could she handle that? Instead she stood at the window and watched the sparrows on the branch. They were noisy and active, jumping between branches and then disappearing in a delirium of feathers. In the morning, the children ran around, calling, climbing stairs, then, in an instant, everyone was gone, and the house became very still. Later, like the sparrows, the children came back and the house was noisy again. She felt safe here, in this room, in this house. In this foreign place, this house full of strangers, she felt out of harm's reach. Also, these strangers didn't burden her with their love, and she did not have to carry the burden of loving them.

"Don't worry about me. I'm great!" she had told her mother on the phone the last time they spoke.

"You're a big girl. You do whatever you want."

"I walked on the Champs Élysées today. It was really...totally awesome. I wish you could have seen it."

"My dinner is not going to make itself."

"Of, course, Mom. Go ahead. I'll call you tomorrow."

Althea knew she would not call her mom tonight. Instead, she lay on her bed and thought of Jared, the new renter on the other side of her wall.

CHAPTER 12

"*D*ear Mark. I am sorry to be doing this to you. I am in New York with the kids for a little while. I need time to think. I am very confused right now about us and about our life. I'm sorry, please be patient with me. Love, L"

Mark put down Lola's postcard, which he knew by heart. He poured himself a glass of whiskey and walked to the refrigerator to find it empty. His rage had not diminished in the week since Lola had left. She better get her ass back home and quick. Here was the bottom line about Lola: She had a pretty sweet situation, and she knew it. She had the house, the help, and crews of cleaners, babysitters, cooks, pool men, gardeners, plumbers, and whatnot. They could easily afford a nanny per kid. He had told her to do it a million times, but she insisted on doing most of the kids' stuff by herself. That was up to her, but if that's what she chose, Mark didn't want to hear any crap about the problems with the kids.

He wasn't going to change. He didn't need Lola's bull. He didn't need her at all, for that matter, if she was going to pull these kinds of stunts. He wasn't budging, and he sure as hell wasn't running after her if that was the game she was playing. He was comfortable with that decision. She'd find herself confused and lonely in New York. With the kids? Where? What? In a hotel room? Hard to picture. Soon enough she'd wake-up, realize the insanity of what she had done, and she'd come back. It was a shock, though. He had to admit, not only because it surprised him, but also because of the staggering sense of loss he experienced at the thought that Lola might hate him.

&

Lola had enrolled Lia at the Lycée International rue de Passy where Paul, Laurent, and Maxence went to school. School enrollment might turn out to be the least of her problems if she were dragged to court, charged with kidnapping her children, but Annie had probed and insisted. Lola got worried that Annie would become suspicious if she did not do normal things such as enrolling Lia in school. So, in a way, she had caved to the strongest will this time again. And in the end, she had avoided being the one in charge of her decisions, again.

Lia kicked and screamed all the way to her first day of school something terrible. Every step put Lola into an agony of guilt, and she would have turned back had Annie not been there. "I won't eat. I won't speak to anyone!" Lia screamed. But once in the school hall and surrounded by strange kids, Lia fell quiet. When the bell rang, Maxence made a sign for Lia to follow him and she did. An instant later the large wooden gate was shut and Lia was gone. Lola looked down at Simon in his stroller, then at Annie, and burst into tears.

Annie steered her away from the gate. "She'll be all right."

"But your children are different than mine. They do what you ask them to do. They don't throw fits."

"The kids aren't different, the mother is. I'm far scarier than you are. Let's go," Annie said, taking Lola's elbow. "I'm taking you to the market."

The invitation had surprised Lola. Every morning she watched Annie march out of the house with the determination of a huntress, a straw basket on each arm, but every time she had offered to come along, Annie forcefully declined and Lola did not dare insist. Besides, she suspected Annie preferred to be alone. "I wouldn't want to slow down your errands."

"What errands?" Annie said. "This, my dear, is called faire les courses. That's an entirely different animal. Prepare yourself for an adventure of the senses." Annie began pushing the stroller and Lola followed thinking of Lia, who by now must be sitting alone, terrified, in the middle of a strange classroom. Had Annie not insisted, had Lola not been weak, Lia would not be suffering right now.

Most of the trendy boutiques on rue de Passy were closed still and wouldn't open until eleven in the morning or so. Only cafés and boulangeries bustled with activity, with men and women stepping in and out hurriedly. The smell of rain, freshly baked bread, and exhaust fumes permeated the air. Lola once again marveled at the sophistication of the people they passed—stylish mothers, men in impeccable suits. She, herself, had adopted a uniform of sweatpants and snow jacket and had stopped wearing make-up. There was something absolutely delicious about having no one to impress, no eggs to walk on, no risk of coming face to face with a neighbor who would know precisely how many pounds she had already put on in her short time eating Annie's cooking. Interestingly, despite her lack of trying to look glamorous, men were looking at her more intently than they would ever dare to do in the United States. Desire, lust, envy, admiration, invitation, flirtation could be communicated with the eyes in Paris. It was as direct as it was not always discreet, but it was quite exciting.

The excitement she perceived was not only about eye contact, it was about a richer texture, a greater dimension to relationships and even to life. The most striking symptom of this richer life she witnessed, taking place in cafés and restaurants, were the conversations, or rather the fact that there were conversations at all. No coffee was consumed hurriedly out of Styrofoam cups; no donut was eaten on the run. This was not a drive through society. The conversations happened between small groups of men and women who seemed engrossed in each other, high on life. This could be what was at the core of Paris' romanticism. It was the notion, the illusion perhaps, that you could suddenly meet someone and it would be the beginning of something extraordinary. Something intoxicating and adventurous. As they walked, and the farther they got from the school, the less bad she felt about Lia. Physical distance had a way of making things less real.

She followed Annie who was still pushing the stroller. They crossed rue de Passy and made the turn onto rue de l'Annonciation. In the blink of an eye, the atmosphere of the street changed. Lola had walked through rue de l'Annonciation just the day before. She recognized the stores, pâtisseries, and cafés, but now it had blossomed into a street-long outdoor market, wild and busy and so very un-city like. The smell of car exhaust was replaced with the scent of flowers, fruit, raw fish, roasted chicken, and overripe cheese. There were piles of fruit and vegetables on the stands. Merchant voices clamored for attention. There were mothers and young children, old ladies dressed like peasants from another era next to women in heels and Chanel tailleurs. Many were holding straw bags that matched Annie's. Sitting at the terrace of cafés, men of all ages smoked, drank cafés serrés, talked and watched.

Annie stopped at a vegetable stand. She pointed to Lola, "Do you like betteraves? Nooo! What are you doing?"

Lola had an apple in her hand. "You don't like Granny Smiths?"

"You're not supposed to help yourself, goodness gracious!"

Lola quickly put the apple down. Annie made a chin

movement toward the wide-shouldered man with a paunch and a thick black moustache who was weighing potatoes on an old-fashioned scale. "You're in his territoire."

"His territory?"

"Just wait and hope that he serves you. And don't think your shenanigans with the apple went unnoticed. His moustache works like an antenna. You've lost points already. If you behave, he'll serve you. If he likes you, he'll be generous, give you his best stuff, and often some extras."

"With that attitude, are you sure you want to give him your business?"

"Ha! He's a pussycat compared to the others. Around here, if you step out of line, you'll go hungry."

"What else am I not supposed to do?"

Annie shrugged. "Just don't piss anyone off."

When their turn came, Annie took her time at the stand, asking the propriétaire for his recommendations. For someone so difficult, the man was in no hurry. He and Annie exchanged thoughts about the weather, and about the Président, as he picked vegetables and fruit from piles purposefully. Lola found it amusing, this air of importance people were taking. Everyone here was a connoisseur. At the fish stand, Annie selected the fish they were having for dinner as though it were a child she was looking to adopt. Surrounded by the opaque eyes of hundreds of fish spread on beds of crushed ice, Lola tried to look at the mounds of shrimp before her with different eyes. She was trying to see the place with French eyes. Obviously, there must have been differences. French women pointed without hesitation towards this mound of antennaed creatures or that one. There were shells of various colors, size and texture but what did they taste like? Wasn't a clam a clam? Some shrimp were pink, some were gray, they varied in size and price, but why?

She followed Annie obediently from one stand to another. At the Boucherie they stood between guinea fowls hanging upside down on hooks—head, legs, and feathers still attached—and a display of hoofs and tongues artfully arranged around a vividly pink pig's head. She wished Lia was there to see this strange and gruesome sight, and she felt a pang of sadness at the thought of Lia, and then a bit of fear. One should not be afraid of one's own nine-year-old. Annie was not afraid of her children.

When their turn came, the butcher gave Annie a lot of attention as he ground beef for the children's lunch of simple biftek haché et coquillettes, then wrapped it in pink paper. They spoke about agneau but Lola wasn't sure if they meant the live animal or a cut of meat. Annie and the butcher laughed a lot and ignored the growing line. Soon everyone in line, who should have gotten mad, instead began to take part in the lively discussion about, again, le Président, who had apparently gotten into some sort of mischief, an indiscretion involving sa maîtresse. His lover.

Once they left, Lola pointed out, "The butcher has the hots for you."

Annie blushed. "You're imagining it."

"I can't believe you do this shopping thing every day. It doesn't seem time efficient."

"That's the fabulous thing about France. Cooking and eating are perfectly worthwhile goals for a day."

Annie's totes were full. On the way back home, Lola was surprised to see her pass a half dozen bakeries on her way to purchase the daily baguette. Lola pointed to a beautiful bakery. "What's wrong with this one?"

"It's all in the details, you see. It gets pretty nutty, choosing the right lettuce, the right bread, the right cheese. Vivre pour manger takes precision, you see. It takes skill."

The baguette they bought was still warm and Lola ate half of it walking to the house not thinking about Lia once. Lia would have to be fine. She wasn't made out of sugar. She was not the first kid going to a new school. Kids adapted. See how she had adapted to the house in a short week? See how she had stopped mentioning her father?

Before they arrived home, they stopped at a small drugstore that looked like an apothecary shop. As soon as he saw Annie, the owner, a tiny man without a hair on his scalp, ran to the back of the store. He returned with a small package wrapped in brown paper.

"You found it!" Annie exclaimed.

"C'est de la bonne!" he said.

At home, Annie showed her how to prepare a marinade for the fish they would have for dinner, how to arrange fresh herbs into individual bouquets that she hung to dry on little hooks on the wall and would later serve as bouquets garnis, and she learned what bouquets garnis were. Once the food was put away, Annie unwrapped the brown package to reveal a jar of old-fashioned wax. She offered it to Lola to smell like it was precious perfume. She then, using a cloth, began rubbing the kitchen table explaining the motion, how much pressure to apply. And it suddenly all made perfect sense. The universe where Lola had spent the last ten years of her life and this one were alternate realities, no less. In this universe, what used to be a chore became an art form, what used to be the work of maids became daily pleasures, what used to be a waste of time became essential. This universe resembled her and the old one didn't!

"I want to learn how to do that," Lola told Annie.

"Wax the table?"

Lola made a wide gesture. "I want to learn to do all of this."

They had a routine now. Evenings after homework, the children were allowed to turn on the TV. Annie and Lola tiptoed into the family room to watch the children in the act of gazing adoringly at a forty-two-inch flat screen TV that Lucas had selected and installed for them. Maxence and Laurent were curled up on one sofa with a beatific expression on their faces, and Paul, bearing the same expression, was lying on the rug. On the other couch were Lia and Simon, she peaceful, he snuggled beside her, sucking avidly on his thumb. No sign of the latest tantrum she had entertained them with just an hour before. As Annie predicted, Lia adapted to school rapidly. The bulk of Lia's obnoxious behavior was reserved for the times when her mother was around to suffer from it, as though she must be punished for some unknown crime. Lia would seem fine until Lola appeared, at which point she would melt into angry tears issued of a perfectly fabricated drama that everyone but Lola could see right through. This baffled Annie. Lola was so patient—so much more patient than she was—so sweet, so utterly beyond reproach. She reasoned that maybe this was what daughters did. Her boys were the opposite. They did ask for things, of course, but never made demands. They knew to get in line the minute she raised her voice. They made her laugh when she looked sad, and tiptoed around her bad moods. Were the boys easy because she was a great mother? Was it because there was a solidarity born of their common loss? Or was it, as she had told Lola before, that she was scary. And if she was indeed scary, was that necessarily a good thing? "I love this machine," Annie told Lola pointing to the TV.

"It's the great unifier. Why wasn't I told about this invention earlier?" She turned on her heels and walked to the kitchen to make dinner hoping that Lola would stay behind. The last thing she wanted to deal with was what Lola called a cooking lesson and what she called misery. Lola had no instinct, no natural inclination when it came to cooking. But already, Lola was following her. "Why don't you sit on the couch and relax with the kids. I'll make dinner," she told her.

The answer was no, unfortunately. In the kitchen, Annie began to work on her endives au jambon, washing the endives, arranging slices of ham, grating gruyère and preparing the béchamel sauce. Lola was in charge of the vinaigrette, a simple enough task she had instructed her on several times. Lola scratched her head before the salt and pepper grinders and the jars of vinegar, olive oil, and mustard asking: "Which one goes in first, again?"

"When do you plan on calling Mark?" she asked, that question often resulting in Lola running away and giving her some freedom.

"I, well, not, I didn't, I mean, not yet. So, it's vinegar first?"

There was also the more bothersome question: Why was Lola pretending to be in the United States? Why this charade? Annie was wondering how to phrase her question when Lia barged into the kitchen.

"I'm not watching stupid French cartoons. Maxence is choosing all the channels. Mom! Tell him!" Lola turned to her daughter with a blank expression. "Mom! Wake up!" Lola fumbled with a response and looked at Annie apologetically. Lia was already raising her voice. "Mom! Do something. Maxence is being an asshole!"

Annie gave Lia a piercing look. "Well, pardon your French, young lady."

Lia stood, defiant. "Well, he is!"

Annie turned to Lola, who averted her eyes, which Annie took as an invitation to set down the rule. "Deal with it, Lia."

Lia's faced turned pale with fury. Annie watched Lia's anger gather energy, her gaze darting around the kitchen like she was looking for something to break, and a second later she was charging towards Lola, pushing her hard with both hands. "I hate you!" she screamed.

"Lia, get out of this kitchen this instant," Annie said. Lia looked defiantly from her mother to Annie, waiting for Lola to come to her rescue. Annie smiled inwardly. If Lola could not take a stand with her daughter, she was not about to take one with her. Lia murdered her with her eyes, stormed out of the kitchen and slammed the door.

"What was that?" Lola said with a little laugh. If someone had disciplined her children, Annie would have seen red, but Lola sounded apologetic. "All this change will be good ultimately."

Did Lola mean leaving Mark, moving to France, or having boundaries set by a stranger? It was as good as any entry into her preferred subject. "Does Lia ask about her father? What do you tell her? What did the judge say about visitations?"

"I'm definitely going to call him."

"The Judge or Mark?"

"Hm...both." Lola presented her bowl. "How much mustard?" She felt an urge to torment her. "Eyeball it."

Lola examined the contents of the bowl, added a minuscule amount of mustard, and pushed the bowl in front of Annie. "Like this much?" Annie made a gesture to add more, and Lola added a tiny amount. "More?" Lola asked. "Still more?"

If Lola could be annoyingly persistent, so could she. "I'm just wondering, I'm just worried that your husband—"

"The one I'm worried about is Althea," Lola interrupted according to her own tactic of diversion. "She's so quiet."

"I know. Isn't it fantastic?" she answered, but Lola gave her a reproachful look. "At least she's eating with us. For a few days, she was eating in her room. Lucas might be a bit much for Althea at mealtimes. You know how he is, the sexual innuendoes, the jokes, the flirting."

Lola beamed at the mere thought of Lucas. "He's a riot. And cute. And so devoted to you!"

"Lucas is a great friend," Annie said, suspiciously.

"A friend who practically lives with you and can't keep his eyes off you," Lola chuckled.

"Seems to me that his eyes are going more in the general direction of your breasts."

"I know...my breasts..." Lola sighed.

They were interrupted by Maxence who barged into the kitchen just as Lia had and said: "Lia keeps switching channels and putting my favorite show on mute!"

Apparently, Lia had taken the situation into her own hands. "You guys figure it out or I'll pull the plug."

"It's not fair!"

Annie grabbed a box of dry pasta from the table, and aimed it at Maxence like a remote control. "You're on mute now too. Go!" Maxence left the room grumbling. She turned to Lola: "I don't think it's Lucas that Althea's trying to avoid. I think it's my food."

"What do you mean?"

"Yesterday she said she'd eat with us as long as she could eat her own food. She said mine doesn't agree with her. Weird, but fine with me. Better than having her bring a heaping plate of Linguini a la Carbonara to her room and shoving it down the toilet behind my back like she did the other day."

"She did?" Lola seemed shocked.

"The pancetta bits refused to be flushed. I guess their high fat content brought them back to the surface of the john's water, an interesting piece of trivia. I told Althea that I noticed her tossing food down the toilet, that I wasn't a complete numskull."

Lola thought for a moment. "Tossed it before or after eating it?"

Annie froze. She had the vision of Althea putting fingers down her throat. "Wow. I am a numbskull! That's terrible! We have to talk to her."

"Well, I wouldn't say a word about it," Lola said as she slowly stirred the contents of her bowl, pausing every so often to observe the result. "Food issues are control issues."

"So, we should let her have full control over starving herself?"

"Those things get better on their own. I had one of those phases. Models all do."

Annie now had the vision of Lola bent over the toilet bowl. "Let's talk to her."

Lola's voice slowed, and she turned her face away. "Bringing unpleasant things up will only make the atmosphere uncomfortable."

Was Lola giving her a subliminal message about her own unpleasant things she'd rather not bring up? "Goodness, the last thing we want is an uncomfortable atmosphere, so I'll shut up."

"It's a difficult subject for her I'm sure."

"And if I really start opening my mouth about what's on my mind, it won't be pretty," Annie said.

CHAPTER 13

$\mathcal{T}$he force of the first blow vibrated his entire body. She was full of shit is what she was.

Larry's voice said, "Take it easy. Take it slow."

Mark ignored Larry and hit the heavy bag with a right, then a left. Larry held the bag with his hairy paws. The guy had hair all over his back. A fucking disgrace. Mark alternated, quick right, quick left. A maid and a nanny while he busted his ass making a living. His face, his arms, and his body were slick with sweat as he punched. He felt the impact in his stomach, felt it in his jaw. Beads of sweat gathered down his neck. The gloves were shiny and red. The place stank like a fucking barn. Hit. Hit. Sweat squirted out of his body like a dog shaking after his bath. And that expression on her face? A professional victim. Hit. Hit.

Larry held the bag tighter. "Take it easy man, you gonna bust a knuckle."

He didn't drink. He didn't screw around, and it's not like there were no opportunities. Mark pummeled the bag. One two, one two. He was a happy guy. That's what he fucking was. Mark let out a roar, and Larry moved away from the bag. Mark hit, hit, and hit again, out of control.

"What the fuck's wrong with you?" Larry said.

He was happy. Mark was fucking happy with what he had and she was wrecking everything.

§

Lia, Maxence, Laurent, and Paul walked through the school gate and Lola followed the four backpacks on legs until they made the turn into the schoolyard. Lia turned and waved to her, and a minute later she was gone. Just like that. Lia had entered school today again without the slightest drama. Could it be possible that Annie's strict rules and unwavering consequences suited Lia better than the respect and freedom she was accustomed to? Lola kneeled next to the stroller. "And you," she said, readjusting Simon's hat. "You're turning out to be a model citizen." She kissed Simon on his cold cheek. "You gave Mommy a whole night's sleep."

She pushed the stroller, light enough to float above the sidewalk. She had thrown all principles — all Mark's principles — to the wind and had let Simon sleep in bed with her. Annie said that women had been doing that from time immemorial, and what was the big deal. Last night she had put him in his pajamas and laid down next to him in her bed and woken up in disbelief after eight hours of uninterrupted slumber. No screams, no bad dream, no night terror, just sweet sleep. She should have listened to her own instinct sooner and claimed her right to soothe her own child. So what if she was "creating sleep issues." Weren't they knee-deep in sleep issues already? She pushed the stroller toward the post office on rue Singer, took an envelope from her pocket and opened it. She read the postcard it contained one last time.

Dear Mark,

The weather is warming up here in New York. I hope this postcard finds you well. The children are doing fine. Simon slept through the night yesterday! We miss you, but I really need this time for right now.

I will continue to send you news weekly. Love. L.

She slid the postcard into the envelope and added the note for Alyssa.

Dear A., Please mail as usual. How will I repay you for your help?! Love, L.

She jotted down Alyssa's address in Manhattan, dropped the envelope in the slot, and walked away from the mailbox harboring a complex mix of guilt and satisfaction. By the time she reached rue Duban, Lola's postcard to Mark was a vague, unpleasant thought that added to all the other unpleasant thoughts she worked so hard to ignore.

She entered the indoor produce market on rue Duban and strolled along the crowded market aisles, marveling at the sights, the colors, the life of it. She wanted to get flowers for the house and took her time looking. She settled for an armful of pink peonies, some still in bud form, some already open and fluffy like cotton candy. She paid the price of gold for them. Mark would be surprised one day to find out she had money stashed away from her modeling days. That was probably a residue from what Mark called her "poor person mentality." She had never told him about the account. It wasn't a lie per se. It was an omission, her secret garden.

The fishmonger beamed his toothless smile at her when she bought half a kilo of shrimp for lunch. She knew her shrimp now, and favored the tiny grey ones so full of ocean flavor. People at the market and the bakery knew her now. They made conversation; they recommended their best products. She waited in line at the crémerie and removed empty, washed glass jars from her straw bag. Simon saw his mother hand over the containers and receive her daily supply of fresh yogurt. He waved his arm at them. "Yayout! Yayout!"

"Simon! Your first French word," Lola exclaimed.

She sat down on a public bench outside the market, peeled off the jar's thin metal seal, ran her hand around the bottom of her backpack, retrieved a plastic spoon, and licked it clean. She put a spoonful of raspberry yogurt on her tongue. "You've earned your yayout, sweetheart." Here she was, feeding her toddler raspberry yogurt on a cold but clear morning in the sixteenth arrondissement of Paris. Here she was, without make-up or acrylic nails, sitting on a stone bench, watching Parisians walk by with their arms filled with produce and bread. Here she was, light. Light as air. She felt the tightness in her throat, that urge to cry. Was it sadness or was it relief? Could it possibly be both?

She ached for Mark far more than he would ever miss her and ache for her. Mark would be fine, really. Oh, there was familiarity in that pain. It was the sweet pain of loving him, the sweet pain in feeling victimized by him even. In her life with Mark, Lola had grown to picture herself as someone who failed at everything and enjoyed nothing. She could not remember a self that did not involve Mark's vision of that self and the consequence, which was for her to feel hurt, neglected, unappreciated. Mark did not do this to her; most of the time, she did this to herself. It was a strange habit, a compulsion. Every decision, every emotion of every instant began with imagining what Mark would say or what Mark would think. But was Mark to blame? Now that she lived with Annie she had to wonder, because now there was a variation on the compulsion. It had become: How would Annie react? What would Annie say? What she needed to get to was: What do I alone think? What should I alone do? With the ultimate question being: Who am I?

She pushed away those thoughts. Right at this precise moment in time, she didn't have a problem. The day was beautiful, Simon had slept through the night, and Parisians carried baskets brimming with produce from the market. Her present was Paris. Her present was the budding friendship with Annie and a new way to spend each day, which made so much more sense to her. This of course was temporary, this lightness, this break from the fear of disappointing Mark, this freedom of movement away from that tentacular Bel Air house. It was temporary but she needed to focus on the moment and just enjoy the fact that she breathed differently here. She even looked different. Her hair was bicolor now, black at the tip with the blonde roots apparent, which gave her a punkish look, an image of rebellion she liked. And she had stopped plucking her eyebrows, those perfect arches that betrayed tension and self-involvement. Here, no power was taken away from her. Here, she could let her baby crawl into her bed in exchange for a full night's sleep. Here, she cooked and did the dishes and didn't feel like a bump on a log. Here, she took care of her own children, and they were doing better than with the nanny!

Those thoughts of Mark were like the Sword of Damocles at times, but only at times. She realized there was something obtuse about the way she had just wished Mark away, or how strangely successful she was at avoiding thinking about disagreeable things such as the consequences of her disappearance, as well as what the future held.

Althea lay in bed, dressed in her coat, boots, and scarf. She was torn between the obligation to call her mother, something she had not done in days and felt guilty about, and the obligation to get out of the house so as to not appear strange. Those, she knew, were no obligations at all. She could stay like this and not make another decision all day. She could stay on her bed and daydream about Jared until night if she wanted to. She didn't move when she heard a tap at her bedroom door.

"Althea? It's Lola. May I come in?"

She felt too apathetic to get up. "Come in," she said.

Lola opened the door and looked at her lying in bed with a coat on. "Were you busy?"

"Do I look busy?" she said. She had not meant to sound antagonistic, yet she did not feel sorry she did.

"Do you want to do the makeover?" Lola asked, dangling a large Vuitton make-up case before her.

Althea wanted to say no, but instead took off her coat and followed Lola to the bathroom they shared but that Althea had come to consider as her own. When she had first entered it, the clutter had been a shock. A cornucopia of seashells and polished rocks marred every surface. The shelves were heavy with glass jars filled with sand and marked Biarritz, Cannes, La Baule, and bottle after sticky bottle of various bubble baths. The bathroom looked clean on first inspection, but Althea had soon noticed mildew on tiles and dull grime hidden beneath the sink, the claw foot bathtub and the toilet. She had spent hours on her knees scrubbing the bathroom tile by tile with an old toothbrush. She had rearranged the blue and white room, polished the jars, even cleaned the seashells and rocks. It was Annie's house, maybe, but the bathroom had become Althea's territory. She liked to spend hours bathing in the massive tub or combing her hair as she sat at the antique vanity imagining she was lost in an entirely different place in time.

Lola, barefoot and in a T-shirt and yoga pants emptied the contents of the make-up case on the vanity. What must have been over a thousand dollars-worth of beauty products — Dior foundation, Max make-up, Crème de la Mer, Estée Lauder anti-wrinkle creams, and twenty or so tubes of lipstick — fell noisily onto the wood. Althea sat down in front of the mirror and Lola began touching her hair, which surprised Althea and made her cringe almost visibly.

"I think you're a spring," Lola said, pulling Althea's hair away from her face and holding it together with a clip. "You have beautiful bone structure and your eyes are gorgeous. And that hair! Your skin is dry. You need to consume more fatty acid. Omega, fish oil, and vitamin D. It's the new fountain of youth."

The warmth of a human body so close to hers felt terribly uncomfortable. Lola's face came to within inches of hers, beautiful despite the thin wrinkles, the skin around her neck a bit tender and loose and betraying her age. Althea watched her face in the mirror as Lola added pink on the cheeks, red on the lips, and mascara. "You know, French women are no better than the rest of us but they know how to make the absolute best of what they have. That's their secret. We have this idea that blonde, busted, and thin is what's attractive, so we become blonde, busted, and thin. French women are individualistic. They would rather look unique than fashionable." Lola was combing Althea's hair now, softly, like Althea had done with her girlfriends when they were little and would go to each other's house. But when it was Althea's turn to have the playdate at her house, her mom refused. She didn't like other children coming over. Althea wasn't invited much after a while.

"Maybe they have good self-esteem," Althea said.

"Annie says that French women always have seduction in mind. They are always open to temptations and romance."

"It seems like too much effort." She was becoming a rag doll between Lola's hands. She felt bad about it somehow, but didn't want Lola to stop.

"This is a new country and a new city. You can reinvent yourself. Find your inner Parisian, have a little fun, be playful. And never go out without lipstick, it will cheer you up, it's automatic. And," she added, smiling at herself in the mirror, "with the gorgeous Jared sleeping in the next room, it should give you some incentive, no? Lordy lordy, is he hot!" she said as she sensually applied lipstick to her own parted lips. "Voilà," Lola said, pleased with her work. "You look just like a Barbie doll." She waved at the mountain of make-up in front of Althea. "You can keep my make-up. It's a gift."

Alone in the bathroom, Althea studied her face. She looked like someone else entirely. What kind of world Lola lived in, a world where lipstick could cheer a girl up. She opened the drawers of the vanity and neatly organized the creams and make-up. When she was finished, she wiped the surfaces of the vanity and the sink with a tissue, all the while observing her own face in the mirror.

She walked down the stairs, feeling like a cardboard cutout, and as stiff as one. Her eyelashes were heavy with mascara like small screens in front of her eyes. No one was in the living room. The only telephone in the house, besides the one in Annie's bedroom, sat on a mahogany table that faced yet another mirror, and Althea watched the strange life-form wearing her hair dial a number and bring the phone to her ear.

CHAPTER 14

MARS

*H*alfway into bringing the groceries back home that morning, Annie noticed a few new things: The temperature was in the seventies, it wasn't raining, and cafés and restaurant terraces were open. Everywhere, Parisians were flooding out of office buildings and onto the streets. Hems were up, coats were conspicuously absent, men had hungry stares, and women looked effervescent. Spring! She understood with a heavy heart. Soon enough she would have to face shedding layers of clothing and expose her winter lard. Winter suited her better, sweaters, pants, no need to tuck in her stomach. This spring would be even harder to circumvent with two skinny women in the house.

Spring was taking her by surprise. In the last month and a half she had barely kept afloat, cooking, cleaning, washing sheets, fighting, and putting up with Althea's idiosyncrasies and Jared's mysterious comings and goings. But she had also adapted to so much, so fast. Lia's meltdowns, at first appalling and unacceptable, she'd come to see as part of the ebbs and flows of the week. She'd grinded her teeth during Simon's night screams, then began sleeping like a baby herself for the first time in years at about the same time he did. She had gone from resenting Lola as her second shadow, to feeling bored when Lola was out and about. She could compare that month of February to a slow incubation period. Like an incubation period, she had not known something was afoot. She had resisted February, all of it, but now that March was here, she had the feeling that things were different, that she felt different and that she might remain different whether she wanted to or not.

She entered the house and listened for signs of life but heard nothing but the low hum of the laundry machine. The kids were in school and Lola, who spent afternoons in subways, museums, gardens, and streets, exploring Paris one arrondissement at a time with Simon, had long ceased asking if Annie wanted to come along. She entered the kitchen, her arms full of groceries and was surprised to find Lola and Simon there.

"It's a beautiful day. We're going out," Lola said.

"See you later!"

"The 'we' includes you."

"I don't think so," Annie said, her voice lacking conviction.

"Why not?"

"I have nothing to wear."

They walked up to her room. This was the first time she let Lola and Simon in since the first day when she gave them the tour of the house. Simon climbed on the bed and used it as a trampoline while Lola foraged in her closet. In minutes, Lola had retrieved a pair of black pants, leather boots and her Burberry Trench coat.

"Here you go. Timeless classics," she said. Annie watched Lola arrange the pants, coat and an orange twin set on the bed and then brandish a silk scarf. "Hermès?" she exclaimed. "You own a Hermès scarf?"

"Johnny was into that designer stuff." Lola would have gasped at the quantities of purses, shoes and clothes Johnny had purchased for her and that she had taken to designer resale stores, partly for the money, partly because she wanted nothing to do with them. This scarf was one of the exceptions.

They walked down the many steps toward the Passy métro station and, judging from Lola and Simon's confidence, it was clear they knew their way around and that Annie was to follow. Already, they were more Parisian than she was. She had avoided mass transportation just as much as she had avoided driving. She had avoided anything that took her more than half a mile away from her house. They squeezed into the already packed metro car. All these people! She held her breath for many stations, until people began getting off and she no longer needed to be body against body. No matter how inconspicuous Lola tried to be, faces turned toward her. A well-dressed man immediately offered his seat to Lola, who declined with a smile.

"French men are the best," Lola said when they walked out of the station. "They flirt but there is a lot of respect. It feels just fun, relaxed. Not like Italians who are like little kids who haven't been taught their manners. Men in some cultures are just frightening."

"You don't think American men are respectful?"

Lola dismissed it. "American men are a bore is what they are. They have no idea how to flirt. In the street, they wouldn't dream of locking eyes with a woman, unless they're in safe accredited pick-up stations like bars or nightclubs. French men flirt easily, not to pick you up, but to give you a nice compliment."

"Yeah, I remember those days. Now the lack of flirting is a slap in the face every time I go out of the house."

"You hardly get out of the house."

"Maybe now you understand why."

"You might want to turn on the 'I'm available' signals."

"I'm not available."

"So they don't flirt. This proves my point."

They emerged Place Saint Germain Des Prés. Annie raised her eyes toward the Café Les Deux Magots. The best hot chocolates in all of Paris. Johnny would have espresso and she the hot chocolate. They would detail the Parisiennes passing by, and Annie would wonder how they did it. Clutching her own purse, she would wonder how, for another woman, it became a fashion accessory.

They walked through the cobblestone streets of Saint Germain des Prés, for a while, entered stores, and admired the buildings. Lola spotted an empty table at the terrace of the Café de Flore. They made their way to the center of the terrace. Next to them were four men at a table and another table with six women in their mid-thirties. Conversations slowed at both tables, and everyone took their time staring at Lola. Again. Annie glared at them and sat down. "When I was in my twenties, and, looking back on it, pretty cute, I'd get intoxicated by the way Parisian men looked at me too. All that sexual energy."

Lola took Simon out of the stroller and let him wander through and under the tables. "Speaking of sexual energy, the testosterone level in the house has gone way up since Jared moved in."

"Tell me about it," Annie said mournfully. "But I wouldn't get too excited about Jared."

"I'm not excited, I just—"

"He's trouble."

"He is?"

"He's had a sort of Dickensian childhood. Or more like out of Zola in his case. No one has ever found out who killed his father. He was raised in an area of Sarcelles, and that's one nasty suburb where even the police don't want to go. They say his father was murdered because of drug debts. Jared was a little kid then. It was all before I knew him. His mother raised him and his sister by herself. Not entirely by herself. They knew Lucas, and asked him if he could be Jared's godfather. Lucas might well be the only person in the world who would take this kind of title seriously. So Lucas helped with money. I suspect he still does."

"Lucas is such a good man," Lola said. "He is," Annie agreed, and as she said it, she realized, maybe for the first time, how true that was. "Jared was about eleven when his five-year-old sister was diagnosed with leukemia. She was gone very fast. That's when Jared's mother all but gave up on living. Jared's way to deal with this was to take on the role of the man. He became her protector and caretaker when he was just a little boy. He dropped out of school, began painting and did very well. He had exhibitions right and left. And then last year, his mother died."

"Is that when Jared stopped painting?"

"So I'm told by Lucas. He kind of dropped everything."

"Is he any good?"

"His stuff isn't exactly decorative. It's on the tortured side. His dying mother was his preferred subject."

They watched Simon totter around. He went from table to table, inspecting the sides of people's coffee cups for forgotten sugar cubes. People smiled at him and gave him paper-wrapped sugar cubes just to watch the expression of joy on his face.

"It's generous of you to let him live in your house," Lola said.

Annie dismissed it with a wave of a hand. "I need the money."

"I enjoy having him around for my own selfish reasons. Talk about eye candy. Just when I thought living in France could not get any better, here arrived Mr. Brun Ténébreux."

Annie considered Lola with a frown. "Come on, you must have led a pretty sweet life in Beverly Hills, with all the money, the sun 300 days out of the year."

"Let me tell you what it's like for women like me," Lola said. "In France, you're only expected to look your best. In L.A., it's mandatory that you remain young and splendid eternally. How about that for pressure? And you can't imagine what it's like to be watched, judged, and demolished by the wives."

"The wives?"

"Women like me, women who married someone rich or famous. My friends, I guess. Women who want to see you fail." Simon came trotting towards them and Lola pried a handful of sugar cubes from his hand. "It's not even personal. In my world, witnessing financial or emotional collapses is a spectator sport."

"How come?"

"Boredom? Or else competitiveness, narcissism. That's the temperament it takes to land a wealthy man. Once those women do, their function in life thereafter is to shop. Accumulation as a raison d'être. All we talk about is weight, plastic surgery, and shopping."

"But you must have friends. You're so nice."

Lola shrugged, "The only people I dare open up to are my personal trainer and my hairdresser. When your social circle is defined by tax brackets, looks, and social status, one has to pay good money to find a friendly ear."

Conflicting thoughts went through Annie's brain. One was that she too might be one of the friendly ears Lola was paying for. But then it occurred to her she was thankful for it. It occurred to her that she too had been terribly lonely and friendless.

"I was feeling so trapped," Lola added. "I felt as trapped outside my house as I did inside. I think we aren't always aware of the intelligence behind our actions. I thought coming to Paris was a spur-of-the-moment reaction. But I think I had put out this intention, you know, at the vibration level. I was asking the universe for a solution, and the universe answered."

That sent Annie into a flurry of head shaking and eye rolling. "It's hocus-pocus."

"You're out of touch with your spiritual core," Lola said. "I think that full-blown depression was where I was headed." A cloud passed over Lola's eyes. She took Simon on her lap and held him tight. "I ran away just in time."

Annie surprised herself by making a deliberate attempt to cheer Lola up. "Well, wherever you are headed now, there will be a place for you. Men are at your feet." She made a joke of it. "All I've got is the butcher at the Boucheries Roger on the rue de l'Annonciation."

"Now you admit it!" Lola laughed.

"Now I'm realizing it." Of course, this wasn't true. The butcher had been courting Annie for years, and though his cheeks looked pretty much like his ground beef, she was guilty of a fantasy or two about being taken by him on the butcher block, amongst rôtis de porc and côtelettes d'agneau.

"Maybe it is the spring thing," Lola suggested. "Look around."

At the terrace, the four men at the one table were now in full flirtatious conversation with the group of women at the next table. At smaller tables, couples were holding hands or gazing into each other's eyes.

"It must be the spring thing," Annie sighed.

Lola's expression was comical. Annie had taught her to gently fold in the egg whites so as not to break the air bubbles, and Lola, stiff, her T-shirt splattered with stains of every single ingredient in the recipe, wore a worried look on her face like she was diffusing a time bomb. Lola raised her eyes for some form of approval and Annie made a little sign in the general direction of Althea, who had stacked cut vegetables into neat little piles on one side and small mounds of vegetable peels on the other. Lola nodded her head in what seemed to be agreement. All week, Annie had pestered Lola about Althea's strangeness and thinness, and finally Lola was acknowledging the problem, or so it seemed. Annie needed no more show of support to finally open her mouth.

"Althea, how come you're this skinny?" she asked. The sentence wasn't out of her mouth before Lola was giving her a look and shaking her head in an emphatic no.

"I'm not exactly skinny," Althea responded as she peeled a potato in one long graceful ribbon. "There are areas that have cellulite on them," she continued in a flat voice. "Like my inner thighs."

Annie worked on her paella, coating the clams and shrimps evenly with juice with one hand while picking uncontrollably at the baguette with the other. "Your inner what?"

Althea wore jeans that were probably the equivalent of a size zero, yet were baggy on her. She stood from her chair and grabbed the inside of her pant leg.

"Here."

Annie laughed, "Well, if you're not skinny, then I'm obese."

Althea considered that information. "I guess you're... curvaceous," she said with an oh-so-subtle grimace of disgust.

"Gee, thanks! I do like to think of myself as curvaceous. Curvaceous is good in my book," she said, but her feelings were hurt. "Althea, how much do you weigh, exactly?" she asked. And then, unable to restrain herself another instant added: "Do you have an eating disorder?"

Lola gave her a very disapproving look. Althea grabbed a carrot angrily and began peeling it. "You're not my mother," she said, not taking her eyes off her task.

Annie wasn't about to get scared away by this. "Do you?" she insisted.

"Annie and I are quite concerned with the fact that you live on apples and tea," Lola said hesitantly, in the same tone of voice that never worked on Lia and was not about to get through to Althea. "People need protein and carbohydrates to maintain their health."

"I'm very healthy."

"You don't look it," Annie barked.

"Fine!" Althea said angrily.

"Don't take it badly," said Lola, "it's just that—"

"I'm not even angry," Althea said. "I mean hungry."

"I'll eat the salad spinner if you're not both," Annie said victoriously.

"I'm not angry," Althea said, raising her voice. She looked at Annie defiantly.

"She's not angry," Lola echoed in a small voice.

"And what's so horrible about anger? Is it too ugly for you? The point is, Althea, that if you're doing something self-destructive under my roof, I think I have every right to know."

"You're not my mom," Althea said again, but coldly this time. She wiped her hands on a towel, got up and left the kitchen, leaving her and Lola to stare at each other.

"Anger's good," Annie said, dropping her wooden spoon in the pan. "I've got it, Althea's got it, and you've got it too. If you don't let it flow out, it will fester inside. Look at the Parisians. They bathe in anger. They are very comfortable with it. I'm very comfortable with it!"

"Maybe," Lola said in a small voice. "Or maybe you've lived in Paris too long."

When she was upset, Annie liked to play scrabble. Lucas had finally understood this through hits and misses. He would come over for dinner and Annie would say "do you want to play scrabble?" and it would end with a fight which had little to do with the game itself, and everything to do with the fact that Annie was upset to begin with and was looking for something to get emotional about. For Annie, this was as close as she would get to therapy. The game was played absurdly, with no respect for the rules. Annie called this bilingual scrabble, and anything went, French, English, misspellings, proper names of people who did not exist. There was no point in trying to make sense of it. The point, he felt, was for Annie to cheat and then get furious as she accused him of cheating. They had barely laid down their first two words when Annie said:

"What are you waiting for? An end to world hunger?"

"Isn't it your turn to play?"

"I meant with Lola. What is taking you so long to make a move on her?"

"What makes you think I want to?"

Annie moved her scrabble pieces around hastily. "Bat, boot, zoot. Is zoot a word?"

"Possibly in Chinese," he said, looking up at her from above his reading glasses, searching for signs that she was about to work herself into a tizzy. She was wearing a white T-shirt that looked good on her. Her bare arms were strong and smooth over the table. Scrabble was good for her, like medicine. Also, he liked it when it was just the two of them, like an old couple. "What are you upset about?" he asked.

"What? I'm not upset. Maybe I'm just restless in comparison to her."

Lola, he thought. Of course Lola. "No one is comparing the two of you," he said.

Well, I am. I'm comparing. "I'm not like Lola. You know, sweet, positive, goody two shoes." Annie peeled away strands of hair that had fallen over her eyes. "I'm going through a phase of…" She thought for a moment. "I think the word I'm looking for is discontent?"

Lucas studied the board. "That's a long word. Where are you going to put it?"

"Discontent is how I feel. And this," she said, laying down the letters Z-O-O-T one after the other, "is my word."

Lucas thought, and added A-N-G under Annie's Z to spell Zang.

"Hey!" she said, her hands on her hips.

"It's Cantonese for cheater."

Annie held her face in her hands, her elbows on the table, searching her letters. "I'm just saying that she and I don't raise our children the same way, that's all. She doesn't raise her children, in fact. She lets them grow rampant like… like crab grass. And Lia is rubbing off on Maxence. That weasel actually rolled his eyes to the ceiling when I asked him to help with the dishes last night."

Lucas arranged his letters. "You can't control everything."

"That's controlling of me? Controlling?" Annie put the word "nasty" on the board. "Lola gets beat up by Lia emotionally and physically and we are all witness to that, my boys included, but Lola never acknowledges it. Maybe she thinks that as long as she doesn't acknowledge it, I won't notice it. Lola has such a pattern of...avoidance! That's the word. A pattern of avoidance."

"How insightful of you," Lucas teased.

"Call me Sigmund."

"She may not like confrontations."

"Oh no, she doesn't. Next to her, I probably seem manic."

Lucas looked up over his reading glasses. "Annie, you are manic."

Annie froze and glowered at him. "Me?"

Lucas pointed his finger at her gently. "You."

"When am I manic?"

"Most of the time," Lucas said, and he put down a word, carefully, took a pen and pencil and methodically added twenty-three points to his column.

Annie looked like she was going to yell, or throw the board across the room. Instead, she pushed her letters away and put her head in her hands. "I'm not likeable," she said.

Lucas looked at her dumbfounded. He hadn't meant to make her feel bad. He had meant to state the obvious. He accepted her manic side, liked it in fact, just like he liked every side of her. Her manic side didn't threaten him in any way. But how to say that and not... he sighed.

"Of course, you are very likeable. Manic is the wrong word. I meant hurried. Reactive. Or maybe the word to use is unpredictable. You're a little bit like having a grenade in the house."

"So you're afraid of me?"

"Me, no. Of course not," he said, though it occurred to him that in many ways, he was. "I was thinking of Lola or Althea, or even the children."

"Which kids? Not my kids?"

Lucas did not like himself very much when he said, "We're all a little bit afraid of your reactions."

Annie let out a huge sigh. She got up, sat down again, and then burst into tears.

"I'm a bitch."

"Of course you're not, Annie." Lucas grabbed a box of tissues. "You're just a little... intense. Where is all this coming from, anyway?"

"Lola told me I was a bitch."

"Lola? Told you?"

"She insinuated. And she's right. With Johnny, I was pissed most of the time." Lucas tensed up like he did every time Annie brought up Johnny. He had told himself long ago, had made a pact with himself, to not say anything against Johnny. "I was just being insecure," Annie continued. She blew her nose; he saw her determination to stop crying. "I was always worried about other women, suspicious. Maybe I don't have a trusting nature," she added.

Lucas took Annie's hand. He felt her sadness. So much could not be said, and so many opportunities to tell her how he felt about Johnny, about her marriage to him, about his death, about the way he chose to conduct his life. So much had never been said that he burned to say. It remained unsaid out of fear. Out of respect for a dead man. Out of a pattern of avoidance. "To the contrary, I think you have a very trusting nature," he told her, and he meant it.

"I'm frigging frozen in time. I don't let myself have fun. I don't even know why," she said, sobbing.

"There is nothing wrong with wanting things, looking

forward to things," Lucas whispered, marveling at how the conversation had shifted to exactly what he wanted to talk about, what they were never allowed to talk about.

Annie cried softly as Lucas gently rubbed the palm of her hand with his thumb. "I'm so afraid to be disappointed that I don't know the first thing about how or where to find it," she said.

"What is it?" Lucas whispered.

"Happiness, I guess."

"Sometimes happiness is staring you right in the face," Lucas said, looking straight at her.

Annie wiped her tears angrily. She was becoming strong again, willing herself to being strong, detached. But Lucas did not let go of her hand. She would have to let go first. "I don't just want to talk the talk," she said. "I want to walk the walk. I find myself wanting more of it for...me."

"That's good," he said.

The phone rang and shattered the moment. Annie sprang to her feet. A moment later, she was handing Lucas the phone.

"It's the commissariat de police. Looks like you're going to have to postpone losing at scrabble."

The cemetery had closed hours before. Jared knew precisely where all this was headed, knew it, expected the outcome, and didn't care. He sat on a stone grave and laid a small parcel wrapped in white paper on the grass next to him. His mother's grave had not completely settled yet; there was a perceptible line between the grass that grew on her grave and the grass next to it, as though his mother wasn't entirely convinced she wanted to stay there. He pictured her full of exuberant energy, laughing out loud from wherever she was, laughing the way she used to when he and Sophie were little. Even after his father was killed, his mother never stopped being strong. She had seemed invincible to him. But with the loss of Sophie, his mom lost all will to live. He often thought of the relief it must be for his mom, to finally be freed of the weight of her pain.

Before Sophie was sick, and even though their dad was gone and they had no money, things were still happy. On Sundays, there was a roasted chicken and for dessert, pastries, éclairs, always the same. He and his little sister both liked coffee éclairs and their mom liked chocolate. They stuffed the éclairs into their mouths trying to finish first. Their mom would eat slowly, and when they had gobbled up their pastries, she shared her éclair with them.

His mom had wanted so much for Jared to make her proud, and he had. He had felt that craving, had sought the success, the acclaim, the money. But he had wanted it for her, not for himself. He had wanted it to make her happy, but also to reassure her that he was fine, that he had a life purpose.

His mother's illness they had called old age, but she was too young for old age. There was no cause of death, no deteriorating organ, no cancer, no tumor, no infection, only a heart that got tired of beating. It had begun when she had climbed into bed one day, years ago, and started to forget taking baths or eating. She had given up and he could not blame her. He had moved in with her and had painted her all the way through to her last dying breath. He understood only after her death how much of his work was connected to her, how it was she, not his art, that was his life's purpose.

He had never been in love. His life did not allow for that kind of attachment, and now he wondered if the strange way he felt, his fascination with Althea, was maybe what love was supposed to feel like. Was love supposed to feel like a macabre obsession? Was he capable of an obsession that wasn't macabre? He had no map for this. He could clearly see what she was doing to her body. It filled him with anger and at the same time made him want to rescue her. He did not accept his attraction because he did not feel sexually attracted to Althea. She looked sick. Did he see her as his little sister? No it wasn't that. She was beautiful and looking at her was like being punched in the gut. If there was such a thing as passion without lust, then this was it. Could the lack of lust be an elevated form of love?

Jared unwrapped the white paper parcel and took out a coffee éclair. Sitting on the cold stone, he ate in silence, absorbing the wetness of the air, the smell of distant spring. In the distance, flashlights were advancing in his direction. He was able to make out the silhouette of the two guards, dark against dark. A moment later they were standing, towering over him.

"Monsieur can't learn to be here when the place is open like everyone else?" the skinny one said.

"No, he is too good for that," the fat one continued.

"This time we're taking Monsieur to the police station."

Jared crumpled the paper and put it in his pocket. "After you," he said.

CHAPTER 15

"*W*e're fine," Althea's mother said vacantly.

"Do you and dad know what to do on weekends, now that I'm in Paris?" Althea asked.

"The weekends are just fine."

"Well, my weekends are very busy, and noisy! With all these little kids around." When her mother didn't ask whose kids those were, Althea moved on. "I finally went up the Eiffel Tower," she said, though she hadn't. "It was so high, you could see everything."

"That's fine," Pamela answered.

Fine? Althea braced herself. "Well, I better go now, someone else needs the phone," she lied. "It's always so busy here, with everyone sharing the phone and all."

"All right then, I'll speak to you later. Goodbye."

"Love you, Mom!"

"Yes, yes," her mother answered.

"Miss you! Give a kiss to Dad for me."

"All right then, bye." And her mother hung up.

Althea's knuckles went white from clenching the phone. Her mother had nothing to say, and worse, no questions to ask. That was the gist of their relationship. Maybe her mother was too depressed to show real interest in her, or in anything, or maybe she had interest only in herself and what affected her. By traveling to Paris, Althea was no longer affecting her. She was twenty-five years old and for the first time she dared contemplating the fact that this was not what mothers were supposed to be like. Living at Annie's for a short month, she could not help but witness what it was that mothers did. Mothers did things with their children, when they were not talking about their children, thinking about their children, or living their lives around their children. Sure, the children of the house were young and she was a grown woman, but her mother had been no different then than she was now. Her mother had always been deadened and indifferent at best, punishing at worst. She, the child, had been the one preoccupied with her mother's well being. Even as a little girl, she had been the one who jumped through hoops and tried to read her mother for signs of displeasure and pain, and maybe the occasional light of joy. And how did it come to this? Why was it that those moments of faint satisfaction came only when she brought her mother accounts of her own failure and unhappiness? Yet, even knowing all this, or not knowing but sensing, she had been hoping that her mother would show an interest in her life in France. Or concern, any concern at all. Crazy as it was, her mother had yet to ask for her phone number or her address in Paris. The simple reality was that her mother would have no way to find her if Althea stopped calling. It would be the end.

"I'm healthy," she had told Annie.

"You don't look it," Annie had said.

All had seemed to be fully in her control in the beginning, but no longer. No longer was it about not eating food, but about food eating her. A war was raging inside. Althea was the assailant and the victim—she was the war zone. These days, the battle wasn't simply against fat. It was for survival. Getting out of bed, having simple desires, not hating everyone, trusting someone, keeping a banana down, having even a few normal moments in a day. How far had she been ready to go to procure her mother some sick joy or to trigger motherly instinct her mother was clearly incapable of? But now she was in too deep to recover or even desire recovery. She had practice only in despair and did not remember what it felt like to feel good, if she had ever known.

Althea walked up the stairs. The house was empty, or so it seemed, the children in school, Annie and Lola on one of their outings. Those two did things together all the time. Althea closed her eyes as she climbed, helping herself to the railing. The railing was smooth and warm. The steps were uneven in places under her bare feet. The house smelled of wax and soup. There were three doors on her floor: her room, Jared's room, and the third room that was full of rubbish and that no one went into. Her floor was the silent floor.

When she was sure everyone was gone, Althea had the habit of walking around the house, opening doors, closets, drawers. Lola's trashcan was filled with crumpled unsent letters to a man named Mark, and her floor was covered with health and parenting magazines. Annie's room was most interesting because of the photo albums, filled with pictures of the boys and of a handsome man, year after year. Here, the father and boys at the beach. Here, they were celebrating Christmas. There, the father and boys skiing. But where was Annie? She must have been the one taking the photographs because she was in very few of them. In the early days, she looked so different than she now did. She looked happy, beaming at the camera with an expression Althea had never seen on her face, an expression that was playful and relaxed. But as the years passed, so did her look of joy, and pictures of her became rare. The man in every image with the boys and with Annie looked like an actor, almost looking younger and better as time passed.

Jared's room remained locked. She wondered if he even lived in the house at all until she began to figure out a pattern. He made sure to never be home around meal times and came in very silently and late into the night, sometimes not until the first hours of the morning. Then he slept, but his room was so silent that at first she had trouble knowing if he was in. She learned to put her nose to his door and recognize his presence though the smell of cigarette, weed, and paint thinner. At some point in the afternoon Jared took a brief shower, always leaving a mess behind him, after which she spent a long time putting everything back in order. She took care of his things. She hung his towel to dry, put the shaving cream and the razor away, closed the shampoo bottle, mopped the wet tile, and scrubbed the sink. Once she left her hairbrush in the bathroom and the next day retrieved several of Jared's black hairs tangled in it. It shocked her to think of her hairbrush, such an intimate possession, being used by him. After that, she made a habit of leaving it behind. One day she left a few of her own long red hairs in the brush on purpose. It made her dizzy when the next day she found some of his hair entwined with hers. She wondered if he ever noticed.

Althea liked her yellow room. She had stopped making her bed or putting away her clothes. She kept her room as messy as she kept the bathroom spotless. She spent hours each day staring out the window. If she remained absolutely still, she became invisible enough for the birds to come very close to where she was, using the metal railing of the balcony as a perch, sometimes even tapping at the window and peering into her eyes.

She avoided Jared and made sure never to look at him if they ever were in the same room. Since he had arrived in the house, the extent of their communications were quick exchanges of "bonjour comment ça va" with both of them hurrying away and not making eye contact. This was how she reacted to men, especially to men she liked, dooming any possibility of romance. And she told herself that she preferred it that way. But she was aware that there were no possibilities with Jared. To someone like him, she would always remain invisible. She almost preferred when Jared wasn't around, so she could imagine him. She would dream him until she could catch a glimpse of him again. She daydreamed of walking the streets of Paris, the two of them holding hands.

❧

This was the last place Lucas should have been in the mood he was in. Outside the café on rue de Passy, tires glided on slick pavement. The icy rain had been pouring for four consecutive days. Inside the café, the noise level was deafening, what with the espresso machines expelling their steam and waiters calling orders and the clanking of dishes and utensils. The counter was so crowded that he had to sip his espresso with his shoulders perpendicular to it. Apparently, no one seemed ready to venture out of the groggy and womb-like atmosphere of the two-hour lunch break. People actually liked being here, even though the air was saturated with the smell of cigarettes and Plat du Jour, and steam from humidity and human heat clouded the windows. A tall man with a lifetime of practice at carving himself a spot in busy Parisian cafés, Lucas didn't usually resent the invasion of his personal space, but today, it was insufferable. His mood was not improved by the spectacle of Jared, unshaven, unwashed, and devouring his second greasy Croque-Monsieur with his left arm and shoulder literally glued to him. Lucas preferred things to be neat and in their places, and he was feeling his stomach turn periodically at the sight of the cheese's grease dripping from Jared's sandwich onto the plate and his three-day-old beard.

"One day I won't be there to bail you out," he accused. "One day, I simply will be out of town, and you'll have to rot at the commissariat."

Jared shrugged and continued to devour his Croque-Monsieur. Lucas took a mental count of the number of times one of the men at his left elbowed him without an apology. They were dressed without any class whatsoever, their ties too colorful, their shirts clashing, the cuts of their suits primitive. They looked like pimps as far as he was concerned. This was Johnny's flashy crowd. What Annie had ever seen in that man remained a mystery to him. The men laughed and eyed a table of pretty women in spring wardrobe. The women giggled, crossed and uncrossed their bare legs. The spring dance has started, again. This realization depressed him. Would this be one more spring of reluctantly chasing the wrong women while the one that mattered continued to elude him? The reason she eluded him, he hated to admit. It could be summed up in a few words: As long as he tried nothing, took no chance, he still had his chances.

One poke too many from the colorful cretin with the pointy elbow tipped the balance and he suddenly felt very irritated. "Annie is constantly alluding to the fact that I haven't made a move on Lola. Why is Annie so invested in this? Does it mean that she wants me to, or that she doesn't?"

"Be a man, Lucas. It's time to make your move."

"I... I'm not ... there quite yet."

"So make a move on Lola and see what happens," Jared said

Lucas waved the notion away. "If I wanted to have an affair with a model, I would already have done so," he said.

Jared laughed, a rare feat that brightened his face. "How humble of you. Why not this particular model, if it's that easy for you?"

"Why of course that would be a terrible mistake for two reasons. Number one, she and Annie are new best friends. So the day the affair ends, it would become really complicated there at the house." He took a breath. "Last but not least, once that story ends, I'll still have to deal with her at Annie's."

"That's the same reason twice."

Lucas waved his hands angrily. "I can't ruin my chance with Annie by having sex with her supermodel best friend in her own house."

"Bien sûr," Jared said. He reached in his pocket for money and seemed to find nothing. "You know, she's a supermodel with a millionaire husband. There is also the possibility she might not want you."

"I'll have you know that according to Annie, she does." Lucas unfolded his napkin, jammed his elbow into the side of the man to his left, and dabbed his mouth with affected poise. "Does that surprise you? You think she is too good for me? I suppose you think Lola might be interested in you. I must laugh," he added with a forced laugh.

"Not my type," Jared said.

"You're too young to have a type. When I was your age, I made love indiscriminately to any woman kind enough to say yes."

"See that's the difference between us. I get to discriminate," Jared said. To Lucas's great relief, he had finally finished his lunch and was wiping his mouth. "Anyway," Jared continued, "I like the other one better."

Lucas cried out, "Annie?"

Jared looked at him like he had lost his mind. "Of course not Annie! The other one."

Lucas opened his eyes wide. "What other one? No! You don't mean that skinny girl?"

Jared stood up, took an orange piece of rag out of his pocket and began winding it around his neck like a scarf. "And why not that skinny girl?"

Lucas burst into laughter. "Discriminating all right!" He opened his crocodile wallet swiftly, took out a fifty Euro bill and placed it on the counter for both their lunches. "You're a funny kid," he said, and with that slapped Jared on his back and left the café laughing out loud.

The rain soaked his hair and covered Jared's eyes as he walked toward Annie's house in long strides. He clutched a large flat package wrapped in brown paper under his coat, hurried through the neighborhood and turned into the street where Annie's house stood. Aside from a man in a grey trench coat and a Burberry umbrella who tugged at a Great Dane's leash, then walked away ignoring the gigantic mess his dog left on the sidewalk, the street was empty. Why were the wealthy neighborhoods of Paris so lifeless?

He ran up the few steps to the front door, slipped on the wet stone steps, nearly fell, and cursed his surroundings. He put his key in the door and struggled to open it with one hand while protecting his package. The house was silent and the lights were off. Annie must have been shopping and the children were probably in school. Jared relaxed, took off his wet coat, and hung it to dry on the coat hanger. He then tiptoed up the stairs to his room, as he had learned to do when he came back in the middle of the night. Once in his room, he dropped the package on his bed, took a breath and stepped into the third floor's hallway which was long, narrow and in the absence of a window, dark as night. He let his eyes get accustomed to the obscurity as he stood in front of Althea's door, and waited. He put his ear against the door and heard a movement inside the room. She was in.

He tapped at her door and the movement inside the room immediately stopped. He waited but was surprised when she did not come to the door to see who had knocked. He tapped again a second time, louder. A third time. She was playing dead. The thought made him smile. Did she have any idea it was he? Probably not. He should have respected her desire to be left alone, but he had come this far, had knocked three times. He nearly knocked again but instead let his arm drop and waited next to the door.

After a long moment the door opened very slowly, and then Althea's head, wrapped in a white towel, peeked into the darkness of the hallway. She stretched her neck to look into the hallway while keeping her body in her room. His eyes were accustomed to the dark and he saw her very clearly. She looked like she had just come out of the shower and wore a white terry bathrobe tied at the waist. She looked to the right, then to the left and found herself inches away from him. She froze. Then in an instant, she retreated into her room like a hermit crab and nearly slammed her door in his face before he could speak.

He stood in the hallway, dumbfounded. Now this was really embarrassing but he wasn't sure whether to laugh or be furious. He was tempted to forget the whole thing, but then his own advice to Lucas rang in his ear. "Be a man. Make a move." He took a step back, and walked back to his room. He grabbed the package from his bed, tore open the brown paper, seized the white canvas it contained, walked back to Althea's door and knocked again, forcefully. "Ouvre la porte," he said. Open the door.

From Althea's room, not a sound emerged, but he sensed her body pressed against the door. Would she be a disappointment? Most women were. Only some of his dreams, once put on canvas, were satisfying.

"C'est moi, Jared," he said again. "Ouvre, s'il te plaît." It's me Jared, Open please.

Althea, in a move that astonished him after the effort she had made to avoid him, opened her door wide, suddenly, and faced him. She stood in the doorway, eyes lowered, arms along her sides. Behind her, her bedroom was a model of untidiness with clothes scattered on the floor, covers and bed sheets in disarray. Jared had somehow expected her to be dressed by now, but she was still wearing that white bathrobe. He wondered if she realized how much her obvious nudity under the robe, the silent house, and the unmade bed behind her could have been interpreted as an invitation. Her face showed no expression but she was blushing violently. She was completely still and he didn't know if she was going to scream, turn to dust, or slam the door in his face again.

"I want to…make a paint…of you," he said, in his butchered English.

"No, thanks, merci, thank you," she said immediately. The one thing she seemed prepared for was rejecting whatever he would suggest. Yet she didn't budge; her door remained open.

"I can come in?" he asked.

"No, no," she said feebly and she blushed even more and looked back at her room. She had not looked him in the eyes once. He understood that he, too, had avoided looking at her all this time. It was the only way he could let her preserve herself. Althea, thoroughly glacial from the neck down, like lava from the head up, continued staring at her feet as her lips trembled slightly. Reading a human being so easily was shameful, and Jared, at once, grasped the extreme responsibility of imposing himself into her protected universe. If she was to let him in, then she might come to depend on him. He might find himself bound to her and this was a burden he wasn't sure he was ready for. But if he left now, said "sorry" and "see you later," he knew there wouldn't be a later.

And Jared let himself into her room, without a word, and gently closed the door behind them.

At first, Althea had to contract every muscle in her body to control her trembling. As soon as he entered her room he filled it entirely. His scent, so dizzyingly strange and wonderful changed the texture of the walls, the bedspread, the air. He was tall and his shoulders were wide, and when he took off his sweater, revealing tattooed arms—muscled, hairless arms and more of his scent—she felt utterly confused. What he wanted she did not ask herself.

He was there and she was overtaken with panic, a panic tangled with pleasure.

"Attends!" he said, putting his hand up like he was stopping traffic. Wait. She watched him disappear into the hallway and heard him enter his room. Overwhelmed, she dropped down onto her bed, sat next to his abandoned black wool sweater and waited. She thought of straightening her room, putting clothes on. Was she imagining this? Hadn't she imagined this before? This could well be the continuation of the dream. But the sweater was there, next to her, giving off the concentrated turpentine smell she had detected while standing beside his bedroom door. She was shocked by that scent; appalled she liked it so much. She moved her hand towards the sweater and caressed its coarse wool with the tip of a finger.

A moment later, Jared had re-entered her room with a cardboard box and a large canvas. "Attends," he said again. He kneeled next to his cardboard box on the floor, inches from her. She observed his unshaved jaw, his neck. His hair fell into his eyes as he retrieved brushes, dirty rags, and paint tubes. It took time, and Jared did not hurry. When he was done, he put some of the objects he had retrieved from his box on her desk and finally looked at her. She felt her heart drumming in her chest. She had not moved from her sitting position on the bed. He smiled a timid smile and came close to her. She was as tense and charged as a lighting rod, hoping he would say something soon or else she might have to burst. But Jared did not feel compelled to speak or to break the silence, and when she understood that, not intellectually but emotionally, when she understood that talk was not expected, or desired, that explanations were not needed, she felt the drop of a terrible weight and her body began to relax. He wanted to paint her!

With gentle hands, he helped her down on her bed. Her body wasn't as tense as she expected; her body was hesitant. Jared put a pillow behind her head, and she lay there, on her side, consenting to she didn't know what. He pointed to the towel wrapping her hair. "Tu peux retirer ça?" Can you take it off? She took the towel off and her hair dropped onto her shoulders, redder, darker now that it was wet. He propped the canvas on the single chair and began to pop open tubes of paints and let large dollops fall onto a magazine. He kneeled in front of the canvas, looked at her. "Tu ne bouges pas. No moving, d'accord?"

Althea nodded. Jared mixed colors and started painting right away, focused entirely on his silent task of gazing at her, or through her, so focused that Althea, after a few self-conscious moments, began to relax her gaze and let herself scrutinize him. His arms were wiry and strong, and his tattoos frightened her because of the intensity they betrayed. He had beautiful thin fingers. There was a mesmerizing point just below his Adam's apple where she wanted to bury her face.

Jared painted, and the only sign that time passed was the growing mass of Althea's hair drying and becoming a red tangle of curls with a life of its own. Periodically, Jared walked up to her and lightly combed his fingers through her hair, rearranging it. When his finger touched her face, Althea shivered, feeling more alive in this silence and stillness than she had ever imagined possible, like a long-forgotten seed that finally receives a drop of water and begins sprouting, inexorably.

CHAPTER 16

AVRIL

*B*eing on the péniche was painful in ways she had not anticipated. Annie was fighting a feeling of claustrophobia that had nothing to do with the movement of the boat. She already regretted being talked into playing tourist on the Bateaux Mouches.

This was the first day of April and the weather was beautiful. The boat was traveling at a slow pace on the Seine River as she sat on one of the uncomfortable wooden benches in the deserted cabin without looking out the window. Lola and Simon were up on deck and she needed time to herself, giving nausea as an excuse. There was no nausea, only a sense of anxiety, like a shallow feeling high up in her chest indicating that something was terribly wrong. Something was terribly wrong with her.

Lola had insisted that she come, but she should have listened to her gut feeling and stayed home. They had boarded and sat in the large cabin filled with rows of benches, waiting for the rest of the passengers to embark. Simon was toddling from seat to seat, climbing on a bench, then another. The tourists were Japanese for the most part. The Japanese women were so pretty and fresh, smiling. Young Japanese men wore their hair spiked. The rest of the tourists were couples, and she suspected many of them were foreigners on their honeymoon. Everywhere couples embracing, couples kissing, couples holding hands, on the boat and on the banks. Maybe it was the sight of all those couples in love that made her feel sick to her stomach. She and Johnny had started out together in much the same way. She wondered if all these lovey-dovey couples would experience Paris as an enchanting, magical place and a few years later see everything change, the memory of lust and love forgotten.

"Are you all right? You look green," Lola said.

"I get anxious when I'm far from the boys," she said, which was also true.

"Is this since the accident?"

"I'm always more comfortable at home sweet home."

"I always feel incarcerated in my own house," Lola said, watching Simon trot between rows of benches. "How come I can't achieve that, a happy home?"

"My guess is that your demonic husband is getting in the way."

"The expectations are so Hallmark," Lola said. "The inviting home, happy children, supportive husband."

"And great sex!" Annie had added, inexplicably.

Lola stared at her intently. "I've been meaning to ask you something," Lola said. She checked to make sure Simon was out of earshot. "But you have to be completely honest with me."

Annie shrugged. "I can try."

Lola hesitated, "Would you like there to be something between you and Lucas?"

Annie looked at her wondering if Lola had recently fallen on her head. "Of course not, silly girl. Why such an idea?"

Lola smiled knowingly. "Just watching the two of you together, I guess."

Annie frowned, shook her head and laughed. "Could you imagine me and old Lucas together?"

"Quite easily, actually."

"Eek, don't!"

Lola looked conspiratorial. "It never crossed your mind, though? The two of you have never... you know?"

It was annoying how insistent Lola could be. "Never," Annie answered in a tone that left no ambivalence.

"I would have bet. And you know the funny thing is, Althea thought so, too."

Lola and Althea talked behind her back? Nobody could talk to Althea. "Why do you ask? Are you interested?"

Lola spoke in earnest. "I happen to find Lucas very attractive."

The first time Annie had met Lucas was on a double date. She and Johnny, Lucas and his girlfriend of the moment. It was at the Rothonde de Passy over an extravagant assiette de fruits de mer. Lucas had been warm and charming and from the get go she had felt very comfortable with him. Lucas's date was a beautiful Parisienne dressed elegantly, her hair, her manners so refined. Annie had thought they made a very glamorous couple. The next time she had seen Lucas, and the next, he was in the company of yet another beautiful Parisienne. As the years passed, Lucas became one of the friends she and Johnny could not do without, and he introduced them to dozens of petites amies. It was only after Johnny died that Annie found the nerve to ask him to keep the women to himself. Maybe he could not grow up but she was tired of pretending to remember who was who. Lucas never brought another girlfriend over, and became very discreet about them.

"I must warn you," she told Lola, "Lucas is a serial dater. He is mister papillon, fluttering from girl to girl. Believe me, I've seen him in action when we went to his house in Saint-Tropez."

"A house in Saint-Tropez?" Lola said. "Now I find him extremely attractive."

"Lucas's family tree can be traced to before the French Revolution, when they were beheaded for the most part. The family lost most of their heads and wealth, but Lucas has managed to remain in that world. He knows people all over Europe, people with houses in Biarritz and Chamonix and London. Lucas has a Paris apartment, a house in Honfleur right on the beach, which he coyly refers to as a 'cabane,' and a dreamy little house in Saint-Tropez that he rents out. I went once with the kids. He invited us last summer." Describing to Lola how much those weeks in Saint-Tropez had been a turning point would have been hard. She remembered crying with relief when they entered the property after seven hours of being cooped up in the old van, as though a vise had been removed from around her chest. The place was so lovely, with the sound of crickets, the smell of the Italian cypress, and that sea breeze from the Mediterranean. "There is a retired couple who lives there year-round," Annie said. "They keep up the property, cook, and clean for Lucas and his guests in the summer months. Madame Denis and I hit it off. She taught me everything I know about Provençal cooking." In truth, Madame Denis had reminded Annie of her own mother and they had both cried when it was time to go. "We went to the beach, we went boating, we discovered the region. In the evenings, we had dinner alfresco under trellises covered in grapes. We ate and ate. No shoes for weeks."

"It sounds like heaven."

"Aside from the leeches."

Lola removed her jacket. "Leeches?"

"There is a type of person that gravitates to the wealthy. Parasites. They might be wealthy themselves, but they basically take advantage of your hospitality. You have to be really hard-boiled to shoo them away, and Lucas is just not that kind of guy."

She had come to dread the sound of tires on the gravel driveway. Madame Denis would perk up and go wash yet more sheets. She tried to instigate a rebellion, but Madame Denis had no idea what she was talking about.

"If it were up to me, there would be some serious friend

reassessing. But it's not up to me. Lucas has always lived that way. Then again, as he pointed out himself, he gets to hop between so-called friends' properties all year long. He skis in Val d'Isère, and paraglides in Ibiza. He's in London for Wimbledon, in Cannes for the film festival. It's a different world altogether."

"A perfect bachelor's life," Lola said.

"Anyway, that vacation was free, and that's our only option lately. So it kind of makes me a leech as well."

"That's totally different. You're a real friend."

"I was quite the pain in his ass regarding the girls."

"What girls?"

"He was pretty discreet about it, but his friends were not. They were constantly picking up women in local night clubs and bringing them home." She told Lola about those suntanned girls that woke up around noon, swooned towards the kitchen, nude under a man's shirt, and asked Madame Denis for breakfast. "Not the best example for my boys. Apparently, Madame Denis was pleased with the men's exploits, as though they were her own sons. She regaled me with the stories of Lucas's past conquests."

"Lucas is unhitched, French, and loaded. I guess it would be expected that he has a sex life."

"I'm just saying, don't get too close. I don't think Lucas can commit to anyone for any length of time."

"I'm pretty committed myself."

"How so?"

"I love Mark," Lola said weakly.

"You have a funny way of showing your love." She looked at Lola's beautiful lips, the angle of her cheekbone. "I guess you can't stay a saint forever. Mark's far away, and you're probably peaking." Lola removed her sweater. Under it, the T-shirt was stretched to its limits. Annie frowned at Lola's chest. "Right as we speak, in fact."

"Hey," Lola said laughing, "same for you. You love an unavailable husband, and you too can't be a saint forever."

"Cute," Annie said, not laughing. She realized that everyone had left the cabin. The boat was now moving smoothly along the Seine river. "Everyone's up on deck, should we go?"

Lola grabbed Simon, walked up and stepped outside. "Before I get all excited about Lucas," Lola whispered, "you and him would have to get things straight."

"What do you mean?"

"Well, it's pretty obvious he's into you."

Annie, to her own dismay, felt a burning blush in her neck and face, which she quickly hid away by turning her head. "I certainly don't think so."

"I'll bet he's great in the sack," Lola added.

Annie laughed. "Well, he does have tremendous self-confidence in that domain."

"He's got some French hotness, he's got je ne sais quoi up the kazoo."

"There is only one way for you to find out," Annie said with a sigh.

"You'd have to swear to me that you have absolutely no interest."

"Me!"

Lola peered at her. "You."

That's when she began to feel uncomfortable. Up on deck, it was windy, too sunny, the light was too bright. "Look, I'm not sure how else to convince you."

"The other factor," Lola added, "is that Lucas would have to want me."

Annie narrowed her eyes. "Could a man possibly not want you?"

"It does happen, you know," Lola said, beaming.

"Lucas has personally told me that you're one of the most beautiful women he's ever seen. Be reassured." Lola hardly seemed shaken by this revelation. Annie clenched her teeth at how easy Lola had it while beautiful, unsuspecting Lola faced the wind with a blissful smile on her lips. Probably picturing herself with Lucas, deciding what she wanted to do.

"I've never considered adultery before. Maybe I should," Lola said finally.

"Maybe you should," Annie snapped. "You know what, I think I'm beginning to feel sea sick. I need to go back downstairs."

"Do you want us to come too?"

"No, please stay."

Annie came down the metal stairs and went to sit on a bench in the cabin abandoned by all except for a young couple who were giggling and kissing passionately. She had to look away. Could she ever inspire lust in a man again? Would she want to? Ten years ago, the Bateaux Mouches had been for her and Johnny alone. They had spent the nights making love and the days strolling around Paris, inhaling the romance of the place, the beauty of it. Paris was brighter then, it smelled better, was imbued with life force, with possibility, with bright shining love. But at the moment, Paris felt grey and small. The Bateaux Mouches were grey and small. She was grey and small.

She got up from her bench, deciding the kissing couple were actually making things worse for her. She went up the stairs and stepped into the light, the reflection of the April sun on the Seine River blinded her and she had to cover her eyes. She walked to the back of the boat. The banks of the Seine stretched before her, the Hôtel des Invalides, and soon, the Musée D'Orsay. There was a gush of cold wind and her hair whipped her face painfully. She buttoned up her coat and removed from around her neck her prized Hermès scarf, the one Johnny had given her for her thirtieth birthday with a request that she start dressing more Parisian. This had been his last gift to her. She tied it over her hair and looked at her reflection in the window of the boat. She looked more Bosnian refugee than Parisian chic. Wrong, wrong. She looked all fucking wrong. She made her way past the Japanese tourists and found Lola, her tall silhouette against the blue sky, standing by the railing, holding Simon and pointing at other péniches. Lola looked very happy, Annie noticed, and so did Simon. He had stopped crying at night altogether. Maybe that's why Lola looked so rested, so carefree.

She leaned against the banister and inhaled the air, crisp and clear. She removed the scarf from her head and opened it to look at the prints on the silk, maybe for the first time. Seashells. Why seashells? Why not walruses or hummingbirds? She held the scarf by a corner, and let it billow in the wind. Simon was watching her intently, his eyes fixed to the scarf like a dare. She smiled at him, and then, let go. They both watched the scarf float in the sky, up and down, gracefully for a few minutes. Simon pointed to the scarf, followed it with his finger in silence. It finally touched the water and became a small point in the distance. She turned around and walked to the front of the péniche. She was surprised to find herself alone at the very front of the boat, like Kate Winslet minus Leonardo. The péniche glided along the Seine River, passed the Pont du Carrousel and made a turn.

And suddenly, inexplicably, Paris rushed in, astoundingly beautiful, and she was taken completely by surprise. Colors became sharper and the ribbon of the Seine was like a silk path between the silhouettes of Notre Dame and the Hôtel de Ville. In the distance, the Pont Neuf, like a bridge made of lace, gleamed in the morning light and she felt alive for no reason at all. Alive and hopeful.

She came back to Lola and Simon and they took turns taking pictures of themselves with Simon in their arms and the monuments as backgrounds. They then sat on a bench and Lola took Petit Beurre cookies from her backpack and hand-fed them to Simon. As the péniche approached the bank, Annie wished the trip had not ended so soon. Closer came the dark, old carcasses of the chestnut trees. Back came her self-imposed limits, the reassuring drudgery of her life. But as the boat approached the banks, Annie noticed that the trees were in fact far from bare, the branches were covered in fat buds, overripe and ready to burst. Spring was under the surface of everything. In a matter of weeks, the trees would recover their leaves, that impossibly green, lush foliage. Nature could start over after almost dying to nothing, time and time again, so why couldn't she?

※

Mark shut down his laptop, ordered a scotch from the flight attendant, and removed the godamned suffocating cashmere turtleneck he and Lola had picked up at Fred Segal's just a few weeks before, when everything was fine, when there was not the slightest sign of her being miffed, no hints, no nothing.

The woman across the aisle eyed his bare arms and his Diesel T-shirt more or less discreetly but he wasn't in the mood. Had he been in a better mood, he might have flirted but nothing more. Truth was, he had absolutely nothing to blame himself for.

Lola was a scatterbrain. That drove him crazy. And she always had an excuse to not do this or that. But when had she become such a professional victim? So, he had a temper. She would too if she was carrying his load. But she was the one he loved, always had been, always would be.

Mark put the laptop away in his briefcase and tightened his grip. Nothing to blame himself for. Lola's move was so transparent. Clearly, she wanted him to find her, sending those postcards from Manhattan, of all places, where her friend Alyssa lived. The equivalent to scattering white pebbles to help him track her down. Manhattan was where he was headed now. For business. If this had been serious she would not have sent the damn postcards, right?

How long did Lola expect whatever money she had brought with her to last, with the lifestyle she was accustomed to? She had used none of her credit cards. He was almost impressed she hadn't cracked yet. He had given her space to think things through, had let her do her charade of postcards and had not budged.

Now the joke was on her. Her manipulation backfired, of course, and now she was at the point where she didn't know how to make the first move to come back. He was going to New York on business, and he'd go get her and the kids. He'd forgive her about that stunt, and she'd come back home. She was very lucky that he would take her back, no questions asked.

The living room whirled, and no sound came out of her mouth. Lola sat down on the couch, the receiver sticking to her burning cheek as she listened to Alyssa's beautiful Jamaican accent trail on the phone. If only Annie had not picked up the phone and saw her turn livid as the tears begin to flow. Now Annie was standing there, arms crossed over her chest, her oven mitts still on. Soon she would know the truth.

"Mark totally expected to find you and the kids here in SoHo, honey," Alyssa was saying. "He was sure you were staying with me. Of course he put two and two together, with me mailing the postcards you sent me. I thought he was going to trash my loft. It was horrible. I mean, I had friends over. I was dying inside. It was embarrassing for everyone, especially Mark. You should have seen his face."

Alyssa was younger than Lola and still worked as a model. She didn't have children, had never wanted to. Lola didn't expect her to understand. And the pressure of Annie standing there, waiting to find out why a friend of hers had called and asked to speak with her urgently, that was all too much "On the other hand it was kind of cute," Alyssa added, "Romantic you know, him flying across the country looking for you."

"Did you tell him where I was?"

"He said he would talk to the police." The shrill tone of

Alyssa's voice showed she wasn't worried, only exasperated. "I told him I didn't know, honey. I really tried to cover your ass. But I just don't want to be part of this. I mean, he talked about abduction, and subpoenas and witnesses."

Lola looked apologetically at Annie. "Alyssa, please don't tell him," she whispered.

"I see his point," Alyssa said coldly.

"Please, wait."

"Look," Alyssa said, her tone sharp, "you better call him. He's at the Four Seasons or on his phone. You tell him where you are yourself. If you don't do it, I'm sorry, sweetie, but I will."

❧

Lucas let himself into Annie's house and found Lola doubled over on the living room couch. Annie was at her side looking like she was having the time of her life. To his silent puzzled expression, Annie raised her eyebrows as if to say "I told you so."

"Mark's on the horizon," she said. "He found her. Or thinks he did, that dope!"

Lola, whom Lucas had never seen looking anything other than serene, sat curled up on the couch in a semi-fetal embrace, arms wrapped around her body and shaking slightly.

"Is he here?"

"Worse. He's in New York looking for her. He thought he was going to find her there." Annie rolled her eyes dramatically. "And now he's really mad."

"What should we do?" Lola said in a small voice.

"We?" said Annie.

"Just stay put and call the police. Tell them your story and they will protect you," Lucas said, all of a sudden noticing Annie's inexplicably smug smile.

"There are no laws that can protect me," Lola said weakly.

"I understand that this is precisely what restraining orders do," he assured her.

"That's the thing," Lola sighed and put her head in her hands.

"That's the thing," Annie echoed, looking thrilled.

"There isn't really a restraining order," Lola said in a very small voice.

"Not really?" he asked.

"Not at all," Annie said.

He looked at Annie disapprovingly. She shook her head to explain this was news to her too. He tried to wrap his mind around this revelation. "But you said—"

"It wasn't really true," Lola admitted.

"I knew it!" he exclaimed.

"But you have every right to protect yourself and the children," Annie said. "You only left him for self-protection, self-preservation."

"He isn't violent," Lola sighed between tears. "Not physically."

"You lied?" Lucas said, sounding utterly shocked.

"Would you have taken my fear of him seriously unless I said he was violent?" She pointed at Annie. "You made me say it."

Annie's eyes widened in indignation. "So, it's my fault?"

Lucas scratched his head. "But isn't taking the children to another country without telling him somewhat illegal?"

"I'm going to jail," Lola wailed. "They will take the children away!"

Annie shook her head. "I just wish you had thought about these small details before you abducted your kids!"

At this, Lola burst into sobs. "It wasn't an abduction. Gee, of course not! I... I sent postcards."

"Do you realize what position you're putting me in?" Annie asked.

Lucas listened as he reorganized his next day mentally, moving appointments so he could drive Lola and her children back to the airport in the morning. With a little luck, the travel agency would find them a plane leaving that night.

"You did talk about it, gave him an ultimatum, something?" Annie was asking. "You told him you were leaving, just not where you were going, right?"

"No, I just picked up my kids and left while he was on a business trip. He came back to an empty house."

Annie held her face. "Merde!"

"Merde," Lucas echoed.

"Did you write to him? To explain, since?"

"I tried... I swear, many times I tried... But, I couldn't...put it into words. I didn't want to make him mad. I didn't want to hurt his feelings so I just sent postcards. I sent them in an envelope to Alyssa, and she removed the envelope and mailed them from Manhattan as soon as she received them."

"A red herring." Lucas stated.

"I didn't want him to worry. And I wanted him to know how well the children were doing. Simon sleeping through the night, and Lia making new friends in... New York. You know... I kept in touch."

Lucas turned from Annie to Lola as though watching a slow-motion ping-pong match and said finally. "So, she just disappeared?"

"You're quick!" Annie said, laughing now.

But Lucas found none of this amusing, and he certainly wasn't feeling a shred of pity for Lola. Behind that beautiful façade was... what? He could now see why Annie might feel vindicated. He gave her a significant look.

"Everyone thinks I've got it so good, so easy," Lola cried. "People, even you two, think that you can just talk things out, and they get solved, but you don't know Mark. You don't know me. He has this...power over me. I can't talk to him. Whatever I say to him doesn't make a dent."

"But how in the world did you expect things to turn out?"

Annie asked. Lucas was surprised to hear a shift in Annie's tone. She sounded suddenly empathetic. Lola didn't respond, she was mumbling almost to herself.

"Even when I really plan what I'm going to say, even if I know I have a point, he doesn't listen. He just puts me down, he crushes me, I mean, mentally. He doesn't need to hit to hurt me. You don't understand."

Everyone was silent for a moment. There was just the sound of Lola sniffling. Finally, Annie said, "Maybe it's not him. You're terrified of conflicts in general. That's what I'm talking about when I say that you need to be in touch with your anger. And you poo-poohed it!"

Lucas could stand it no longer. He turned to Lola and pointed his finger at her. "You say you didn't want to hurt his feelings? Well I think you wanted to hurt him and you chose the cruelest way to do it! And the most cowardly." Lola buried her face in her arms and began sobbing quietly as he continued. "I can't believe you women. You think men are just big idiots with no feelings, no emotions."

He was interrupted by Annie grabbing his arm and dragging him out of the room and into the hallway out of Lola's earshot. She leaned against the wall and looked at him smiling. "Of course we know you guys have emotions," she whispered. "Only not as important as our own." Annie was actually having fun with this. No, he would never understand this woman.

"I'm disgusted. It's not cooking lessons you need to give her," he said. "Maybe you need to teach her how to ... I don't know... grow a backbone."

"Nah, who needs a backbone when you have her cheekbones," Annie laughed.

"Well, personally, I find a lack of backbone particularly unattractive."

Annie looked at him as if for the first time. "So, it's not style over substance for you?"

In the darkness of the hallway, Lucas stopped pacing and put a hand on the wall, coming close to Annie in a sudden move that surprised even him. "Very few women come with the full package," he whispered, looking her in the eyes. Annie searched his face for signs of irony. He waited for a repartee. It did not come. Instead she continued looking at him.

"You want me to look into plane tickets?" he asked to break the awkward silence.

"Tickets? What for?"

"For a honeymoon in the Bahamas bien sûr"

"You think I'm going to just send her back? Let her be eaten alive by that jerk?"

"Yes."

Annie opened the door and led him out of the house. "Never. Lola is my friend, Lucas."

❦

If Annie was clear on one thing, it was that Mark and Lola needed to speak, and not about the weather. Silence in a marriage, Annie knew now, was the real killer. The assumptions one makes, the secrets one lets the other get away with, the slow creeping into one's own role, the impossibility to change within the confines of non-communication were all part of that silence. How easy it was to play one role and one role only for an entire marriage, even when there was love. Especially when there was love. In her marriage to Johnny she had painted herself into a corner. Because she loved him so, she had not wanted him to see sides of her that he had not chosen her for. He had chosen her as a spouse, the mother of his children. He had chosen her for her independence, her lack of neediness. Indeed, she had been the most independent, the least needy of wives. But only in appearance.

After she and Lola put the children to bed and cleaned the

kitchen in silence, they went into the salon. It was after ten at night. Annie moved the logs around the fireplace waiting for Lola to dial Mark's number. But Lola wasn't dialing. She was sitting stiffly on the couch's armrest. The piece of paper with Mark's hotel number was at the tip of her shaky fingers, and she was staring at the telephone as if it might any moment uncoil and jump at her throat.

"Aren't you going to dial?"

"I don't know if I can," Lola said. She looked so white Annie wondered if she might throw up.

"Seriously, how bad can it be?"

"Bad," Lola whimpered.

There was a master plan. Lola would not mention Paris since Mark assumed she was in New York and there was no advantage in telling him otherwise. Annie was to listen in on the conversation on the cordless phone for moral support. She'd help Lola be strong, level headed, and firm. This was an excellent plan.

"You want me to dial for you?"

"Okay, you dial."

Annie dialed, handed Lola the receiver, and picked up the cordless feeling perfectly confident about the plan. She began to feel some sense of alarm when she heard Lola give the Four Season's receptionist Mark's name and room number in the voice of a six-year-old. After an interminable silence and the sound of muzak, a man's voice on the line said: "Yes?"

"Mark?" Lola said in a minuscule voice. She looked like she might faint.

Annie was walking towards the living room with the phone against her ear when Mark uttered his first sentence to his wife in weeks. "Lola, where the FUCK are you?" This somehow was not what Annie expected. What had she expected? She realized in an instant she had no experience dealing with an abusive, yelling spouse. She had been the yeller in her marriage. Johnny was the quiet, calm one. She promptly came back to the couch, sat right next to Lola, and squeezed her free hand with her own. Lola's eyes widened, filled with tears and she shook her head as if to say she wasn't up to this. Annie sent her a look that said, "You'll be all right."

"Hi honey," Lola said still in the smallest of voices.

"Give me your goddamn address," Mark said coldly. "I'll take a cab."

Lola's voice had turned plaintive. She sounded like a scared little girl. "I'm not—"

"Give me the address."

Annie recognized from the adrenaline that suddenly pushed through her veins a sudden and unequivocal hatred for the guy. She wished she could soothe the stricken expression on Lola's face, but how could she when she felt overwhelmed herself. Lola might have been right. It could be that bad.

Lola tried to speak: "I just wanted to say that—"

Mark's voice came, cold, matter of fact. "You have nothing to say. You're in no position. You listen to me Lola. I've run out of patience for your bullshit. Give me your address. I'm getting really pissed. Believe me, you don't want to see me really pissed off."

"I wanted to say," Lola continued, "that I'm not...in New York."

What about the plan! Lola wasn't sticking to the plan! Annie wiped her sticky palms on her jeans. But as long as she said nothing about France...

"Then where the fuck are you?" Mark roared.

"I'm...in France, honey," Lola sing-sang.

There was a silence, and Mark said and Annie mouthed in unison: "What?"

"Lia really likes her new school," Lola chirped. On the line, there was a long silence. Annie could almost hear Mark's brain gears making painful rotations. Lola timidly added, "She's learning French so rapidly. And you should hear Simon!"

"Listen," Mark said, his voice no longer containing his rage. "You can't take the kids out of the country. That's kidnapping. Is there another guy? That's it? There's another guy? Some sissy French guy with a fucking beret?" Annie found herself chuckling. This was playing out like a bad soap opera.

"No, of course, not," Lola said.

"Bull—Shit!"

"Really, Mark, it's just that...I had to...I needed to take some time off."

"Some fucking time off what? Your life is loaded with time off. That's all you fucking do, take time off, flee your fucking responsibilities."

Annie wasn't the most verbally scrupulous person, but to hear curse words barked like this made her shudder. Lola swallowed and looked at her with despair. By now, Annie's bloodstream was laced with adrenaline. She scribbled furiously and handed Lola a piece of paper, which Lola looked at, frowned at, but nonetheless read to Mark verbatim.

"Time off from your tyranny," Lola read flatly.

"My motherfucking what?"

"Tyranny," she repeated, rolling the word in her mouth like a piece of chocolate. She smiled at Annie. It must have felt good.

Annie smiled back, and they braced themselves with heads sunk in shoulders. But Mark stopped yelling.

"What are you talking about?" he asked. His voice was calm again. In fact, he sounded surprised.

"Well," Lola stuttered, "It's hard to say..." She looked up at Annie apologetically, and Annie sensed Lola was about to say something horrible in the vein of "you don't buy me flowers," if she didn't get involved. There was no time, so Annie, figuring that her one advantage over Mark was that she was in the room and that Lola seemed to respond well to intimidation, looked at her with lightning in her eyes.

It worked. Lola swallowed and spoke fast. "You, you...put me down, you abuse me emotionally, you treat me like I'm an…idiot. You…scream."

Another long silence, then Mark said, "Who's coaching you right now?"

Lola and Annie had an identical silent nervous laugh. The guy was no dummy. Or else he knew his wife well. Annie had an unfitting jolt of appreciation for him.

"No one," Lola assured him. His lowering his voice seemed to instill her with some form of strength. "I…had to leave because I couldn't stand the abuse anymore."

Mark had little he could say to that. "Tell me where you are, exactly."

While Lola stuttered, Annie scribbled frantically on the pad and brandished it before her eyes.

"I have every intention to come back," Lola read. "But if you don't make some changes, this relationship is over. Think about that. I'll call you tomorrow at the same time."

"I'll be back in L.A. tomorrow," Mark said matter-of-factly. "I have meetings."

Annie sliced her throat with the side of her hand.

"I'll call you tomorrow at the same time," Lola repeated like a robot, looking at Annie. And before anything could ruin this perfect moment, Annie tore the phone out of Lola's hand and hung up for her. For an instant, they were stone-faced, a second later they were breathing a collective sigh of relief. Annie brushed her hand across her forehead. It was drenched in sweat.

In Althea's room, a dozen canvases stood on the floor next to every free inch of wall space. She kneeled next to a painting of a desolate urban land that reminded her of home. At the very bottom, lying on her side was the fragile silhouette of a small girl with blonde hair. How did this painting have anything to do with her?

Every night that week, long after the rest of the house had gone to sleep, Jared had tapped at her door. Each time she let him in and he apologized for being late, which made no sense at all. It took him a while to decide on a position. He moved her and she made herself like soft clay in his beautiful hands. Once he moved to his colors and started mixing, it was her clue to freeze in position. From there on, and unless he came to her and moved her again, she would not budge for hours; her body as outwardly still as it was pulsating wildly under the surface. She kept her face still as well while her mind buzzed with a mix of euphoria and burning questions as to the whys of this.

Jared mumbled to himself in French and asked her dozens of questions per session in terrible English. Was she comfortable? Was she cold, hungry, thirsty, tired? But he asked her no personal question, and she told herself that she preferred that. He sometimes spoke about his painting in French, saying "tu comprends" and she nodded yes. He did not enquire as to how much French she knew, and she did not offer the information, which might have then forced her to speak, something she did not want to do for fear of breaking the enchantment.

Sometimes Jared drew instead of painted: the back of her neck, her hand. Sometimes he mixed colors and looked angry. Sometimes he mixed color and did not or could not paint at all. After an hour, or five, Jared stopped. He thanked her. He seemed shy then. Apologizing, he left her room like a criminal, and Althea felt flustered and ashamed. But then, the following night, she'd hope he'd come, and he would, amidst the mighty smell of turpentine fumes that made her dizzy.

On the glass of her bedroom window droplets of condensation collected like a testimony to the unacknowledged heat their bodies generated.

CHAPTER 17

*A*nnie and Lola closed the front door and descended the steps on a crisp morning that smelled of spring. Lola had done her share of crying and wringing her hands since the phone call to Mark, but this morning she was back to her own calm self and Annie wondered if she was witnessing an expression of Lola's denial at work. Lola was barefoot in her Birkenstocks, a gross overestimation of the shy sun's progresses. She was dressed for yoga in black leggings that made her slim legs appear even longer, and carried a rolled mat in a cotton bag. Annie held her grocery baskets tightly as she walked down the stairs toward the street and wondered if she too shouldn't be barefoot and in leggings instead of in heavy boots and wrapped in that red poncho that made her look like a tent.

Together they walked down rue de Passy. Lola had found an English-speaking daycare willing to take Simon for a few hours every day so that she could take a yoga-teaching course. She had organized things to give herself free time, just like that. Annie had always lacked the ability to delegate. Besides, being a mother was what she did best. Perhaps the only thing she did well. So,

Lola was from another Galaxy. She was an alien. And she was her friend.

The word dismayed her. Friend. A friend is someone you trust, and she somehow trusted Lola. She trusted her in the sense that she believed that Lola was absolutely benevolent towards her. Benevolent and admiring, which baffled her even more. Maybe this was not the kind of friendship where she would reveal her innermost thoughts. No, that was something she reserved for Lucas, the poor guy. Not that she told him everything either, but with Lucas she let herself be more vulnerable. With Lola, she was the grown up. The mother. Always the mother. She probably would have been The Mother with Lucas but he never let her. He let her feed him yes, but not mother him.

Lola was possibly the first woman friend she had made in ten years. How she mistrusted these Parisian women. How she mistrusted all women. And most men.

Annie tried to unbutton her poncho as they walked, looking for air, for more skin to air contact. "How can you go to yoga with what's going on with Mark?"

"I can't think straight when I don't meditate. I have to de-stress first."

"What I mean is that you're putting Simon in daycare, and you're taking a class. It's like you're planning your future here. But you know it's not going to be that simple, don't you?"

Lola gripped her mat. "You mean I should go back to him?"

No, Annie did not want Lola to go back. She wanted Lola to stay. But she had to wonder at her own motives. "I don't know what I mean," she said.

"France happened to me for a reason." Lola said, walking. "I can't just go back home as though nothing happened. I'm so terrible at making decisions."

"You've made a decision if I ever saw one made. France didn't just happen to you."

Lola stopped in front of the door of the yoga studio and looked into Annie's eyes. She always searched her eyes like that. It was unnerving. "So what do you think I should do?"

"Take action legally, not illegally," Annie said. "Get some child support out of that cretin."

"You're right," Lola said feebly.

"You always say that I'm right, but you go on doing the opposite. Like yesterday when you told him you were in France. Now the shit is hitting the fan."

Lola shuffled her weight. "You're right that I should want a divorce."

"Should, shmould."

"But I don't. What I want is for Mark to change. Back to the way he used to be. I know he has it in him. He was different at the beginning of our marriage."

"Then give him an ultimatum." What she wanted to say was "grow a backbone," but she refrained.

"I can't jump into things. People distribute ultimatums like chocolates. I'm different. I won't give an ultimatum I'm not willing to follow through on." Lola paused, then said, "And I don't want to leave. Not yet. I'm happy here, Annie. I'm healing. Being under your roof is very healing for everyone. It's good for me, it's good for Lia, and it's good for Simon. Just take a look at them. I leave Simon at a daycare for the first time in his life, and not a peep!" Lola put her hand on the yoga's studio door and added "Even Althea is not poor little Althea anymore."

"She isn't?"

Lola smiled mysteriously "Looks to me like she's in love."

"What love? What's going on?"

"Althea and Jared spend a whole lot of time together in her room."

Out of the loop again. Annie stepped onto the sidewalk. "What? I refuse to believe it."

"Three hours yesterday. In her room."

"What are you talking about? Jared has the hots for you."

"Oh, come on," Lola laughed. "First Lucas, and now Jared? You're being paranoid."

"To be paranoid I'd have to care. I'm just concerned about Althea."

"She's young, pretty, and has her life ahead of her."

"I don't know what he sees in her," Annie said as she walked away.

Annie hurried down the street and after a few blocks set her straw bags on the sidewalk, removed the Poncho, made a ball out of it and stuffed it in one of the bags. Cool air billowed under her shirt, a button down flannel shirt that Johnny used to wear only on weekends. She had not imagined it would be so warm out today. Even the flannel shirt was too much. She stopped walking, set her bag down again, removed Johnny's shirt and rolled it into a ball. If she put the shirt in her bag she would run out of room for groceries. She thought of tying the shirt around her waist. So hot. She held the shirt in her hand, looked around. There was a city trashcan. She picked up her bags, opened the trashcan and tossed the shirt into it.

ॐ

Lola had spent the night rehearsing her future conversation with Mark, and rehashing the one they'd had. She felt utterly exhausted, utterly weak and confused. Still she went on as planned and took the first of a series of classes toward a yoga-teaching diploma. This was an accelerated program where she would be learning and practicing yoga for five to six hours each day. In just a few weeks she could get accredited to become an instructor. No matter where life led her thereafter, this diploma could not be taken away from her. This was the first time, probably in her life, that she was making a decision by herself, meaning without an agent, a manager or a husband's advice—not even with Annie's advice—to do something for herself with the grander scheme of things in mind.

By the end of the very first class, she felt somehow stronger, more empowered. Taking the class, she sensed possibilities for herself, and felt that she was closer to being able to finally take action. But the evening came, and the time to call Mark, and she felt weak again.

"Tell him what you want. Do you even know what you want?" Annie asked her.

Lola knew her plan had never gone this far. "I don't want him. Not the way he is now."

"Tell him. Set ground rules. He isn't in front of you, so you can be a bit more aggressive."

"Isn't passive–aggressive good enough?"

Annie patted her on the back. Don't worry, "I'll listen in and help you."

How to tell Annie she did not want that. She hesitated, "I'm pretty sure I'm ready to take sail on my own."

"No, really, let me," Annie said excitedly. "I'll put some serious wind in your sails."

Lola hesitated. "I'll be... fine?"

"You were crumbling yesterday. You could not wait to cave in and tell him about France. Trust me. I'll tell you exactly what to say."

"To be honest, I don't want to feel harassed from both ends." Lola said. This might be the most insensitive thing she had ever said to another human being, but Annie only shrugged it off.

"Suit yourself. I'll grab a shovel and start digging your grave in the backyard meanwhile."

Lola's hands shook wildly as she dialed her own phone number in Bel Air, a place where she'd lived eons ago, in another lifetime. There was one ring, and Mark picked up. "How are you doing?" she asked the instant she heard his voice, these being the only words she could utter.

"I'm doing," Mark grunted from somewhere in the mansion, maybe the bedroom. Was the housekeeper coming every day now that she was gone? It would have been unnecessary. Lola could hear the TV in the background. Football it seemed.

"How're the kids?" Mark asked. This could have been a conversation between them a month ago. She almost melted with joy at the normality of it all.

"They're wonderful."

"How well could they be doing, without a father?" he barked. How could she have responded without hurting him? But Mark spoke before she could. "The kids know I have a temper, big deal!" Something in Lola's chest sunk. Mark knew. He knew. "How do you think I grew up?" he continued. "I got my ass kicked all the way to adulthood. If you think you're doing them a favor by protecting them from real life, well you're wrong! Life—I'm talking about real life, not the cocoon you live in—is tough as shit."

"You make it tough," she responded, picturing the thumbs up Annie would have given her for this.

"It doesn't mean I don't love my kids," Mark said.

Lola felt her tears, irrepressible. "I know you love them," she said softly, "and I know you love me. But you don't show the love you feel."

"Lia hates both of our guts equally, I'll have you notice. And Simon—the kid isn't missing a limb for God's sake. They need a dad that's a real man. Not some faggot French guy that...Are you fucking a French guy?" His voice rose. "Is that why you left? For a French guy?"

Lola was incredulous. "No, of course not."

"So, what's the point? What is it you want, Lola?"

"I want … I need for things to change."

"Like what?"

"I … I want to be a useful part of society, find a career." She imagined Annie would want her to tell him, tell it to him like it was. "But mostly, I'm very ... anguished by our marriage." She waited for Mark to respond but he didn't. "I'm so sorry, Mark. I need this time. I was losing ground. I was so ... unhappy and confused." Lola wanted to tell Mark how she felt free in France, boundless. How she cooked, ate, drank, laughed, flirted, explored Paris. How she felt light, playful, and happy with the children. Instead she said, encouraged by Mark's silence, "Here, I'm discovering who I am and what I like, and even what I'm good at."

His answer came, glacial. "And what might that be?"

Did he mean who she was or what she was good at? "I'm going through training right now," she continued weakly, "to get certified, as a yoga instructor."

"Certified at putting your legs behind your head?"

This was precisely the kind of remarks she was leaving him for, but she let it pass, regretting immediately having done so. "I can be a yoga instructor in L.A. just as easily," she said.

"And earn peanuts? Suit yourself."

"I needed to be away from a materialistic lifestyle, the facade, the arrogance."

"So, you went to France?" Mark chuckled.

"My self-esteem was so low."

"Don't hold me responsible for your low self-esteem," Mark said, "That came long before you met me, honey."

Mark might be right about that. But he was certainly not innocent. Lola surprised herself and snapped. "Then why do I only feel low self-esteem when I'm around you?"

"You tell me."

Lola took a deep breath, stared at her feet, at the wall, and said, "You're a fault-finder."

"You're the fault-finder," Mark retorted, "as you just proved. Only you're a hypocrite."

"I'm a hypocrite?" Lola said anxiously.

"You never said anything."

"I was afraid that you'd stop loving me. I was afraid that you'd leave me."

"So instead you leave me? What a joke."

"I'm sorry."

"It suits you to see yourself as victimized and me as the tyrant, but you constantly insinuate that I'm a bad father, a bad husband."

"I never said that."

"Oh, spare me. I read it in your eyes."

Lola was dumbstruck that Mark allowed himself to be so candid. "But I..."

"And sex," Mark interrupted. He paused, "There's always an excuse. Your libido."

Lola's shoulders relaxed suddenly. Sex, that time-honored weapon of conjugal life. "Maybe I was just resentful."

"Well, I'm sure glad you admit it at last. I knew it was a crock of shit."

"You know it's not that I don't love you."

"What do you want me to do, Lola? You want me to crawl back to you on my hands and knees? You know me better than that."

"We need to communicate."

"Girlfriends communicate."

Lola's heart sank. "So what do we do?" she murmured.

"I'm not running after you, if that's the game you're playing. I won't be waiting long. You're not the only mermaid on Malibu Beach, as you well know."

"Are you saying you want to see other ... people?"

"Hey, not a bad suggestion! You know, try out a French guy." He laughed nervously.

"There is no French guy."

"After you've finished gut-wrenching communication with the perfect wimp of your dreams."

"But it's not what I want."

"I'm what I am," Mark said, "It's my way…"

"Or the highway … I know."

"Well, fuck you! I'm hanging up," Mark said, and he did.

Lola stared at the receiver and burst into tears. Annie was there in an instant, an arm around her shoulders, letting Lola sob against her. "I listened to the whole thing," Annie admitted. "You're making real progress."

"You think he's beginning to see my point?"

"Well, no. What I mean is that you're closer to standing on your own two feet."

"You know what's bothering him the most about having us disappear like this?" Lola wept. "It's that he can't explain it to people without looking like a complete loser. He doesn't care at all about us … about me."

❧

In Bel Air, Mark hung up the phone. It was dark now and he had not bothered turning on the lights in the living room. So when the headlights of a passing car in the distance briefly brightened the room, Mark lifted his head, startled. For a second he was disoriented and took it for Lola's car coming up the driveway, which was absurd.

The house had a different smell now, a different sound. From the couch, Mark counted the interval of the security system's light, red against the wall, and green lights of the message machine that showed thirty unheard messages. He better have the doctor check that hollow feeling in his solar plexus that felt kind of like acid reflux, but not exactly.

Far away, in the kitchen, the refrigerator hummed. He searched the darkened room for signs of life but there were none, no movements and no voices, only the echo of his breathing bouncing off the walls. He got up from the couch, turned on a few lights, then turned most of them off. He walked up the steps and wandered through the immaculate house—immaculate, the way he thought he liked it. The sound of his steps muffled on the carpet but echoed like in a museum when he entered the bathrooms. He opened the kids' bedroom doors, smelled the air for signs of them. He was a good man. Unlike his own father, Mark would never have raised his hand to his children or his wife. He only raised his voice. Only his voice.

CHAPTER 18

$\mathcal{T}$he kitchen air was thick with heat and steam when Lucas entered. Annie was tipping a pot of boiling water the size of a small car into a giant colander. From Lucas's angle, steam from the angel hair pasta appeared to rise from Annie's body and she looked good enough to eat.

Annie glanced over her shoulder and saw him. Did she know he had been looking at her back and her beautiful butt in those pants? "Where's Jared?" she asked.

"How should I know where Jared is?"

She poured the pasta into a bowl and dabbed steam from her cleavage and forehead with a kitchen towel. "He's gone M.I.A for three days."

"And you can't live without him suddenly?"

"Not me..."

Annie went quiet when Althea materialized in the kitchen cradling an oversized gray clay mug in her bony hands like it was life support. Lucas could not help but feel uncomfortable around this strange woman. Maybe it was the white sweater and pants that gave her that air of translucence, but today she looked more like a ghost than ever. "Bonjour!" he bellowed gregariously to hide his dismay. Again, he thought he must have misunderstood. There was no possibility that Jared was interested in her.

"Hello," Althea mumbled without looking him in the eye. She advanced slowly towards the stove like a somnambulist, wrapped her long fingers around the handle of the teapot, poured boiling water into the mug that already contained a used-up tea bag, and vanished from the kitchen through the backyard glass door.

Annie nodded toward the door. "That's why I need Jared, and quick."

"You think they have a thing going?"

"Of course. How could you not notice?"

"Well, Jared did mention something."

Annie frowned. "So, it's true? Why didn't you tell me anything? Anyway, he's disappeared for three days and nights and Althea's waiting for him, I know that much. But no one can talk about it. Oh no! Or the way she eats! I asked her why she looked so haunted. She said she was fine and had no idea what I was talking about. It's like a frigging 800-pound elephant in the room."

"Or an 80-pound elephant in her case."

"Since Jared's been gone, she has barely left her room during the day, and she roams through the house all night. She's not even calling her mother. I heard her crying in her room at four in the morning."

Lucas approached the stove. "What smells so good?"

"And Lola's no better since that last phone call to her husband three days ago when he essentially told her to come back to the marital bed or bug off. She's crying all the time. I'm thinking of adding a surcharge for Kleenexes."

"What are we eating?"

"Fish stew."

Jared's voice came behind them. "I'll have some."

"Look who's back!" Annie exclaimed. "God's gift to mankind! Where have you been?"

Jared made an evasive hand gesture. "Is it all right with you if I bring the food to my room?"

Annie gave Jared a dirty look, shrugged and took a large plate from the cabinet. Lucas watched her fill the plate with pasta, pour over it a heaping serving of fish stew that overflowed with mussels, shrimp, and red sauce, and top it with a sprig of parsley. She handed the plate to Jared. "You want something else? Dessert? Bread?"

"Non, c'est parfait," he said. He thanked her and left the kitchen like a robber carrying his loot, the aroma of fish, white wine, and tomatoes following him up the dark stairs.

"The hell with these people," Annie said.

Lucas uncorked a bottle of Pouilly-Fuissé, poured it in a glass, and handed it to Annie. "Even me?"

Annie put down her towel and took the wine glass. She leaned against the kitchen counter and took a sip. "No, you get an A-plus for entertaining me."

The dinner turned out to be a real dîner de fous. Once their mothers mellowed out thanks to the wine, the children, sensing a window of opportunity, began making bullets out of bread and throwing them at each other. Simon's apparent function was to retrieve the bullets that had landed on the floor and pop them into his mouth. Lucas struggled to make conversation but it was no use, as Lola and Annie roared with laughter every time his accent sounded particularly hilarious to them. No one paid any attention to Althea who ate her own meal in the most peculiar way: She was cutting cooked beets into even squares, placing them between her fingers and dipping them in moutarde extra forte. The result was that her fingers and mouth were stained red and made her look as if she'd just feasted on someone's neck.

"I hope you can find me a couple cases of this fabulous wine,

Lucas. I'm throwing a party," Annie said, emptying her glass and handing it to Lucas to be filled.

"A party?" he said in surprise. Annie had not mentioned a party, let alone attended one in the last three years. "What does it mean?"

"It means, I am back, baby!"

"She's back!" Lola howled and burst into laughter.

Wasn't this the same woman who, according to Annie, had been crying for three days? Lucas pondered the unpredictability of women. Scientists have demonstrated that as they live together, they can fall hormonally in synch. Could this be what was going on? Both of them on their emotional time?

Annie proceeded to tell Lola about what she had in mind, which made it apparent that this was not a spur of the moment decision, but something Annie had been planning for quite a while. This might not be drunken or hormonal talk, but perhaps a rebirth of enthusiasm for the very things Annie had shunned ever since Johnny's death. Maybe she was indeed coming out of her shell in some way. "It will begin as a kids' party and transform into an adult party toward the evening. An all day and all night affair. Something huge," Annie explained. "You remember my old parties, Lucas?"

Lucas groaned. "I thought they had been outlawed."

"You're an old party poopydoo!" Annie said.

"Please allow me to give Lola an account of past events," Lucas suggested. "About thirty well-mannered children under the age of ten arrive here, and within moments, they become raving hooligans. Memorable indeed. They'll look back on it and say 'You know that party at Annie's, the one where I lost my left eye?'"

"My parties are a riot," Annie agreed.

"Alas in the proper sense of the term."

Annie ignored him. "Later in the evening, the grown-ups

arrive. They bring something to drink, but the French don't do potluck; they don't even have a word for it. So the food will be up to me. I'm thinking of cooking a whole lamb, méchoui style. It will be served under a tent in the garden. That's what the pillows I've been working on are for."

This announcement confirmed the deliberate, premeditated nature of Annie's decision. This was news he should have rejoiced about, but he could not help but be aware of the fact that his friendship with Annie had started, been possible even, when Annie had isolated herself and become antisocial. "See Lola," Annie continued, "you have never partied until you've partied with the French. We'll be dancing, drinking, and eating all night. This thing won't end until the wee hours of the morning, with fresh baked croissants from the bakery, espresso, smeared make-up, and hangovers for everyone."

"How fun!" Lola cried.

"I've seen many couples created and destroyed during your parties, Annie."

"Oh, it's a meat market! People bring people, and I usually make a few new friends."

"And lose one or two."

"Let's party!" Lola bellowed.

At that moment, the dining room door opened. Jared was standing in the doorway, his hair a tangled mess, his black shirt riddled with moth, or perhaps acid, holes.

"Did you like the food? How come you..." Annie began, but before she could complete her question, Jared had walked around the table to where Althea sat, taken her beet-stained hand, grabbed bread from the bread basket, and taken her away from the dining room table and out of the room, the whole thing without uttering a word. Althea had appeared violently surprised, or embarrassed and had turned a shade of red that would have made the beets envious. The door shut behind them and the kids giggled hysterically. Lucas looked at Lola and Annie who looked at him perplexed.

"No one told me that Frankenstein and his fiancée lived here!" he told the children who burst out laughing. Even Simon, who did not know why, laughed out loud showing the content of his mouth, filled with bread.

"What the hell?" Annie whispered to Lola.

Althea was too rattled from her abduction from the dinner table to understand what it was she was looking at. Inside Jared's room, on the small pine desk, the table was set for two. There was red wine in coffee mugs, two plates framed by forks, spoons and knives, and in the center a bowl covered by a third plate. In a tall glass were two long-stemmed white roses that threatened to topple over. Jared placed the bread he had just taken from the dining room table next to an overflowing ashtray, then, realizing the ashtray did not belong, he emptied its content into a trashcan and put it back on the table. He took out a cigarette, lit it, put it in the corner of his mouth, took off the plate to uncover the bowl which was filled with the same food Annie had served for dinner and said "Ta-dah!" sounding apologetic.

She looked at him, still not understanding. Althea's stomach turned at the sight of that dish. She had not touched it at dinner, not even glanced at it, and now it was there, facing her like a reproach. The shrimp, mussels and pasta looked congealed, like those plastic meals one might find in the window of some Japanese restaurants. Did he mean for her to eat this? But what panicked her the most, what she could not take her eyes away from, was the attempt at a bouquet that stood on the table. Were those store-bought roses for her?

Jared gave Althea the one chair and sat Indian-style on the bed, across from her, the desk between them serving as a dinner table. He was close, much closer than those times he had painted her, and he was peering into her eyes. There was absolutely nowhere to hide. Jared put the single bowl of food in front of him and she breathed in relief. She watched him wrap pasta expertly around his fork with the elegant ease that French people have when it comes to table manners. She followed the fork from the bowl, then up. The fork seemed suspended in the air for a moment, then began to advance toward her mouth.

Her eyes widened as Jared brought the food an inch from her lip. "No, No, Merci, non," she said, shaking her head furiously.

Jared gazed intently into her eyes and whispered a soft command. "Mange. C'est bon."

Althea blushed terribly. She was cornered. She opened her lips slightly.

"Plus grand. Bigger," he said gently, but with extreme seriousness.

She felt she had no choice but to part her lips and let him slide the pasta into her mouth. Her taste buds sent conflicting information to her brain about salt, tomatoes, danger. Her lips noticed the food was in fact still warm. The roof of her mouth and her tongue remembered the lusciousness of the sensation of eating forbidden food. She chewed slowly, not knowing where to look as Jared scrutinized her face. She chewed all the while eyeing the door, planning an escape. But already Jared had wrapped more pasta on the fork and aimed it at her mouth, his eyebrow raised in concentration. And again. And again. Althea chewed and swallowed powerlessly while her body rebelled, while, under the table, her fists tightened and her legs wanted to spring from under her and run out of the room. But, tangled with that rage, her heart ached for the way he gathered the pasta and slightly opened his own mouth like a mother does, how he whispered encouraging words, and smiled approvingly when she swallowed.

By the fifth forkful, she was gagging and her eyes were watering.

"Good for today. Très bien," he seemed pleased. "Demain aussi, d'accord?"

Althea nodded.

He did not offer to paint her that evening. Instead he helped her up from the bed, away from the table and out of his bedroom, then walked her back to her own room. At her door, he filled her hands with bread like a grandfather gives candy to a child. Then he seemed to remember something. "Attends," he said suddenly. She stood in the hallway and watched him hurry to his room, then come back with the two roses. "Belle comme toi," he said, handing them to her. She took the roses, shaking from head to toe.

Althea waited five minutes after Jared had left and ran to the bathroom. Once there, she fell to her knees in front of the toilet, and put two fingers down her throat.

The next day, they were in the kitchen attending to dinner and homework. So this was her new life, Annie pondered as she sat at the kitchen table picking at the baguette. She was enjoying the spectacle of Lola's frightened attempt at soufflé making while her own chicken with tarragon was gently bubbling on the stove. How familiar those strangers were already, and how surreal it was that she actually liked this new life. And how fun it was to watch Lola squint anxiously at the cheese soufflé recipe. The ingredients were all on the table. All Lola had to do was read, measure, and mix, but by the look of her you'd think she was navigating a crocodile infested swamp. Also at the table, Lia and Maxence were studying less than half-heartedly and Althea was peeling the carrots necessary for the carottes rapées, prompting Annie to wonder once again why Althea insisted on joining them in the preparation of meals she would not eat. Meanwhile, Paul, Laurent and Simon ran around the kitchen, throwing ill-designed paper airplanes at each other that invariably landed on Althea who ducked them humorlessly.

Lola jerked up like a jack-in-the-box. "I can't make this. We're out of Parmesan."

"Substitute," Annie said.

"Substitute with what?"

"You could try cement. If the soufflé rises, it will make a very practical door stop."

Suddenly the kitchen went silent. "What? What did I say?" She turned to see that Jared had entered the kitchen.

He mumbled hello and went about the room gathering plates, utensils, bread, and fruit. Annie exchanged a meaningful glance with Lola, silenced Paul's giggles with a death stare and got up. She didn't miss a beat. She took a ladle and a medium-size serving bowl, scooped out a generous portion of tarragon chicken, and handed it to Jared as though this were the most natural thing in the world. She might be festering with curiosity but she'd be damned if she showed it.

"Don't forget to come back later," she told him, "Lola is making concrete for dessert."

Jared left with inaudible grumbles, and, on a tray, the makings of a setting for two people.

No one made a comment about what had just happened. A few minutes later Althea finished peeling, cleaned up the table, and was gone.

Lola approached the stove and whispered so the kids wouldn't hear, "Do you think maybe he is helping Althea with her anorexia?"

"What anorexia?" Annie said through a mouthful of bread. "She's weird about food and too skinny, but she's a grown woman. If all it takes to be an anorexic is to whine about your thighs, then I'm anorexic."

Lola considered this and said "I'd say your thing is more bulimia."

Annie stopped chewing, opened her mouth wide. "Yaa reaaaaly thhhink?"

"Who am I to judge anyone," Lola sighed.

"You think I eat like a pig, don't you?"

Lola looked at her apologetically. "Sometimes."

Annie considered the baguette in front of her. A good half was missing, and this was before dinner. She was a bottomless pit of hunger. Food: hunting it, preparing it, and ingesting it was how she self-medicated. "I'm glad Jared's paying attention to Althea," she said. "Because I sure as hell don't have that kind of patience." She turned to the children. "If your homework is finished, put it in your backpacks and go watch a few minutes of TV before dinner." The children were out of the kitchen before the end of her sentence.

"What am I going to do when I'm back in L.A.?" Lola asked the contents of her bowl. "My life is out of control. My own husband is encouraging me to have an affair." Her eyes filled with tears. "I've been faithful to him all these years and this is the appreciation I get? He's right, I should have an affair. That's what he deserves."

"No one deserves that," Annie answered. It occurred to her at that moment that sooner or later, Lola would be going back to that ape she had married. That was obviously what she really wanted to do. Annie removed her apron that read, "Don't Provoke the Chef" and threw it on the kitchen counter. "Well, I don't know what I'm going to do with my life either."

"You? But you're happy!" Lola exclaimed.

"Who says?"

"You have your house, your crafts."

"Realistically, how many times can one sofa be reupholstered? One wall stenciled? What am I going to do with myself for the next forty, fifty years of my life? And will I ever get laid again?"

Lola contemplated her quizzically. "Is that what you worry about? Love?"

"I'm a frigging tub of lard," Annie said, holding whatever was left of the baguette against her chest.

Lola wrestled the baguette out of her hands. "Sorry, but that's it. No more bread for you until further notice Madame."

CHAPTER 19

MAI

*B*etween the surprising heat and the cobalt blue of the sky, Annie asked herself how those people in the office buildings were going to make it through the day. She was drenched just from walking three blocks. Granted she was walking kind of fast. Okay. She was exercising. She had retrieved a pair of forgotten gym shoes from the closet earlier in the week and begun walking around the neighborhood at a brisk pace. This was something she kept to herself. She did it while Lola was at yoga and the kids in school. No need to make a big statement about it since she couldn't guarantee she'd stick with it. Also, she cut pasta and bread out of her diet cold turkey, and the combination of both made her feel lightheaded, almost saintly.

On this first day of May, rue de Passy was overtaken by the sweet smell of Lily of the Valley. Street vendors had basketfuls of the small white flowers at their feet, and since Annie wasn't carrying any yet, she could not make a step without someone shoving a small bouquet towards her nose.

The store windows she passed were in full spring regalia. The spring fashion, it seemed, had a nautical theme. It was in the streets as well. "French women never go out without lipstick," was the circular thought in her mind. She did not look too French at the moment. Her hair was a disaster. No cut, no color. She slowed her pace and stopped to look at the mannequins in a boutique's window. That T-shirt with navy and white stripes looked fresh and youthful. She had not bought as much as a new T-shirt in three years. She flattened her hair with the palm of her hand and entered the boutique.

What size was she now? She looked at piles of jeans, mountains of them. Where to start? A young woman in a flowery dress walked out from behind a curtain and looked at Annie disapprovingly from her toes to her head. Annie turned on her heels and made a run for the exit.

"Je peux vous aider?" the woman said.

"Non, je regardais, c'est tout. Anyhoo, ciao and sayonara as they say in Bangladesh."

"I speak English," the salesperson said. She had a nice smile, not that ice queen Parisian attitude.

Annie slowed down.

"I'd love to help you," the woman insisted.

"Help me?" Annie inhaled. "Do you perform lobotomies?"

The woman considered her. "I can do better than that."

Oh the power of a good salesperson. An hour later, Annie was leaving the store with a bag filled with pretty clothes on her arm and the address of a hairdresser in her hand.

Althea had lit up all the candles in the room and set them around her desk. A Parisian landscape was taking form in black and white under her fingers on a piece of paper she had found around the house and with a sharpie borrowed from the kitchen: a café, passersby holding umbrellas, rain, silhouettes of a woman and a man in dark coats holding hands. It was almost eleven at night and Althea was dressed to go out. She had spent the last hour on her make-up, perfecting the eyeliner above her top lashes. Her coat was laid on her bed, ready to be put on. In a few minutes, she prayed, Jared would knock at her door and again would take her out for the evening. He had brought food for them to eat two hours before, in the strange ritual that was now theirs. Then he had left with a promise to come back.

Now that Jared fed her, painted her, and by some miracle seemed to want to show her the city at night, her time alone was spent on nothing but waiting for him. She counted hours, and she counted minutes, and she counted breaths inside of those minutes.

In the short month since Jared had begun painting her, everything had changed for Althea. She could hardly remember what she did with her thoughts before she knew him. She loved every instant of those nights, even if she was cold to the core, and tired, even if Jared never did what she most wanted him to do: kiss her.

Some nights with Jared, icy gusts of wind beat down on them without mercy. Other nights the air felt soft and smelled of lilac. His long black coat like the sail of a night ship, Jared ignored the elements altogether. Her hand in his, she floated, her feet barely skimming over the asphalt. Paris and Jared became confusingly entwined in her understanding, each inconceivable without the other.

It was on those nightly walks through the blur of light that was Paris that she was slowly discovering her voice. Jared never pressured her to speak. He could be silent for an hour and then speak for another hour, fervent monologues in French about politics, art, and religion. She spoke very little at first, she preferred to listen to him, watch his beard creep on his face as the night went on, and inhale his scent. Then she dared answer his questions, first a few words in French, then stringing words together like beads, then composing sentences more musical to her ear than music. Speaking in French, in Paris, was like a blank slate. Her voice was different in French; her thoughts were different in French. She never wanted to speak English, her mother tongue, again. But she loved being with Jared in silence too; she felt great freedom in simply being present.

Jared advanced through the streets of Paris rather than wander through them. He did not explain where they were going or why, and she did not ask. When they were not walking, they sat in deserted subway cars that meandered under the city and screeched through long stops at every station. There they sat shoulder to shoulder, hand in hand, often not speaking a word. Yet, even doing nothing in silence, she felt more intensely awake in Jared's company than she ever felt in her life.

Once they reached a destination, a party, a restaurant where people he knew were dining, or the home of a friend, Jared never really seemed to settle or plan to stay. In fact it wasn't uncommon for them to walk or ride the métro for an entire hour to get somewhere, only to leave that destination minutes later.

Everyone they met in Paris, in cafés, in train stations, in the streets, seemed to know Jared. In the darkest corners of the city, homeless people, prostitutes or junkies would speak to him, seeking his attention for a few moments. The same happened in glamorous areas of Paris where the beautiful people of an intelligentsia Jared seemed welcomed to join tried to seduce him into staying longer. All looked at her questioningly, some bold enough to ask who she was. Only then would Jared tell her name, but he never volunteered other information, and never introduced her. He had been one, and now he was two, and no explanation was given.

After several nights of this, Althea arrived at the conclusion that Jared liked places more than people. He pointed out the architecture, and the history behind the architecture. There was a narrative to each place he took her to, she could tell, but often she would have to guess that narrative herself.

One night, on the quays of the Seine at dusk, couples were

soon replaced by a furtive crowd. He asked her to wait in a dark corner under a bridge while a conversation took place between him and a man. The exchange chilled her, though she heard not a word. It lasted only a few seconds, an eternity of separation between her body and his. Later, she told him she had been scared and he only smiled and squeezed her hand tighter.

Once they had walked fast on rue Botzaris when Jared came to a stop. There was a torn patch in a chain link fence, and he helped her crawl under. The moon was bright that night and she recognized the park of the Buttes-Chaumont where he had taken her the evening before, just before closing. It was a different park in the crepuscule. Gone were the voices and children, gone the dogs and the grass. Instead, shadows layered like Japanese inks, trees, grass, rocks, and ponds all turned shades of gray.

Walking on a graveled path, Althea thought she heard moaning. She squeezed Jared's hand hard. Past a patch of tall bushes, two men, barely hidden, were having sex. They were close enough that the reflection of the moon shone briefly in one of the men's eyes. Jared didn't hurry or slow his pace any more than if he had passed a mother and carriage in broad daylight.

"That was horrible," Althea whispered.

"Why? Because of the sex or the fact that they were both men?"

She loathed herself, but said, "The idea of sex outside of love." Realizing she had brought up sex, she backtracked. "Paris is sad."

"It depends on the mood you are in to begin with," Jared responded. He removed his hand and she died a little, but he slowed his pace and put his arm around her shoulders.

One time, after wandering through Paris all night long, seemingly looking for someone, they ended up in Rungis. "This is the largest wholesale food market in the world," he told her "Whatever you want to buy, someone will sell it to you here."

It felt like the middle of the night but the market teemed with frantic activity. Althea gasped at the scale of what lay before her eyes: Entire animals hung on hooks, live geese in cages, piles of dead rabbits, croaking frogs, snails, fish by the bushel, head and tails attached. Odors. She should not have been surprised. In France, she had discovered, everything, the most disgusting things, were intended to be eaten. The ground was littered with bruised vegetables, feathers, crushed ice, straw, cigarette butts. She was overtaken with nausea between wheels of cheese piled like tires and black mushrooms that smelled of rot.

"The French are obsessed with food."

"Whatever little happiness you can steal in a day seems like a good idea to me," Jared had said.

There was never an instant when she was not terrified that Jared could turn towards her and realize his mistake. There was no reason he wanted to spend time with her at all, at least no reason he cared to give her. Just the same, at every street corner, every pause in this frenetic search for nothing, Althea dreamed, hoped, begged new and ancient gods that Jared would kiss her. But though he incomprehensibly held her hand tight and sat close to her in the métro, this he never did. Her nights with Jared were spent in a state of awakened dreaming and ended when he eventually took her back to Annie's house, opened the door for her, walked up the stairs with her, deposited her back in her room, in her world, and then left. The first time he took her out, she thought it had been a fluke. The next evening though, he had come back. Every night after that she had wondered if it was the last time, but every time he had come back.

In her bedroom, Althea was done with the drawing. She tossed it in the trash. There was no more paper. She looked at the clock. Ten at night. Jared would soon be there she hoped, to rescue her for her main preoccupation, defined in her mind as "Not Calling Mom." The obsession took over most of her waking hours and resulted in crippled sleep and circular thinking. She was in turns heartbroken and furious with her mother, emotions that soon morphed into self-loathing and confusion as she waited for sundown. It was in that state of anguish and suspended animation that she counted the minutes until Jared reappeared into her life.

❦

Annie had not mentioned anything about her new clothes, the cute striped T-shirt, the new sandals, the pedicure, nor had she talked about her desire to cook leaner food to Lola who, she felt, was a bit too self-involved to notice details about other people. Annie tossed her cookbooks one by one onto the kitchen table. How was it possible none of them contained a single recipe that wasn't laced with butter, cream, starches and carbohydrates? No more buying cookbooks on an empty stomach.

She heard the distinct sound of her front door opening followed by mild cursing en français announcing that Lucas had let himself in and that she had therefore forgotten to lock the front door again. How predictable the man, how predictable the woman, how predictable the situation. Never mind food, a battle of a different nature was afoot. She braced herself, pretended to be absorbed in her cookbook.

Lucas entered the kitchen in a huff. "Your front door was open."

"Hello to you, too," she cooed.

"You didn't lock. Again!"

"And?"

When Lucas was mad, his accent was even cuter. "Eets not safe to leave your front door open."

She didn't look up from her cookbook. "Eet's my house so I do what ees good for me!"

Lucas paced around the kitchen. "Is this new?" he said.

"What's new?"

"Your clothes?"

She shook her head, feeling terribly embarrassed, like she had

231

been caught in the act of being vain. "Nah," she answered. Lucas was getting a tad hunchbacked with age, but to be objective, he was still a pretty handsome guy. That's how nature was so unfair. The Sean Connery Syndrome is what she called it. Ameliorate versus deteriorate, the unjust advantage man gets over woman as age ripens one and withers the other.

"You could be wrong about leaving your door open," he said. "You just could be wrong! And what happens then?"

"There's nothing of value in this house except for your god-awful TV."

"My TV?" Lucas choked on the injustice. He stirred the air with wide arm gestures. "I don't care about robberies. I care about some maniac," which he pronounced maniackeh, "coming to...I don't know..."

"A rapist?" Annie pondered. "Now of course the upside is that I'd finally get laid."

"Don't say things like this!" Lucas said, horrified.

She looked up from her cookbook at last and flashed him an utterly innocent look. "Now what did I say?"

Lucas stopped pacing and crossed his arms. "Are you telling me the reason you leave your door open is that you want sex?"

She shrugged. "No one's exactly banging on my door to...bang me, so why not?" The conversation was turning to a direction that had very little to do with the unlocked door.

Lucas uncrossed his arms, tapped the side of his cheek as though he was deep in thought. "Are you saying that all that stands between danger and a locked door is sex?"

Annie challenged him, raised her chin with apparent relief. "Are you finally offering your services here? At last! I thought you would never offer."

In the kitchen, a spring breeze gently moved the muslin curtains, and Annie heard the chirping birds that were taking over her blossoming garden. What in the world was she saying?

Lucas's eyes smiled with the kind of blazing gaze that only

Frenchmen can muster without commanding an immediate slap across the face. "It would be my pleasure," he said.

It was the way he said it. With that voice and the smirk, she found herself cooking from her head to her toes. A deeper shade of crimson than anything Althea could have produced. Annie sprang to her feet and advanced towards the sink to hide her face and that stupid blush. "Yeah, right, anytime!" she muttered.

Lucas walked backward out of the kitchen. "I... have to go. I'll lock the door behind me, d'accord?"

"D'accord, whatever," she yelled back.

She sat back down, and read the same line in the cookbook twenty times, smiling to herself like a nincompoop.

CHAPTER 20

$\mathcal{A}$lthea instinctively began to shadow Jared's rhythm, like a mother resigned to getting sleep only when her baby does. She first fought the self-discipline that had always dictated she rise and go to bed early, but after a few days of staying up all night with him, she surrendered to going to sleep at sun up and not rising until the early afternoon. When they came back from their night in the city, Jared accompanied her to her room then went to his. If he fell asleep easily or not, her own sleep was uneasy, her ears vigilant for the familiar stirring in the next room, the moment when he would wake up sometime after two in the afternoon. Through difficult dreams where she was at war with the world, she heard him take showers in the bathroom, dress, walk down the stairs, and leave the house. After he was gone, she was left to wait for him. She passed the time by taking interminable baths, experimenting with Lola's makeup, working the eyeliner with increased expertise, drawing on everything she could put her hands on. She waited impatiently for the times when she could find herself alone in the house. Then she felt free to move about and inspect the bedrooms, the closets, inside the refrigerator, the content of trashcans, cupboards, laundry baskets. She thought of what she would change, what she would clean, what she would keep and what she would throw away if this were to be hers and Jared's house. In Lola's room, there weren't any more letters in the trash, but in Annie's trashcan she was surprised to find strange new things. Today a pair of men's shoes, the next day a man's hat, photographs, even a watch one day. This bothered her. She had preferred Annie's compulsion to keep her dead husband's belongings. She herself had a small stash of things that Jared had left behind in her room: a T-shirt, an old métro pass with his photograph, an empty lighter which she hid under her bed in the darkest corner next to the wall.

She liked being in the kitchen alone the most, boiling water, making and sipping tea and feeling the twists and turns of hunger traveling through her body. While the water boiled in the teapot, she passed her fingers over shelves sticky with honey, oil and crumbs. In the back of the shelves were small bottles, walnut oil, truffle oil, and tiny jars of mustard, maple syrup, broken pepper grinders, Asian spices, Tagine mix, flour in paper bags. She climbed on chairs to peer through deeper discarded layers of hardened packets of brown sugar, expired cans of beans and corn, two hundred euros in a tin can, and little glass bottles she opened one by one and smelled. They had pretty names: vanille, essence d'amande, eau de rose, eau de violette. Some were full, some so old the contents had evaporated and all that was left were thick smelly substances at the bottom. She was fascinated with every corner of the house, the smell of mildew and food, the dust, the mess, the discarded objects, the abundance of useless things, the dough rising on the counter top, the fabric littered around the sewing machine, the seedlings growing under windows, everything in progress, nothing ever completed. She felt the burning desire to put things away, to discard, to clean, to make it perfect, to finish things for Annie. But this was not her house. She was not allowed.

Jared did not need a house, she thought. He might need a

place to sleep and bathe, but the rest of the time, he was in motion. What was Jared doing between the time he woke up in the afternoon, and sundown when he came back to the house to eat with her, an occupation she now thought of as 'feeding time'? She wished she could ask him that question, but such was not the nature of their relationship. But what was the nature of their relationship?

Was it a relationship?

What she ought to do, while she waited for Jared, was call her mother. But this simple act was beyond her capacity. All she could do was think of calling her mother and marvel at the relief she experienced from not calling.

When the house filled with noise again, she retreated to her bedroom, sat at her desk, and doodled on Post-Its, bits of construction paper leftover from the children's homework, even cigarette paper and the backs of subway tickets.

A few nights earlier, she and Jared were sitting at a bar. While Jared spoke with an acquaintance in a French much too rapid for her to follow, she had doodled on the back of his beer coaster. She had felt Jared's eyes on her hand. "Tu dessines bien," he said. You draw well. This was a statement, not necessarily a compliment, neither was it a mark of surprise. She did not see him pocket her drawing, a jumble of branches and birds, and she was shocked to find it pinned above her desk the next day. "Tu ne jettes rien, d'accord?" he told her. Don't throw anything away. "You exhibit, now." So now she kept her doodles and scotch-taped them next to the first one and watched her wall come to life in a way that somehow made her proud.

Around dinnertime, they had a ritual. She waited in her room and Jared tapped at her bedroom door. He looked happy when he entered, smelling of cigarettes and coffee and carrying a tray with their dinner. Here too she had resigned to follow his cue. This would be her only meal of the day. They ate it as they sat cross-legged on her bed, the tray of food between them. Jared ate but mostly watched her eat. When he was not satisfied with the way things were going, for example if she took too small a bite, or if she slowed down her eating, he would take his fork and food to her lips. She agonized about every bite and worried about the food that would be digested before she could get rid of it in the bathroom.

She wasn't sure what to make of Jared's obsession with food and began to hope it meant that he loved her. She wondered what would happen if he did not come. She wondered if she would be too embarrassed to go downstairs and ask for food herself.

❦

Lola sat on the edge of her bed next to Lia in the girly pink room, under the canopy sprinkled with silk daisies. Lia was inconsolable. Her face was in her hands and her thin shoulders moved with each silent sob as Simon, seemingly oblivious, nudged coins between the cracks of the old wood floor and under the rug.

She wanted to caress Lia's hair, but stopped herself—Like Mark, Lia had trouble expressing emotions other than anger—and waited. She hoped this was about a fight with the boys. She hoped it was about school. She hoped it was anything but the topic of Mark, a topic avoided in an unspoken agreement. Why did Lia no longer bring up her dad? Did her daughter understand it all but refuse to ask for fear of getting her worst fears confirmed? Was Lola tricking herself into thinking that Lia and Simon weren't traumatized?

Lia lifted her head finally, and looked at her through tears and fire. "You're so mean!" she cried.

Up until she met Annie, Lola believed it was a good mother's job to be her child's emotional punching bag. If not your mother, then who? Now she wasn't so sure how to react to Lia's anger. "What did I do this time?" she asked. Her sarcasm was really Annie's sarcasm, but in her own mouth it sounded awful.

Lia looked at her in disbelief. Tears sprang from her eyes. "Why aren't we going home? Why can't we see Daddy? Why isn't Daddy calling? Why aren't we calling him?"

There it was, Lola thought. There it was. Words throbbed to get out. Lia needed to know that Lola was the victim! Lia needed to know that it was in fact Mark who had abandoned them by not loving them the way they needed to be loved. But really it was all so unclear. Who was the victim and who was the perpetrator? It took every ounce of her strength not to fall to her knees and beg Lia and Simon for forgiveness. What little strength she found at that moment she extracted from herself by thinking of Annie, who knew better than to frighten her children with her own weaknesses.

Simon walked toward the door. "Where are you going, love," she asked.

"I play with the boys," Simon answered casually as he left the room. Lola saw it as a parable of women's condition. Boys went into the world and women stuck around and wrung their hands.

"Lia, these are very good questions," she said, her words like cotton in her mouth. "You know things between grown-ups get very complicated sometimes. Your daddy loves you and your brother so much, but right now, he and I are taking some time apart. We're taking a little break from each other." Those were vapid words she would have considered an insult to Lia's intelligence if she hadn't been the one forced to use them. "It's just temporary," she added, not knowing if this was even a possibility any more.

"I want to go home. Why aren't we going home? We're not going to stay here forever, are we?" Lia cried. She was working herself into a tizzy. Girls. Lola had never been like this, maybe there lay the problem. Not that she wasn't feeling hysterical herself, panicked suddenly, because, though theoretically Lola never gave Mark a way to reach them in France, had he really wanted them, had he really wanted her... For a man of such means and resourcefulness, there must have been ways....

"Don't you like it here?" she asked emptily. "We've made good friends...we're pretty happy here, aren't we?" That was, of course, beside the point.

"This isn't our real home," Lia spat. "They aren't my real friends. I hate French people. I want to see Daddy." Then she added, her voice calmer, "Do you think Daddy could come here and live with us in France?"

Lia liked it here! "Honey!" Lola mechanically braided Lia's hair. But Lia didn't want physical contact. She might have needed it as desperately as Lola needed it, but not now, and not from her mom. She cringed and moved away, and Lola hated her daughter for a flashing instant.

The hope, she realized now, had been that Mark would crack. That he'd crack and run back to her. She had read too many romance novels. Mark's aloofness broke her heart. She was much more comfortable with his tantrums that gave her the illusion of attachment. In more ways than one, she was the one who was "cracking."

"It's your dad and me, Lia. We're not getting along. We both love you guys so much." Lola cringed at her own cliché. "But there was so much screaming and fighting at home."

"Daddy is always screaming at you," Lia said. She wasn't crying suddenly. "Are you going to get a divorce?"

Lola swallowed, "We haven't used that word," she lied. "We're taking some time apart to figure things out." Lies and clichés.

"Rebecca at school, her parents are divorced," Lia said matter-of-factly.

"That's...that's true."

"But she sees her mom every weekend."

"Her dad takes care of her?"

"I don't want Daddy to take care of me. I want you to take

care of me, and Simon. I don't want to go back home to Bel Air and never see you anymore." She burst into tears again. "Is that what would happen?"

Lia had just articulated Lola's deepest terror. Her throat constricted, she was only able to let out a small "You, you're going to see me every day."

"I want to see Dad every day, too."

"Of course, baby. Of course you do. And he wants to see you."

"I think he doesn't care about me so much," Lia wept.

"That's nonsense. He's crazy about you!"

"But he's not crazy about you, is he?"

The comment hurt Lola terribly. She had believed for so long that she and Mark couldn't live apart, that they loved and needed each other despite the indignities, that the family was the priority to both of them. "I...just don't know...what he thinks. Sometimes, loving someone is good, but not enough. You have to treat the people you love right. That's what I want Daddy to do. Treat me nice."

"I hate it when he screams."

"It's scary," Lola agreed.

"Did you tell him that?" Lia raised her shoulders and her mouth made a grimace of contempt that made her look like the teenager she would one day become. "What's the point, he never listens."

Lola felt small. "Not as much as I'd like," she whispered.

"I'll tell him then." Lia jumped to her feet and faced her mom, her expression tight with determination. "That's what I'll do. I'll tell him that we'll come back if he stops screaming all the time. That's what I should tell him." Lola, felt too overwhelmed to answer. Lia continued, "I'll write him a letter, that way he can't interrupt!"

Despite her anguish, Lola burst into laughter. "You know your father pretty well."

"I'm a good negotiator, too. Remember when he didn't want

me to go to that sleepover at Joshua's, and I convinced him, and he said I was a good negotiator, remember?"

"I remember."

"Okay. I'll do it right now."

Lia went to Lola's desk, took a pen and paper and began writing. She watched Lia and felt elated. They had communicated. This was for real. But as Lia wrote, hunched at the desk, Lola understood what she had to do next: Follow her child's example and face Mark.

A superhighway of ants crawled from under the garage door to the kitchen, to the sink, and industriously blackened every inch of the dirty dishes that filled the sink and marred the countertop. Mark observed the ants from his seat at the kitchen island as he chewed his Stouffer frozen pizza. Selena had quit two weeks before and things were going to the dogs but he didn't really care. He swallowed the last of the pizza, reached for the can of Raid, and discharged a long spray of ant-and-roach killer in the direction of the sink. He watched the ants wither and die wondering if this would be enough to send him to hell.

What he thought was the flu had turned into something else. He wasn't going to the office and when the office called he had a hard time picking up the phone. He had decided to stay home, skipping showers and shaving for a few more days. The phone was ringing. Again, he hoped it was Lola and not the office. But it was never Lola and it was always the office. He picked up the receiver.

"I think I've found her," said a man's voice.

Mark sprang to his feet. "How? Where is she?"

"She's definitely in Paris," the voice said. "I have an address. Do you want me to fly there? Take pictures?"

"No, no…not yet. I need to think. I'll call you back."

Mark hung up the phone feeling lighter than he had in weeks. He imagined himself arriving at the door of some French hotel, she falling into his arms, the kids... but the memory of their last phone conversation came to him again, like a vice on his heart. He had tried to play it smooth and had said all the wrong things. It had started with Lola asking him if he was "doing okay" and it had pissed him off that she would do something so wrong and selfish and then expect reassurance that it didn't affect him.

He had tried to be funny. "Oh, just peachy," he had said. "You know, making money, playing strip poker with my girlfriends."

There had been a mundane exchange then Lola said, "I've been thinking of the reasons I left. I think it also has to do with needing to do something worthwhile with my life."

"That's ridiculous," he had answered. "Of course you do things that are worthwhile."

"I'm not even raising my own children."

"What kind of bull is that?"

"The nannies. You think the nannies are better than me. You won't even trust me to be a mother to my children."

Mark had rolled his eyes to the ceiling. "That is bar none the most ridiculous accusation I have ever heard. The nannies are for you, Lola, not for me. Everybody does it. You can free up time to—"

"To accompany you on business trips?" she had interrupted. "I end up leaving the kids for days at a time. You don't know how much I've cried in those hotel rooms while you were doing business."

"You never said anything!"

"It's always about what you want, and what you think, Mark. I was afraid to disappoint you."

"It looks like you've conquered your fear all right. Well good news, the nanny quit, and so did the maid. When you get back home there will be no one left to blame!"

"You want to know why I left? For this! This very comment!"

"What? What did I say?"

"Do you even hear yourself?" Lola said angrily. "Calling me a parasite all the time?"

"But I didn't call you a..."

"And screaming at me and putting me down?"

Lola barely sounded like herself. He did not know how to respond to her aggressiveness. "Is that all?" he asked.

"You won't change," Lola had said flatly.

"I'm too dumb, eh?"

"To change, you'd have to see that the way you do things doesn't work."

"Oh, spare me the psychoanalysis."

"It's always about what others have done wrong. Heads have to roll."

"If you were so miserable, why didn't you say so?"

"I was terrified of speaking to you."

"What stopped you?"

Lola had sounded incredulous. "What stopped me?" She breathed in. "You can't be asking that question! How about your uncontrollable, violent anger? How about the names you called me? Do you at all realize how unforgivable you've been, and how much I have forgiven you anyway?"

"Oh!" he said, furious now. "Because you think that your resentment didn't seep out continuously?"

"You've got an anger problem. Of course I had resentment," Lola had exclaimed.

"Disappearing like this, and now all this crap about being afraid and not wanting nannies? Make up your fucking mind, Lola."

"You're out of control, and I can't stand it!" she said.

The bitch! He had felt the rage rise in him like a damned Godzilla out of the waters. He had yelled, "You want a divorce? Say it, for Christ's sake!"

"I don't want a divorce," Lola had cried. "I want a good marriage."

He was not listening anymore. He was screaming. "We have a good marriage! We have a freaking mansion, we..." Mark searched for proof. "You have a life of leisure!"

"Mark, you're in denial," had come Lola's cold voice.

"You have to come back Lola, by law! I'll sue your ass!" was all he could think of saying.

By that point, Lola was sobbing on the line. "I...I'm not ready. And with that attitude, I don't know if I ever will be."

"Then screw your attitude," he screamed. "Fuck you, Lola!"

When he realized that Lola had hung up, he had hurled the receiver against the wall. The phone had smashed into pieces that scattered around the kitchen with earsplitting violence. Days later, the shards of phone were still there on the floor, telling him more about himself than he wanted to know. He could have picked them up, yet part of him was interested in what the remnants of the telephone were saying. Never mind the ants, this was what he would go to hell for. For that broken phone. For that fury that overtook him and was long past his ability to control.

Up until this moment, he had been focused on the private investigator and finding Lola. But now that he had tracked her down, he realized it might be too late. She had not really been found. In fact, she might be lost to him now.

Mark opened his wallet and took out the card. Larry had given him the card, Larry, his boxing coach, of all people. The irony wasn't lost on him. When your boxing coach hands you the card of a shrink who deals with anger management, you know you've got a problem. Mark rubbed his eyes and neck and dialed the shrink's number.

CHAPTER 21

*A*nnie slipped into her shorts, and it was a delicious feeling. The zipper zipped a nice smooth zip. She didn't even need to hold her stomach in. She turned around, looked at her butt. Nice! Feeling like a runway model, she descended to the garden in shorts and a tank top. The heat wave, unseasonable for May, had metamorphosed the garden in a few days. The clematis burst with pale pink flowers, the air was heavy with the scent of wisteria and leaf buds practically opening before the eyes. The children in their bathing suits were running in and out of the house and Lola was sun tanning in her bikini, her skin gleaming with suntan lotion.

Annie had spent the winter hauling car-sized flagstones around and now the planting could start. She knelt in the musk-scented earth and got that feeling again. That feeling of urgency, that feeling that she was about to burst with…what? For half an hour, she raked the earth with her fingers, making small holes, separating flats of creeping thyme and baby's tears into small chunks and placing them in between the flagstone while the children pursued each other armed with loaded water pistols.

Lola turned away from the French magazine she was leafing

through. "I hate sunbathing marks. Would you mind if I do like the French and go topless?"

"Do I mind that you look this good? Of course no, why would I mind," Annie answered. She surprised herself for saying what was on her mind, and then realized that the reason she could say it was because Lola's beauty no longer raised red flags in her. She and Lola were as different as night and day, but she had dropped at least twelve pounds and felt better than she had in years, light and diaphanous, practically waif-like. But it wasn't just the weight. It was something else that had to do with Lucas telling her she had a backbone, and that she was the full package and whatever other silly thing he had said but that for some reason made her suddenly feel attractive.

She lifted her face towards Althea's bedroom window, and sure enough, there was Althea, watching them. Was she waiting for an authorization to join the fun? Or was she just being creepy? She waved at Althea to come down but Althea disappeared from the window. A few minutes later, to her surprise, Althea materialized in the garden. She wore winter clothes, black pants, black turtleneck and heavy black makeup around her eyes. She would never understand how this girl functioned. Althea was, according to Maxence, "Turning emo" which she understood was the new Goth. Althea plopped down on a plastic chaise like a teenager who wants to be there but resents it all the same.

"Take some clothes off," Annie suggested. "Lola did and she feels much better. See…look."

Althea glanced in the direction of Lola's bare breasts and quickly looked away.

"Lola is busy acting French so she cannot be disturbed at the moment."

Lola glanced above an obsolete Paris Match. "You betcha," she said and resumed her inaction.

The children came running from the house and spilled into

the backyard followed by Lia in tears. Althea sprang to her feet in reflex, and Annie had the notion that Althea was experiencing Lola's nudity like it was her own.

"What's going on in there?" she asked Maxence.

Lia was drenched, "They ganged up on me," she wailed. "They wet me!"

"So, isn't that the whole point?" Annie wondered out loud to Lola who shrugged behind her magazine. Lia noticed her mom.

"Ewww...Mom!"

"Maxence, no water balloons in the house," Annie yelled without conviction.

Maxence, followed by Paul, Laurent, and Simon, stomped into the yard. Her boys all ignored Lola. They had seen bare breasts at the beach their entire life. "It's just a few tiny drops. It's not gonna kill her."

"Just sit out there and be quiet. All of you." Annie said.

"Can't you find anything to keep yourselves occupied without killing each other?" Lola asked behind her magazine.

"No, we're bored." Simon said.

Althea got up from her plastic chair and walked towards the kitchen. She almost entered the house, then turned back towards the garden, looked away, and said to no one in particular, "We can do something if you guys have washable markers." Annie had to hold onto her trowel not to fall. She did a quick glance in the direction of Lola who glanced back.

"It's not a school day. I'm not doing crafts," Maxence said.

"I mean," Althea said timidly, "maybe, if you want, I'll tattoo you."

Maxence perked up. "Cool!"

Lia shook her head. "I'm not doing it."

"Not on the face, no blood, no profanity, no weapons," Annie said.

Lola folded her magazine and got up. Her bare breasts shone with oil and looked a lot like torpedoes. "I'm off to yoga," she said.

Annie pursed her lips, "Not in this accoutrement I hope!"

Annie resumed her planting and watched from the corner of her eye the unlikely scene unfolding. She didn't know what was most unlikely, the children cooperating, Althea taking an initiative, or the fact that Althea had a secret talent. Out in the sun-drenched garden, Althea used a thin black marker and began to draw patterns of entangled animals, dragons, lizards, bees, and unicorns on Maxence's arms and torso. She drew precisely and without hesitation, as if she were merely reproducing the figures. She was indefatigable even as the boys wanting their turns harassed her by calling out names of animals or superheroes they wanted on their bodies. She drew without small talk and certainly without pretending to play with them. In her expression, all Annie could see was an artist at work, completely engrossed in what she was doing. When Lia volunteered to color in the drawings to make them look like real tattoos, Althea let her without seeming the least bit territorial about her creation.

After a while, Annie stopped pretending to garden and went to sit next to them to watch Althea work. By the time Lola came back two hours later from her first yoga class as a teacher, the children were covered in drawings and Althea was putting the finishing touches on the garland of flowers that circled Lia's arms. Annie, sunburned and covered with dirt was taking pictures.

"She's good," Lola whispered.

"She's damn good," Annie said.

They both looked at Althea, not knowing what to think.

Lucas peered above his Armani sunglasses. On the north side of center court, in the bleachers, Jared's black silhouette moved past pastel Lacoste shirts and wide-brim hats. Then back the other way when he realized he was on the wrong side of the bleachers.

Second row seat at Roland Garros, and Jared was forty-five minutes late!

Jared came to sit beside him. They followed the yellow ball from one racket, to the clay, to another racket and back, the set ending with a murmur of discontent from the audience. Lucas wore a white polo shirt and light seersucker pants appropriate for the time, place, and heat wave. "Aren't you hot?" he asked. Jared seemed to realize only then that he was, and removed his coat. He was too pale and did not look healthy at all. Lucas took a sip of Evian and offered him a bottle.

"You need some sun," he said. "You live at night—" He was interrupted by a cheer from the crowd. One of the players had removed his shirt. "American players have no class. Do you see Europeans doing this? No. How are things with your damsel in distress?"

Jared looked at him and frowned. "Who?"

"That, that creature. Althea. Lovely, really. Only—"

"How is it going with Annie?" Jared interrupted.

Lucas shook his head. "Ah! Annie. The other day in her kitchen, I came on to her." He sighed. "I don't know what possessed me. It was unpremeditated, awful. I made a terrible fool of myself. There's so little alone time with her and with Lola being there all the time, there is so much flirting and joking going on. I'm at the mercy of two irresistible females. The last thing I need is for Annie to see me as a buffoon with too much testosterone."

Jared shrugged, "Don't you think it's about time to be more direct? Haven't you wasted enough time? Years, in fact?"

Lucas continued with his train of thought. "Annie's more self-sufficient than ever. Of course, it also confirms my positive opinion of her. She is not needy. I don't think I've ever been with a woman who wasn't needy one way or another." Lucas turned and looked at Jared. "I want to warn you about that."

"What?"

"Needy women."

"I don't need any warning."

"That lovely young woman, of course. Althea? Right? Youth, beauty, they can be quite manipulative. Annie is a different woman entirely: strong, smart, autonomous."

"Annie's a pain in the ass."

"That's because you're not living up to your potential! At least with Annie, I know where I stand."

"Do you really?"

"At least I'm not manipulated."

"Not manipulated?" Jared stood up. "You're the Testosterone Buffoon."

"Ah, merde!" Lucas said as the players walked back on the court. "How am I going to fix this?" he asked. But Jared was already gone.

❦

Althea had taken to wandering the streets around the house while waiting for her time with Jared. The day was overwhelmingly hot and the house had no air conditioning, which turned her room under the roof into a furnace. She walked and stopped in front of a store she had noticed before. The name of the shop was "librairie traditionelle," an old-fashioned book and art supply store. As she entered, she was welcomed by the jingle of a bell placed on the door. Inside, it was as cool and quiet as the street had been sweltering and busy. The store smelled of chalk, books and ink. She moved around the cramped alleys and shelves heavy with merchandise, letting her fingers caress the various surfaces. She did not know why she had stopped there or what she was looking for. Her fingers recognized the sensation first. Papier Canson, one of the finest papers in the world.

Her dad had given Althea her first drawing pad for her eighth birthday. It had a black cover and the pages were thick and smooth. Each year on her birthday, she'd go to the store and choose a new one. She drew everything and everywhere. She drew during school. She drew at home when her parents watched TV. She'd sit on a bench at the playground and draw. She liked that kids and even adults looked over her shoulder as she drew, and often complimented her. She wanted to take lessons one day to become an artist. By the time she was fourteen, she had filled every page of six sketchpads. When she was fifteen, they moved. In her new bedroom, Althea had already put away the content of every box of her belongings when she realized her pads were missing.

"Mom, I can't find something."

Her mom had been frazzled from the move, her patience was thin that year and she was smoking more than ever. She blew a cloud of angry smoke at her. "What's missing?"

"My drawing pads."

"I can't keep every single shred of paper this family produces. Don't be ridiculous."

Althea had screamed and sobbed and yelled at her mom. As a result, she had been slapped and grounded. She then stopped drawing.

Althea admired the ancient wood shelves, the rows of inks, paint tubes and pigments arranged by hues, then she went back to the area for drawing paper and pads. She opened a couple of pads, smelled them, felt their grain with the palm of her hand. There was something noble about blank white paper, something that made her heart flutter.

Jared saw things the way artists did, which was also the way she used to see things. He noticed every inch of her face and body when he painted her. He looked at what she ate, and how she ate. He looked at how she walked. He observed the way she held her spoon, the way she put on her shoes. It was exhilarating and terrifying, to be watched like this.

Her mother was the opposite: completely self-involved. She

didn't care about her daughter's needs, or talent. Her mother had neglected Althea and rejected anything she did that was short of devoting her life to her mom. Her throat tightened.

She bought a vellum pad and a box of expensive pastels. Forgetting the heat, she hurried back to the house, holding the paper bag against her chest like a shield. She immediately dialed the number. In Cincinnati, it was the heart of the night. Her mom's voice came, apprehensive, disoriented. "Hello?"

"It's me."

Apprehension dropped out of her mother's voice to be replaced by anger. "Why are you calling us at three in the morning?"

Althea's fists tightened. "Hi."

"I certainly hope you're not waking us in the middle of the night just to say hello."

"I. Said. Hi," Althea repeated between clenched teeth.

Her mother's voice turned to ice. "What is your problem?"

"You're not dying. That's the problem!" Althea screamed.

"What's wrong with you?"

Althea looked at her face in the mirror as she screamed at her mother. "Everything is wrong with me, and you don't give a shit about me."

"At three in the morning—"

"I've worried about you my whole life. I've spent my whole life thinking you'd die if I weren't around. I'm in Paris, and you're not dying. You're just fine without me. You've never even bothered to ask for my number here. You only think of yourself."

"I won't stand for this."

Althea wasn't sure of the nature of her tears. Sadness, relief, rage? "It's me, Mom. ME! I exist, you know."

"I have no idea what you are saying."

"How sad I feel? How depressed I am? How lonely I am? I'm invisible to you. And to Dad."

Annie entered the room carrying a pile of dinner plates.

Althea didn't care. Annie placed the plates in the cabinet, gave Althea a quick two thumbs-up and left the room.

"Are those French people putting ideas in your head?" her mother screeched. "You hate America now, and your parents? Why am I not surprised?"

"Well, at least I'm not invisible here." Althea understood now. It wasn't just about Jared. They accepted her here. More than her mom ever had. Here she was herself. She didn't have to be pleasing. She could have a fit. They all could. It was all right.

"Good for you. Stay there then. We don't need that attitude here in America."

"I can stay in pajamas all day here, and leave my room in a mess. I can be lazy. I can be useless!" Althea knew how silly this was, yet how true.

Her mother's precise voice came across the phone line. "Useless? Isn't that what you've always been, Althea?"

This, Althea saw, wasn't going to be the usual pummeling. This was her first fight with her mother, a fight where she could punch back. "I'm glad you're saying that, Mom. I'm glad. Because it shows you're a mean bitch. And a shitty mother."

"You, you...Look at yourself in the mirror."

"As a matter of fact, I am looking at myself in the mirror," Althea said. "I'm looking at myself in the mirror, and I'm holding my head up. I'm looking straight into my own eyes and making the decision not to talk to you anymore."

And Althea hung up.

After dropping off Simon at daycare, Lola walked fast along rue de la Pompe. Her previously frightful anxious baby had simply waved goodbye. She and Lia had changed in just a short time in Paris, but Simon was the one who had made the most astonishing transformation.

Lola looked so unlike herself these days, and at the same time, she looked at long last like herself. Oh, she was a mess by any standard. Her hair was bicolor now: an inch of blond hair at the root, and an inch of jet black at the tip. She used Lia's barrettes to keep her hair out of her face while it grew out. She wore no make-up and lived in Birkenstocks. Over her yoga clothes she had put on a sweater that had belonged to Johnny and that she had rescued from the trash can.

Why did she feel perfectly at ease looking entirely unstylish in a city where appearance was laced with codes and rules? Why was it that unlike in Los Angeles where she felt she never looked perfect enough, in Paris she felt just fine dressed in rags? Of course, there was the daily reinforcement from unknown men willing to stop her in the street just to tell her she was beautiful, the fact that age didn't seem to matter here as French men celebrated women of all ages and flirted almost as though not flirting would have been the rude thing to do. And women flirted right back. She saw it happen all around. French life was all about men and women playing, enjoying each other.

She had other reasons to feel beautiful. She felt much lighter on an emotional level. Mark had set her free in a way during their last phone conversation. He had been despicable. Out of control. His absolute inability to reach out to her, his condemnation of everything she represented, his utter lack of effort to win her back had been sobering. That conversation had been followed by an entire night of tears, much like a giant draining of every cell of her body. In the morning, she had felt brand new. It was as though years of anxiety and tension had melted off her shoulders, her face, her skin. If Mark did not want her anymore, if he wasn't planning on taking her back, then she needed to start life anew, just like Annie had after Johnny had died. Wasn't it almost the same? Mark was, in fact, dead to her, and she to him.

She entered the building through the arched doorway, she felt the coolness of the stones reverberate on her skin and climbed the stairs towards the Yoga studio. In the staircase, she said bonjour to two women who had come a few minutes early to get a better spot in the room. She wondered if he would come today. With her own key, she opened the door to the studio. It was the first time she had done that, and her throat tightened. How long since she had last felt in control of her life? How long since she had last experienced her life through her own perceptions, not Mark's? Owning a key to the studio made her the official teacher. Substitute teacher, but teacher nonetheless. She belonged here. Even as a model, she had been somebody's tool. With yoga, she was not only belonging, she was contributing. For the first time in years, she felt capable, and important.

Fellow yogis walked in behind her and unrolled their yoga mats at the front of the class, close to where Lola would be putting hers. As yogis entered the yoga studio, they exchanged the French ritual of a kiss on each cheek and whispered a few words.

Lola turned on a switch. In the center of the ceiling, where intricate stucco molding remained from a time when the superfluous was essential, the single immense crystal chandelier reflected the light like drops of sunshine. She opened a window to let the warm air mix in with the pungent scent of the room, a mix of wood wax, incense, and humidity, that timeless scent she associated now with yoga, and with Paris.

The room was vast and the walnut floor, which the instructors took turns waxing meticulously, a floor probably as old as the building, had a patina so lustrous that it seemed alive under her bare feet. Lola had fallen in love with this room the first time she had come here for a class over three months ago. Now, she was the one giving the class. Those years of practice when she clung to yoga like a buoy did have a purpose in the end.

The room filled with mats and students. Lola discreetly searched among the faces and glanced too many times in the direction of the door. She inserted a CD of Indian chants into the CD player and felt a thrill when he entered. He was German and she had found out his name was Gunter. He looked younger than she by a good ten years and had the graceful musculature of a cat. The first detail she had noticed about him was the blond hair on his arms. He looked absolutely delicious. There had been enough looks between them to give her a sense that he was attracted to her as well. When her glance met his piercing blue eyes, he always seemed to smile in a slightly ironic way that made her feel weak in the legs.

Once he asked her if she'd like to have coffee after class. She had said, "No thanks." He had said, "Maybe another time." She had flirted back, "Maybe," before running off. Since then he had always left before she could continue to play hard to get.

She read some well-prepared words in French that Annie had translated for her.

"Thank yourself for coming to practice today."

She began her class by demonstrating, then moving among the mats to alter postures. She walked by Gunter's mat and paused, mesmerized by the pearls of sweat on his flexible back. She moved on to the following asana.

Later, when the mats were rolled back, and the class had ended, when shoes were gone from the floor and the students had waved good-bye, Lola gathered her CDs and closed the window. She turned toward the door, and her heart leaped in her chest.

Gunter was standing by the open door, watching her with his smiling eyes. Her heart started beating way too fast. He extended an arm and shut the door. Now it was just the two of them in the beautiful room. He turned the key in the lock and walked toward her, still looking into her eyes until they faced each other.

She liked that he was taller than she was. She didn't budge. I'm breathing in. I'm breathing out, she repeated to herself, but her breath was heavy. They stood in the center of the wooden floor, surrounded by the whiteness of the walls and the soft light in a room that suddenly felt immense. He kissed her neck. She stopped breathing. He kissed her mouth and she opened her lips. He slowly proceeded to undress her, right there in the middle of the empty room and she had never felt so deliciously naked. He caressed her body with the tips of his fingers, taking his time as she waited, breathlessly for more.

ॐ

Outside Bistro de l'Aval, the thunder and lightning came simultaneously, and rain began dropping from the sky with the force of a waterfall. The humidity was quickly transforming the place into a sauna as Parisians began flocking in for refuge. From their table near the fogged-up window, Annie watched the servers, the maître d', the owner and his wife, all of whom she knew by name, go into overdrive. In minutes, tables for four had to accommodate six, the floor was becoming dangerously slippery, and the smell of wet coats and wet hair overpowered the smell of Plat du Jour.

Lola, using her fork to hunt bits of olives and anchovies the chef had refused to leave out of her Salade Niçoise, was describing in whispers what had happened at the studio with Gunter. Annie stabbed her grillade for relief, but it gave her none. She gave up on eating, stopped chewing and dropped her fork and knife on the side of her plate as Lola went on, giggling away as she spoke, not even bothering to mask how thrilled she was.

"I don't think your husband actually meant it when he said you should have an affair," Annie said.

Lola beamed. "Do you think I planned this?"

"You took off the ring!" Annie accused.

"I must have been sending out 'I'm available' signals. Unconsciously."

Annie thought about this. If that was all it took, her own

signals must be very weak. "But what about Lucas? You told me you liked Lucas?" she said breathlessly.

"I like Gunter better."

"But you don't even know him!" she blurted out, scandalized.

Lola laughed. "Believe me. I know plenty now! And the best part is how perfectly uncomplicated it is." Lola put her hands over her face. "And oh my goodness... If you only knew the things he... did to me..."

"Tell me every detail," Annie said grimly as she cut a piece of grilled meat and put it in her mouth. Her grillade tasted like cardboard now.

"I don't know if I should, I'm a married woman," Lola said coyly.

"Now you feel married?"

People were continuing to crowd in. Wasn't it obvious they would never be able to accommodate everyone? Weren't there restaurant regulations about this? Annie's eyes searched for a sign indicating a maximum occupancy. The wool of her sweater made her neck itchy. Outside, thunder roared.

Lola leaned over the table. "It was the single sexiest, kinkiest experience of. My. Life!"

The word came out of Annie despite herself. "Ouch."

Lola opened her eyes wide, innocently. Was she finally aware of how insensitive she was being? "What's bothering you?" she asked. She really had no clue.

"No, please go ahead, rub my nose in it. I can only get laid vicariously, as you know."

Lola frowned, "Annie, you can get laid whenever you choose to."

"A widow with three kids, one mortgage, and an ass the size of the Arc de Triomphe doesn't choose when to get laid, Lola."

"This is Paris, the City of Love. Women are treated like goddesses. You can have any man you want!"

"Let me rephrase, Lola. You can have any man you want."

Annie felt dangerously close to crying, and over something so stupid. The bistro de l'Aval's owner, Monsieur François, a jovial man with a wide stomach and luxurious moustache had seemingly solved his crowd control issue by distributing glasses of wine and small dishes of olives, and now everyone was standing, chatting and drinking merrily. Annie cut her meat angrily and, without meaning to, raised her voice. "I've had four lovers in my life. Four! One, two, three, four. One I married, and the others were awful one-niters in my twenties. I'm aging and flabby." The end of her sentence distorted into a loud cry. "And no one is looking at me!"

Lola recoiled in her chair, her eyes darting to the other patrons. Tears began falling from Annie's eyes, as uncontrollable as the storm outside. Lola seemed to duck under the table, but she was only retrieving her purse, in which she hid her face in search of a tissue and whispered frantically "Shhh. I'd say everyone in the restaurant is looking at you now."

"They don't understand English," Annie wailed.

Lola looked supplicating. "Please... I hate being a spectacle."

Annie pointed an accusatory finger and raised her voice. "You get laid in the middle of a yoga class, and I'm the spectacle?"

Lola looked over her shoulder to discover half the restaurant staring. "Shhh... Annie, we were alone, of course!"

Annie gave up on controlling anything. She was bawling in front of the whole restaurant. "But what about meeeee?"

Lola looked about to run away from the table, but instead she said, "Here, I'll bet you a kilo of Gascogne foie gras that the owner thinks you're fetching."

"I'm only thirty-five!" Annie sobbed softly. "I could still have more babies."

"And I bet he would love nothing more than to get into your panties."

Annie blew her nose but tears were still falling freely down her cheeks. "I'm not dead down there you know."

Lola called out in despair, "Monsieur François!"

"Stop it," Annie said, wiping her eyes quickly. "I thought you hated being a spectacle."

"Well, this is a crisis." Lola made big motions with her arms. "Monsieur François!"

"Oh shut up, Lola! No! Don't do this! I forbid you!" Annie dabbed her eyes and smoothed her hair with the palm of her hand as Monsieur François approached their table, smiling and readjusting his necktie.

"We need your expertise," Lola said. "My friend here thinks that no man could possibly find her attractive."

Annie, her eyes red and puffy, recognized the absurdity of the situation, so she looked up at Monsieur François as though he were a worldwide authority on the matter.

Monsieur François straightened his posture and looked around him as though he was looking for hidden cameras. "C'est une blague?" Is this a joke?

"You see a lot of people every day," Lola said in her best French. "And as a man, what do you think?"

Monsieur François readjusted his sports coat. "I cannot speak for all men, bien sûr…"

Lola smiled encouragingly. "Of course."

He bent down so that his face would be at the same level as theirs and whispered in a seductive breath that smelled of cigarettes and red wine. "I can't be speaking for all men, but, I'd personally be happy to prove Madame l'Américaine, heu—"

"Annie," offered Lola.

"Madame Annie, can count on me to be her…Chevalier Servant. It would be a pleasure. As long as ma femme is left out of all this, of course." He stood up, caressed his moustache, and declared with loud panache as he walked off, "Two Moelleux au Chocolat, Gérard, on the house."

Annie and Lola had to duck under the table at the same time to hide their laughter.

CHAPTER 22

*A*lthea had been standing close to Jared at métro station Beaumesnil, her icy hand in his warm palm. It was just after dawn and they had been walking all night or so it seemed. Sleepless nights in the streets of Paris were adding up. She felt spent, exhausted, cold to the bone. Jared, unperturbed by the temperature or the early hour, seemed lost in his thoughts. What were his thoughts? The station was mostly empty aside from a dozen men and women already on their way to work. It smelled of coffee and perfume, of warm sheets and hot showers, of dreams being put back together like pieces of a jigsaw puzzle. Despite her exhaustion, she could not quiet down that newfound ability, that curse; she felt things now. Now she had desires and wants, she who had not cared about much of anything in her adult life. Even as they stood there in silence and exhaustion, she felt especially overwhelmed by her maddening need for Jared to tell her why he spent time with her. Who or what was she to him? Of course she did not dare ask. How she wanted Jared to kiss her. Why was he not kissing her? Did he not want to? But why then did he never let go of her hand? A frigid gust of wind found its way through the tunnels of the métro and through her clothes and she shivered violently.

"Tu as froid?" Jared asked, turning towards her. She nodded yes. What Jared did then was something wonderful and awesome. He opened his coat and let her take refuge against his chest. He then wrapped the coat around her and held her there. In one moment, she was engulfed in the incredible pleasure of his scent, the muscles of his chest, of his warmth. At that moment, she could take it no longer. She raised her face toward his, dared to hold her body tight against his, and dared look into his eyes.

"You're very beautiful," he told her.

She had closed her eyes, raised her chin, and whispered, "Embrasse-moi." Kiss me.

When she felt his lips on hers the inside of her body, her heart, swelled, rose and spun. When the train arrived, she let Jared drag her like a rag doll into the car where they kissed all the way to the sixteenth arrondissement.

Nothing would taste or smell the same the week that followed; the espressos she drank in small cafés engulfed in the smoke cloud of Jared's many cigarettes, the wet scent of deserted public gardens, the warm bread he hand-fed her at dawn when the boulangeries opened. She could now feel the world, see the world in new ways that astonished her. When Jared pointed to a strange person, a poster, a newspaper headline, an advertisement, a building, a tree, Althea saw those too for the first time. What Jared did, saw, thought, ate, and drank suddenly existed for her. And there was joy. Sometimes the sound of her own laughter would surprise her, and she'd be stunned by the possibility of her own happiness. She, Althea, had a boyfriend who found her beautiful, painted her for hours, kissed her, fed her. She lost herself in the sight of him. How he scratched his day-old beard, how he walked, how his hands held a glass, a fork, a paintbrush. She lost herself in his body next to hers, his scent, and now his kisses. But soon it was no longer enough, She began wanting for him to touch her body, but he didn't. Why didn't he? Did he not want to? What was wrong with her?

And then, just like that, they had a fight. It was late, almost dusk at the Cimetière du Père Lachaise. Jared had stopped in front of names like Méliès, Piaf, and Balzac and rambled on about their genius while Althea watched the way his mouth moved. When they passed Jim Morrison's tombstone and the dozen people taking pictures, she asked Jared if Jim Morrison was French.

He laughed. "Français? You don't know who he is? You're American."

"I wasn't sure," she said impatiently. Jared should have known that she had not had a normal life where people have friends, listen to music, care, take pleasure in things. She had told him about herself, in simple sentences and he had listened. He knew about a lifetime spent in suspended animation, he knew about her jailor, the mother she never wanted to see again, the father too shut down from life to pay attention. Jared knew almost everything. Almost. He did not know there was a third jailer. And when she was with him she almost forgot she too was a monster.

The cemetery closing time was near and Jared took her in a corner to hide. They waited in silence for people to leave, the guards to make their rounds, the gates to close. "Why do you like cemeteries at night anyway?" she asked when they were finally alone and could move from their hiding place and sit on a bench.

"For the silence," he answered. "And for the cats." He looked at her and winked. "C'est plus romantique. Non?" She watched Jared take out a small boulangerie box from the depth of his pocket. "On mange," he said and he opened the package and placed it between them on the bench. She took one look at the contents of the package, two coffee éclairs with glossy light brown icing. She felt anger rush through her. "I don't want to eat that," she said.

Jared ignored her, picked up one éclair and moved it gently

toward her mouth. "They're my favorite," he told her. She jerked her head back and he considered her reaction with amusement. "Take a bite."

Althea felt the familiar repulsion, the tightening of her hands into fists. "What happens if I don't eat this?" she asked, rage in her voice.

"Then I'll eat two," he shrugged.

She fought to contain her tears. "What I mean is, I just think you should stop trying to feed me."

Jared put the éclair down, licked his fingers. "You don't like me to?"

She needed the truth. "I'm worried about being fat."

He looked at her and frowned. "Tu es trop maigre," he said shaking his head, "Much too thin," he added with vehemence. "C'est pas bon ça."

"Sometimes I feel that all I have in the world is my thinness," Althea whispered.

Jared looked away. "That's very strange."

Althea's eyes were full of tears. "Do you hate me now?"

Jared scratched his day-old beard looking unsure. "No, why?" He thought for a moment, then said, "Do you think that maybe you are sick?"

Althea's body hummed with energy. She had heard this before. "I just want to be thin. What's wrong with that? Everybody wants to be thin, but for me, suddenly, it means that I'm sick."

"I'll kiss you if you promise to eat some éclair, maybe not today, but one day." Jared had moved close to her and held her face in his hands.

"You don't understand, I'm really afraid to be fat. Really, really afraid," she whispered when Jared's lips were an inch from hers. Her secret out, tears fell freely from her eyes and down the side of her face.

"Promise you will try one day," he said, "or I don't kiss you."

"But not today, right?"

"No, today, I'm the one who will be fat," he said.

Lola brought the silk sheet to her chin to hide her grin. Everything was too perfect about this loft and about Gunter. What kind of man puts his mattress in the center of a room and sleeps on immaculate white silk sheets? She watched naked Gunter's catlike body glide towards the bathroom. No bathing suit marks. She hoped he wasn't the kind to go to the tanning booth, what a turn off. He had a perfect body. No, the perfect body. And this was the perfect room, white, light and airy, with high ceilings, piles of books on the shelves and the floor, incomprehensible artwork on the walls. Clean, Zen, and sensuous. Gunter was a travel journalist. He scoped the world for an upscale travel magazine, slept in lavish resorts, ate in opulent restaurants. And judging from his in-plain-sight selection of condoms—the ribbed, the fruit-flavored, and even the humorous ones—lovemaking was to him a lighthearted affair.

She stretched under the sheet. Wholly comfortable in his nudity, Gunter walked back to the bed, a joint at his lips. He crouched down next to her, offering her the joint along with a front row seat to his perfect genitalia. "No, no, no," she said. "I don't smoke. I've never smoked! Oh, fuck it!" She put the joint to her mouth, feeling completely silly. Every one of her moves in the last few weeks had been a source of utter self-amazement. She was already an adulteress, what further harm was there in being a pothead?

Lucas could tell that Annie was not in the best of moods. When the temperature went up like this, the only reasonable thing to do was leave Paris. Within a short hour-and-a-half train ride he could be in his cottage in Honfleur. But instead of packing his duffle bag and heading north in a first-class TGV, instead of looking forward to a few days of sailing along the coast, he had stopped by Annie's house and invited her to take a stroll around the Bois de Boulogne. Annie had accepted, and now she was blaming him for the weather.

"I'm sensing a heatstroke coming," Annie said when they had barely stepped out of her house.

Lucas took her elbow, "It will get cooler by the lake."

They walked down rue de Passy toward La Muette. "Give me my breeze," Annie implored. "You promised me breeze!" Humidity wrapped around them like tentacles, but the tension and exhaust smell of the city did seem to wane as they approached the dark mass of sycamores and chestnut trees that was the Bois de Boulogne.

"The theme of the party will be Arabian Nights," Annie said. He wondered again what guests she planned to invite since she had made sure to alienate everyone she and Johnny used to know. The thought had occurred to him that she had done it on purpose at the time, severing old relationships with Johnny's crowd. She had been impossible, antagonistic, finding any pretext to shut off one friendship after another. He still saw a lot of these people, but she had made it clear that she didn't want to know who was sleeping with whom and who had cheated on whom. Too many memories, too many worries.

For someone who felt too hot, Annie was walking fast, intent on getting from point A to point B, instead of enjoying the stroll. She was preoccupied, he could tell. He noticed that her clothes were new. Had she lost weight? She was wearing a floating white blouse with folkloric motif, maybe something Russian, and cute shorts. Inside her sandals, her toenails were painted bright red. She continued walking fast beside him and talking about the party, but it felt as though she was making a point of not talking about something else. She seemed mad at him, in fact. "I bought scraps of fabric at the Marché Saint-Pierre," she said, "and I've been sewing pillows since February. I really want the party to be outdoors in the backyard, a pillows-on-the-floor, eating-food-with-our-hands kind of party."

"Because of the heat wave?" He asked, absentmindedly.

"I need a bloody project. My newfound sexual frustration's so thick you could cut it with a machete."

Lucas was glad she wasn't looking at him as he fumbled with his sentence. "B-Because of the heat wave?"

"While Lola is joyfully going at it with her cute German guy. Gunter! Gun-fucking-ter! How tacky! Could one have more of a cliché name?"

Clearly, this was going to be about Lola again. "What about her husband?" he asked.

"What husband? He's playing dead. We're all playing dead. Lola's been heavily into tantric yoga. Down Dog, you know, head down, butt up for the last week. Her head's in the sand, and she's getting it on daily with the 'Fuckanator.'"

Lucas wrapped his brain around the visual. "I've got a bad feeling about all this," he said. "Someone needs to talk to her husband."

They were finally entering the Bois de Boulogne, the temperature dropped by a good ten degrees and the air suddenly smelled of leaves and decomposing bark. Annie stepped over a dead branch.

"And why would that be? He's a dick."

"That is unfortunate, but not a crime. Am I the only one with a moral compass?"

"Oh puh-leeze," Annie said. She bent down, picked a blue campanula, and put it behind her ear. "So, in terms of the party, you've kept in touch with people. Are there any couples we know that are not doing too hot?"

"Should I wonder about the morality of that one?"

"What morality?"

"In coveting thy guests' husbands."

Annie turned around. In the mottled light filtering through the canopy of trees, her face was shining. "It's time to announce to the world that this respectable widow isn't in mourning anymore." She had a small smile. "I thought you'd be happy for me."

As they emerged from the woods, light bounced off the surface of the lake's water and blinded him. His eyes adjusted to the light. Around the lake, the large grassy areas were bright green. He was taken aback by the sight of dozens of couples, men and women dressed in business attire who lay entwined on the grass. The entire park was a grown-up's recess. The business crowd from the nearby buildings had descended to the Bois de Boulogne Lake for a refuge from the heat, and was clearly taking full advantage of their two-hour lunch break. Those who were not already kissing or groping each other sat in the grass, biting into baguette sandwiches, and flirting. Everywhere, tucked in the shade of trees, on the freshly cut lawn, on the benches, couples kissed. Lucas felt embarrassed.

Annie whimpered, "I need to stop thinking about my loneliness, not have it thrust upon me at such a vulnerable time, thank you very much."

Lucas guided her toward the dirt path that circled the lake. Would Annie let him rent a rowboat for an hour? Would that sound too romantic? She would probably laugh at him. What had she meant by not "being in mourning" anymore? But Annie began walking faster. He had to hurry to catch up.

They passed a couple lying in the grass. The woman, in her forties, pretty but not stunning, had her business skirt as far up as decency permitted in a public park. She stared up at the sky as the man, in a white shirt, caressed her thighs with the tip of his finger and whispered in her ear.

"The French in heat!" Annie mumbled after they had passed.

"The way men can be so completely satisfied with themselves is beyond me." Annie was apparently going from edgy to furious before his eyes and for no good reason. It was one thing to sense when Annie was egging him on for a fight, but stopping her was another thing.

A pack of strollers advanced on the path, pushed at high speed by closed-faced nannies. Inside the strollers, babies looked right through them. Annie and Lucas stepped onto the grass to avoid a stampede.

"And look at this," Annie cried out. "Where are the moms? Can you tell me where these poor babies' mothers are? I'll tell you exactly where they are: frolicking in a park like this one. They're busy cheating on their husbands while their babies turn into zombies."

Lucas thought he saw tears in Annie's eyes, but she was walking fast again. Good mood or not, he was glad to be with her in the park on a hot day like this one. He enjoyed her furious presence, the now cooler breeze, the lace of fresh new leaves above their heads, the tiny wild daisies on the grass, the baby ducks on the lake, the dirt path that absorbed his footsteps, and the smell of Annie's shampoo when she was close enough. She wasn't in mourning anymore.

Annie came to a halt, made a 180-degree turn and brutally put her hands flat on his chest. It felt nothing short of being punched. "What's with you?" she muttered in a rage. "You've gone mute? Have you turned into a fucking zombie too?" Her eyes were filled with tears. Her cheeks were red, and there was a mist of sweat over her upper lip. As always, her bangs were too long and fell over her eyes. She was beautiful. Her hands on his chest made Lucas's breath quicken.

"I'm not sure what we're talking about," he whispered.

"Of course, you never listen to a word I say."

"Men are self-satisfied, the babies are zombies, and the mothers are…irresponsible?"

"Exactly," she cried out. She stood erect facing him, shorter than he was by a foot. Her bangs covered her eyes completely.

Lucas did not mean to move his hand. His hand moved itself, rising slowly, approaching Annie's face, and his fingers brushed away the hair from her eyes. Annie did not move. She looked at him. And the way she looked at him... he didn't know what that look meant. But his thumb stayed on her forehead, then he caressed her cheek. Her wet eyes had a crazy glow, an angry glow, maybe an expectant glow. Lucas knew that if he stopped right now, everything would return to normal, his relationship with Annie would go on as it had, crucial, reassuring, unfinished. But he did not feel reasonable at the moment. He enveloped her chin with the palm of his hand. Annie was motionless, still looking at him with eyes overflowing with tears. With his other hand, he cupped her neck, and he felt Annie softening. A slight softening, but a softening, nonetheless. He approached her body, did not let go of her chin and her neck, that elusive suppleness guiding each one of his moves. When he brought his mouth to hers, the impossible happened. Annie, instead of tensing, instead of jerking back, became lighter and softer, a surrendering with which he was very familiar. He kissed her and she melted further, and his heart beat wildly, as wildly as he always hoped it would, the day he would, at last, kiss her.

He was the one who stopped. They were still in the middle of the dirt path. Annie was lost for a moment. He, however, knew that he would have the rest of his life to kiss her if he played this moment just right. He had, after all, nearly a lifetime of experience seducing women. He guided a now weightless Annie away from the path and laid her onto the daisy-sprinkled grass. He lay down next to her and kissed her again, and she kissed him back like any other couple on the lawn by the Bois de Boulogne Lake.

CHAPTER 23

JUIN

*N*ot much, even the sight of Jared with a five-day-old beard and bloodshot eyes, could have dampened Lucas's enthusiasm the next morning. Outside, the temperature was thirty degrees cooler than it had been the day before. In the café, the collective mood was glum. This first day of June felt like January, and the blustery rain seemed to scoff at the suede shoes now covered with mud, and the linen suits ruined by rain. The heat wave had ended as abruptly as it had begun but it didn't matter. It had lasted just long enough for him to kiss Annie!

By the look of him, Jared had not gone to sleep yet. He was drinking his second espresso without a word. It suddenly seemed almost impossible for everyone to be in such a cranky mood while Lucas felt like getting up on the counter and bellowing his love. He turned to Jared and said, beaming, "You might want to consider taking a shower in the next few days."

Jared stared into his coffee. "You might want to consider getting off my back."

Lucas whistled "Singing in the Rain" softly between his teeth. "Another round of espressos, Monsieur Jean. My friend might not make it through the hour otherwise. And how is business today, with all this rain?"

Monsieur Jean didn't bother responding and walked to his coffee machine. So what if everyone gave him the cold shoulder for transgressing all rules of common sense by being happy on a nationally observed day of depression. "Aren't you going to ask me why I'm so serene today?" He asked Jared.

Jared slammed change on the zinc counter. "I got to go."

"Ask me," said Lucas excitedly.

Jared turned to Lucas exasperated. "You banged Annie?"

Lucas was caught by surprise. "Well, it is far, far more complex than that."

"You banged Lola?"

Lucas's mood was fading. "You want to hear what happened or not?"

"Not really."

"We kissed! Yesterday! We did! We really kissed like teenagers. It was unbelievable."

"And then?"

"She was late to pick up the kids from school so she took a cab home."

Jared dropped two words like they were rat poop. "That's it?"

"You can't rush perfection."

Jared shrugged it off. "You lost your one chance, man."

Lucas was taken aback and stuttered, "You th-think?"

"Women are horny one day a month, two tops. Yesterday was her day, and you blew it."

"She was sincere. Best kiss I've ever given...or received. I'm in love! I'm utterly in love."

"You're just horny."

"Past the age of forty-five, people actually become capable of other human emotions." Lucas considered the gaunt color of Jared's skin, the slight shaking of his hand on the cup. "I hope you'll reach this ripe age of wisdom before you die of cirrhosis of the liver or some other alcohol-related degeneration. Or worse, cynicism."

Jared put a cigarette in his mouth. "Your only chance at this point's to play it cool." He lit the cigarette and inhaled. "Maybe she'll forget the whole thing happened, if you're lucky."

"It's on me," Lucas said. He folded a bill under a saucer, and walked away. As he exited the café, he covered his head with his newspaper. He stepped into the rain, and made a little dancing step in case Jared was watching.

❦

The morning rush was over. Thick raindrops pounded at every window in dramatic gushes. The children had left for school accompanied by a neighbor and her children. Annie and Lola waved good-bye to the cortege of colored raincoats and umbrellas and ran giggling to the kitchen as soon as the front door was shut. Lola put Simon down on the kitchen floor and gave him pots and pans to stack, wooden spoons and metal ladles to bang. They poured themselves coffee into mugs and ignored the remnants of the children's breakfast that were still scattered on the table, crumbs, milk spills and half-empty mugs of cold cocoa. Annie put a sugar cube into her cup and plopped another one in Lola's, realizing too late that Lola took it black.

"Sorry."

The order of business was the incident they had titled The Kiss.

Lola tossed the contents of her mug down the sink and poured herself a fresh cup. "He puts you in a cab yesterday after all that kissing, and nothing since?"

"It wasn't that much kissing, maybe forty-five minutes tops."

"That's a whole lot of kissing. Not exactly an accidental kiss. Did he tell you anything? Do you think it was premeditated?"

"We didn't talk at all. I mean talking was not what we were doing. And I was too embarrassed to talk."

"Does he usually show up here by this time?" Lola wondered, reading her mind.

"It's not like that. He shows up sometimes every day, sometimes not for days. It's not like we have a relationship. He doesn't owe me an hourly account of his schedule."

"Still," Lola said, her hand wrapped around her coffee mug. "This is not business as usual."

"That's the understatement of the century."

"So what do you think is going on?"

Annie put her mug down on the table and began pacing the kitchen. "Oh I'll tell you precisely what's going on: He made a mistake. He is mortified and doesn't know how to get out of this one. He doesn't dare present himself at my door, and neither can he dump me since nothing has officially happened between us."

"Don't rush to judgment."

"I rush to judgment. That's what I do," Annie said, shuffling around the kitchen in her hole-ridden slippers. Her pajama legs were too long, and made her trip. At least Lucas wasn't around to see her look like a hobo. It dawned on her that he had probably seen her dressed like this, unwashed and uncombed time and time again. There was something very wrong with this picture. "I will die of embarrassment," she said. She stopped at the table, added a third sugar cube to her cup and offered the sugar to Lola who put a hand over her coffee to protect it. "I can't think straight. What do I need to think?"

"You need to think positive."

Annie rolled her eyes to the ceiling. "It was the heat of the moment. What an idiot I am! Lucas so regrets this."

"Maybe he doesn't."

"Take a look at me." Annie pointed to her troll-like hair and her ill-fitting pajamas as sufficient evidence.

"I bet Lucas knew exactly what he was doing."

"I've known him for ten years. He's never looked at me once!"

"You are so blind."

"I am?" Annie plopped down on a kitchen chair. "The last time I had sex was almost three years ago," she said. "That's a lot of years without an orgasm."

"Shhh!" Lola signaled in the direction of Simon who was happily banging away. "None at all?"

"None that involved another human being."

"At least you had you-know-whats with Johnny, whereas I haven't had a you-know-what with Mark in years."

"No you-know-what whatsoever?"

"In the beginning I did, but he rushes through things. I can't be rushed. I wasn't really missing it per se, but now I can compare. Gunter is a master at giving me you-know-whats."

Annie sighed heavily. "I would not know how to get—she mouthed the word naked—in front of a man, and the idea of getting—she mouthed the word naked again—in front of someone I know so well. I would be mortified. Do you know how perfect the women he goes out with look? Besides, should I introduce a man into my life, I mean for the kids' sake."

"He seems like a master you-know-whatever to me, that Lucas," Lola mused.

"And I like things done my way. And I'm hardly a catch."

"Stop the self-flagellating!" Lola said. "You're the biggest flirt. You've been flirting with him for years. This was going to happen, and you know it."

Annie could not help a grin from growing on her face. "I do not flirt with Lucas!"

"Not just with Lucas. You're a flirt."

"But not with Lucas."

"Absolutely with Lucas."

Annie grabbed her face. Things had happened that could not unhappen. Things that she had not meant to happen. But then again... "And don't start telling me that life needs to go on," she said.

"Life needs to go on," Lola responded.

Annie made a little pile out of the breadcrumbs on the table. "With Lucas, though?"

"There are many reasons why it could be with him," Lola mused.

"Well, he is cute, and supportive, and a great friend." Annie looked at Lola. "He is funny, too, don't you think?"

"Very funny."

"Don't you find him cute?"

"He's cute, yes." Lola agreed.

"And don't you just adore the way he dresses?"

"Yep."

"And the kids like him a lot."

"They do."

Annie felt the tears, tried to contain them. "But he can have any girl he wants," she said.

"Maybe he can, maybe he can't. The fact is, he kissed you."

Annie said the words that she had not dared tell herself and let herself cry openly, "Oh, Lola, I'm so afraid to hope."

Lola nodded. She seemed to understand precisely what Annie meant.

"Listen, I'm not holding my breath. Okay, so he kissed me. He will realize this is going to ruin our friendship. We have a very special friendship." Annie blew her nose loudly. She stopped crying as abruptly as she had started.

Lola shook her head in disbelief. "You never realized that a single, handsome, heterosexual man wouldn't spend so much of his time with you if he didn't desire you all along?"

Desire? Now the big words. But could Lola be right? "So you think he might actually like me? Wow," she added. "Far out." She laughed out loud.

"You do like him!" Lola exclaimed. "You've always liked him!

Of course! Even the kids can see it. In fact, I spent my first month here convinced you were together, remember?"

"So you think he might like me, and you think I might like him?"

"This conversation is really weird. The real question to me is how come you haven't kissed before?"

"No, no, the real question is, how can I get him to kiss me again and not look like a total slut."

Just as she was saying the word slut, Althea entered the kitchen. Annie exchanged glances with Lola and they waited in silence as Althea opened a folded-up Kleenex, retrieved a used tea bag, and dipped it into a mug filled with cold water. Strange. That girl was strange. They watched as Althea placed the mug into the microwave and the three of them stared as the seconds went down on the microwave screen for a whole minute. The microwave beeped and Annie noticed she was holding her breath.

"May I?" Althea said, taking three apples from the fruit bowl.

Annie shrugged yes. They waited for Althea to leave and Lola said, "I've tried to not seem like a slut all my life, and for what?"

"Yes, for what? Sluttish is good!" Annie said, and laughed ferociously.

"But you'll take it slow, right?"

"What do you think I am? A slut? I have all the time in the world."

She did not yet know just how little time there was, and how frantic the next twenty-four hours would turn out to be.

Lying on Althea's bed, his arms behind his head, a cigarette in his mouth, Jared watched Althea as she stepped over canvases, tubes of paint, dirty glasses, a filled ashtray and picked her clothes up from the floor. It was pouring outside and rain whipped the tree branches against the bedroom window. "I'm getting breakfast," she said, leaving the bedroom. It was eight in the morning and they had not gone to bed yet. They had gone out until five in the morning and then he had wanted to paint her. He realized this was unfair to Althea for two reasons: he knew she would not be able to say no, and she did not know he had taken speed at the beginning of the night. But now it was the morning and he hated himself for it, for invading her space, for taking advantage of her, for not letting her sleep. He had meant to paint her to capture her stomach-churning beauty, her smiles so quick to vanish. As a small boy, he tried to make his little sister smile, and then his mother smile, and it worked for a while until they got too sick to smile at all. He had always been surrounded with sick women. Now he could see that Althea was more of the same and he was furious at her and at himself.

Althea re-entered the bedroom, carrying a cup of tea and three apples.

"That's our breakfast?" he said, feeling mean.

"They were there," Althea said as an explanation.

"Who?"

"Annie and Lola. And they were laughing. They always laugh. I mean, I went in and out of the kitchen, I don't think they even noticed that I was there."

Althea looked spent. What kind of selfish bastard was he to not let her sleep? Was this love? Would he love her if she were well?

"And I'm a burden to them," Althea said. She reddened, looked away. "Sometimes I think I'm also a burden for you. Like you feel that you have to take care of me or something."

Was he the angel of death, killing one by one all the women he loved? "What burden?"

She sat on the bed and looked at him. "Every day I know you're going to feed me, and I don't want to say no to you."

He had wondered how long they could go on, not saying what

needed to be said. "You need to eat." He moved his chin in the direction of the tray. "And not only apples."

Althea looked at him with a sort of defiance. "When you feed me I eat too much. So then I end up eating nothing else the rest of the day or..." she stopped herself.

Jared searched his memory for the word in English. "Do you throw up?" he asked.

"It just kind of happens sometimes, after I eat like a pig."

He could see her ribs under the thin sweater, hidden behind the red mass of her hair. He felt sick. His cowardice made him sick, feeding her all this time without talking about why, letting her be insane.

"Althea, you can't do that to yourself. You're too skinny," he said, knowing this was more of the same cowardice.

Althea spoke more to herself than to him. "Models are skinny, but they don't have the veins and the bones that show like I do. I don't feel skinny. I feel fat." She looked at him, powerless. "I'm too fat and too skinny."

Jared sprung up and sat next to her before he knew it. He grabbed her by the shoulders. "This has to stop, Althea," he growled.

Althea's eyes widened in horror. "I'm not doing anything wrong."

"You know damn well you're doing something wrong. Don't lie to me."

She shook her head and began crying. "I'm not lying."

"I can't always be here to make sure you don't starve yourself!" he yelled.

"Then don't!" she yelled back. "I don't need anybody. I'm so sick of eating, and not eating, and being hungry, and throwing up. And Lola and Annie couldn't care less; they're eating wads of butter. Like my mom, always cooking greasy food. And selfish." Defiant, Althea raised her head and, through her tears, said, "I know why they remind me of my mom. I could be dead for a week, and they would not notice. Maybe then they'd realize they should have paid attention."

"Is that what you want? Starve yourself and die?" he yelled. He let go of her.

Althea collapsed on the bed and he suddenly understood. His desire to paint Althea was no different from his desire to feed her. It was, in fact, an urgency to keep her alive. Jared had been there before. Up until his mother died, he painted her desperately. He had painted her so that there would be something left of her, like an insurance policy.

Jared stood up and felt wobbly. He was not with Althea because he loved her. He was with her because he was supposed to sit with her and watch as she slowly killed herself. "I can't take care of you, Althea," he whispered.

As Althea sobbed in silence, Jared grabbed his clothes. He didn't have the words, or the courage to explain. He left the room, ran down the stairs, left the house, and felt that he was followed by the cloud of stench, of darkness, of illness he carried everywhere with him. He left taking with him his destruction.

CHAPTER 24

A t four-fifty the next morning, Annie opened her eyes. Closed them again, tight. What in the world? The irreversibility of the last few hours, her wanton and libidinous self, in the dreadful lucidity of the early hour all came to her in a rush. Horrific! She dared open her eyes again. Judging from the last of the moonlight reflected on the ceiling above her bed, the rain had wiped the sky clean and today would be a beautiful day. She ever so slowly glanced to her right and barely repressed a giggle. There he was! Lying right beside her on his stomach was Lucas, his head buried in the pillow—Johnny's pillow—sleeping like a gentle brute.

Without moving a muscle, Annie contemplated Lucas's bare back, which was on this side of hairy. She found it hysterically funny that it hadn't bothered her in the least a few hours earlier.

She slipped a leg out of the sheet, her cutely painted toes, her freshly waxed calf, and had to admit to herself that what had happened wasn't entirely free of premeditation. The cellulite on her thigh gleamed in the early morning light and she thanked her good stars for the chance to gather herself before Lucas saw her au naturel. She felt as giddy as a teenager at the thought, and sight, of a nude man in her marital bed. She had done it! Boy, had she been at the end of her rope after those years of forced abstinence. But with Lucas? She was glad it was with Lucas. Of course, it had to be with him. Her cluelessness baffled her and she almost laughed out loud. She pulled the sheet under her chin continuing to feel in turns embarrassed and elated.

What would happen when Lucas woke up, both literally and figuratively? Would he wish he hadn't followed her after dinner, after they had cleaned the kitchen, after a few drinks too many. Would he wish he hadn't dragged her into that dark corner of the stairwell?

Lucas had invited himself to dinner after a day of nerve-racking silence. He just appeared as though nothing out of the ordinary had happened between them. What had first felt like a relief quickly turned to wrath. How could he say nothing? She had felt the deep burn of humiliation. Lucas continued to be tactlessly normal during dinner, that asshole, so cruelly without conspicuous eye contact.

She had lost at her own game of planned aloofness in a matter of thirty minutes. It was one thing to act as though the kiss in the park had been insignificant to her, but that it be insignificant to Lucas flustered her so much that she had behaved erratically. She had drunk too much wine with dinner, spoken too loudly, been heavily opinionated —so much more than usual that she had read it in Maxence's air of sulking disapproval.

After dinner, she had put the boys to bed only to come back downstairs to find Lucas and Lola sitting together on the loveseat. The loveseat! They were so wrapped up in one of their trademark flirtatious conversations that they didn't even acknowledge her being back in the room. She could have murdered them both. That's maybe what triggered the whole thing. She would not, could not, let either of them perceive her as a fool.

All three of them drank vodka, too much of it. She maybe,

possibly, got a little flirtatious at that point. Nothing too obvious, though it is hard to tell how obvious she got. Things got blurry. She did remember going into the kitchen around midnight and opening the two top buttons of her top. When she got back in the room, Lola sent her eye signals that her brand new black lace bra was showing.

They drank some more, joked around, flirted heavily, and suddenly, out of absolutely nowhere, Lola stood up, teetered a little, said she was going to bed, and just disappeared. Annie had enough brain left to sense the danger. She got to her feet and called it a night, but Lucas didn't leave. Instead, he followed her into the hallway, and before they reached the kitchen, he had put his hand around her waist and dragged her into the corner of the staircase where she had turned to mush.

Should she pretend to be asleep, see how Lucas would handle the morning, take her cues from him, or pounce on him like the starving she-wolf she was? She sat up and gathered the sheet over the negligee purchased the day before when she still believed herself above suspicion. Lucas had nice skin. And he was a deliciously attentive lover. Better than Johnny. And to think she had accused Lucas of being a legend in his own mind. She took a look at the clock and watched it turn to five a.m.

That's when the shrill ring of the telephone pierced through the sleepy house.

Althea was awake and curled up at the base of her bed when the phone rang somewhere in the sleeping house. She looked up at the clock. It was precisely five in the morning. Jared had left her room at nine the morning before, twenty hours ago. After he had yelled at her and abandoned her she had put her clothes on, bundled herself up in her coat and sat at the base of her bed amongst freshly painted canvases and dirty socks. There she had drifted in and out of sleep and counted the hours until Jared came back. But this time, for the first time, he had not come back. Her make-up was smeared from crying and her nose and mouth were swollen with tears. Within arm's reach were the tea and the three apples she had brought up twenty hours ago but she was too desperate to reach for them. She did not deserve food or water. There was nothing in her stomach but a nauseating loneliness. During the night, a hundred times she almost rose to her feet, a hundred times she stayed down. Her stomach was empty, and her chest was full with a dry rage she couldn't contain or understand. Soon day would come and the house would wake up. Happy noises of life, like a slap in the face. The children would complain and fight for the bathroom. She would smell the coffee and toasted bread that made her stomach scream. Lola and Annie would bark endless commands to the children who would ignore them.

The way the phone rang, or was it the time that it rang, Althea knew immediately that something was wrong. After the phone stopped ringing, there was an interminable silence, then doors began to open and close throughout the house. There were hurried footsteps down the hall. Althea stood up and put her ear against her bedroom door. Her whole body began shaking uncontrollably. Footsteps rushed up the staircase. A violent knock at her door. Nausea. She opened her door and faced Annie, who was barefoot and clad in a short lacy nightgown. Annie eyed the incredible chaos that was her room with incredulity and frowned with surprise at the sight of Althea dressed and wearing a coat. "Do you know?" she asked.

Althea felt faint. "No! What's wrong?"

"It's Jared." She put her hand on Althea's arm. "He's at the hospital. They think it might be a drug overdose!"

Althea put her hand to her mouth. Her legs stopped carrying her and she held onto the doorknob. Annie looked at her face with suspicion. "Did you guys have a fight?"

Althea answered the truth: "I don't know."

"Look, you're already dressed. You should go ahead of us. He's is at Hôpital Bichat in the eighteenth arrondissement in the emergency department."

"Is he all right?"

"Honey, they say he's in critical condition."

Althea received the news like a punch. Annie continued. "Lola will stay here with the kids. Lucas and I...he's here. He spent the night but we're getting dressed. Grab a cab now. We'll meet you over there. Run, honey, all right?"

Overdose? But Jared didn't take drugs. Althea needed to tell the doctors. Maybe they didn't diagnose him correctly. Althea ran with legs that couldn't run, thought with a brain that couldn't think. Her body moved out of the house and onto the street. She nearly threw herself at a passing cab. "Hôpital Bichat. Urgences s'il vous plaît. Vite!" The cab, a BMW, accelerated to sixty kilometers per hour within seconds. "Stop! Stop," she yelled. The cab's tires screeched, and the car stopped just in time for Althea to open the door and vomit bile.

In the hospital room, Althea stood in her coat, her hands tight on her purse, her eyes scanning the room for a blanket, for Jared who laid there, unconscious, and whose body was covered by only a thin, white sheet. He was like a wax rendition of himself. He was very pale. The wiry muscle on his forearms almost flaccid. Clear plastic containers filled with liquid dangled above him, dispensing their fluids through catheters. The only sound in the room, the rhythmic beeping of a heart monitor, failed to reassure her.

Voices came from outside the room. Through the small window in the door, she saw the doctor speak to Annie and Lucas. The same doctor, repeating the same words he had given her: There was no evidence that Jared could hear at the moment, but they could speak to him anyway.

Lucas and Annie would enter the room in an instant and she would no longer be alone with Jared. She ventured a small step toward the bed and had the hardest time getting her body to obey her. She glanced behind her shoulder, through the window. Annie and Lucas who had just arrived were still speaking with the doctor. She bent down and brought her face close to Jared's. He did not smell like himself. She came close enough to feel his breath on her face. She had tricked herself into thinking that he loved her, but the brutal truth was that she knew nothing about him. He had never trusted her enough to let her in. They didn't have a relationship. She couldn't have despised herself more. She whispered in his ear the truest words she knew "I love you. And I hope that you love me, too," and stood up as Annie and Lucas entered the room. Their faces displayed the same fear the doctor's words had inflicted on her. Jared was in a coma. There was no evidence he could hear, no indication he ever would again. Althea refused Annie's hug, walked past her and Lucas, and ran out of the hospital room.

Lucas couldn't imagine himself staring at Jared's still, waxy face another instant. "Why did Althea run out like that?" he asked Annie. "Isn't she supposed to be his girlfriend? How come we're staying here and she is gone?"

Annie was sitting in a gray chair next to the bed, her hands clasped, her eyes glued to Jared's heart monitor. "You can go," she said.

"Go? Go where? Why would I want to go? That's not going to help Jared if I go." Lucas paced in the small room full of awful medical smells. Everything in the room was gray, the walls, the chair, Jared's face. "I need to go," he finally said.

Annie looked at him. "So? Go."

"I need to find an answer," he explained.

"I'll stay."

Answers. Yes, he needed answers. What kind of answers he wasn't sure. The hospital staff described precisely what drug Jared had used and how much, and no amount of additional information would improve his condition. Lucas left the hospital and walked down boulevard Boissière like a somnambulist. There had been no time for shaving or a shower and he was still wearing the clothes from the evening before—his charcoal Dior sports coat, a tailor-made baby blue dress shirt, and a gray raincoat by Karl Lagerfeld. Who knew Jared? Did Althea? He certainly didn't know any more than what Jared deemed to show or tell him and that wasn't much. Besides, Jared had a distaste for answering or asking questions.

Across the boulevard was the entrance of the métro Porte de Saint-Ouen. Lucas took taxis through Paris when he was not driving his own Mercedes, but he suddenly felt the commanding need to take the métro, something he had not done in perhaps fifteen years. Jared was always in the métro; this would be just like getting into Jared's mind. He walked down the foul-smelling steps, odors of trash and urine, and waited in line to purchase a ticket, feeling self-conscious. He was shocked to discover how much a ticket cost these days.

He stood on the platform, waiting for the next subway amid African workmen, maids, and elderly men. His clothes suddenly felt deeply inappropriate. This attire had been meant to dazzle Annie, certainly not to wear in the métro in an undesirable neighborhood early in the morning. He discretely removed the folded silk pocket square from his suit jacket and buried it deep inside the pocket of his raincoat. He imagined he'd get himself mugged in this attire but all he got was indifference. He stepped into the subway car and held onto the bar rather than sit down. He studied the faces around him with great interest but no one looked at him. Men and women on their way to work, closed to the world. This was how people lived.

He changed trains at Place de Clichy and headed toward Place Blanche and Pigalle, reasoning that if this was the Paris he never set a foot in, it therefore had to be Jared's territory. Only by attempting to retrace Jared's footsteps, no matter how futile an endeavor, would Lucas have a chance to understand what might have happened.

He emerged from the métro station Pigalle and was surprised by the heat of the morning. Yesterday had been a day of storm and thundering rain and today would be a scorcher. A record heat had been predicted for the day. He removed his raincoat and folded it over his arm. Everything was upside down: the weather, Jared, and he and Annie.

At Pigalle, he stood in the middle of the boulevard and surveyed his surroundings. He had somehow expected stench and prostitutes in broad daylight, but instead found only a few tourists looking for a place to have breakfast, he assumed, looking as out of place as he did. A group of Senegalese men armed with brooms were laughing contagiously as they cleaned the front of closed stores still protected by metal screens.

A drug overdose made absolutely no sense. As a child, Jared had a charming intellectual curiosity and a promising gift for art. In adolescence, after the murder of his father, his sister's death and his mother's illness, he had taken refuge in a form of self-protection disguised as aloofness. Secretive, yes. A drug addict, no.

Though what just happened to Jared was neither his fault nor his responsibility, Lucas blamed himself. He had made a promise to Jared's mother to watch over her son. She had not burdened him with that request, not at all. Yet he had promised. What sickened him was that small sentence by the doctor: The combination of drugs and alcohol could have been intentional. The insinuation outraged him. But when he learned that Jared had been discovered by night guards at Cimetière de Montmartre, the cemetery where Jared's mother and sister were buried, Lucas had a sinking feeling.

When he'd just turned eighteen, years before his mother died, Jared had materialized at Lucas's doorstep. He said he was making a living with his art and that he and his mother would no longer need Lucas's financial assistance. That was when he and Jared became friends, a friendship based on the mutual understanding that Jared, as far as Lucas was concerned, would never have to meet his expectation, search for his approval or even give signs of life, as well as a mutual understanding that Jared could always count on him.

No, Jared was a good boy. Lucas came to the only possible conclusion: Althea was the one who introduced Jared to drugs. It all made sense: she was uncommunicative, unhealthy-looking, antisocial. She definitely had something dark and self-destructive to hide. He would personally see to it that she be sent back to her country, her and her drugs.

Lucas walked in the empty streets, feeling the heat of the sun. Althea had ruined everything. This terrible tragedy could not have come at a less auspicious moment. He felt guilty to feel a smile on his lips: Annie!

The evening before had been a whirlwind and this by no choice of his own. Since the kiss, he had planned-out his seduction. He had envisioned a slow and romantic progression, a rediscovery of sorts, with tête-à-têtes, dinners, dating, kissing. After a while, ideally, Lola would have stayed home with the boys so that he and Annie could go to Normandy for a couple of nights and stay at his maison on the beach in Honfleur. They'd eat plateaux de fruits de mer, oysters, shrimp, crab. They'd walk on the beach hand in hand. Oysters are an aphrodisiac.

But with women, one had to know when to go with the flow. When he'd arrived at Annie's house the night before, he was nervous. He needed to get a sense of how she felt about their kiss at the park before he began his planned romantic seduction. Apparently, Annie was not in a romantic mood. He went with the flow, took his cues from her, and it was fantastic.

He spotted a taxi and hailed it. What to do now? It could go several ways from here. One of them involved Jared not waking up and Annie rejecting him. Another scenario was that Jared would wake up and that Annie would pretend that nothing had happened between them. Lucas was far from the hospital now, far from the two people he cared most about and whose next few hours would define his own destiny.

Lola played the last two hours back in her mind again and again like an incomprehensible movie where the plot and the sequence of events made no sense, where the protagonists acted bizarrely out of character: Annie banging at her door explaining in a run-on sentence about Jared, the hospital, and waking up in bed with Lucas. Althea emerging into the hallway, rushing down the stairs and out of the house, her black coat floating behind her like Batman's cape. Lucas and Annie escaping out of the house like robbers at the crack of dawn to rush to the hospital.

And then, silence. Lola was left in the house with the sleeping children. So she did what needed to be done. Alone, she went and woke the children, one by one, hers and Annie's, five kids in all. Five sets of breakfasts, teeth to brush, scattered clothes and shoes to extract from various bedrooms and closets, five sets of passive or active resistance techniques at the prospect of school or, in the case of Simon, daycare. She explained to the children that Jared had fallen sick and that everyone was at his bedside.

By eight, Lola had gotten four children to school on time, appropriately dressed and with full stomachs. After she said good-bye to the children and told the teachers they would be staying at school for lunch, she took Simon to the daycare for the day so she'd be free to go to the hospital or do whatever was needed. She felt senselessly proud of herself as she pushed Simon in his stroller toward the daycare. It was an exceptionally beautiful morning, and she could not help but be happy despite what was happening to Jared. It wasn't happiness she felt exactly, but self-worth. Mark would have found ways to criticize her and to paste a couple of negative labels on her already bad record. Without Mark's judgment, she saw how perfectly capable she was, and that felt better than any collagen injection, better than Bikram yoga, better than Pilates, even better than sex with Gunter! She arrived home and luxuriated in the feeling for a few more minutes, until Annie called and told her of the gravity of Jared's condition.

"How is Althea?"

"Althea flipped, apparently," Annie said, in a high-strung tone. "She left the hospital. She looked freaked. I was hoping you had heard from her."

"I haven't. And how's Lucas?"

"Looks like he flipped too. I don't think he felt too comfortable being in the same room with me. Everyone is freaking out right and left."

"How about you?"

"I'm fine, of course," Annie snapped. "Someone has to be."

"You sound tense."

"I'm perfect."

Lola hung up the phone wondering about Annie's choice of word.

Althea let the revolving door of the hospital's windowless lobby sweep her away from muted light and stagnant air, and propel her into the street. The heat of the day after the cool hospital temperature shocked her. She recoiled, swirled back inside the revolving door and back to the lobby. She stayed there, panting. Jared did not want her, and he did not love her. Whatever she had done had made him want to run away, and he had taken drugs, suffered an overdose. If he died it would be her fault for not giving him a reason to live. He had given her a reason to live. But if he did not want her anymore, or if he died, then her reason to live was gone. She rushed to the bathroom. In the stall, she heaved but she had nothing in her stomach left to vomit. At the sink, she put both hands on the cold, smooth marble, waiting for the nausea to subside. She faced her image in the mirror, studied her reflection for another unsparing moment and felt such pain in her heart, in her stomach, in her head and in her limbs that she thought she might be dying. Panic grabbed her. She ran out of the bathroom, expelled herself from the hospital through the revolving doors and thrust herself into the street.

In her black coat, her black scarf, her black pants that stuck to her legs, she ran along the boulevard. She ran in small streets, between cars and tall, ornate stone buildings. When her body stopped being able to run, she walked. She knew none of the streets and though she was losing her bearings to the point of toppling down, she continued walking. She was so thirsty. Her body would not go on for much longer without food or water or hope. All she needed now was a place to curl up and wait for death.

When she realized she was completely lost, she began following a single boulevard hoping to cross a river or a railroad where her life would end. But there seemed to be no end to this street, no end to the city. She advanced on wobbly legs toward a horizon that did not exist.

In the distance, she thought she saw something. It was strange. It was far away at the end of this interminable boulevard. From where she was, it looked like what might be the canopy of a circus, a series of white awnings or tents with colorful flags and balloons, red, yellow, pink floating above them. She advanced toward the floating colors, which appeared farther the more she advanced. She thought of her black tea still at the house. It was cold now. She needed it. She needed to get back to the house and drink her black tea. But first she would need to reach the flags and the canopies. But the flags were so far, and her body so weak that she could hardly make any progress toward them. She cried tearless tears and reached with her arm toward the tents.

Suddenly tents and flags expanded and reached toward her, and a moment later, she was swallowed. Wherever she was now was loud, blinding, filled with people and exotic shops. Strong smells of trash and spices emanated from the doors of buildings, the pavement. There were groups of children playing on the sidewalk. Was she in Africa? Maybe this was China, Egypt. There were people everywhere, hustling around, in a hurry. Busy, determined people from no country and from every country.

The sun, straight above, tracked her without mercy. Her heartbeat was loud. It was as loud a sound as Jared's heart monitor. But she realized the pulsating came from outside her body, like the rhythmic throb of a distant drumbeat. As the crowd became more dense and determined, she found herself carried by it. Her movements became easier, she was no longer one but part of a human wave made up of entire families. There were women covered in burkas pushing strollers, and babies with dark hair and skin like golden silk. Everywhere, excited children were running and calling to each other. Men walked in groups, some with turbans, some kippas, all gesticulated, waving their hands, and speaking loudly to each other in strange languages. There were women in saris, women in miniskirts, women who carried young children and large totes.

No one paid attention to Althea, as always. So she made herself one with the crowd without intention or thought other than to get to water. Suddenly, she was right under the flags and colorful awnings, engulfed in the scents of exotic food, grilled meats, spices, mint. There were perfumes too, musk, patchouli. A market? The drumbeat became more insistent as new instruments joined in the rhythmic melody of Arabic music that grew louder and more exuberant as she approached. There were piles of fruit, huge legs of lamb turning on skewers with blades like swords, their juices oozing out over the flames that licked them, vegetable stews cooking in immense pots. Men and women waited in line to be served. She recognized couscous. Annie had served it once and she had not dared taste it at the time. But today she would. She would wait in line and be served steaming couscous, and maybe one of the thin spicy sausages. But before she could get closer to the food stands the crowd carried her away, toward an area of vibrant color: rugs, gold, jewels, beads, and Indian fabrics, piles of it, caressed by a woman in a sari so green and vivid it was fluorescent; the woman's wrinkled hands like leather on silk. Everywhere, there were children with cotton candy in their hands darting around their mothers like flashes of lights. An old man was setting up copper pots, pans, and jars, all gleaming in the light, and smiled broadly at her, the porcelain white smile against his dark face. He told her something, something she did not understand. She wanted to stop moving but her body was in motion, her body had someplace to go; her body that wanted water or food but knew only how not to eat and drink. She did not feel in control of her senses. She could smell, and see with such delicious and heartbreaking clarity despite her thirst, hunger and exhaustion. Her senses had expanded in wild surges. Everything she saw and smelled and touched was intensified, magnified. A knobby man with slick hair was holding a voluptuous woman, his thin arms around her bare waist. Her skin was made of melted chocolate. Althea loved that beautiful skin, she who had never noticed skin before, hers or anyone else's. But already the couple had disappeared. A small man in a dark suit walked toward her holding a sandwich. As he walked, he bit into the overflowing sandwich, juices dripped onto the ground—a disgusting sight, a fascinating sight. Althea wanted to tear the sandwich out of the man's hand. Food was everywhere again; Kebabs folded in pita bread. A fruit salad a woman cut before her eyes, her wet hands holding peaches and splitting them into chunks. Lemonade, the lemons dancing with ice cubes. Her head spun. This was the throbbing life that had been accessible to the rest of humanity all along. It did exist. It was real. And she did not need to be with Jared to experience it. And she liked it, yes, she wanted it. She wanted to touch it and be touched by it. She wanted to taste and feel. She wanted to bask in the immense sensuality of being alive; she wanted to learn how to make it happen to her every day like it was happening now.

Her heartbeat raced, involuntarily catching up to the rhythm of the drums. The burning sun baked her hair, shoulders, and back. Her tongue felt swollen inside her mouth, and her hair stuck to her face and neck. Under her coat, she sweated the last drop of her body's moisture. The crowd grew denser, more jubilant with every step. She needed to get back to the hospital and Jared. But where was the hospital? She didn't recognize anything in this blinding light, this crushing heat.

And suddenly, shade. She stopped walking and lifted her head. The dense shade under the canopy of giant sycamores poured on her like a liquid blanket. There was a breeze suddenly, a delicious breeze. Althea began spinning in place, looking up at the leaves playing in the breeze. The shade of the tree seemed to be there for her only, like her own private oasis. Soon there would be peaches, lemons floating in iced water, and love. She laughed. But first, she had to strip her body of this armor of a coat that choked her. Her arms had trouble getting out of the sleeves as she slowly whirled and looked up at the canopy. When her coat came off, she let it drop to the pavement.

There were faces, people watching her. Some had surprised faces. Some were laughing. She twirled and removed her turtleneck, the drenched T-shirt that clung to her chest, until she was down to her minuscule bra and the horror of her devastated body. She felt the cool air, the refreshing spin, and the strange well-being that came upon her. She stopped, looked down at the ground where her shed clothes lay like fallen black wings. The floor danced. The crowd danced and laughed. There was a bright white cloud before her eyes like gauze, and then darkness.

CHAPTER 25

*A*nnie bent cautiously over Jared's bed. Had she really seen his eyelid flicker? She sat on the edge of her chair, kept her eyes on his and held her breath. Jared blinked. She sprang to her feet like a madwoman and pushed on the call button over and over. Instants later, nurses and doctors were hurrying about Jared, checking machines and life signs. A beautiful Algerian nurse whom Annie had spoken to earlier gently took her by the elbow and guided her out of the room. She was made to return to the hallway to wring her hands. She looked around, trying not to jump out of her skin simply from being here. She hated this damn hospital, and the hospital hated her right back. The smell of the place alone sickened her. The terrible bright lights and the nauseating pink of the walls were like an ever-present menace. No one knew her here, of course, but she and the walls of this place remembered each other well. Being in the emergency room on this day, of all days, was bitter irony.

Thirty minutes after Jared had regained consciousness, Annie was allowed back into the room.

"Heavens thank you! You're alive!" she said.

Jared shook his head feebly and whispered, "Je suis désolé."

Sorry? He was sorry? She looked at him, horrified, furious. She opened her mouth to say something but decided against it. "I'd better call Lucas," she said. She turned on her heels and walked out of the room. She asked for a phone and called Lucas on his cell. "Jared will be fine," she said.

There was a long silence, then a longer sigh. "Thank you God."

"All he could say was 'je suis désolé.' You know what that means?"

"What does it mean?"

"It means it was suicide. That's what it means. The asshole tried to kill himself."

"It doesn't have to mean that."

"Then why did he not ask what happened, or why he was in a hospital room?"

Lucas let the thought sink in. "You have a point."

"Please get your ass over here before I rekill him."

"You're upset."

"You let me open my house to a drug addict who also happens to be suicidal. How do you expect my mood to be?"

"Who are we speaking of here?"

"Jared of course"

"I've known Jared most of his life, but only when that bizarre young woman enters his life does Jared get into trouble with drugs."

"What are you saying?"

"I'm saying that she is the one who got him into trouble. She's the drug addict."

Annie let it sink in. Althea's erratic behavior, the strange moods, the physical clues that something was off. Could Lucas be right? If he was right, then she was the one who had opened her house to a drug addict.

"I'm already in a taxi on my way," Lucas said.

Annie walked back to Jared's room with the sense that she

was forgetting something. Walking through the halls she held her breath and tried not to look at all these terribly sick people. All morning, the doors of the emergency room had swung open to the clamor of ambulances and an endless flow of human beings on stretchers. She went to the emergency room desk and demanded to speak to the triage nurse.

"He's awake. Here, do you see?"

"Yes."

"So, he doesn't belong here. He's no longer an emergency."

The nurse raised a bored eyebrow. "The doctors decide who is an emergency, and who isn't."

"But isn't he using up important time and resources?"

"We have the space and we have the staff."

"In my country…"

"I know my job, Madame, now please sit down or leave."

Annie left the desk grumbling, then came back and found the beautiful Algerian nurse, the one with the nice smile.

"Look," she said. "I don't mean to be difficult here, but I know this emergency room. I know how this place works. This is where I showed up in the middle of the night three years ago to find out that my husband was dead."

Jared was promptly transferred to the recovery floor. She followed Jared's rolling bed toward the elevator and up to the fourth floor. She glanced toward the hallway where they had taken her that night. At the end of the hallway was a very cold room. There, in that cold room she had identified Johnny's body. She had shaken so much in that room, shaken so violently, that they had to hold her. There, she had wept and she had hollered like a wounded beast. She had wept with grief and with murderous rage. Mostly she had wept for herself. It was in that room that she did the first and the last of her crying. She had left the morgue resolute to pull herself together, to focus on the boys and what she was going to tell them and how.

In Jared's new room, the walls were white and there was a

window. In the next bed a small black man with a large bandage across his head was sound asleep. She sat beside Jared, not sure what to say or what not to say. Lucas needed to be here soon. She wondered where Althea was. Jared's eyes were shut, and she took it to mean that he didn't want her to be there. She was conscious of how difficult it was for her to speak to certain people. She let words storm out of her mouth to fill voids, and she amused some, but with Jared, her words did not feel welcome or amusing. It was a familiar theme. She had often sensed in Johnny's friends a hint of indifference to her. Maybe worse than indifference: dislike. Maybe she lacked glamour. Maybe she did not know how to behave in Parisian society. Of course, she could have simply been insecure and imagined the whole thing. Those daunting parties... Johnny glowing with that peacock certainty, and the women looking at him, and Johnny, not paying attention to her a single instant. Why was bitterness coming in through the back door simply because Jared's eyes were closed?

"Do you need anything?" she asked abruptly, ignoring the fact that Jared might be sleeping.

"I'm starving," Jared answered, his eyes still shut.

"I'll go ask the nurses," she said.

She asked the hospital staff if Jared could be fed, then realized that she had forgotten to call Lola. She passed the nurse's station on her way to the pay phone when she heard her name.

"Madame Roland?"

She approached the nurse's station. "That's me," she said, figuring Lola had tracked her down. As a joke, she put both elbows on the counter like she was ordering at a café. "Un Croque-Monsieur s'il vous plaît."

"They're asking for you in the emergency room," the nurse said.

"We were just there," Annie said cheerfully, determined to make friends with the staff on this floor. "He's been transferred here, to room 402."

The nurse spoke slowly to make it sink in. "This," she said, "is for someone who just came in. A new emergency."

Annie saw it, the image as crystal clear as anything she had ever imagined. She distinctly saw one of her boys, any one of her boys, it didn't matter, the head crushed, the left side of the face a pulpy mass of crushed bones and burned flesh, dead on arrival, like Johnny. "Is it my child?" she screamed.

The nurse jumped to her feet, widening her eyes and speaking fast. "They did not say." She pointed to the elevator. "Three floors down and to your right."

Annie sprinted across the hall, pushed the button on the elevator, changed her mind and ran down three sets of metal stairs. Her heart was like a stone in her chest and her whole body tingled with panic. Visions of Maxence, dead, Paul, dead, Laurent, dead. All three of them, dead.

Once on the ground floor she ran to the emergency desk and practically screamed.

"Someone called for me. Annie, Annie Roland."

The triage nurse recognized her and rolled her eyes to the ceiling. "Not her!" she said to the beautiful nurse.

"Are we having a busy morning?" the nurse said with a smile, and Annie understood instantly from the nurse's casual attitude that whatever it was, her boys were not in any danger. She was flooded with instant relief. Tears ran down her cheeks that she did not even bother to wipe. Her relief was complete when she was told that a 'demoiselle' had arrived on a stretcher a few minutes before and had woken up, realized where she was and asked for her. The demoiselle, was Althea. Althea who had passed out only a block away from the hospital after having, the report said, taken off most of her clothes in the middle of a street fair, of all things.

Annie entered the room still high on adrenalin. But the sight of Althea took her aback. She lay on the hospital cot looking as frail and vulnerable as a newly hatched chick. A bag filled with clear fluid was hooked into her arm via an IV. Annie had wondered before why she had never seen Althea without a sweater or a jacket on, and now she knew why. The barely there, sleeveless hospital gown revealed it all and she was struck to the point of nausea by the impossible thinness of Althea's arms, the large knob of an elbow above the bandage that kept the needle of the IV in place. In the room, a nurse as tall and wide as a lumberjack was scribbling on a pad. Maybe Annie should have felt compassion, and maybe she did, but mostly she felt cheated, furious. It must have been the adrenaline let down, but she felt ready to bludgeon Althea to death. Lucas's theory that Althea had introduced Jared to drugs now made perfect sense. Jared and Althea, two young people with so much going for them both calling for negative attention like nine-year-olds. She had let them into her life, tried to take care of them, and this was what she got in return? Both acted like she was difficult, like she was the pain in the ass.

"Why in the hell are you here?" she said coldly.

The massive nurse advanced toward Annie, her arms crossed over her large breasts. "Doucement," she growled.

"It's been a hard morning," she told the nurse between clenched teeth, but the nurse continued standing in front of her, unconvinced. "I'll be fine," she had to say before the nurse finally stepped aside. She walked around the nurse, sat on Althea's bed, and willed her tone into cooperation. "What happened to you?"

Althea's gaze was absent. "Jared?"

"Jared's up and running," she told her. Althea's eyes brightened, and Annie felt sorry for her suddenly. "He's fine," she added. "The coma didn't last. Lucky bastard. What a scare." She forced herself to laugh. "He is devouring his hospital lunch as we speak, food, tray and all."

Althea did not speak but began sobbing tearless sobs. Annie reluctantly patted her bony hand. "There, there, everyone's fine," she said, but Althea was not fine, that much was clear. Althea's arms, her shoulders, her chest looked awful. This is what drugs did to bodies, it was all so clear now. Something about the way Althea had looked from the start was so dreadful, so different and wrong. But then again she had not known, or she had preferred not to see. "Jared's doctors want to run tests, keep him for a while, and then off to rehab if I have a say in this," she said. She searched Althea's forearms for a sign that she had used drug needles. How could one tell? Not all drugs came in a syringe. Were there drugs hidden somewhere in her home, in a drawer within reach of her boys? A part of her brain was quickly thinking up schemes to get Althea and Jared out of her house by any means necessary.

But another part of her brain was screaming something too. Something she could not hear, and there was this terrible hollowness in the pit of her stomach. "This is a warning sign for both of you," she said. "You both need to go to rehab."

"I didn't take drugs," Althea whispered.

Annie smirked. "Yeah, right!"

"No drugs," said the sergeant nurse. She read from her pad, "Dehydration, and exhaustion, but mostly starvation. Looks like a concentration camp victim."

Annie turned toward the nurse, flashed her best death stare, and turned back to Althea. She took a deep breath, "No drugs," she echoed, and then, stuttered in anguish. "My home's... hardly a concentration camp!" Her voice broke, and she tried to hold those burning tears, but they squirted out of her eyes irrepressibly.

"Weighing in at 90 lbs," the nurse added. "A clear case of anorexia nervosa. And a bad one. Very sick that girl. Been going on for quite a while."

"I thought you were on a diet. I didn't mean..." Annie said. She was bawling now and there was nothing she could do to stop herself.

Althea's exhausted voice tried to appease her. "It's not your fault."

"But I knew you were not eating. I knew it."

"It's all my own fault."

"I saw," Annie sobbed. "I saw and I didn't make you eat."

"It's not like that."

"I don't... understand," Annie sobbed, her shoulders shaking.

"Me neither," Althea said, shaking her head. "Me neither."

"But did you know?"

Althea hesitated. "Kind of."

The two of them became silent. Annie grabbed Althea's hand. "I'm so sorry."

"But Jared is going to be fine?"

Annie blew her nose. "As it turns out, it's only drugs. He's probably the healthier of the two of you."

"I was thinking," Althea paused and looked away, "maybe I need to go home."

"Sure, absolutely!" Annie sprang to her feet. "I'll take you home right now. Let's get out of this joint."

"Hospitalization is mandatory," said the nurse who was obviously a sadist and did not want to miss a second of this.

"I mean, go home, to the States."

Annie sat back down on the bed. She knew what she was going to say and she knew she would regret saying it. "Your home's here," she affirmed, her voice calm, her eyes steady. "We are your family. Dysfunctional, yes, but family, nonetheless."

"I'm afraid to go back to my mother. I don't think I'll get better there."

Annie tried a joke, as she contemplated how she was essentially screwing herself up, but some things have to be done and cannot be undone and some words have to be said, and cannot be unsaid. "Well, I'm far too young, but please consider me to be your temporary dysfunctional mother."

Althea looked at her with clear eyes, eyes that were full of a certain light, a hopeful light, and said, "Thank you."

§a.

Lola knew from watching E.R. that each passing minute could mean irreparable damage to Jared's brain. She hurried through the house, made the children's beds, picked up enough dirty socks to practically fill the diminutive machine à laver, then, armed with a bottle of Monsieur Propre, she scrubbed both bathrooms to a shine. As though she were hired help, as Mark would say. But she liked cleaning the house. Or rather she liked cleaning this house. This was a house with a soul and a spirit, not like that thing that resembled an over-decorated wedding cake and that Mark pompously called The Mansion.

After cleaning, she filled the bathtub with bubble bath and very hot water. She brought candles into the bathroom and lit them one after the other for Jared, saying a small Sanskrit prayer with each one. She placed the candles around the bathtub, the telephone on the sink, undressed and slipped into the steaming water. As she floated, she did Pranic breathing and visualized Jared's recovery by focusing on the color blue-green and sending him healing thoughts. Her hands floated to the surface. She took them out of the water and contemplated her nails now freed from the tyranny of acrylics. The sick-looking stumps at the tip of her fingers were a disagreeable memory, and now her nails were short, clean, and real.

She wondered why she needed to look perfect for Mark. Was it really something he asked of her? She did not look her own idea of perfect anymore. A couple months of Annie's food and she had gained at least ten pounds—pounds her body needed so she could feel normal, and real. Real was a theme that kept coming back. Real, as opposed to perfect. Annie had helped her trim off what was left of her dyed black hair, and without the dye to give it some weight, her hair grew like hay in all directions. It was interesting how her face, scrapped of artifice, was back to the androgynous look of her teenage years. The fine lines around her eyes and mouth were still there, but they no longer bothered her. Wrinkles added charm, that's what Annie had said. Because her face was rounder and her eyebrows were now blonde as well, her expression was softer. She looked more average maybe, but also infinitely more relaxed. There was very little of her old appearance she wanted to go back to. She liked the way she looked now. But would Mark?

It wasn't only the way she looked that had changed. It was the way she felt. In Paris, she felt more capable, more centered, stronger, independent. Maybe it had something to do with basking in sexual ecstasy at the ripe age of thirty-nine with this man who had obviously descended to earth for the sole purpose of giving her pleasure. Mark would not like that either.

After her bath, she patted her body dry in the foggy bathroom, stole some of Annie's Chanel No 5 crème pour le corps, the one that Annie had bought the day before when all was well, when the frivolous was acceptable. She slipped into a favorite pair of lavender leggings and a matching T-shirt. Her wardrobe had narrowed down to whatever was wearable in the lotus position. She was putting on her socks when the phone rang.

"Jared's going to be fine," Annie quickly said. "I'm sorry I did not call you sooner. He's been out of the coma for the last hour, but it's been one struggle after another."

Lola felt the tension melt out of the muscles in her back. "How is he?"

"They're running some tests on him, but it all looks good so far." Annie sounded exhausted. "You won't believe this, but the question of the moment is not how is he, but how is she."

"Who?"

"Althea," Annie said weakly. "She's been hospitalized, too, one floor above Jared. I'm guessing that the emotion around Jared precipitated things. Listen," she paused before adding, "according to the doctor, Althea was on her last leg. She fainted in the street near the hospital. They said they had rarely seen such a severe case of dehydration. Besides, she is so malnourished. Lola, I..."

"It's the anorexia. This was going to happen sooner or later. We knew that."

"We didn't know that! I certainly didn't know that!" Annie cried out. "I didn't know anything about that."

"I guess I've seen anorexia at work before. There is little you can do."

"There are tons we could have done," Annie screeched, "and even more we should have done." There was a long silence on the phone. "You're right," Annie finally said. "I knew she had an eating disorder. How could I knowingly let her do this to herself?"

Lola searched for soothing words. It had been a difficult morning. Annie acted tough, but she was a marshmallow. On the phone, Annie was blowing her nose.

"I've been so wrapped up in my shit," Annie said finally.

"Think of all the things you were dealing with. Jared and Althea are adults. We'll help her. I don't know how but we'll help her and she'll be fine. I know tons of ano..."

"On the bright side," Annie interrupted, "Lucas spent the night!"

"The two of you did look highly suspicious this morning." She heard Annie giggle, and she was once again amazed by Annie's gift for joy, her ability to either swing away from negative emotions or embrace them. "How did that happen? How was it?"

"I have so much to tell you. Things are a little tense around here. Lucas just arrived. He's acting all perplexed and embarrassed, and you should see me. At any rate, we've spent the whole morning running between Jared and Althea, one crisis after another, and we haven't exchanged one word about the subject."

"This is so romantic!"

"In our case, it was strictly pornographic."

"Even better."

"I want to stay at the hospital for Althea. I told her I would."

"Not a problem. I'll pick up the kids at school at 4, and visit Althea and Jared later. I'm so excited about you and Lucas." A loud banging coming from the front door interrupted her. "Wait," she said. "Someone's at the door. Are you expecting a delivery?" Lola nudged the phone between her ear and her shoulder and ran downstairs. "We'll help Jared and Althea get back on their feet, and everyone is going to be happy, you'll see." She unlocked the entrance door with two hands with the phone tight against her cheek. "Now it's your turn to describe your wild night," she said chuckling while pulling hard for the front door to open. "How did you finally..." Lola faced the open front door, and her body turned to granite.

Annie's voice echoed in her ear. "Lola?"

But Lola could not speak. She heard the faint "Lola? What's going on?" coming from Annie at the end of the line. Lola managed to articulate "I...I have to go."

On the phone, Annie screeched. "What's going on? Who's at the frigging door? Talk to me!"

Lola had forgotten how tall he was, how she needed to look up when she faced him. "Annie... It's my husband," she said, "Mark. He's here... Mark.... How did you...? Annie, I have to go," she stammered before hanging up.

❦

Jared attempted to lift his arm, but it was strapped to the IV so he brought it down. His voice was weak. Lucas had to lean toward him to hear what he was trying to explain. "One thing led to another," Jared said.

Lucas decided to ask. "Did you mean to do this?"

"What?"

"To overdose, Jared. Did you mean to kill yourself?"

"I was having a bad day."

"A bad day!" Lucas blurted out, and Jared closed his eyes. Lucas softened his voice to a whisper. "What happened exactly?"

"Well, I had this...thing with Althea, and I drank a lot of booze on top of some coke and then some other stuff that kind of landed in front of me. I usually know my limits. I fucked up."

"Who got you into drugs? Althea?"

"Believe me, I don't need anyone's help to get into trouble."

"But why?"

"You know how it goes."

"No, I have no idea how it goes, Jared." Lucas rubbed his eyes. "Tell me."

"After Maman died. It was part of a learning curve, I guess. I'm not a junky."

Lucas's throat tightened. "This is not what your mother would have wanted."

"Maman is dead." Jared looked away. "That's as definitive as it gets. It's my own business. I didn't bother anyone."

He squeezed Jared's arm. "Well, it's bothering plenty of people now. You could have died."

"Look, not that I want to die, but what's the difference to anyone if I die now or later?"

"Your father died early, and I think it made a great deal of difference to everyone who loved him and depended on him."

Jared remained silent, and neither one of them spoke for a while. Lucas could not bring himself to mention how this affected him personally. And it would have been bad form to point out that it could not have been worse timing. Lucas's shoulders stooped. There had been no time to speak to Annie about their night together, and he had the feeling that Annie was trying to avoid him. "And Jared, this is already having a snowball effect. Althea is... ill right now. Listen, I hate to tell you this, but she fainted in the street. She's in the emergency room downstairs."

Jared tightened his fist but was too weak to move another muscle. "What happened?" he asked softly.

Lucas did not want to get into it. "It's…unclear. We're still waiting to hear."

"Look," Jared said, "I'm not addicted."

"Not yet."

"That's right. Not yet."

Lucas felt overwhelmed with sadness. "I'll help you out, Jared. You know I will."

"Thanks. I know."

Annie peeked her head inside the room and coughed. "Lucas, may I borrow you?"

"Is Althea okay?" Jared said feebly. He looked ashen.

"She's stable. They gave her something to sleep while they pump her with fluid and stuff. Things her body needs. She's okay for now. Lucas, do you mind coming out here for a minute?"

Once in the hallway, she whispered frantically "You won't believe this. The shit is totally hitting the fan! Lola's husband just showed up at the house!"

Lucas raised an approving eyebrow. "At last! What took him so long?"

"What could you possibly mean? It's total chaos! She can't fight him alone. She's got as much defense as a newborn kitten. I have to rush to the house right now. Can you keep an eye on Jared and Althea? I'll go home and see if Lola needs my help, and…" Annie's eyes widened. "The kids! The last thing we need is to add children to the equation."

Lucas looked at her, waiting for a rest of the sentence. Then it dawned on him. "What do you need me to do?" he said in resignation.

"Pick up the kids at school at four, and then walk to the

daycare, the kids will tell you where it is, and get Simon. And no matter what, don't bring them home."

"Vraiment? And where do you suppose I should take them?"

"I dunno. Your place?"

"All five of them? Je ne peux pas." Discouragement must have showed on his face because Annie planted her eyes right on his.

"You owe it to me," she whispered. "Didn't I just give you the most memorable sex of your life?" She beamed at him.

"Wait a minute," Lucas's spirit soared. He tried to sound extremely offended. "I thought I gave you the best..."

But already she was running away.

CHAPTER 26

a t the door, Mark wasn't exactly smiling, but he did not look angry. He was closely shaven and dressed with extreme care. Did he just bring his small Hermès bag neatly stored in the overhead compartment of his first-class direct flight? Did he already have their flight booked for the way back? Was he planning on taking the children only and leaving her in Paris? She instinctively searched his jaw for tension, his eyes for the cold light of controlled anger, but instead found in his expression a weariness she wasn't familiar with and assumed must be jet lag. Strangely, he looked glad to see her rather than victorious. Her heart was in her throat.

"Aren't you going to let me in?" Mark said. This wasn't a question. Lola moved slowly away from the door to let him in. The absurdity of her situation was so apparent to her now. She had imagined in minute details how Mark would be searching for her, yet had not for an instant prepared herself for the moment he would find her.

She followed him into the house, her mind blank. He stood in the hallway, looked at the collection of small antique mirrors of all sorts and shapes and at the yellow walls stenciled with naïve suns. He waited until it occurred to her to guide him into the living room. She instantaneously began seeing the house through his eyes. The living room was too dark, too heavy with antique furniture and velvet curtains, too provincial French. "Can I give you something to drink?" she asked. Whether he asked for a drink, and the type of drink, the tone of his voice, were all subtle signs she was desperately seeking to read. She searched the walls for traces of Annie's strength and common sense. Hers had abandoned her.

Mark walked around the room taking his time, inspecting objects from a distance that appeared to be physical and emotional, like he was visiting a second-rate museum. He did not touch anything and she was thankful for that, because she would have perceived it as an invasion of Annie's home. She wished so much she had not let him in. And it was terrible how she already felt battered by his unspoken disapproval. He turned to her and stared at her, cocked his head with an amused expression. "You look different." This sounded neither like a criticism nor a compliment. She instantly became terribly self-conscious. "I do hope this is a wig," he said, pointing at her hair. She felt relief like cool water running though her body and smiled. This was his sense of humor. She fluffed her now blond hair. "I let it grow out. This is my real color actually."

"Who lives here?" Mark said.

"Well, there's Annie, my... good friend, and her three sons, Maxence, Paul, and—"

"Any guys living here?"

She was about to give him a convoluted answer when she remembered something Annie had said. "You don't owe him an explanation. Just remind yourself that he is the bad guy, not you." So, Lola did something very out of character. She answered with a question and mirrored his tone.

"Is there a woman living in your house?"

She chose the word "your" on the spur of the moment, and it

felt good. Mark ignored the question and returned to inspecting things. Her shoulders had turned as hard and heavy as stone, and her jaw felt sore from clenching it. She was able to gather enough distance from what was happening to understand that her body was awaiting the blow up. Mark had not blown up yet but he was about to, because that's what he did. Something stirred in her, indignation, determination. This was no way to live, this walking on eggshells, terrified of a human ticking time bomb.

"What money have you been using?" Mark asked softly. "Nothing came out of our accounts."

On the phone with Annie, she had wanted to shout out for her friend to come to the rescue, but with Mark right in front of her, it had been impossible. So she pictured Annie in her mind for strength.

"I'm using my own savings. From before us."

"Clever girl," he said. "You had a secret account all this time? I never knew you to be secretive."

There was something different about him that she could not put her finger on. He seemed...not humble, no, not quite, but less self-assured, and also less edgy. She wondered if maybe he was sick. "I guess I thought I knew you, but the joke's on me," he added.

"Do you want to sit down?" She asked and she was surprised to see him sit on the couch immediately, as though he had been waiting for permission. He crossed his legs with one foot over the knee, and spread his arms on either side of the couch. She knew his body language, had learned to read its minutest fluctuations. Mark was trying to appear relaxed in a way that screamed that he wasn't. "Okay," he said, trying to smile. "So what's the plan now that I'm here?"

She had seen him do this a hundred times—let the other person talk too much, get confused, emotional. He'd reveal nothing of himself or his desires until he was completely in control. "Information is power," he always said. She didn't have to fall into the trap. All she had to do was the opposite of what she usually did. No excuses, no glib explanations, no pitiable display of emotion. So rather than sit down, she crossed her arms and said relatively firmly and with as little feeling as possible, "You tell me what the plan is."

Mark examined Lola from head to toe with amusement. "What's wrong with the way your hair was before? Is that part of the incognito thing? Are you trying to change identity?" he laughed a bit too loudly. She wanted to tell him that this was the real her, and that the identity she had assumed with him was the false one. She saw him follow her gaze toward the clock. The children needed to be picked up from school in just a few hours. As on cue, Mark asked: "Where are the kids? Are they here?"

He would take the kids away! He would have every right to. She had been found out but she could still hide them from him. Panic set in and she was slowly falling apart starting with the knot of tears that was irrepressibly forming in her throat.

"I want to see them," Mark said.

She was about to burst into tears like a five-year-old when came the unmistakable pushing and yanking sound of someone opening the front door, followed by the loud thump of the wooden door closing again. Mark, from his sitting position on the couch, looked at her interrogatively. What followed was almost comical. Annie barged into the room. Her hair was electric and she seemed to have been sprinting.

"Cheerio!" she said, panting. She walked right to Mark without the slightest pretense of surprise. "I'm Annie. This is my house," she huffed, holding her hand out to shake his. Mark slowly unfolded from the couch and got up to face her. Standing, Mark was a good foot taller than she was but to Lola, Annie was the Rock of Gibraltar. For what seemed like an eternity, Mark did not take the hand Annie continued to keep firmly outstretched toward him. When he finally shook it, it felt to Lola as though Annie had scored a touchdown. She had made Mark do

315

something he did not want to do! But Lola's elation did not last. Instead of looking at her and speaking to her, Mark looked at Lola and said, "Where are the kids?"

"You haven't introduced yourself," Annie said aggressively as she stood in front of him, hands on her hips.

"Annie, this is my husband, Mark…"

Annie looked at Lola with an expression that said, "Duh!"

"Lola, I need to see Lia and Simon," Mark said. He was beginning to look agitated.

"You're out of luck," Annie said. "The children are out of town." Lola knew it was a bluff, but she felt a nonsensical sense of relief. "As I said," Annie added, "this is my house. As far as I know, there is no reason why you shouldn't be welcome. But things can change very quickly."

"Lola," Mark said between his teeth, "I need to talk to you in private."

Annie turned to Lola, who was petrified. "Lola, do you wish to speak to this man privately?"

"Not really," Lola said, and she meant it.

"All right," Annie continued. "In that case, I will be present during your conversation, as a mediator."

"You're dreaming," Mark chuckled.

Annie walked toward Mark. Was it Lola's imagination or did Mark back off ever so slightly. "Then you can leave," she said. "Should I be calling the police?"

Mark let out a big friendly laugh, and put both of his hands up in surrender. "All right, ladies. Let's be friends here."

Lola's face lit up with relief. Annie's expression was unflinching, and she was certainly not laughing. "Are you saying that you're agreeing to me serving as mediator?"

Mark was still smiling widely, "All right, all right…whatever. Lola, where did you find your friend here? You gals crack me up." Lola detected tension in his jaw, but he could have fooled anyone else. Thankfully, Annie didn't appear the least bit fooled either.

She had heard enough accounts to know what Mark was capable of. Lola caught herself wanting Mark to go crazy and demonstrate one of his trademark temper tantrums so she could be vindicated. Annie would see how terrifying Mark was, and it would excuse her lies, all of them.

But for the moment, Annie didn't seem terrified at all. She guided Mark to the kitchen and had him and Lola sit on opposite sides of the kitchen table. Mark was even more of an incongruous apparition in Annie's kitchen, which had so recently overflowed with kids, cereal boxes, and cups of hot cocoa. Mark had to love the kitchen, she thought. Everyone loved Annie's kitchen. It was so French, so quaint. But moving from the living room to the kitchen did not change the fact that time was ticking. The kitchen clock was just as mercilessly accurate as the living room clock. She breathed with increasing difficulty. She stopped looking at the clock, which she decided was going to give things away, and, resting all hope on Annie, she waited for someone's next move. While she and Mark fell silent, Annie flattened her crazed hair with the palm of her hand, brushed some crumbs leftover from breakfast off the table with dignity, and turned on the coffeemaker. She opened the kitchen glass door wide. The chirps of birds and summer heat found their way into the kitchen. In the distance, someone was playing the piano, a lighthearted piece that sounded like something by Vivaldi.

"Let me grab something to write with," Annie said. She walked out of the kitchen while Mark and Lola sat in silence. Lola scrutinized her hands and considered how docile Mark was at the moment as he looked around the kitchen and rocked on the back legs of his chair. A minute later, Annie was back and she was holding a pad and a pen. She sat down on the chair across from Mark, and sat at Lola's side. Annie was in her element, in her kitchen, in her house. The sun and the smell of coffee flooded the kitchen like a promise of better days.

"Let's get started, shall we?" Annie said. "Oh, and Mark,

317

please, could you stop doing that to the chair. It's an antique, and you might end up on your ass."

Mark stopped. Lola looked in despair at the clock. It was three forty-five. The children! She glanced in panic at Annie who discretely mouthed, "Lu-cas."

😀

A violent ray of sunshine darted through an opening in the curtains of Althea's hospital room. That light attacked her in her sleep, and she awakened with difficulty. She lifted an arm, wiggled her toes, and was surprised when they responded. She dropped her arm, exhausted by the effort. Her head hurt terribly, her brain felt too large for her skull, and it was nearly impossible to open her eyes. The scary nurse who had made Annie cry barged into the room, her voice boomed.

"I see Sleeping Beauty's up!"

Althea felt compelled to apologize. "I'm ready to go now. I'm sorry."

"Sorry?"

"I'm fine really. I just need to pee."

The nurse moved about the room. "You don't need to pee. You're connected to a catheter. It's just uncomfortable."

Althea, horrified, imagined what that meant.

"Anyway," the nurse added without looking at her, "no one's going anywhere."

"You don't understand."

The nurse shrugged and looked at her with cold eyes. "If someone doesn't understand, it's you." And she left.

The throbbing pain in her head erased all thoughts for a while, but Althea didn't have the strength or courage to face the nurse and ask for a pain reliever.

Soon, the doctor, a tall black man in a white lab coat, walked in. In his footsteps walked an elegantly dressed round woman in her sixties. The woman was as short as the doctor was tall, as pale as he was dark. She wore an expensively cut gray suit that didn't belong in a hospital room. Both the doctor and the lady had matching expressions of unhurried kindness. The doctor took her pulse and spoke with a hint of an African accent. "How are you feeling?"

"I have a very bad headache," Althea whimpered, and saying those words she nearly burst into tears. The doctor called the nurse on the intercom and asked her to add something to Althea's IV. The nurse entered, syringe in hand, and her face lit up when she saw the older woman. The two spoke in French about grandchildren while the doctor continued to examine Althea, pausing every so often to take notes. Althea's head throbbed. The nurse emptied the content of the syringe into the IV bag and left the room. The doctor scribbled in a file and the round little woman dragged a chair next to Althea. "Hello, my child. My name is Madame Defloret." She added the obvious, "I speak English."

"Good," Althea whispered. She was glad it was her turn to get this stranger's attention. The nasty nurse had seemed delighted to speak to her.

The lady took Althea's hand. "I'll tell you what is going on, and what we suggest you do about it, and you decide if you agree to it." Madame Defloret's voice seemed to turn liquid. Althea felt a release of every muscle in her body. "I'm ready to go. I'm feeling just fine. I'm so sorry I..."

"You've been diagnosed with an acute case of Anorexia Nervosa. Are you familiar at all with what this illness signifies?"

Althea felt the distant alarm in her brain. She was in dangerous territory, but her headache was melting away, and she could only notice the wellbeing. She did not answer.

"It is a very real illness that requires treatment," Madame Defloret continued without letting go of Althea's hand. "For too many it is a deadly illness. It is considered by many as a mental illness. Have you been diagnosed or treated in the past? Are you receiving treatment now?" Althea turned her face away. Mental illness? What the woman said did not matter, but the kindness of her tone made Althea's throat tighten. "Have you, my child?" Madame Defloret insisted. "Have you been diagnosed or treated, ever? In America maybe?"

"No...no, never. I'm all right, really. I think I can go home."

"As far as this hospital is concerned, it would be assuming too much of a risk to let you go until you are better."

"I feel better," Althea answered, and she did feel wonderfully relaxed at that moment.

Madame Defloret looked straight at her. "You need to listen to this, Althea. This is a serious matter. You might not be able to assess things accurately. Your body is completely run down by this, and most likely there was a grave toll on your emotional welfare as well. In my experience, even with the best of intentions and family support, you won't be able to overcome this on your own."

Althea blinked, her eyes wanted to close. "On my own," she echoed.

"I work for the eating disorder department at Sainte-Anne Hospital. We have a wonderful service that deals specifically with your kind of problem. We don't always have spaces available, but I have a spot for you."

Althea looked incredulously at Madame Defloret. She couldn't think of anything to say.

"Do you have any questions, dear?"

Althea's words and thoughts struggled to come out "How...do you know...for sure If I have a mental...anorexia?"

"Honey, you weigh ninety pounds and measure five-foot-seven. The ratio alone is a real indication of malnutrition. When was the last time you had your period?"

"I don't remember."

"I'm here to help. Do you want to be helped?"

Tears swelled up in Althea from way down in her throat. "I don't think you can help me."

"Oh," Madame Defloret said with a smile, "I've helped young women such as yourself time and time again, even some whose lives were only hanging by a thread. I absolutely can help you. But you have to want to be helped. It will be hard work, but, dear, there is a light at the end of the tunnel."

Althea could no longer think or speak. She only found the strength to say, "Please, yes."

"Here is the paper you need to sign." She placed a pen in Althea's hand and Althea watched her hand sign on the line. In the far distance, she heard a voice. "She's in. Let's have her transported to Saint-Anne right away. Lucky girl." And a moment later, Althea surrendered to sleep.

Leaning against the school gate, Lucas rubbed his chin, surprised to find it rough with beard. He had not showered, brushed his teeth or shaved since the morning before and was still wearing the same clothes. Why, he practically looked like a transient. Now that Jared's life was no longer in danger, Lucas had returned to worrying about Annie, or Annie as she pertained to him. The last playful words exchanged as she was running out of the hospital and back home to assist Lola had only reassured him briefly. He replayed the evening and the night in his mind, going from smiling to himself to feeling despondent. And now, why was he here at the children's school taking part in the charade between Lola and her husband? Maybe he should be at the house instead to make sure things were safe. Even if Lola's husband wasn't violent, Annie was just as likely to escalate a confrontation.

The children came out, cutely dressed in school clothes and wearing backpacks. But the warm welcome he had expected did not happen. The children weren't delighted to find him standing outside the school gate. Maxence looked at him accusatorily. "Why are you here?"

"Your mothers," Lucas started and then cleared his throat, "are visiting Jared and Althea at the hospital."

Maxence looked dubious. "I thought it was just Jared."

"What's wrong with them?" Paul said.

"It's a complicated question and—"

"Did he shoot her?" said Laurent.

The children asked and asked, he noticed, but seldom waited for an answer. "Nothing of such a dramatic nature, I'm afraid."

"Are they dead, though?" Paul wanted to know.

Laurent pushed him. "If they were dead, they'd be at the cemetery, not the hospital you turd-head."

"Are they bleeding at least?" Paul asked.

Lia trailed behind. "Where are we going?"

"We're picking up your baby brother and then to the…"

"When's Mom coming back?"

"…park," Lucas continued, wondering about his blood pressure.

Maxence raised an eyebrow, "Oh yeah? Why not the house?"

Lucas had figured out a long time ago that the boy was exceptionally sharp. "That would be because…"

Paul interrupted. "Which park?"

Laurent made an awful face and held his throat. "I'm thirsty."

Lucas strained to continue, "…they forgot to give me the key."

"Whatever happened to your own key?" Maxence said.

"I…misplaced it."

"Well, that sure is bad luck!" Maxence exclaimed, not buying it for an instant. Before he asked another one of those disagreeably inquisitive questions, Lucas took Maxence aside. This was the best thing to do, the only thing to do.

"Lia's father has come, quite unexpectedly I'm afraid, and there needs to be some grown-up discussion before…"

Maxence nodded knowingly. "We're in hiding then?"

"Well... we... but... In a way…"

Maxence patted Lucas on the arm. "Don't worry, man. I'll cover for you."

The group walked gingerly to Simon's daycare and Lucas decided that his fear had been just plain silly. At the daycare, Simon was busy at work with Legos and did not want to leave. Finally, he got up from the rug and followed them. But as soon as they were outside, Simon stalled.

"What is it now, small one?" Lucas asked him.

Lia shrugged. "He hates to walk."

"You could just carry him," Laurent instructed. Lucas lifted Simon up onto his shoulders. The child was light but strangled him with his powerful little arms.

There were too many of them, so a taxi was out of the question. Strong from his morning experience, Lucas decided he would take the children on the métro. He was a bit miffed when the kids casually took passes from their pockets and entered the station as easily as he would have entered Fauchon. Lucas studied the map and came up with an itinerary. They would have to change trains three times, but to get to Buttes Chaumont would present the advantage of being near the park and steps away from his apartment. They rode the métro from La Muette to Buttes Chaumont. At each métro change, Lucas lifted Simon onto his shoulders and huffed and puffed to the next train, the children complaining of thirst, heat and hunger the entire time.

When they finally got out of the métro, Laurent said, "How come we didn't take the métro at Passy? We would have had to change only once." Lucas planted his gaze on the child and wondered if he should put his own understanding of the world into question. As they climbed up the steps out of the subway and toward the street, he nudged Simon. "Come on, little one. You can walk. I've seen you do it plenty of times."

"Mamma," Simon began wailing.

"How does your mother do this?" he asked Lia. "This gigantic baby must weigh over fifteen kilos!"

"Mom?" Lia said. "She doesn't carry him like that."

"She takes the stroller," Paul added.

"What stroller?" Lucas heard himself wail. "Where is it?"

"At the daycare," Laurent answered.

Lucas wailed, "Should you not have told me about the stroller?"

Lia just shrugged as if to say, "What is the problem with you?"

At the park, Lucas was desperate to rest on a bench, but the children saw the ice cream vendor. From there on, things worsened. Lucas purchased five ice creams, but by the time the last child was served, the other four were a mess. The ice cream melted faster than they could eat it, and already their clothes and faces were smeared in horrible ways. Lucas made a silent prayer that Annie would call him and that he would not have to bring them up to his apartment. The playground was shaded and Lucas moaned with relief when he finally sat on the bench.

"All right now. You can play," he said and waved in the direction of the jungle gym.

Lia planted herself in front of him.

"I need to pee."

The bathroom was within eye distance. He pointed to it.

"Mom takes me into public bathrooms," Lia told him, making a face.

Indeed, the toilets of public parks had to be squalid, and what about the strange people that might be lurking around. But how could he take one child to the toilet and leave the other four unsupervised. The boys were busy amusing themselves with fighting other children on the playground. They called it play, but it was more like war. Youngsters could be remarkably aggressive, Lucas noticed, but he also noticed with contentment, and maybe a hint of pride, how his children formed a tight little clan against the others.

Lucas turned to a mother on a nearby bench who had heaven knew how many children of her own. "Would you mind keeping an eye on those boys there?" He pointed to Lia. "This little lady needs to use the restroom."

He stood with great discomfort at the door of the girl's bathroom. "The lock is broken," he apologized to the mother and daughter waiting in line behind him.

Lia's voice came out of the stall. "There is no paaa-per! Can you hand me a Kleenex?"

"Dear," Lucas whispered, "I do not carry such things."

The woman behind him laughed and produced Kleenexes from her purse as though she were some kind of genius. Lucas thanked her as graciously as he could, considering he felt like clubbing her over the head. But already, on the playground, the woman allegedly supervising his children was yelling at Paul for hitting one of her brats with a plastic shovel.

It was getting late. Annie had not called him and he knew better than to call her. How he was ready to bring the children back to their house. To hell with keeping them! But the thought of taking the métro again was more than he could bear. Of course, his own apartment was five minutes away, but the thought of five children with shoes filled with sand and hands sticky with ice cream residue all over his Persian rugs made him shudder.

The children, sensing his weakness, began making demands.

"We're hungry!"

"You just had ice cream."

Laurent shrugged. "Ice cream doesn't fill you up."

"It's just sugar. Empty calories," Lia added.

"Empty?" Lucas echoed.

"I have an idea. You go get the food," Maxence suggested. "We'll stay here and play."

"I regret, but this will not be possible."

Laurent pointed an ice cream smeared finger toward a yellow

arch Lucas had never noticed in the past. "McDonald's is right there," he said.

"Me want chicken nuggets," Simon blurted out, followed by frantic orders from every kid:

"I want a Whooper."

"They don't do Whoppers, dumbass."

"Can I have a toy with my happy meal?"

Lucas stopped them by raising both palms. "Let me make something clear," he said, "I refuse to set a foot in that horrible place."

"You never had MacDo?" Maxence was flabbergasted.

"Never have, never will. Not only is it rubbish, but it is the symbol of American imperialism."

"What?"

"France is the world's capital of gastronomy, so why ingest the worst that the world has to offer?"

"How do you know you don't like it if you've never had it?

"You're like Sam I Am."

The children explained that it was an American joke about eating green eggs.

"But it's sooo good."

"But we're really, really hungry."

Lucas discovered he was walking on the edge of the razorblade too late. "No McDonald's! Never!" He yelled.

The playground turned silent. Birds stopped chirping, dogs quit barking, and mothers and children froze. Everyone was staring at him as though he were a child abuser. Lucas hurried the children out of the playground. He felt quite famished himself. With the circus at the hospital, he'd had neither the time nor the enthusiasm for breakfast or lunch. He, too, needed to go to the bathroom but he could no longer ask those hostile mothers for favors. He resigned himself to bringing everyone to his apartment. He would make some pasta; maybe he had enough for a salad. He hoisted Simon on his shoulders, and now was also carrying Lia and Paul's backpacks. He was fuming. The children could see he meant business and cooperated. But they all came to a stop in front of McDonald's, jumping up and down, begging and claiming starvation. The fact was, he was starving. Really starving. He had not eaten a thing in nearly twenty-four hours.

The double cheeseburger with bacon turned out to be surprisingly tasty.

CHAPTER 27

*G*iving a bathroom break as an excuse to leave the kitchen, Annie left Mark and Lola alone and rushed to her bedroom to call Lucas. She wasn't going to miss much. Mark seemed on his best behavior in her presence, asking only carefully crafted questions about the children, which Lola answered happily. Whatever was really on Mark's mind was well concealed and he sounded nothing like the a-hole he had been on the phone. In her bedroom, Annie sat on her bed and dialed Lucas's number. It was well after six p.m.

"What's the news on Althea and Jared?" she asked right away.

Lucas answered with an injured voice. "I called about every hour, both are stable and safely hospital bound at least for the weekend. And Althea is being transferred to that service that takes care of her ... issue."

"That's a relief."

"My apartment is ransacked, I have a terrible headache and I still haven't had a chance to take a shower," he said.

Annie smiled to herself. "Welcome to the last ten years of my life," she said.

"I'm glad you called," he said. "There's been this thing on my mind, I wanted to ask you if —"

"Mark is so smooth," Annie interrupted. "You'd think he's just here on a little visit. If I did not know better, which I do because I heard with my own ears what he is capable of, I'd think Lola was a lying sac of dung. But so far, he's been entirely in control and he's not said the least aggressive thing. I'd bet he's waiting for the moment he can be alone with her to rip her a new one."

"Do you believe him to be dangerous?"

"I can't imagine he would be, unless I'm a poor judge of character. Still, you should see how much power he has over Lola."

"Who doesn't have power over her?" Lucas sighed.

"I'm enjoying the challenge."

"I'm delighted you're having such a wonderful time," he said with defeat in his voice.

"Oh come on, how bad can it be? They're wonderful children."

"Yes, wonderful. And absolutely filthy. And all over my nineteenth-century Kurdish rug. They're watching television now."

Annie took a breath, mustering courage for what she was about to ask of him. "I really think we should keep the children away from the house. Lola and Mark need to be alone to sort things through. The kids' presence would jeopardize any chance of an adult conversation." On the line there was silence, then a heartbreaking moan. Annie braced herself. Of course, Lucas already knew what she was about to say. "We need to find a solution for the night," she added.

"I can't possibly— "

"You have to."

"But there is no room, no beds. I can't very well make them sleep on the floor, can I? And doesn't this man have the right to see his children?"

"He's got no rights in my book."

"Meanwhile, I'm being an accessory to a crime."

She sighed, "Oh now the big words."

"Annie," Lucas hesitated, "I need to ask you something—"

"Besides he'll see them. Only not tonight. Listen, I have to get back to Lola and Mark."

"There is the possibility of my cabin in Honfleur. We could get there in about two hours by car. There are enough beds. But my car is too small. We would need your van."

"Honfleur! The beach!" she yelped. "Oh Lucas, I could hug you right now!"

"About that, I wanted to ask you if—"

"I'll load up the minivan and pick you and the kids up and off to Honfleur!"

"You! Pick us up?" he asked.

"So what?"

"You don't drive anymore, remember?"

"I'll drive the darn thing to your place, and you can do the drive to Honfleur."

"Lola's not coming?"

"That's the whole point. She needs to stay and humor that Neanderthal." She teased, "Are you worried to find yourself alone with me?"

"Alone? With five children?" Lucas said. "Let me ask you something."

"I better pack bathing suits!"

"Annie, we're not going anywhere until you shut up for a second and listen to me!"

"I'm all ears," she said after a long pause.

"Did you...?" Lucas cleared his throat, "Well, was last night meaningful to you?"

"Meaningful? Of course, it was meaningful," she mumbled.

"Annie, help me out here."

"Don't we have the weekend to talk about this?"

"Would it be more towards the positive-meaningful, or the negative-meaningful?" Lucas asked.

Her mind went blank. She was not prepared to answer that question, any question.

"Annie?"

Her nose felt prickly. "You're pretty cute, you know."

"I'll take that as a positive, then?"

She looked around the room for a Kleenex. She'd be damned if he heard her cry. "I would. Yes, definitely."

"Are you really sure about driving the van?"

"Listen, I can drive the van, okay?"

"All right, all right. We're waiting. Bring vast quantities of aspirin."

The drip into her arm was gone and replaced by a small bandage. She did not feel weak anymore, but she was exhausted despite sleeping so deeply for hours that she did not even feel herself transported by ambulance from the hospital to where she was now. Althea dressed herself, stepped into the hallway, and asked for the room where she was supposed to meet Madame Defloret. She walked through several hallways, refusing to make eye contact. It was after nine p.m. and the light of the day was only now showing signs of waning. Outside, the sky had a purplish tint. Every window in this place had a metal screen over it, like a prison. She entered a room that resembled a classroom. In the center of the room, ten chairs had been arranged in a circle. Madame Defloret sat in one of the chairs. A long strand of pearls rested on her motherly bosom. "Have a seat, Althea," she smiled. "The rest of our little group is about to arrive for our evening meeting."

Althea wrapped her arms around her body. She instinctively

searched for the way out as one by one girls and young women entered the room, all thin. Much too thin. She observed the women as they entered the bare room and sat reluctantly without acknowledging each other. Althea searched the girls' eyes and faces for a thread of connection. But the eyes weren't interesting in seeing and the faces were closed. What did she have in common with this punk-looking girl who wore torn black pantyhose, a bobby pin in her ear and who sat staring down at her feet, clearly resolved not to speak or listen. What did she have in common with this small girl dressed in pink jeans and pink T-shirt who looked straight in front of her with fire in her eyes, ready to kill? These girls were trapped inside themselves she could tell. She wanted to have nothing in common with them, yet she knew why she had been brought here, and that she was here for the same reason they were. They shared a single purpose, a single common obsession: food, or how to avoid it. There was no hiding it to herself anymore.

As more patients came in and filled the chairs, she realized with sadness that by entering this place, by leaving Lola, Annie, the children and their earthly preoccupations, she had left humanity behind in a way. This sisterhood was devoid of empathy or closeness. Here, it would be each woman for herself. Lola and Annie had offered her kinship at a time when she couldn't accept it. She had also experienced being cared for and a sense of connection when she was with Jared. She would find none of it here. She was glad to know connection with other humans existed, and how good it felt. It helped to hang on to that thought as she found herself in a room full of women dead set on avoiding it. In a way, she did not belong in Annie and Lola's life, and she did not belong with these girls either. But where did she belong? She had hoped to belong with Jared but it was all so clear now that all along he had to be on drugs to tolerate her. That thought, strangely, made her more furious than sad.

She thought of excuses to get up and leave. She understood the bars on the window all of a sudden. This was a psychiatric hospital. Surely, they could not keep her here against her will. But if she left and went outside, she would be reduced to confront whatever was haunting her without help, support or guidance, just as she always had. There was no outside. Outside was a metaphor for life, and to her, inaccessible. This was a psychiatric hospital, and she, Althea, was mentally ill. She knew she could not do it alone, and for the first time in her life, she did not want to do it alone. Sitting in her chair, surrounded by women who, like her, suffered unimaginable pain, Althea made the most important decision of her life. She decided to trust she could get better. For Jared. For herself.

Madame Defloret started to speak, and Althea listened.

Lola knew that the so-called couple mediation Annie had in mind had little to do with anything other than gaining time. Neither she nor Annie knew what they were doing, and if Mark realized this, he showed no sign. Lola controlled the shaking in her voice and asked him mundane questions about his flight, and when he had arrived and where he was staying and he responded in a perfectly civil manner. They could have been two strangers meeting for the first time. Annie pretended to take notes, but clearly had no clue how to mediate a thing. As for Mark, he might have agreed to Annie being there but that did not mean he had any intention of revealing the least bit about himself or his intentions in her presence. Mark wasn't the type to air his dirty laundry in public anyway. Anger and yelling were the only way he showed emotion, so for the time being he was careful to show none. An outburst, threats and insults would arrive all too soon but this gift of time, the knowledge that the children were away and Annie was present helped Lola gather herself.

When Annie left the two of them alone in the kitchen, they faced each other in silence. She could tell that he wanted to say something, that he was mulling it over, something he had trouble getting out. She waited. When he finally spoke, it was to say only one thing: "I missed you so much, Lola." She was too astonished to respond.

Annie came back a few minutes later and discretely put a scribbled note in her hand. "Picking up kids and Lucas with van and taking them to ocean for weekend (he-he!) if that's ok with you??? You 2 go out to restaurant so I can pack."

So Lola suggested that maybe she and Mark could go out and talk just the two of them. Annie made a big show of asking if she was absolutely sure that is what she wanted to do, and should she come along. Dinner in a restaurant was agreed upon.

Lola was still wearing yoga clothes, an outfit that seemed perfectly good a few hours ago. She had felt very much a woman in it. She had seduced Gunter in it, but now it felt all wrong. She asked Mark for time to change for dinner. She asked him, she realized.

Mark waited in the living room while she ran up the stairs and rummaged in her tiny closet, her cheeks burning. Mark had dropped everything and flown thousands of miles just for her, just to find her. The only decent clothes she owned were the pants and turtleneck she had not worn once since her flight to Paris. She put them on anyway. Mark liked her boobs when she wore a turtleneck. Underneath, she wore a silk camisole just in case. Mark hated waiting so she hurried to the bathroom and found all her make-up neatly arranged on the vanity. She applied mascara and peach-colored lipstick, and brushed on some powder foundation. Her confidence rose as the image in the mirror began to resemble more the Lola Mark was used to. There was a violent knock at the bathroom door.

"Open, it's me!" Annie said.

Lola let her in, twirled, and flashed Annie her movie star smile as a joke. "What do you think?"

Annie looked indignant. "Making yourself all pretty?"

Lola frowned at Annie's angry tone. "What's the problem?"

"You tell me what the problem is! We just went through hours of drama, shams, schlepping of the kids, leaving Althea and Jared on their frigging deathbeds, and all this shit only to end up at a romantic dinner between you and this schmuck?"

"What do you expect me to do?"

Annie's rage was barely contained. "Certainly not to fall back into his arms like this."

"Annie, I'm sorry. I just don't know how to deal with him."

Annie raised her voice, "Can't you see you have to stop trying to please everyone?"

"Shhhh…"

"I'm sick and tired of people doing what's wrong for them."

Lola thought of the children. She thought of Mark, who was probably in a state of advanced agitation waiting for her. She thought of the life she had here that she didn't want to give up. She thought of the life that was waiting for her in Beverly Hills. The soulless mansion, the bleak runs to generic stores, the right shirt always at the dry cleaner. Watching her step. Watching her back. Her breathing was constricted. She felt a strange rush of energy throughout her body. "Why don't you tell me what's best for me then, since you have all the answers," she said between clenched teeth.

"You don't want to hear what I think," Annie barked.

Lola's pulse raced. "Try me," she said coldly.

Annie put her hands on her hips and said, "How about you end the charade and tell him the truth. Tell him you want a divorce."

Lola felt a heat wave engulf her. Who was Annie to give her orders on how to run her life? Who was she to talk to her as though she were a little girl? Despite herself, she raised her voice. It was entirely unlike her to raise her voice. "How can you be so sure?"

"It's so obvious!"

"You don't know him at all. You're not in my shoes."

"One life! We have one life! And if you go back with him you know what your life is going to be. It won't change mine. You ran away from him. You disappeared. You hid for months. Can't you remember how bad it had to be for someone like you to do something that drastic? You were in hell! Your life was horrible!"

Lola paced angrily from the tub to the door and back. It was so ridiculous, this fight in the bathroom. "No matter what, I'll have to go back and live in the States. Otherwise, you know what he'll do? He'll go after the children. I kidnapped them. I could go to jail!"

"Ha! You realize that now, after all these months?"

"And the children...And Mark still loves me. He said so. He said he missed me."

"Ha! Famous fucking last words! He loves to own you, haven't you noticed?"

Lola had noticed. She tried to resist the volcano brewing inside her. "No, I did not notice!"

Tears flew from Annie's eyes. She didn't even bother wiping them. "Fine, I'm out of here. I'm very fucking disappointed in you."

Lola erupted. "Stop saying fucking! And I'm not here to make you happy! You want me to stop pleasing him so that I can please you? Trade one tyrant for another?"

Annie opened her mouth in shock. "I have zero invested interest in your decision!"

"Stop fixating on my life, okay? Why don't you start working on yours if you're so evolved...and leave me alone."

"Fine! Let him use you as a rug. You love it!" Annie wiped her tears, all anger suddenly out of her voice. "Am I still taking the kids to the ocean?"

"Yes! Take them to the fucking ocean," Lola yelled. It felt good to yell. So good.

Annie raised an eyebrow, as though she wondered what Lola was so mad about, shrugged, and left the bathroom.

Lola sat on the edge of the bathtub, shaking. Mark was still waiting downstairs. He would have to wait. She looked at herself in the mirror and saw pure rage. She barely recognized herself. Her hands were folded into tight fists. If Annie hadn't left, she would have whacked her, she knew she would have.

Suddenly, the door opened, and Annie peeked in. "Okay, honey, keep in touch with the anger. It's good, excellent!" and she closed the door.

So this was how it worked? Lola ran back to her room and nearly ripped her clothes off. She replaced them with an old pair of jeans and a baggy sweater. She wiped her lipstick with the back of her hand. She kept her fists tight. She was ready for Mark.

It was an eerie feeling to be walking down the steps of Annie's house and in the streets of the sixteenth arrondissement of Paris with Mark. Her heart was beating hard. How had she managed to push away the thought of him? Now that he was here, he filled all the spaces in her head, and unfortunately, in her heart. He wore that lavender aftershave she liked so much, and that did not help. It was irrational of her, but she was just thrilled. It was as though his presence in Paris was a sign that he loved her. It wasn't like this at all, of course, but she so badly wanted this evening to be romantic. Had he taken her in his arms, would she have buried her head in his neck, or would she have been able to resist? But Mark only walked and did not try to take her hand. Thank goodness he didn't take her hand.

The sun was slowly setting. They walked in silence, neither of them managing small talk. They passed all the familiar shops closed for the night. She would not be able to show him the jewelry-like spread of pastries behind the window of the boulangerie, the quaint cheese shop. She longed to share the marvelous Parisian sights and experiences with him. But now, glancing at his profile, the strong angle of his jaw, watching him hurry through the streets as though lost in his thoughts, she doubted he would be the kind to enjoy Paris at all. She was catching herself remembering Mark as she wished he would be, as opposed to how he really was.

They advanced toward rue de Passy in search of a restaurant. There was the building where she taught Yoga. There was rue de l'Annonciation, where she bought peonies and fromage de chèvre. Here was the very mailbox where she dropped the postcards. Over there, at the end of rue de Passy, was the métro and the city beyond. Between the centuries-old buildings, the sky was deep blue with streaks of pink clouds. Mark marched without looking and she walked along without sharing, her heart tightening with each step.

As they walked, she also began to sense something different in the air that had nothing to do with Mark's presence. The streets were unmistakably livelier than they usually were at this time on a Friday evening. The neighborhood, polished and upper class, did not usually attract the kind of Parisians who party at night. But the more they advanced, the more she saw men and women, couples and groups of teenagers everywhere. Was it music she heard? There was a sense of anticipation and excitement in the air she did not recognize.

It wasn't until they were halfway up rue de Passy that she remembered. Today was June 21st. Summer solstice. Tonight, was the yearly Fête de la Musique. This also meant that tonight was the third anniversary of Johnny's death. No wonder Annie was a basket case.

Bands were setting up, and Parisians were flocking out of buildings and onto the streets. Small crowds were beginning to gather around musicians, and many were already dancing. Was

Mark noticing any of this? Paris was en fête and she was stuck with her own personal party-pooper.

They slowed their pace as they passed restaurants dressed in long white tablecloths and flickering candles on diminutive tables set right on the sidewalk. At the terraces, couples gazed at each other over stiff menus. The rainstorm of the day before and the heat of today had turned the evening warm and balmy. The quality, the texture of the air reminded her of the Hawaiian breeze of their honeymoon. They had made love on the lanai for days. They had lived naked for a week and had fed each other mango and pineapple, drunk with each other's touch. She closed her eyes and thought she smelled the salt of an improbable ocean.

Mark came to a stop and pointed up to a restaurant sign. "What about here? Chinese?" A Chinese restaurant? In Paris? Mark always chose the restaurant, and there was a time when she would rather not have made that kind of decision. Already Mark had entered the restaurant, but she surprised herself by not following him inside. She remained standing by a table nudged between the wall and the sidewalk, a table set for two with a small bouquet of orchids in the center.

Inside, Mark was speaking to the maître d' in boisterous English that was clearly getting him nowhere. Lola watched him through the glass window. Had he noticed she had not followed him inside? Her body was filled with the kind of energy that could have launched a rocket; an energy that rushed through her arms and accumulated in her fisted hands. Mark finally turned to speak to her, and seeing that she wasn't there, stormed outside. When he found her standing by the small table, he looked so flabbergasted that she almost laughed. "You're not coming?" he asked, and there was a tinge of despair in his tone.

She waved in the direction of the white tablecloth: "I want to eat right here."

She marveled at how easy it was to state this simple fact.

Mark turned on his feet; returned inside, spoke to the same

maître d' who hurried outside with him, menus in hand. As they sat down, Mark did not seem upset, as though what had just happened was of no significance. Could it be this easy? Simply ask and you shall receive?

Mark, with much arm movement, ordered a scotch. The waiter had to be playing dumb, squinting and shaking his head emphatically in incomprehension. Lola found it very amusing to watch his Majesty Mark the Great, Ruler of All He Saw, struggle with a society for which the American's concept of "service" is seen as humiliating subservience. Clearly, Mark had rubbed management the wrong way by bullying his way to a table. This meal would be fun to watch. Paris would chip away at Mark's arrogance real fast. Lola couldn't hide a smile.

"Anything you can do to help here?" said Mark, not amused.

"Bonsoir, pourrais-je avoir un whisky pour monsieur et pour moi un verre de rosé, s'il vous plaît," she said. The waiter beamed at her "bien sûr, Madame," and left.

"I guess you speak the native dialect. You learned fast."

"I took French for years."

"Didn't know that."

"Don't know much about me, do you?" she said, surprised at the animosity in her voice.

Mark seemed taken aback by her confrontational tone. "Please spare me the attitude," he said.

What would Annie answer to that? Lola looked Mark straight in the eyes. "If I were you, I'd put the diplomatic gloves back on," she said.

"Diplomatic? You're the one who disappeared." He paused, looked away. "You took the children with you. You left me. I think you owe me an apology," he paused again, "and remorse. Don't you think it would be appropriate, now that your pitbull friend is not around? And..." Mark stopped what had sounded like the introduction to one of his tirades and studied his menu. Lola didn't respond. If it weren't for her pitbull friend, she would have had no time to regroup and things would have taken a very different turn. Right now, she felt strong, stronger than she had ever felt. She waited for an end to Mark's sentence, ready for a fight, but the end of the sentence did not come, and Lola wondered again about the strange discrepancy between the way Mark looked at the moment, weary, almost unassuming, and the way she knew him to be.

CHAPTER 28

*a*s soon as the door to the house closed behind Lola and Mark, Annie rushed about the house, grabbed a couple of duffle bags, and hopped from room to room gathering clothes, pajamas, soap, toiletries, teddy bears. She found the umbrella in the attic, the suntan lotion in the bathroom, water guns in the garden. Within half an hour, she was ready to go. She pushed and shoved the duffle bags and the umbrella down the garage stairs. The kids would be surprised to go on a trip. The weather was perfect. They would have a blast. They'd make a fire pit in the sand and barbecue there. She and Lucas would have ice-cold beers. Beach and beer mixed great. She felt twenty years old. Or fifteen. She had been riding this crazy adrenaline wave all day and she still felt pumped! Thinking of her night with Lucas, she laughed. What in hell was this all about? Was she actually having an affair with Lucas? She dropped the content of her arms on the garage floor by the van and climbed back upstairs to fetch her razor and cellulite cream. She ran back down to the garage, back to the house for the car keys, and again to the garage. She had a vague recollection of Althea, and Jared, and Lola, and Mark. The hell with them all! She opened the trunk, stuffed it with bags, towels, and beach balls. She walked around the van and put her hand on the door.

There was a strange hollow feeling in her stomach. She opened the door, climbed in and sat on the cold leather of the front seat, the van as familiar as the palm of her hand, yet so alien. The smell of the cold car, the dust on the dashboard, even the broken toys, her sitting in the driver's seat, everything so terribly unchanged since that night exactly three years ago. She put the key in the ignition and the engine started. She rested both hands on the wheel and had the creepiest of sensations throughout her body. She quickly turned off the engine, put her hands back on the wheel, and tried to breathe.

Something awful was taking hold of her chest. Her fingers. All of a sudden, she wasn't sure she recognized her own fingers. Her vision blurred. Cold sweat sprang from the nape of her neck and her hands began to shake. The flu? Something she ate? A heart attack? Does a heart attack come with an abominable sense of dread? A scream threatened to come out of her, but her lips refused to open. She had the urge to jump out of the van and run! Run out, now! But she was powerlessly stuck, unable to feel her arms, her legs, her body, unable to move. She had enough presence of mind to realize what was happening to her. This had happened before. She knew what this was. The events of the day, the van... She was having a panic attack.

How could he? How could Johnny do this to her?

She waited. It would pass. She would die or it would pass. It had passed before. Where was Lucas? She needed him now. Cold sweat and shaking, nothing could be done about it. She waited, waited, waited. She wanted to scream but even that was impossible. And then, abruptly, it stopped. Her body stopped shaking. She could breathe again. She sat panting, her hands on the wheel. Sweat streamed down her face, and suddenly, tears sprang, bitter tears. Tears of rage.

Johnny had robbed her. He had died like a coward. He had

died without explaining. He had quit. And she would never know. She would never find out who she was—the woman Johnny was leaving her for.

She began sobbing, each sob like a laceration in her heart. The children had been spared by Johnny's death. But she hadn't been. In the darkness of the garage, the scene unwrapped before her eyes. The lie, the reality she had created for herself and the children practically the moment when she saw Johnny's corpse in the cold room. She would never tell a soul that Johnny was leaving them. The children would never have to know.

Three years ago, to the day. Summer solstice. Fête de la Musique. Something was off that night, uneasy. She had spoken continuously in the car. He said he wanted to go out with her to discuss something important. She hadn't let him. He said he wanted to go out to dinner. Did he really know her that poorly? She was far more likely to have a scene in a restaurant than at home where children could hear.

She had felt close to him that night, that entire year, but it was the wrong kind of closeness, born from unrequited passion. Her parents had pointed it out early on in their marriage: Wasn't Johnny a bit too handsome? It was a mismatch. The mismatch, so obvious to everyone, herself included, was apparently of no concern for Johnny. He had wanted to marry her, he had said. He had loved her. He had chosen her.

Then, just like that, ten years and three children later, Johnny had dumped her. In a van, in the middle of Paris. The words from that night seeped into her brain, invaded her heart, taking hold deep in her soul. Those malignant words of his, so carefully buried within her for three years. She had been driving the van through Paris while Johnny sat in the passenger seat, trusting her.

"Annie, I met someone."

"Someone who?" She said as she drove. She was not going to understand easily.

"A woman."

The dread had come upon her. It had to be a misunderstanding. She turned right at the light, any light. What street they were on, which city, which country, she could not have said. "What kind of woman?" she asked.

"A woman, Annie. I fell in love with someone." He added, "I'm sorry."

"Who is she?" She hadn't wanted to hear the answer. Johnny said her name, but Annie didn't know her. "How old is she?" It mattered without mattering. They had been together for two years, he said. In love, behind her back, a joyous, carefree betrayal. Tell her the prognosis. Cut the crap.

"We want to live together," Johnny said.

We? A new we that did not include her. The cancer of his words was aggressive, spreading fast. Annie's life as she knew it would never be the same. The horror of another woman jumped at her, filled her with poison. She drove mechanically as Johnny spoke in his warm reasonable, charming voice. You could not be mad at Johnny. No one could be mad at Johnny. Everyone loved Johnny.

It did occur to her to stop driving, every part of her was still intent on going out on a date with him, only with a shattered heart. She had only allowed one thought to echo in her mind: she could, she would, win Johnny back from that bitch whoever she was.

"Annie, I want a divorce," Johnny finally said.

The words barely registered. So, she would have to fight harder. Johnny was smitten by this woman but he would not break up his family over her. But then he told her the terrible truth.

"We want to start over in Australia. She's from over there. She can't stay here, professionally and legally."

There was Johnny, in the car, letting her drive, trusting her completely. Her man. Her funny, charming man. Her love, her best friend. He'd obviously had plenty of time to get used to the

whole idea because he spoke with patience and compassion. He
was putting himself in her shoes. To him, the news had been
digested. He had become comfortable with the idea, with the
logistics of abandoning her and the boys.

"But the boys?" she screamed. "Australia?" This couldn't be. He
could break her heart all he wanted. But her babies' hearts?

The heat of the rage that followed was memorized in every
cell of her body. How she had wanted to slam on the breaks to
send Johnny flying through the windshield. How she had wanted
to pierce his heart like he was piercing hers. How she had
pictured glass shards deep in his chest. It would have only been
fair. How else could he have felt the abject pain, the
abandonment, and the battleground of their souls for the years to
come. Instead, she had stopped the van in a street near Avenue
Victor Hugo, any street, put the car in park and put her forehead
on the wheel. He didn't love her.

Johnny foolishly put his hand on her arm. "I realize I'm doing
something shitty to you guys. But you'll be fine. The kids need
you more than they need me."

"But that's not true," she yelled, yanking away from his hand.
Johnny had the uneasy smile of the one who knows that shit
would soon and inexorably hit the fan. "You have to live near
them," she cried out. "You can't go away that far."

But she had known he absolutely could. He had done it
before, in fact. He had left his own family in order to move to
France. He never called his parents. They called France and
complained, and she'd be the one to shrug impatiently, the phone
nudged between her cheek and her shoulder as she changed a
diaper or cooked dinner. Couldn't they just get over him,
already?

She was the one who called Johnny's parents with news. She
was the one who remembered to send gifts, letters. She
remembered birthdays, apologized, covered for him, protected

everyone's feelings as best she could. Johnny couldn't be fenced in; couldn't they see that?

In the parked van, somewhere near Avenue Victor Hugo, she began to scream, sounds that were not human. Her strength had not been human either. She punched him in the shoulder. "Leave! Get out! Out! Get out of my fucking car!" She watched powerlessly as Johnny got out of the van, and walked away on the boulevard, away from her, and toward his fate.

His fate happened two hours later, when Johnny was at the wheel of his brother's car and drove it to his death. The very night she thought she would die, Johnny had ended up killing himself.

Oh, she had massaged that night over and over in her head. Every night of the last three years and almost every day. Was it her fault, this accident, since she kicked him out of the van? Or was it his fault? Had she killed him or had he killed himself? If the boys knew, would they blame her? Would they hate him? Would they hate her? And again and again for three years: He didn't love her.

Now that the panic attack subsided, a strange calm swept through her. She'd survived that one. She was alive and sitting in the driver's seat of her van, which was still parked inside her garage. She breathed with relief, dug in her purse for a Kleenex, and wiped her eyes and nose.

Something felt odd, hollow. What now? Something was missing all of a sudden, but what was it? It occurred to her that she had in fact, for all intents and purposes, been stuck in that van ever since that night, that she had been sobbing inwardly for three long and lonely years. And she had been angry. So angry. But suddenly a long-forgotten sense of lightness was emerging out of thin air. What was this? Something was not there anymore?

It took several minutes for Annie to understand that what was strangely missing was her pain.

It was past bedtime. She pictured the kids, their faces pale with exhaustion. The sandy eyes. This was mommy time, and they were piled up in Lucas's apartment wondering about going home. Lucas. Johnny's friend. Lucas knew about Johnny and that woman, but he had never said a word. He had tried but she had not let him and now she knew why. By not letting him speak, she didn't have to let him, or anyone, know what she knew. By not telling anyone she could keep Johnny intact, their story intact, for the children, and maybe, also, for herself. Lucas had let her keep her secret. A secret about being unlovable, carelessly tossed away. A secret much too heavy to carry alone.

Pain for the boys had come the morning after. Unfathomable pain, but a pain of a different nature. A pain possibly easier to digest for them, one day, than the trauma they would have experienced had Johnny been able to carry out his plan to abandon them all. As long as she would have a say in it, the memory of Johnny as a loving father and husband would be preserved. Not for Johnny. No, not for Johnny, but for the boys. So that they would continue to feel loved by him.

She turned the key in the ignition. "Fuck you, Johnny," she wailed in the garage. "Fuck you, asshole, disgusting liar, cheater, coward, selfish bastard. You were right, loser! We didn't need you after all!"

Annie started the engine and stormed the car out of the garage. She drove as the sun went down, radiating a red glow on the stones of the buildings. Music and warm air flowed through the van's open windows, and her hair floated wildly behind her. She drove the van through Paris to take her boys to a weekend at the beach. She drove the van through Paris to meet her lover.

Jared waited for the nurse to leave his room to rip the IV needle from his arm. He stumbled out of bed and had to hang onto the wall to not fall, but by the time he reached the closet and found his clothes neatly folded, he was able to stand almost normally. When the nurse came back to his room, he was gone.

Minutes later he was riding a cab through dense traffic. The purple glow of sundown and the last of the day's light reflected on the Seine, transforming it to a river of pure silver. The deep green sycamore leaves were almost black against the cobalt blue sky. The act of breathing alone was exhausting and his vision was still altered from the drugs he had taken and those they had given him in the hospital.

Tonight was the Fête de la Musique, he realized. He rolled up his window to protect his throbbing head from the discordance of competing music that came from every street, every house, and every room in every apartment. The interior of the silent cab became a pocket of quietness that floated through the city like a bubble. The carved stones of buildings gleamed in the street lights, every light was a blurred star. The statues seemed alive, churches like giants in helmets and coats of armor, the wooden doors of century-old buildings like gaping mouths.

Had Althea been with him, he would have shown her the restaurants filled to capacity, people dancing and drinking at café terraces, awestruck tourists wondering where they had landed, wild kids zigzagging through traffic on their mopeds, hair in the wind, lovers walking hand in hand along the streets, body against body, kissing, waiting for the night, for passion. If Althea had been with him in the cab, he would have put his head on her lap and let her caress his hair until he drifted to sleep. But Althea was not with him and he needed to find her. The cab drove on boulevard Richard-Lenoir and suddenly, a hundred people on roller skates surrounded the car like a school of fish in the dark ocean. A girl tapped at his window and flashed her bare breasts. An instant later, they were gone.

Time away from Althea was wasted to him. He hated that she was fragile, and needy, and sick. But as fragile and needy and sick as she might be, he was going to find her despite the nurses making excuses, saying she had been transferred to another hospital they couldn't disclose.

෨

Sitting across from him, in that French Chinese restaurant, Lola had settled into her chair and had an air of contentment and serenity that maybe did not mean she was serene or content, now that Mark thought of it. There had been nothing to indicate she was unhappy with him the very day she left. Or so little.

Lola was even more breathtaking as a blonde, and he wanted to tell her that. It was strange to be in Paris, a city he had trouble understanding. People were still arriving for dinner at eleven at night accompanied by their dogs. This was a city where heterosexual men dressed gay, where sexy women of all ages danced in the street, where waiters ignored you and your empty plate, where Chinese restaurants had few recognizable Chinese dishes on the menu, and where the preferred modes of transportation were roller blades and mopeds. In Paris, music was everywhere.

Lola removed her jacket. She was luminous. He loved the soft caramel color of her skin, the roundness of her lips, the washed green of her eyes without makeup. Lola's face was calm. Lola was always calm. Her calm had allowed him to act out his rage at the world with impunity. He wanted to tell her that, too.

It had been a while since the private investigator had given him Lola's address in Paris. Mark had kept the address in his wallet and had looked at it several times a day to remember what he was doing and why he was doing it as he went through the work. Therapy, it was called, anger management classes where he had faced the depression and the rage. The depression, especially, seemed like a bottomless pit. Once he saw a problem he was not the kind of guy to shy away from it. He tackled it head on, and methodically. Hired the best, gave it his best. He had taken the drugs they gave him and refused to lie to himself. He had done the group thing too, and had not needed more than that session to recognize himself in those men around him, out-of-control bullies guilty of emotionally battering their women. Those were not facts he wished to advertise at the moment. He wanted to win Lola back as the new him. Besides, he wasn't sure much would be gained from Lola learning he had turned into a wimp who cried himself to sleep.

Watching Lola, it was difficult not to display the emotions that overwhelmed him. Then he remembered what the shrink had said: To the contrary, he was supposed to be feeling the emotions, not bottle them in, which might have caused the problem in the first place. How to feel the emotions and not bawl like a six-year-old, that he had not figured out yet.

Lola drank her wine with small sips, her skin caressed by the balmy night air. "How did you find me?" she finally asked.

"Well," he chuckled, "it was a bit of a challenge, but when you throw enough money at a problem, the problem usually disappears."

"Not all problems, though," Lola said, and she looked at him intently.

"No, not all problems," he said.

The waiter removed Mark's untouched appetizer and Lola's empty plate, and brought their entrée. Mark was unable to swallow a bite, and here she was, eating happily, her head swaying faintly with the music.

"When did you find out where I was?"

Mark hesitated. "About a month ago."

"A month?" Lola looked pained. "That's a long time," she said reproachfully.

Mark hesitated again. "I had stuff to take care of."

"What kind of stuff?" she asked.

He watched the tip of Lola's chopsticks go to her plate,

expertly grab some food, and gracefully come to her mouth. "You know... stuff. I think that what we need to talk about is what's going on now and come to some kind of understanding about the future."

"Things cannot go on the way they were, Mark," she said, looking upset. "I've changed. I simply can't go back to the old me."

Mark shrugged. "You changed a long time ago. But you didn't dare tell me, for some reason."

Lola put her chopsticks down. "Some reason? And what reason might that be, in your opinion?"

Mark didn't respond. They both knew the reason. Instead, he said, "I could have reported you. I could have sent the police after you a dozen times, and you know I didn't. Obviously, I care about you. I'm not some kind of monster. I gave you the space you needed and all. And I'm here to solve whatever little problems we might have."

Lola's voice became sharp. "Except they are not little problems, Mark. They're huge problems. I don't know that we can solve them."

"I'll tell you what. Nothing's going to get solved between us as long as you're in France."

"I'll come back to L.A., of course. I owe it to you and the kids. And I need to make changes in my life."

Mark relaxed. "Yeah, you need a life. I get it. You want to work. Do your yoga, right?"

She shook her head. "I don't think I can come back to that house."

Mark raised an eyebrow. "You want to move?"

"I won't go back to the marriage."

Mark didn't look at her. He was trying to hide the apprehension, the drop in his shoulders. "What do you mean?"

"I'll come back to California, but," she looked down at her plate, "I'm sorry Mark but I'll rent a place somewhere."

"Come on, Lola! I know that we both have our grievances. It's not the end of the world!"

"No, Mark! It is the end of the world," Lola said with such force that Mark hardly recognized her. Her eyes shone with anger. He'd never seen her openly angry. "How can I say it in words that you will finally understand? Especially if you refuse to hear me out."

"Why do you think I came all the way here if it wasn't to hear you out?"

Lola looked at him. "Very well, then. You say things changed after we had children. Well, that's because you were just fine as long as my world revolved around you!"

Mark opened his mouth to respond, then closed it. Lola pointed her chopsticks at him angrily, her voice never rising as she spoke. "Do you realize how much of myself I've given up to be with you? And how much more I give up daily to meet with your approval? It's always about you—your nice little shirts, your stupid house, your business trips I have to endure with you instead of being home with the kids. It's about your ideas on entertaining and decorating, which by the way suck." She whispered that last word, but she might have well been screaming it.

"I get it Lola. I get it. I'm an asshole."

"I'm saying that if you don't change, I will divorce you."

Mark took a large gulp of his drink and said, "What kind of changes do you want me to make?" They both let those words, incongruous in his mouth, float between them for a long minute.

"Huge changes, Mark," Lola shook her head. "I don't know if you'd be up for the task."

"I can change."

Lola snapped. "Then why don't you start right now, by apologizing for your uncontrollable anger? The yelling, everything you have put me through, and I…"

"I apologize," Mark said.

Lola looked at him stunned.

"I apologize," Mark repeated. He held her gaze now. "I've been everything you just said. I can change. I need to change. I've started to change."

"You would need to see someone, a professional, about your anger."

"I have already started. That's the 'stuff' I was talking about. I've been going to this kind of program. I... I'll do what it takes."

Lola opened her eyes wide. "A program?"

"A program. Anger management, spousal abuse." He smiled apologetically, "The works."

"A program?" Lola said again, seeming completely shocked by this revelation.

For a long moment, neither of them spoke. Lola had stopped eating. A musician had set up a few feet away from their table and was playing something like flamenco on the guitar. They both watched the man's fingers float over the strings. Of course Mark should have said more, but what? You can't make someone love you. The dice had been thrown. It was out of his hands.

"All right then, maybe," she finally said.

"Maybe?"

"Maybe if you're willing. And able."

His throat tightened painfully. "I'm willing. And I'm definitely able."

"Maybe then," Lola said again. She looked at him and had a soft smile, but her smile froze when she saw the tears well up in his eyes. He tried to hide them but it was too late.

"Are you all right?" she asked.

Mark stretched out his hand, and after a few seconds, Lola finally stretched out hers. They did a slow motion high-five, but Mark did not let Lola remove her hand. He entwined his fingers in hers and began weeping in plain sight in that Chinese restaurant in the middle of Paris.

CHAPTER 29

$\mathcal{L}$ucas felt like a human being at last. The children were watching a movie and he had finally shaved, washed and changed clothes, all the while rehearsing how he would give Annie a piece of his mind for leaving him to fend for himself with five children. But when Annie arrived at his door, her face washed with tears, so distraught that she immediately threw herself into his arms, he thought she'd just been beaten or worse. Had Mark attacked her and then murdered Lola in a fit of crime passionnel? She stayed there against his chest, sobbing for a full minute he guiltily enjoyed. To hold this body in his arms felt so right and wonderful. Finally, she gathered herself, dried her eyes, and to his silent interrogation she responded, "I don't want to talk about it."

She ran to his bathroom and emerged having washed her face and applied lipstick. She was strong again, or at least had decided to appear that way for the children. She peeked into the salon, which at the moment bore no sign of his afternoon ordeal. The children were piled on the sofa, all eyes riveted to the television set, except for the baby who had fallen into the deepest of slumbers two hours before. Maxence saw his mother, jumped up from the couch, and turned off the television, which seemed to raise her suspicion.

"What were you watching?" she asked as a form of hello.

"Nothing," Lia and Laurent said together.

"Arachnophobia," Paul screeched.

Annie turned to him reproachfully. "You let the kids watch horror movies?"

"They-they said they do," Lucas stammered. "They said you let them. All the time."

"I sure would have expected better of you," she told Maxence coldly.

To the news that they were leaving for a surprise vacation, the children jumped up and down crazily. "We're giving your mom a lovely weekend to herself," Annie assured Lia. They did last-minute bathroom runs, and turned off the lights. Lucas put sleeping Simon over his shoulder. They shut the front door and stepped into the elevator. In the street, they reached the van. Lucas fastened Simon into the car seat without him ever waking up, and the children piled in excitedly after.

The city was enthralled by the Fête de la Musique. The citywide party atmosphere affected the children in no time. They wanted, begged, to get out of the car and "see the music." Annie simply said, "Not a chance," and they stopped asking. How did she do this? He drove the van through Paris and Annie let the children open all the windows wide. The streets were closed to traffic in many places that he wondered if they would ever find their way out of the city. Maxence and Laurent began to terrify Lia with imaginary tarantulas and her screeches went through Lucas's brain like swords. Meanwhile Annie sat next to him in the passenger seat, her hands in her lap, lost in her thoughts. Now, how did she do that?

"I didn't see your bag," she finally said over the children's screams. Her first sentence in the twenty minutes since they left his apartment.

Lucas pondered what she meant, then said in amazement, "Why, I believe I forgot to pack for the trip."

"What?" Annie buried her head in her hands. "You forgot? How could you forget to pack?"

"This was a stressful day."

"It sure as hell was, but look at me, I'm perfectly prepared."

"You'd think you have nerves of steel when I see you with children, but the slightest little irritation coming from me..."

Annie made a quick turn, faced the children, and yelled, "Shut up!" The children went quiet instantaneously. They drove toward a huge moon. The city was far behind now, and the sky filled with stars. One by one, the children fell asleep. They seemed alone on the highway, aside from the occasional car that passed them at breakneck speed and made the minivan tremble.

"So, how are you?" he asked tentatively when the children's eyes were closed.

"Shh."

"They're sleeping."

"Not Maxence. Not until he snores," Annie whispered.

Soon they entered the Département de Normandie. Aside from the loud rumbling of the engine, the darkness and silence were almost complete. Lucas sensed Annie's body beginning to relax. Her breathing became more peaceful and he felt his own stress dissolve with each of her breaths. He moved one hand off the wheel and reached for her hand, which was still in a tight fist on her lap. He brought her tense hand to his lips and kept it there until it became soft. This made Lucas very happy, happy to be here with Annie, at night, in the car, with five sleeping children in the back seat. Like a family. His family. No matter how messed up other people's lives around him were, his was just starting to make sense.

He drove through the sleeping town of Honfleur, then slowed down and followed the small road he knew so well. He stopped the van in front of the property's wrought iron gate, left the engine on, got out, and pushed the heavy gate open, got back inside the van and drove on the gravel driveway for a hundred yards under the bright moon. The night was clear and warm. Tomorrow would be a gorgeous day.

Annie's eyes opened wide when she saw the small house, the dark half timbers alternating with white plaster that glowed in the moonlight. "Lucas, this is too perfect! Look at the climbing roses going all the way up the roof. It reminds me of Nantucket!"

"What's that?"

"Martha's Vineyard and Nantucket, Islands off Cape Cod."

"This is much better," he said.

Lucas parked the van by the house. Annie was out of the car before he even turned off the engine. The children were so deeply asleep no one noticed they had arrived at their destination. Annie was walking away from the car toward a dark expanse ahead. Lucas got out of the car and walked after her. A fresh breeze smelling of ocean, sand, and seaweed swallowed them. Annie pointed at the ocean. "You never said your house was on the beach! Right on the beach!"

"Why, yes."

Perfectly prepared or not, Annie was wearing a sleeveless shirt and goose bumps covered her arms. Lucas removed his sweater and wrapped it around her shoulders.

"Let's leave the kids in the car one more minute. They'll be fine," Annie said.

"Are you sure?"

"Yep." She was joyous suddenly, and playful. She looked beautiful.

She grabbed his hand and started walking fast toward the ocean, and then they were both running. They reached the sand and she kicked off her sandals. They climbed up a small sand dune, pushing and shoving each other. The air cooled, but Lucas was hot. Annie kneeled and put Lucas's jacket on the sand that was smooth and grey in the moonlight and still warm to the touch. She grabbed his hand again and laid down there, pulling him down beside her. Lucas's pulse started to race. He took her face in his hands and kissed her, and Annie reached for his belt.

❧

The sun was blinding and Annie put on her sunglasses. Waves swelled in the distance only to end, docile, near her feet. The ocean air, rich and thin, swelled her lungs and her heart. She sat in a low beach chair in her retro red one-piece suit that made her look like a pinup girl, and buried her feet in the warm sand. Next to her, but not too close, so as to not raise the children's suspicions, Lucas, still wearing the clothes he had on the day before, sat in another chair. His unbuttoned white shirt billowed in the breeze, his pants, rolled above his ankles, were soaked and he squinted in the sun looking not unlike Clark Gable. A few yards away, the children glistened with sunscreen, water, and sand. Maxence and Lia were up to their waists in a hole the children had dug in the sand. The two talked incessantly as they dug away. About what, Annie could not hear over the rumble of the ocean. It was amusing to watch how Maxence dispatched Paul, Laurent and Simon to get more water or seashells, making them run to and from the ocean with overflowing buckets as though their lives depended on it. It occurred to her that Lia and Maxence were absorbed in each other, oblivious to their surroundings, their desire to be alone together palpable.

Lucas's foot began teasing hers under the sand more or less discreetly. That contact alone provoked immediate erotic sensations throughout her body. They had made love in the dunes the evening before, because she had initiated it. How deeply aroused she had been baffled her. This was a beautiful

359

moment, as beautiful a moment as there ever could be on this Earth. Lucas was a wonderful human being and a wonderful man, and he seemed to want her. He was the man she could start over with, the man who made her laugh and laughed at her angry jokes. The man who got her. The man who'd seen her whole, scarred, and flawed and was still interested.

But didn't life remain picture perfect in movies only? In real life, summers ended, children went back to school, grew up, and left their mothers. Best friends ran back to their pathetic husbands. People collapsed of self-inflicted starvation or drug overdoses just when you thought you had helped them. Husbands betrayed you and then died. And new lovers found ways of nipping things in the bud before anything too intimate set in, before happiness lured you all the way, only to crush you later.

"Lucas, this is not going to work," Annie said softly, her eyes scanning the shimmering waves. His own eyes still on the ocean, Lucas stiffened. He knew her well enough to expect this and waited. "What exactly did you have in mind?" she continued, aggressive. "I mean, this is all very cute and all, the house, the beach, the torrid sex on the dunes. But you and I know it is all a lie."

"Who is lying?" Lucas asked after a moment.

"You, me. I mean, this was fun, but we know each other too well. This is almost incestuous, this relationship. I really like you... I mean. But I really like the way we were, you know, before."

"When we were just friends?"

"Right."

"You're saying you'd rather stay friends?"

She hesitated, not long enough, "Yes, just friends."

"Speak for yourself!" he said, gazing at the ocean.

She gave a little laugh. "Sex is not everything."

Lucas got up from his chair. He walked away from her for a few steps and faced the waves. She thought he was about to walk away, but instead he turned on his feet and came toward her, then plopped down on the sand to face her. His chest hair was salt and pepper. She liked the lines around his eyes when he smiled. A happy person's wrinkles. Right now, he was not smiling. He brought his hands to her glasses, took them off, and all of a sudden, she was exposed.

"Annie, I'm not interested in this. I don't want to play Le chat et la souris."

"I'm not playing cat-and-mouse," she said, indignant, but she knew she was lying. She was playing hard to get. She was ready to throw everything out the window if need be. This was a test after all.

"Annie. This is not an accident. Maybe for you it is, but not for me. I've been waiting and hoping for you, for… years."

She said nothing. Please tell me more.

"I was always hoping for more," he added, searching her eyes.

"Always?" Please tell me, tell me more.

"Even when Johnny was alive, I had a crush on you."

"A crush?"

"A big crush, Annie. Don't make me use the word."

"What word?" She quickly put on her sunglasses, because her eyes were like her feelings, blurred. Lucas was an expert at that, seduction. So many girlfriends. Of course he was an expert at appearing sincere. She'd seen him at work. All he wanted was to get his way.

"All you want is to get your way," she exclaimed.

"Bien sûr, I want to get my way. And what do you think my way is? And could you please take off those glasses? They're annoying."

"Too bright. I'm blinded."

"By the sun or the truth? Face it. Face me. Be blinded for God's sake. Take off those ridiculous glasses."

Annie did.

"You are crying," he exclaimed. "I am relieved."

"Relieved," she echoed, unable to come up with her own words.

"You," Lucas said, touching her nose, with his index. "You have feelings. For me."

"What are you talking about? Of course I have feelings."

Lucas wiped the tears off her cheeks with the back of his hand, and she could smell testosterone—his or hers?—and suntan lotion in that brief contact. She wanted him to bite the side of her neck and tell her that she was beautiful like he had on the dunes.

"You are beautiful."

She laughed, she cried. "You are a womanizer. I would be crazy."

"What? Was I supposed to stay celibate for the last twelve years?"

"You expect me to believe you were screwing around but that I was the woman of your dreams? Lucas, I'm not a teenager. I don't buy this shit."

"You need to buy it. It's the truth."

"The truth?"

"Okay, Merde!" He made a fist and punched the sand in front of her feet. "I want you, tu comprends? I wanted you. I couldn't be celibate while you were a respectable and devoted wife, and then a respectable widow in mourning, all the while shaking that sexy ass of yours in front of my eyes all these years."

"The nerve! I never...I never shook."

"Oh, you shook."

"The nerve." She laughed out loud. He found her big ass sexy.

"But, you know, it's not just your body. I like everything about you, even...even your extremely difficult personality. And I'm not giving up. I'm not going to be a friend. I want to be your lover. If you let me."

"Oh, all right, dammit," she said.

Lucas put his hand near her neck as though he was considering strangling her. "All right what?"

"I'll let you."

"At last!" Lucas took her chin in his hand and kissed her.

In the distance, she heard Lia's clear shriek. "Look, Maxence! Lucas and your mom are kissing!"

And she couldn't care less.

CHAPTER 30

JUILLET

The women here were as sick as they were desperate. Only six months ago, Althea would have been in no better shape than they were. Six months ago she too would have lied to the staff and to herself. She too would have secretly burned calories by walking around the hospital corridors or by taking her showers cold. She too would have cheated on the amount of food she was ordered to eat, and she too would have perceived the program as an impediment to her deepest and most profound compulsion, which was to not eat. But things were different now. She wanted to resist eating with every fiber, still, but she could no longer ignore the pathology of it. This, this disease, could kill her, was killing her and might as well because living with it was hell.

Also, things were different because, unlike six months ago, she now wanted things. There were more things she wanted than she ever would have thought possible.

She did not want visitors. She was doing this alone by choice. Annie had called her parents to let them know what was going on with her. Where was her mother right now, she wondered? Where had she been her entire life? She tried to imagine a future without her mother, and the ultimate of all rejections—the rejection of a child by her mother. This had been at the heart of all her fears and now that she was facing it, she felt safer, rather than more vulnerable.

Abandoning the toxic connection to her mother was a death of sorts, and her only chance for freedom. This desertion allowed for something new, a reinvention. But despair came as she tried to envision a future that did not include Jared. If she were to live at all, she would need to believe that, for a brief moment, in that chaste and careful way of his, Jared did love her. But most importantly, she needed to believe that she loved him—that the feeling of love that had always eluded her was something she was capable of.

Althea left the bedroom she shared with Valerie, a forty-year-old mother of three who never talked but spent her time doing push-ups and sit-ups in her room even though it was against the rules. She and Valerie were the oldest women in the department. Valerie's teeth were rotted out from years of self-induced vomiting. Valerie scared her, disgusted her as only a person who represents your future can. Althea moved through the familiar white corridors of the hospital. In the elevator, she stood next to Veronique, a sixteen-year-old, eighty-two-pound girl with a head too big for her body. Another sick girl. The girl and Althea didn't acknowledge each other. Althea tapped on a door and let herself in. She sat in the chair across from Madame Defloret's mahogany desk, brought one knee to her chin, and waited for Madame Defloret's phone conversation to end. Even here, the window had bars. Behind the bars, under the canopies of trees in the hospital's garden, mentally ill people strolled.

Madame Defloret hung up the phone and smiled at Althea. "Althea, you have been with us ten days already. You've done well, my dear. You are a brave and strong young lady."

Althea measured those words. Brave and strong. Yes, she had

been brave and strangely strong. "Thank you," she smiled. "It's been as good as mental illness gets."

"I can see you have a sense of humor. That's wonderful! It takes a lot to embrace the concept of an illness as unflinchingly as you did. Not everyone dares."

"Thank you." Althea understood that she had been ready, that the shift had happened over the last six months without her even realizing it. Without living in Annie's house, that crazy house where people argued, and food was rich, and children played, without Jared painting her and kissing her, without Paris and the abundant messy life of it, she would never had been ready.

"You and I have talked about a plan to move you to outpatient as soon as we, you and I together, would feel ready." Madame Defloret added, "I suggest that the time has come."

"I'm not ready to leave!" Althea said, suddenly terrified.

"You will need extensive therapy, but you don't need to be hospitalized. It will be a long hard journey, at least as long as it took you to get here. Don't expect immediate results, but I believe you can do it."

"But I..." Althea's throat was useless. "I can't do it alone."

Madame Defloret smiled kindly. "Things will be different now. We've discussed creating a support system that—"

"My parents didn't even call. They don't care."

"In the interest of healing, you need to spend your focus on those who do care." The ringing of the phone interrupted her. "Yes," Madame Defloret said. "In the waiting room please." She hung up the phone. "As a matter of fact, you have a visitor."

Althea looked at her hands, at the bars at the window, at Madame Defloret. "I don't think I'm ready to see anyone."

"Visitors can be an olive branch."

Mom! Althea felt nauseous. "It would be throwing me into the lion's pit."

"He's certainly not taking no for an answer," Madame Defloret said. "Should I let him in?"

He? Althea curled up in her chair, ready to lick her wounds. Her hope was formidable. "Yes, please."

The door to Madame Defloret's office opened.

Jared seemed taller maybe, or thinner. He was closely shaved and had dark circles under his eyes.

"I'll leave you two alone," Madame Defloret said as she got up and left the room.

In her chair, Althea didn't budge. She had the sensation of sinking.

"No one wanted to tell me where you were," he said with an awkward smile.

"Why? Why not?"

"They said a drug addict is bad for you."

"Oh, Jared. I'm so sorry." She didn't know what she was sorry about.

"I looked for you. Then I went to rehab for a few days. Now I'm here."

"Oh, that's all right," she whispered. "I understand, of course."

Jared kneeled next to her chair, took both of her hands, and brought them to his face. "I'm crazy. You're crazy. Together, we would be less crazy. What do you think?" Althea fiercely fought tears of yearning, despair, and joy all at once. "But you have to promise me to get better," he said.

Althea looked at his beautiful, manly hands encircling her thin wrists. A wave of disgust shook her. Of course, she had to get better. She had to stop this right now. The old way wasn't necessary anymore. She was no longer alone. He wanted her whole, not broken. Not sick. She was going to do this for him, for herself. Althea stood and let Jared hold her in his arms. The scent of his shirt was like coming home. She looked out the window, and it all came rushing in, the warmth of the sun like a caress, the sound of the birds, the wind coming through the trees, the smell of the wet grass that was being mowed. Now. Right now. It was so simple. And she could feel all of it.

§

Lola's hair stuck to the back of her neck with sweat. She had hurried up and down the stairs, washed several loads of laundry, finished last-minute shopping, her heart bouncing in her chest from activity and fright. Everything was coming together; everything was falling apart. Jared and Althea had emerged from their respective treatments and announced they were moving in together in Jared's apartment on rue de Cambronne. Annie and Lucas were careful to show no signs of affection in public, but the pink on their cheeks and the smiles on their lips showed how thrilled they were to be catching up with ten years of unattended lust. Annie's happiness was a beautiful thing to watch. Was her own life coming together or falling apart? Lola wasn't sure. All she knew was that she, Mark, and the children were going home. They were leaving Paris the next day.

Of course, Mark's arrival changed absolutely everything. Had he not found her, she might have stayed in Paris eternally. But he had found her. As long as she was away from Mark, it had been possible to convince herself that running away was a legitimate response to her problem. But watching Mark be reunited with Lia and Simon, she was appalled by her cruelty to him and the children. Her cruelty and selfishness, she realized, had been a by-product of fear. The fear had led to what Lucas called cowardice. Yes, she had behaved in a cowardly way that now disgusted her. But if there was one thing that those six months in France had changed about her, it was that she now realized she never needed to feel like a victim again, or act like one. She could take action, make demands, draw lines. She had made a pact with herself to never be a coward again. That which she feared most, she must now do. What she feared most to say, she must now say.

She contemplated the beautiful small bedroom that had felt so safe. The woman who had entered that bedroom six months ago was no longer. She liked the new Lola much better. She fastened the last suitcase and left her bedroom. In the stairwell, the smell of cooked lamb and spices, the lamb for Annie's party, was overwhelming. Lola's heart was unbearably heavy for leaving. She had burst into tears three times this morning alone. Yet she needed to go through the motion of helping Annie. Everybody, in fact, moaned over the undertaking—Mark especially, who could not fathom why they could not leave before the party and why he was made to wait to get his family back home. Lola's desire was to stay until after the party for Annie's sake. In the old days, she would have yielded to Mark's desire. In the old days, barely six months ago.

Everyone was expected to help, and everyone did, though no one understood why Annie insisted it had to happen. Why this party was so important to her, no one dared ask. Lola suspected that Annie was celebrating the death or the birth of something deeply personal, too personal to talk about. By throwing this party, Annie seemed to be officially reclaiming her life.

In the stairwell, Lola was too slow to prevent Simon from hurling a tennis ball at Laurent's head. "Simon, you're on my team, dimwit," Laurent shouted. Simon hollered gleefully and ran away without acknowledging her presence. The boys ran wildly throughout the house, shouting and arguing, and Lola wondered how lonely it would be for Simon without them. He would go to preschool, of course. He was an active boy, she had discovered, a fearless boy who liked balls, and guns and fighting. He was not a boy who needed to be protected from life.

Earlier, the children had rolled up the salon's big rug, gathered every pillow in the house, and brought those outside to the garden under the giant canvas canopy that now covered it. They had hung lanterns and set out small tables made from cardboard boxes covered with fabric. Inside, the tent looked roomy, cozy and exotic, and straight out of Aladdin's world. She found Lia under the canopy arranging flowers. She looked lovely in her party dress, a sari made out of crimson and pink silk. She looked exactly like a princess, yet gone was the princess attitude. Gone was the frown, too. Lia had learned that bitchiness did not serve her well in a house full of rowdy boys, which was a testament to her adaptability. She may want to turn back into a diva once back home surrounded by mini divas, but things were going to be different now that Lola was done being afraid of her children. Children craved guidance and boundaries, Annie had said. Wimpy mothers made for confused children. And she had learned at Annie's school of motherhood that she need not fear losing their love if she asserted herself.

"Honey, did you decorate those tables yourself?" she asked Lia. "They're beautiful!"

Lia's face glowed. "I'm going to be an interior designer when I grow up!"

"You'll be a talented one."

"You think Daddy will like the party?"

"Whether he does or not, we'll enjoy it, right?"

"I'm happy Daddy's here."

"I'm glad too, my love."

She was.

She and Mark had shared her small bed, and under the daisy-sprinkled canopy, they had talked and talked. Even about the painful stuff. They had cried and they had held each other, but they had not made love, not yet. Not until her anger subsided. Not until they came to an understanding of how things should be from now on, or how things should never be again.

Their plane was leaving in twenty-four hours. Mark was out under the pretext of finding an Internet connection, but she suspected he needed to get out of the house where the chaos was overwhelming. Annie's disapproval for Mark, for which of course Lola had no one to blame but herself, was palpable. Mark had been nothing but friendly and pleasant with everyone. He and Lucas had charmed each other right away. Still, it hadn't stopped Annie from fuming the instant she entered a room he was in.

Lola kissed Lia on her braided hair and walked out of the tent and into the kitchen and braced herself for Annie.

The heat of the last few days had given way to a humid and rather threatening weather, but Annie was steadfast in her decision to have the party outside, even if the storm decided to break. Tonight, rain or not, there would be over a hundred people, adults and children, under the canopy. They would eat, drink, and dance until the early light of the morning. Then there would be croissants and coffee for everyone who had made it through. It would be a party to remember.

Annie had been cooking for two days. A Méchoui, an entire lamb, had been roasting for hours in the kitchen's giant fireplace, sending its extravagant aroma through the sixteenth arrondissement. She was also making piles of couscous and had baked Tunisian pastries and Moroccan buns with anise seeds. The food would be rich, and sweet, and heavy, and happy, and excessive all at once. It would be wonderful. If only Annie could stop being so angry. Lola had cried and cried today, and she was not done crying. But sentimentality was not Annie's way.

Lola entered the kitchen where it was hot as the inside of a furnace with the strong aroma of mint and roasting lamb clinging to every part of the room. Annie's elbows were up as she stirred taboulé in an immense pot. She looked a bit like a witch by her cauldron. Lucas and Jared walked in and out of the kitchen, carrying baguettes, cases of wine, and crates of fruit. At the table, Althea was chopping and peeling carrots, turnips, and zucchinis with a glow in her eyes that was new and beautiful.

"The floor, Annie, look at the floor!" Lucas bellowed. The kitchen floor was caked with mud from everyone's back-and-forth and resembled the pavement of a train station on a rainy day. "It will never come back," Lucas insisted.

"The floor has seen worse," Annie said. "Look at my hair. Now that's worrisome." Her hair was frizzy from the steam and all over the place. "I look like Don King's mama."

"Your hair is the most beautiful thing I've even seen," Lucas said as he huffed and puffed under the weight of the last case of wine.

Lola approached Annie at the stove. "I'm done with the packing," she said. "How can I help?"

Annie continued stirring without looking at her. "I don't need help," she responded coldly.

Lucas and Jared dropped the last box and left the kitchen.

"Please, don't be mad," she told Annie. "I'm sure you need me."

"I better get used to being on my own." Annie stirred the contents of the pot with violence. "You can't even help yourself. Tell me how in the world you're going to help me?"

At the table, Althea sat still and looked up at Lola in a way that said, "she's going to blow," and promptly put down her peeler, wiped her hands and left the kitchen.

"Come on, Annie," Lola began, her voice weakening already, but she was not a coward and she was going to tackle this. "This couldn't last forever. You know that."

Annie turned on her feet, both comical and threatening, a wooden spoon tight in each hand. The frizz of her hair sprinkled with what looked to be fresh parsley.

"And why not? You're happy here and you'll be miserable there."

"You might not approve…"

"Rushing back home solves absolutely nothing. In fact, it's idiotic."

"But it's no more idiotic than what you're doing," Lola said, her tone more confrontational than she had meant it to be.

"And what might that be?"

With amazement, Lola heard herself speak. "Well, for example, renting out rooms to people and expecting them to live their lives according to your whims and desires."

"That's a low blow. Well, fine, Lola. Run back to stupid

Beverly Hills. Go paint your toenails for hours on end and wonder where your life went."

"Annie," she said softly, "we'll still be friends."

"A phone call every so often is not friendship, it's pitiful! You're not doing what's right for you, only what works for Mark."

"What is it I should do, since you have all the answers?"

"You came here to start over, remember? That was the whole point. Look at Althea, she's starting over! Right, Althea?" She turned her head and saw that Althea was gone. "All you're doing is crawling right back to the womb."

Lola felt heat rise to her neck. "Oh, don't worry, I'm not going to let him walk all over me. I'm not going to let anyone walk all over me." She paused and said, "Starting with you."

"Me? I walk all over you?"

"That's right. You can't have tantrums every time someone disappoints you. It makes it very hard to be around you." Lola regretted her words immediately.

Annie stopped, set down her wooden spoon, and sat at the table. She put her face in her hands and her back began to shake. Lola thought she was laughing at first, but soon she was appalled to realize that Annie was weeping. She sat next to her.

"Are you all right?"

"Is that why people leave me?" Annie said through her sobs. "Because I'm too horrible to be around?"

Lola wasn't sure which "people" Annie was referring to, but suddenly there was nothing amusing about Annie's fit. Her sorrow came from somewhere deep. Lola wondered if she should rub her back. "Of course not. I'm going to miss you terribly." Lola searched for the right words. "You are the best friend I've ever had. You're not pushing people away. I take it back. I'm sorry. It's the opposite. You attract people. People love you. I...love you, all right? Gee, I wish we didn't have to go through this."

"Sorry I'm making you uncomfortable," Annie said. She lifted her tear-streaked face toward Lola. "So why are you so damn uptight? Give me a hug and cry a little."

"I'm not going to cry. But, I'll give you a hug. I just hate goodbyes."

Annie was now laughing and crying at the same time.

"Get over here!" She gave Lola a big old hug. Lola wiped her own tears.

"What a pain in the ass you are," Lola sniffed. "I can't believe it!"

And they went back to cooking, sniffing away all afternoon.

"Am I clownish in this dress?" Annie asked Lucas over the sound of Lady Gaga's music. Lucas took her hand and led her into a twirl on her pole dancer's heels. Her Flamenco-style dress, a low-cut, ruffled, black-and-red polka-dotted thing that seemed sewn to her body, twirled along.

"Clowns have never given me erections in the past," Lucas said seriously.

The atmosphere was getting raunchy. Women were showing a lot of skin, and Annie was sober enough to notice joints popping from pockets.

"I better take the children out of harm's reach," she told Lucas. She swayed her hips to the music as she walked away from him. Cutting through the dancers, she began searching for Lola. She went upstairs and quietly opened her bedroom door. Six little kids, including Simon, were fast asleep on the bed and on the floor. Lola wasn't in the room. She went down the stairs and said a few words to people she knew only vaguely but had invited anyway. Maxence, Paul, Laurent, and a dozen other children were running wild throughout the house. It was past midnight.

"Kids, we need to settle down. Come to the salon in five minutes. I'll put a movie on."

She went back outside. Under the canopy, couples danced to a reggae beat, while others sat on pillows around the low tables, drinking, eating, and talking. The party, as far as Annie was concerned, was fabulous.

Mark alone did not seem too happy. He sat alone in a corner, watching the dancers. She had observed him from a corner of her eye and saw that he was mostly watching Lola, who turned out to be an indefatigable dancer. But where was Lola now?

In another corner of the tent, Althea and Jared were huddled like conjoined twins. Althea spoke in Jared's ear, who in turn put food in her mouth. Hey, who was she to judge. It worked for them.

She found Lola involved in a whispered conversation with a gorgeous guy. She waved at Lola who left the man to walk toward her. Together they entered the tent.

"And who might that be?" Annie asked. "He looks good enough to eat."

"That," Lola said proudly, "was Gunter!"

"The Fuckenator?"

"Shhh! I've been trying to reach him for days. He was in Nepal. I just about fainted when he showed up. Anyway, I just told him all about my husband."

"What did he say?"

"That he wasn't jealous! The break-up was as satisfying as the affair."

"Lola, we need to create a diversion, gather the kids, and put them in front of a movie. People are smoking pot, and some of the salsa dancers are getting borderline R-rated."

As if to illustrate, a couple was slow dancing and the man's hand was surreptitiously creeping under the woman's skirt.

"You're not kidding."

They gathered the children and put on a movie in the TV room, and closed the door.

"You're having fun?" she asked Lola.

"Yes, but it would be a hell of a lot better if Mark wasn't around. He's not dancing or drinking. Meanwhile I have the urge to rip off my shirt and show off my sexy top."

"What's stopping you?"

"Mark's definitely the stern parent in this relationship."

"You allow him to take on that role. You don't have to shiver under his disapproving glance, hand him your life, and then blame him."

"Now you're defending Mark?"

"Well, he does look absolutely miserable at the moment. Save him from himself."

"But what if he won't—"

"Make him!"

Annie watched as Lola walked to the bar and mixed vodka with orange juice in two glasses, took a big gulp of one and coughed. Then she proceeded to remove her shirt and reveal her black lace top, the one that propelled her breasts like missiles. She swooned languidly toward Mark, holding a glass. Mark looked up at her and stared at her cleavage uneasily.

"Are you finally going to get stinking drunk and dance with me?" Lola told him. She offered him a drink with one hand and reached out for him with the other.

"You know, I'd rather stay clear headed. We're leaving tomorrow," Mark answered without moving.

Lola put the glass in his hand almost by force. "It will be good for both of us if you just loosen up a little bit."

Mark brought the glass to his mouth and took a long sip. "Not bad. I'm just not sure, you know, with the pills I'm taking." He nodded toward the dancers. "How do you do that thing?"

"The salsa? Let me show you." She gave him her hand and he got up. From there she grabbed his hips and showed him.

Annie thought she was going to burst before the night ended, and it wasn't just the corset of her crazy dress. She was bursting with joy. She was bursting with sadness. She had been right about the party. It wasn't a luxury; it was a vital necessity. Everything she thought she knew was on its head. Her old best friend was now her lover. The woman she had been so envious of was now her best friend. It had become perfectly legitimate to hate Johnny. And as much as she loved her house, it was not all that important to her anymore. The house was where her life happened to take place. She no longer needed the house to live.

She walked around, swaying her hips with the music, saying hello to old friends who, one by one, were thrilled to see she was back to her old self and told her so. She picked up empty cups and plates. A wild Latin beat came on. She saw Gunter dancing with a beautiful woman Lucas had once dated. Where was Lucas? She felt a pang of nervousness and scanned the dancing couples, searching for him. He was dancing indeed. With a woman. It was a frenetic salsa, and the woman was a great dancer. Lucas, stiff like a dignitary on a mission, was trying to keep up. Annie marched toward them, and in an instant, she had pulled Lucas away from the woman.

"C'est mon homme."

"I feel very in demand, and I like it," Lucas told the woman as Annie dragged him away.

Holding his arm, she took him through the house and out to the street. Outside, the air was clear, and the sounds of the party came muffled. The only light was that of an old streetlight. She stopped and faced him. In an instant, water was flowing freely from her eyes and onto her cheeks. "I'm sorry," she said, as she stepped a couple feet away from him, shielding her face with her hands.

"Why? What?"

"I didn't mean to come on so strong. It's the kind of thing that has gotten me in trouble before. Johnny said I have a jealous streak."

Lucas took her arm and brought her close, "Of course he did!" he said. "Johnny was a philandering bastard."

Annie sniffed, wiped her eyes. "Yes, he was."

"You'll never have to worry about that with me," he said and kissed her nose.

"By what miracle?"

"I'm not planning on being away from you more than three minutes at a time. How does that sound?"

"Terribly claustrophobic."

"Tomorrow's the happiest day of my life with everyone leaving. I can finally get some attention," Lucas said. "Let's take the kids to Saint-Tropez for a week or two."

She wrapped her arms around his neck and kissed him. "Wow. Now you're talking!" She was silent for a few breaths. "I wonder what they will be like," she muttered in his ear.

"Who, what?"

"My future tenants."

Lucas looked at her in horror. "Ah, non!"

THE END

ACKNOWLEDGMENTS

My eternal gratitude to my readers. It is you who transformed my humble dream into a best-selling novel now translated into nine languages. It is you who helped perfect the book through your many emails of support (and admonishment when I got something wrong) and your uncanny ability to spot typos. It is you who encouraged me to write a cookbook because the recipes in the novel made you hungry. It is you who keep asking me what I am up to and what it is I will write next. It is for you that I get up happy every morning, rush to my keyboard, and write!

Thank you to my husband Joe for suggesting I self-publish long before it was fashionable.

Thank you for my boys, David and Nathan. You guys are my life.

ABOUT THE AUTHOR

Corine Gantz was born in Neuilly France and studied at the Sorbonne before falling in love with a handsome American artist who brought her to the U.S. kicking and screaming. She spent the next 35 years with her heart torn between France and the United States and writing to make sense of it. She likes to daydream. Her happy place is an isolated cabin in Vermont, walking on a beach – any beach – or in front of a good coq au vin. She has two talented sons and is still married to the handsome American.

Email her: corinegantz@live.com
Visit her website: www.corinegantz.com

A NOTE FROM THE PUBLISHER

Thank you for reading this book. If you enjoyed it please do consider leaving a review on Amazon to help others find it too.

We hate typos. All of our books have been rigorously edited and proofread, but sometimes mistakes do slip through. If you have spotted a typo, please do let us know and we can get it amended within hours.

info@bloodhoundbooks.com

ALSO BY CORINE GANTZ

NOT PUBLISHED BY BLOODHOUND BOOKS

THE HIDDEN IN PARIS COOKBOOK

Recipes from the novel, personal stories and photographs.

THE CURATOR OF BROKEN THINGS

The new family saga trilogy

Book 1: *From Smyrna to Paris*

Book 2: *Escape to the Côte d'Azur*

Book3: *Resistance in Algiers*

Synopsis for The Curator of Broken Things

With her twins in college and her ex-husband off to a younger pasture, Cassie is resigned to a disappointing life in Los Angeles, until she reluctantly returns to Paris to visit her ailing father. There, she discovers the existence of an estranged aunt, a woman of many secrets who lives in a beautiful house in Paris's exclusive Cité des Fleurs. Dumbfounded by what she learns, Cassie sets out on a quest to understand her family's past and make sense of her father's cold indifference toward her.

In Paris, as the truth about her failed marriage begins to take form, Cassie fights with her family, grapples with French idiosyncrasies and her own, and attempts to resist the charms of a good-looking Parisian who rides a vintage motorcycle.

From the last gasp of the Ottoman Empire to Paris of the 1920s to the prewar French Riviera to the World War II Allied landing in North Africa, the extraordinary story of her family unfolds to reveal the burdens Cassie has carried her entire life.

The Curator of Broken Things is a family-saga trilogy that takes place over a century. The novel weaves multiple narrative threads, each revealing new sides of the story until three generations of secrets are revealed that might bring a family together or tear it apart.

Ingram Content Group UK Ltd.
Milton Keynes UK
UKHW040634220523
422126UK00004B/64